D0235601

PASSIONATE TIMES

EMMA BLAIR
PASSIONATE TIMES

BANTAM PRESS

LONDON · NEW YORK · TORONTO · SYDNEY · AUCKLAND

TRANSWORLD PUBLISHERS LTD
61–63 Uxbridge Road, London W5 5SA

TRANSWORLD PUBLISHERS (AUSTRALIA) PTY LTD
15–25 Helles Avenue, Moorebank, NSW 2170

TRANSWORLD PUBLISHERS (NZ) LTD
3 William Pickering Drive, Albany, Auckland

Published 1995 by Bantam Press
a division of Transworld Publishers Ltd
Copyright © Emma Blair 1995

1011361Ʒ4

A catalogue record for this book is available from the British Library.

ISBN 0593 028317

Typeset in 11/12pt Plantin Medium by
County Typesetters, Margate, Kent.

Printed in Great Britain
by Mackays of Chatham plc, Chatham, Kent.

PASSIONATE TIMES

Chapter One

He woke to find himself staring at a pristine white ceiling from which a large fan hung, slowly rotating. He was covered in sweat and had a blinding headache. Closing his eyes again, he groaned.

'Corporal Douglas, are you awake?'

She was pretty, wearing a grey dress, a scarlet cape that reached to her shoulders. 'Yes,' he whispered in reply, as he licked paper-dry lips, now aware of how parched he was.

'Water,' he croaked.

She disappeared for a few moments, returning with a white porcelain vessel that had a handle at one end and a long spout at the other. He sucked greedily when the spout was slipped into his mouth.

'Not too much,' she chided. 'That wouldn't be good for you in your condition.'

The disappointment, and eagerness for more, showed clearly on his face when the spout was firmly removed.

She had dark hair, green eyes and a winning smile, he observed. 'Who are you?' he asked, his voice rough and cracked.

'Sister Parkin, Corporal.'

There it was again, corporal. And what was round his head? Something tight. He groaned again when he tried to reach up and touch it.

'Now you lie still. You're not to move, understand?'

'What . . . ?' He trailed off, confused, bewildered.

'You were shot, Corporal, in the head. You're a very lucky man to have survived.'

'Shot?'

'In the battle to take Patra. You were flown here by Dakota.'

He'd never heard of Patra, or a Dakota. 'Patra?'

'It's in Greece, the Gulf of Corinth. You were quite a hero from all accounts.'

He had no idea what she was talking about. 'What did you call me?'

Sister Parkin frowned. 'Corporal Douglas. That's your rank and name.'

Despite the heat, and the warm sweat trickling down his face, a sudden deep chill seized him. 'And this is Greece?'

'No,' she said patiently. 'This is Libya. You're in a hospital just outside Zuwarah. Tripoli is the nearest big town.'

He tried to digest that. He'd vaguely heard of Libya, and Greece. Countries, they were countries, he told himself. But he couldn't have said where they were located.

He closed his eyes again, willing the headache to go away. But it remained, a throbbing, pulsating pain. 'I'm in the Army then?'

'A paratrooper. From what I understand you were in the first wave to be dropped.'

'And I was shot?' he repeated dully.

'In the head. Half an inch lower and it would have been curtains. As I mentioned, you're a very lucky man.'

He looked into his mind and saw nothing. Blankness. He couldn't remember this battle she'd referred to, or anything else.

'More water, please?' he rasped.

Sister Parkin's lips thinned in indecision, knowing from experience how extremely careful you had to be with head injuries. 'I'd better consult the medical officer first,' she declared, and moved swiftly away.

His eyes were drawn back to the fan whose slow rotation had a mesmeric quality about it. He was dimly aware of beds on either side of him, and somewhere close by of the rustling sound of a skirt in motion. Another nurse? He imagined it had to be.

Time passed, but he had no sense how long. It might have been a couple of minutes, it might have been ten.

'Hello old chap, back with us I'm informed.'

The speaker was short, fat, bald and wearing a white coat with a bloodstain on its left lapel.

'I'm the bod who did your op. And a damned difficult one it was, too. For a while it was touch and go.'

The MO peered at the bandages swathing the top of Douglas's head. 'How do you feel?'

'Headache.'

'Not surprised,' the MO replied. 'Quite natural in the circumstances.'

'I . . .' Douglas swallowed. 'More water?'

The MO nodded and Sister Parkin picked up the white vessel from Douglas's bedside table. He drank his fill.

'Thank you,' he said.

'You'll be here for a while. Then, when we judge you fit enough, it's home to Blighty for recuperation.' The MO beamed.

Douglas was beginning to find the doctor irritating. 'I can't . . . can't remember anything. It's all . . . just empty space.'

The MO's forehead creased. Bending over Douglas he lifted up an eyelid and gazed at the eye. He grunted, then did the same with the other one.

'Shock, trauma,' he murmured. 'Only temporary I should imagine.'

Relief washed through Douglas. 'Can you give me something for my headache?'

'Of course, old bean. Nothing easier.'

The MO turned to Sister Parkin who was hovering nearby and issued various instructions.

'I'll stop by and have another natter later,' the MO stated, once more addressing Douglas. 'In the meantime the best thing for you to do is get some sleep. Are you tired?'

Douglas realized he was exhausted. 'Yes.'

'Good, good!' the MO enthused. 'I recommend sleep, and lots of it.'

When Sister Parkin returned with the prescribed pills she found that Douglas had already dropped off, but she felt it was prudent to wake him to administer them.

Douglas watched a little lizard dart across the ceiling. It stopped, looked around, then sped off in a new direction. He was fascinated.

'So, how are you after your nap?' Sister Parkin enquired, approaching so quietly Douglas hadn't heard her.

'I still have a headache.'

'But is it as bad as before?'

'No, not quite,' he admitted.

9

Sister wiped his face with a damp cloth. 'I'll never get used to this heat, not in a thousand years,' she grumbled.

'How long have you been here?'

'Three months.'

'And where were you before?'

'Egypt for a spell, and some place I can't mention prior to that.'

Douglas was desperate for information. 'What's my Christian name?' he asked.

'You can't remember that either?'

'As I said, it's all a blank.'

She pulled up the single sheet which covered him, then consulted the notes hanging from the foot of his iron-framed bed. 'Your Christian name's Reith. Unusual, but nice. Has a ring to it. And you're from Glasgow.'

'Glasgow,' he repeated quietly. No vision appeared. 'That's in Blighty, I presume?'

'Of course. Scotland to be exact. You're a Jock.'

Scotland, no recollection of that either. Rage suddenly swept through him, together with a sense of hopelessness. He felt so . . . lost.

'It must be difficult,' Sister Parkin sympathized.

'Is there anything else you can tell me about myself?'

She shook her head. 'Sorry, that's all that's here.' She paused, and exclaimed. 'Oh, you're thirty. Born nineteen fourteen.'

'Nothing else?'

''Fraid not.'

She returned the notes to the foot of his bed. 'Now I must get on. Is there anything you want?'

His bloody memory, he wanted to say, but didn't. A little later his friend the lizard reappeared.

He woke with a start, panic stricken. His heart was beating wildly, his throat constricted, his eyes starting in their sockets. And he still had a headache. Had he been dreaming? He wasn't sure. He thought he might have been.

'Christ!' he muttered.

Someone in the ward was snoring, someone else coughing. It was night, the ward illuminated by moon and starlight.

How had he been shot? How had it happened? In a battle, that he knew. But in what circumstances? Sister Parkin had said he'd been quite a hero from all accounts. What did that mean? He concentrated, trying to remember, someone, some place, anything. But there was only the same blankness that had been there since coming to earlier in the day. It was as if . . . he'd been born a second time.

It was only temporary, he reminded himself. That's what the MO had told him. Only temporary, he mentally repeated. Then he spoke the word aloud. 'Temporary.'

He took a deep breath and that helped control the panic. 'Reith,' he murmured. 'Reith Douglas. Hello Reith Douglas.'

He fought back the urge to giggle hysterically. It was all so stupid, farcical. Who was Reith Douglas? He was. A corporal in the paratroopers, from Glasgow, Scotland, aged thirty, who'd been shot in the head during a battle in some place called Patra, Greece.

He took another deep breath, noting that his heart had stopped pounding. But the panic remained, if not quite so intense. He twisted his head round and noticed a shaded light at the beginning of the ward with a hunched figure sitting behind it. A nurse watching her charges throughout the night. He found that comforting.

'Reith,' he murmured aloud again. Sister Parkin was right, it did have a ring to it. He decided it was a name he liked.

'How are you doing, mate? You're new, aren't you?'

Reith glanced at the patient who'd halted by his bedside. He was the first patient in the ward to address him as the two on either side were too ill to speak. The man was missing an arm.

'I'm fine, and yes I am new.'

The soldier gestured to where his missing arm should have been. 'Gangrene, they had to take it off.' He laughed. 'That fucked me for civvy life good and proper. Know what I was?'

'What?'

'A fucking juggler in a circus, that's what. Whoever heard of a one-armed juggler? I ask you! Fucked, like I said.'

The soldier moved closer. 'What happened to your head?'

'I was shot there.'

'Tough. But you look all right. You'll pull through. What's your name squire?'

'Reith Douglas.'

'I'm Cyril Hoskins from dear old London Town. You're a Jock by the sound of you.'

11

'From Glasgow. I was with the paratroopers.'

'Hard as nails that lot,' Cyril acknowledged. 'Too hard for me. They treating you all right here?'

'No complaints so far.'

'The grub's good, and plenty of it. You could do a deal worse than ending up in this hospital.'

'I've lost my memory,' Reith heard himself declaring.

Cyril's eyebrows rose. 'That a fact!'

'I can't remember anything. I even had to ask Sister my name.'

'Dear me,' Cyril sympathized.

'Everything's just . . . gone.'

'And will you get it back? In time I mean.'

'The MO seems confident that I will.'

'There you are then!' An amused smile lit up Cyril's face, and then he barked out a laugh.

'What is it?' Reith asked.

'Just thinking cocker. Losing your memory might not be so awful after all. Not if you were married to my wife it wouldn't. It would be a relief to forget about her, even if it was only for a short while.'

Reith smiled. 'She can't be that bad?'

'Bad! I've never known anyone nag like her. Nag and rabbit, non-stop rabbit. From first thing in the morning till last thing at night. It's a wonder she didn't drive me mad years ago.'

Cyril stabbed a nicotine-stained finger at Reith. 'So maybe losing your memory is a blessing in disguise. You never know.'

Reith hadn't thought of that.

'At least it beats losing an arm. That'll never come back. I can be certain of that.'

Cyril's visit cheered up Reith, as he put things somewhat in perspective. It could have been a lot worse. At least he was whole in body which was more than could be· said for many of the poor buggers in the ward, some of whom had lost limbs, and several their eyesight. Oh yes, it could have been a great deal worse. No doubt about it.

His first day out of bed was a big day for Reith. And he knew exactly what he wanted to do. He took it easy as he progressed down the ward, walking slowly, smiling and nodding to various patients *en route*. Cyril spotted him and gave him the thumbs up sign which he acknowledged with one of his own.

Sister Parkin had said the toilet was out through the ward doors and to the right. He went in hoping to find a mirror, and sure enough, there was a large one above the washbasins.

He hesitated before looking into it, wondering what he would discover. He knew he had light brown hair, but as for the face, that remained a complete mystery.

Reith walked sideways up to the mirror, swallowed, then turned to stare into it. He sighed with relief. Without the bandages swathing his head the chap gazing apprehensively back at him was passably good-looking. Certainly not ugly, not by a long chalk.

He touched his smooth cheeks which a Libyan orderly had shaved every morning for him. His eyes were blue, his nose neither large nor small. His was a pleasant face, he decided, pleasant and fairly strong in character. It wasn't the face of a weak man.

Of course he could have asked for a mirror while confined to bed, but he hadn't wanted that. He didn't want anyone else to witness his reaction in case he was disappointed and it showed. Besides, it was such a personal thing, a grown man viewing himself for the first time.

'You'll do,' he murmured, then turned, and, humming jauntily, left the toilet.

Shafts of vivid colour pierced the night sky which then began to lighten gradually. The desert sand shimmered, a billion individual pearls seeming to dance in the pale glow enveloping them. The wind that had been blowing died away leaving behind an eerie, almost unearthly, silence. Then the sun, like a great blood orange, appeared, climbing slowly heavenwards. Dawn, another day had begun.

Sister Hollins came hurrying along the terrace to halt beside Reith. 'So there you are, Corporal. I've been searching everywhere for you.' Julie Hollins was Night Sister on Reith's ward.

'It's breathtaking,' he breathed.

'What is?'

'Dawn coming up in this land. I've only ever previously watched it from my bed.'

'You shouldn't be out here,' Sister admonished. 'Apart from anything else it's freezing.'

'I'm wearing my dressing gown. And anyway, I couldn't sleep. I've been lying awake for hours.'

'You should have said and I'd have fetched you some pills.'

'I didn't want pills. I was thinking.'

'You'll get me in trouble if anyone finds out about this,' she declared, shaking her head.

'It isn't long since Matron did her last round so I knew you were safe enough.'

She sighed with exasperation, knowing that was true. 'Even though! I was only off the ward for a minute.'

'That's when I went,' he said. 'Sneaky, eh?'

Despite herself she smiled.

He gazed out over the desert again, wondering.

'What are you thinking about?' Sister Hollins asked softly, noting his expression.

'Glasgow.'

'What about it?'

'And Scotland. What they're like.'

She understood now. 'You still haven't heard anything further about your personal details?'

'They haven't come through yet. I don't know whether I'm single, married or what.'

She glanced down at his left hand. 'You're not wearing a wedding ring.'

'No. But that doesn't mean anything. Several of the blokes in the ward are married and don't wear one.'

'I went to Scotland on holiday some years ago,' she stated.

He turned eagerly towards her. 'And?'

'It's beautiful. We were in the Highlands and fortunate to have good weather. I was most impressed. It has a unique rugged grandeur that's spectacular. It does rain a lot mind, with sudden wet mists that can spring up from nowhere. But as I said, we were fortunate.'

'It's a pity there are no other Scotsmen in the hospital,' he said. 'And to date you're the only one I've found who's been there.' Only a portion of the patients were British, the others were French, Australians, Canadians, all sorts, including captured Germans and Italians.

'I know little about Glasgow except it thrives on heavy industry. Ships built on the Clyde are renowned throughout the world,' she informed him.

'That I have learned.'

'A fairly dirty place as well I understand. But that's to be expected.'

Shipbuilding. Had he been involved with that before the war? And if so, what had he done?

'MO Chappelow mentioned you the other day,' Sister Hollins said.

'Oh?'

'In cases like yours the patient often forgets how to read and write. But that's not true with you.'

He nodded. 'That's correct.'

'And there are no other side effects?'

'None. I can walk perfectly well, use my hands. Everything's functioning as it should, except my memory.'

'It's a funny old thing the brain, there's so little known about it. Doctors hate to admit that of course, but it's true.'

'I just hope MO Speed is right about my memory coming back eventually,' Reith said quietly. Speed was the surgeon who'd operated on him.

Sister Hollins bit her lip, realizing that she hadn't been very tactful. She'd put doubt into Reith's mind, perhaps even alarm. 'I'm sure he is,' she declared, injecting as much conviction as she could into her voice. 'He's an excellent and widely experienced surgeon.'

Suddenly Reith was tired, wanting to return to his bed. He shivered.

'That's it, inside for you. I'll tuck you up personally,' Sister Hollins told him.

Reith glanced out once more over the desert, the blood-orange sun rising steadily in the sky. Soon it would be hot, and the large bloated flies with shiny bodies that they all loathed would appear.

'I wonder . . .' Reith mused, and trailed off.

'Wonder what?'

'If my mother is still alive.'

Sister Hollins took him by the arm and led him in, keeping her word by tucking him up and draping the mosquito net over his bed.

As the last bandage fell away from Reith's head MO Speed stepped forward to make his examination.

'Hmmh,' he murmured, gently probing the wound.

Reith was sitting up in bed, surrounded by Sister Parkin, a

Voluntary Aid Detachment nurse and an elderly Sudanese orderly called Hussain.

Speed exhaled. 'You're coming along nicely Corporal Douglas, very nicely indeed. In fact I'm so impressed that I think we can ship you home as soon as possible.'

Sister Parkin beamed, not only pleased for Reith but delighted that a much needed bed would be released. 'I'll make the necessary arrangements,' she declared.

'The voyage will do you the world of good, and then there will be the recuperation period at the other end,' Speed went on.

'Where will I go for this recuperation?' Reith asked.

Speed straightened and shrugged. 'That's not up to me old sausage. But you'll find out soon enough.'

The MO gestured to the VAD. 'You can put fresh bandages on, Nurse.' Under the eagle eye of Sister Parkin, the VAD hastened to obey.

Home, Blighty, Reith thought. Understandably this news was greeted with mixed emotions.

'Well goodbye Corporal, have a safe and happy trip,' Sister Parkin said. While she was delighted that Reith was well enough to travel, she was saddened to see him go. He'd been a model patient and won a special place in her heart. Not that she'd ever have admitted it. She'd been taught that all patients were the same, but in practice she knew that wasn't quite true.

'I'll miss you Sister,' he replied, a lump rising in his throat.

'And we'll miss you Corporal.'

'I know you're an officer, but . . . what the hell! They can only court martial me.' And with that he kissed a scandalized Sister Parkin on the cheek.

'Well I never!' she exclaimed.

'Go on. I bet you have been kissed before.'

Her eyes twinkled. 'That's for me to know and you to wonder about Corporal.'

'A cracker such as yourself, every single MO in the hospital must be after you. And quite right too.'

'Enough!' she admonished, wagging a finger at him, thoroughly enjoying the flattery.

He smiled. 'I'd better get on the bus I suppose.'

'You'd better. We don't want it leaving without you. I've already got someone else in your bed.'

16

He was reluctant to go. The hospital had become his life, *was* his life. It was all he knew.

Realizing what was going through his mind Sister Parkin grasped his hand and squeezed it. 'You'll be all right Reith, you'll see.' It was the first time she'd ever called him by his Christian name.

'It's . . . well you understand?'

'I do,' she nodded.

He was going to cry, he thought, appalled. How could a paratrooper, and so-called hero, cry merely saying goodbye? 'I did thoroughly enjoy your dancing at Christmas,' he said, referring to the ballet number the Sisters had done at the Christmas party.

Sister Parkin coloured. 'It was awful!'

'But very funny. We all roared.'

'Funny unintentionally. It was supposed to be serious.'

'Which was why it was so hysterical. But you were better than the others.'

Which wasn't saying much, Sister Parkin told herself, remembering only too clearly the débâcle of eight Sisters prancing out of step and often going quite the wrong way. 'The Skater's Waltz' could never have been danced so badly.

'Never again,' Sister Parkin swore. 'One humiliation like that is enough, thank you very much.'

Reith grinned, the threatened tears now under control. 'You say that now, but wait till next year. The Colonel, who laughed as loud as anyone, will insist.'

Waiting patiently the bus driver now beeped his horn to encourage his passengers to get on board.

'Take care Corporal. And good luck,' Sister Parkin said.

'And you.'

'Now I must get back,' she declared, efficient and businesslike once more. 'There's lots to do.'

But she waited till Reith was seated and they'd exchanged waves before striding off.

The hospital ship *Oranje* slowly steamed away from Tripoli, and Reith was lucky enough to be one of those allowed to remain on deck to watch the departure. Their next stop, he'd been informed, was Gibraltar. Southampton was their ultimate destination.

He thought of Sister Parkin with enormous affection. She and the others had become like a family to him. Now he was leaving

17

them behind and who knew what lay ahead. He was sailing into the unknown.

Tripoli shrank into the distance, an exotic city that had enthralled him. Such sights, smells and sounds! So different to England, he was aware, and Scotland.

If only he could remember. If only his memory would come back. But it all remained stubbornly blank. But it would return, he reassured himself. He was certain of that, not knowing quite why.

As Tripoli and the Libyan coast finally disappeared over the horizon he whispered a final goodbye.

Chapter Two

'How are you this morning?' enquired Sister Nell McIntosh joining him on a wooden bench overlooking the gardens of Harrington Manor. She was another Glaswegian with whom Reith had become friendly.

He smiled, always pleased to see her. 'So so.'

'Just that?'

'Better than yesterday.'

'Well that's something anyway.'

The violent headaches had returned aboard the *Oranje* and had continued since he'd arrived at the manor, which had been turned from a private house into a nursing home for members of the forces.

'How about the nausea?' she further probed. She knew he'd been troubled by recurring bouts recently.

'Not for three days now,' he answered.

'That's good.'

'But still no memory return. Not even a glimmer,' he said, smiling thinly.

'That can take time as you've often been told. You simply have to be patient.'

'Do I have a choice?' he joked.

She laughed. 'Not really.'

'But it will come back. I'm convinced of that.'

She approved of his positive attitude, just as she approved of Reith to whom she'd taken a shine. He was popular with all the staff at Harrington.

19

'There is always the possibility it won't though. You mustn't blind yourself to that,' she continued softly.

'It will,' he reiterated stubbornly.

Not for the first time she prayed he was right.

'According to the papers the war continues to go well for us,' he said. 'The Allies have crossed the Rhine.'

'One thing I think we can say for certain, you've seen the end of it. The whole ghastly business is over and done for you.'

'But a ghastly business I have no recollection of whatsoever. For now anyway.'

She stared out over the gardens, thinking how gorgeous they must have been in peacetime when lovingly tended by diligent gardeners, who were now off fighting, if not dead. Since then they'd run riot. 'I have some news,' she stated quietly.

'Oh?'

Nell McIntosh tapped the buff-coloured folder she was carrying, drawing Reith's attention to it. 'What you've been waiting for has arrived.'

'You mean . . . ?'

She nodded. 'Your personal details. They came this morning.'

Suddenly Reith's throat had gone dry, his breathing shallow. He stared at the folder in fascination. At last, at long last.

Nell handed him the folder. 'There you are.'

He reached out to take it, hesitated, then withdrew his hand again. 'Have you read it?'

Her expression confirmed she had.

'Then . . . you tell me.'

'Are you sure? Don't you want to read it for yourself?'

'Tell me Nell.' They used each other's Christian names when alone, a mark of their friendship.

Reith glanced away, waiting for her to speak.

'You're married Reith, with two children.'

Married, a family. 'Called?' he queried hoarsely.

'Your wife's name is Irene and, according to this, she's twenty-eight years old. Your son is Mathew and he'll be ten now. Your daughter is Agnes and she'll be eight.'

So there it was, now he knew. Irene, Mathew and Agnes, names that meant nothing to him. His wife and children.

'I don't suppose there are pictures?'

Nell shook her head.

'What did I do for a living?'

20

'You were, are, a cabinet-maker by trade. A highly skilled job.'

'Cabinet-maker,' he repeated in wonderment.

'There's more,' Nell said.

'Go on.'

'Your father and mother are both dead. And you're an only child.'

He rose from the bench, stuffed his hands into his pockets, and took a few short steps. 'I live in Glasgow?'

'You do. The address is . . .' Nell flipped open the folder. 'Twenty-three Mill Street, Bridgeton.'

'Any more?'

'You enlisted in the Black Watch before transferring to the paratroopers.'

There was a chap from the Watch at Harrington whom he'd spoken to on several occasions, but who obviously didn't know him from his time with the regiment.

'Irene,' he mused. 'I wonder what she looks like.'

'It doesn't mention that.'

'Hmmh!' he murmured and gently kicked the ground. He was a husband and a father.

'How do you feel?' Nell asked quietly.

'I don't really know. Elated I suppose. Relieved that I now know something more about myself.' He spread out his hands. 'Shocked too I think.'

'Shocked?'

'That I have a wife and two children whom I can't remember anything about at all.'

'Of course,' Nell nodded.

He kicked the ground again. 'I think Nell, if you don't mind, I'd like to be alone for a while.'

She understood perfectly. 'I'll see you later.'

After she'd gone he turned round and found she'd left the folder on the bench. Hesitating slightly, he opened it and began to read.

Blonde? Brunette? Redhead? Reith was sitting in the day-room gazing blankly at a yellow distempered wall speculating about Irene. He sighed. The permutations seemed endless. Was she pretty? Not so pretty? Did the children take after him? Her? A combination of both?

The door opened and Nell came in. 'Enjoy your lunch?'

'Powdered egg will never replace the real thing.'

21

'Ah!' she exclaimed, eyes lighting up. 'You remember what they taste like? You *remember*?'

He laughed kindly at her eager expression. 'No, we had the real thing at Zuwarah on many occasions.'

Her face fell. 'Pity. I thought we might have something there. A tiny breakthrough.'

'No such luck.'

'Well cheer up, it's spam for tea.'

She was teasing him because she knew he loathed spam. 'Oh terrific!' he answered, which made her laugh.

'I'm lying,' she confessed.

'So what is for tea?'

'No idea. But I do know it isn't spam. One of the cooks happened to mention earlier that they've run out.'

'They can stay run out as far as I'm concerned. It's hideous.'

Nell agreed with Reith. Her heart always sank when presented with spam. She decided to change the subject. 'There's a group going to the pictures this evening. Want to come?'

'Are you going?'

Not what was on, but was she going Nell noted. 'Yes.'

'Then I will too. But only if I can sit beside you.'

'Why Reith!' she exclaimed. 'And you a married man too.'

'That's something I'm going to have to get used to,' he reflected with a frown.

Nell broke eye contact with Reith and smoothed down her apron, a quite unnecessary act as there wasn't a crease or wrinkle on it. 'You must write to her,' she said casually.

'Irene?'

'Of course. She must be worried sick.'

'I've been thinking,' Reith said slowly. 'All this time, these many months, why hasn't she written to me? I appreciate letters get held up, but surely at least one would have reached me by now?'

Nell shrugged. 'Who knows? There could be all sorts of reasons.'

'Perhaps we weren't corresponding?'

'That would be odd,' Nell murmured.

'Nothing in Zuwarah. Nothing here. Not a single line.'

Nell wondered if Reith and his wife were separated. That was possible. 'There's all kinds of muddle in wartime,' she said. 'Look how long it took for your file to catch up with you. It went to Libya you know, arriving there after you'd left. Then it had to be forwarded here having been returned to source. It could be the same with Irene's letters, they could be all over the place.'

'Strange all the same, considering the time involved,' Reith persisted.

Suddenly Nell disliked this conversation about Reith's wife and why she hadn't written. 'The group is meeting in the hall directly after tea,' she said, moving on to other things.

'Which isn't spam,' he grinned.

'Which definitely isn't spam,' she smiled. She enjoyed his sense of humour which was very similar to her own and explained why they got on so well together.

'And I get to sit beside you?'

She pretended to be unsure. 'That would smack of favouritism.'

'So?'

'So that's not on.'

Reith pulled a funny face. 'Then make an exception. Please? Just for me.'

She laughed at his antics. 'I don't know.'

'I have some chocolate which I'll bring along. And you *love* chocolate,' he cajoled in a seductive, tempting tone.

'That's bribery,' she admonished.

He hung his head in mock shame. 'True,' he admitted. 'Just shows how far I'll go for the pleasure of your company.'

Nell was deeply touched. 'I'll have to think about it. I'm not making any promises.'

'That's good enough for me!' he declared brightly. 'But you won't get to share my chocolate unless we're together. And it's lovely chocolate, I promise you.'

Nell glanced at her watch. It was high time she was elsewhere. 'I'm still not making any promises.'

But she would sit beside him, Reith was certain of that. And would have done so without the chocolate. They were good pals.

Reith passed the rest of his chocolate to Nell. 'You finish it off,' he whispered.

'Are you sure?' she replied.

'Positive. I've had enough.'

He focused his attention back on the screen, not really all that interested in the film. Called *The Spider* and starring Derrick de Marnay, Diana Churchill and Cecil Parker, it was a thriller about a theatrical agent who kills his partner on a train.

Reith was acutely aware that Nell was wearing powder and scent which he thought smelled heavenly. He was also very conscious that her thigh was jammed against his own.

He glanced sideways, watching her as she ate the chocolate. She returned his glance and smiled. When she'd finished, her hand fell into her lap. He longed to reach out and clasp it. 'Boring, isn't it?' he whispered, referring to the film.

'Sshhh!'

'You're not enjoying it, are you?'

'Yes I am. Now be quiet.'

'It's a load of old codswallop in my opinion.'

'I said be quiet Reith,' she whispered back fiercely.

Nell was as aware of Reith's closeness as he was of hers. They'd been close before but somehow it had never felt like this. With a shock she realized he'd come to mean more to her than a mere friend, which disturbed her greatly.

She forced herself to concentrate on the picture, trying to disregard Reith's presence and the recent revelation, failing totally on both counts.

'Have you written to your wife yet?' It was now a week since Reith had found out he was married.

Reith shook his head.

'You really should.'

'I know but . . .' He took a deep breath. 'I've started twice, but simply didn't know what to say. How do you write to your wife and tell her you can't remember her? Or anything about your life together?'

Nell regarded him sympathetically. 'Not easy,' she murmured. 'But you must. You have to.'

He'd had enough of Irene for the present. 'How were your two days off?'

'Fine.'

'What did you do in the end?' The last time they'd spoken she'd been undecided about how to spend the forty-eight hours.

'I went and stayed with some friends who live not far away. It was very relaxing.'

'I missed you. A lot,' Reith stated quietly.

She refused to meet his gaze.

'I did,' he added.

And she'd missed him. In fact she'd spent nearly all her waking

24

hours thinking about him. If she'd been uncertain of his feelings towards her then the plaintiff note in his voice confirmed that he felt the same about her as she did about him.

'Any headaches?' she asked.

'A minor one yesterday that only lasted a few hours. Nothing like those I was having before.'

'Good,' she enthused. 'Perhaps you're finally getting over that stage.'

'I hope so,' he said, wanting to take her into his arms and hold her tight.

'Nell . . .'

'No,' she interrupted, knowing what he was about to say.

'No?' he queried.

'No,' she stated firmly.

'I see,' he murmured.

'I'm glad about the headaches,' she declared, and bit her lip. She then strode off leaving him gazing forlornly after her.

Sister Moynihan burst into the day-room, her face ablaze with excitement. 'It's official!' she blurted out. 'The Prime Minister has just announced it over the wireless. The war in Europe is to end at midnight.' It was news they'd been expecting, but its arrival still stunned all present.

'Thank God,' a naval rating called Williams breathed, and hastily crossed himself.

Then bedlam broke loose in the day-room. A crutch was brandished in the air, while two other patients grabbed one another and did a jig. Hands were shaken, backs pounded, whoops of glee burst forth.

Sister Moynihan found herself being whirled round and round by an NCO from the Royal Artillery and she shrieked when her feet flew from the floor.

Reith didn't know how it happened, but suddenly his lips were on Nell's. She melted against him, her hands coming up to clasp the back of his head. Her scent was so strong that it made him almost giddy, while the kiss went on and on. Simultaneously the realization of what they were doing struck them both, and each went still. Their lips parted and they gazed at one another.

'Nell,' he croaked.

She broke away quickly to join the end of a conga that had started up, weaving its way amongst tables and chairs.

'Isn't it wonderful!' exclaimed Jimmy Bell, a commando, to Reith, who nodded his agreement.

'Wonderful,' Reith repeated.

Nell danced past without looking at him.

'You've been spending a lot of time with Corporal Douglas,' Penny Moynihan, Nell's roommate, commented.

Nell, who was vigorously towelling her recently washed hair, paused. 'Have I?'

'A few of the girls have mentioned it. And I've noticed it myself.'

Nell resumed her towelling. 'I like him. He's fun. There's no harm in that.'

'I just hope Matron doesn't hear about it. She wouldn't approve.'

'There's nothing to disapprove of,' Nell answered casually.

'She might not see it that way.'

Nell tossed aside the towel and reached for her comb, dragging it through her thick blond hair.

'Nell,' Penny said patiently. 'There's something going on between the pair of you. It was obvious from the way he kissed you in the day-room yesterday.'

'You were kissed as well, by more than one man,' Nell protested.

'Come on! There's kissing and kissing. What you and he did was the latter.'

Nell knew she could trust Penny who wasn't a person to gossip. They'd shared many confidences since being thrown together at Harrington.

'He's different,' Nell said softly. 'There's just something about him.'

'He's also married.'

Nell glanced at her roommate. 'Not to mention he's out of bounds as I am an officer. But the war in Europe is over which surely means it's only a matter of time before Japan also capitulates. Then the whole thing will be finished and we can all return to some sort of normality.'

'Do you love him?'

Did she? She didn't really know. 'I think I could. The possibility is there.'

'And what about his wife?'

'He doesn't remember her. He firmly believes his memory will return one day, but there again it might not. I'm in the present for him, the here and now. His wife Irene is in the forgotten past.'

26

'Forgotten by him maybe, but not her,' Penny pointed out. 'And there are children, too, I understand.'

Nell nodded. 'Two. A boy and a girl.'

'Hmmh,' Penny murmured. 'Another obstacle, wouldn't you say?'

Nell laid down her comb, picked up a pale pink dressing gown and shrugged into it. She was tired, it had been a long and difficult day.

'It is classic after all, as you well know,' Penny went on. 'Male patients are always falling for their nurses. I've seen it happen often.'

Nell didn't reply, knowing that was true.

'I must admit though,' Penny smiled, 'he is extremely attractive, with tremendous charm.'

Nell couldn't have agreed more. 'And easy to be with. It's so relaxing being in his company. Soothing almost.'

'I think you want to consider the matter very very carefully before you go any further,' Penny counselled. 'I wouldn't want you getting hurt. Anyway,' she continued, jumping to her feet. 'I'm off. A few of us are going to The Wheatsheaf for a drink.'

Penny left Nell alone with her thoughts, brooding about Reith and their relationship.

'Hello.'

Reith was sitting on the same bench where he'd read the folder containing his personal details.

'Hello,' he smiled at Nell.

'It's a gorgeous afternoon, isn't it?' The sky was blue without a trace of cloud. It was the hottest day of the year so far.

'Beautiful,' he agreed.

She saw then that something was wrong. 'What's up?'

He glanced away and several seconds passed before he answered. 'I had a reply from Irene today.'

Nell's heart sank. 'Oh?'

'She sent me a photograph of her and the children.'

Nell sat beside him. 'Can I see?'

He fumbled in his jacket and produced a white envelope which he handed to her.

'Well well,' murmured Nell as she studied the photo. 'Your wife is pretty.'

'Yes,' he agreed. 'I never imagined her to be so tiny though.'

27

'Petite,' Nell said. 'And the boy's handsome. Takes after his dad.'

Reith gave a small laugh. 'Flattery will get you everywhere young lady.'

Nell thought Mathew was very serious looking, frowning quizzically into the camera. The girl, on the other hand, had a happy-go-lucky air about her. She too was pretty in a tomboyish sort of way.

Nell then turned over the photograph and read, To Reith with all my love Irene xxxx.

All her love. Nell's heart had sunk when she'd heard about the letter, and now it sunk even further.

'She's very sympathetic about my amnesia and says she can't wait to have me home again. She also says she's missed me dreadfully,' Reith declared tightly.

'I'm sure.'

Nell tapped the photo. 'You must be proud of the children.'

'I suppose I am.'

'As I'm sure they're proud of you.'

Reith had felt wretched ever since the letter had arrived. 'There was a lot of confusion after my being wounded in Greece,' he went on. 'For some while I was apparently even thought to be dead. A real cock-up.'

'Which explains the lack of letters.'

He nodded.

Nell slipped the photograph back into the envelope and returned it to Reith. 'There we are then,' she said, her smile strained.

He put the envelope back in the same jacket pocket. 'It's the oddest sensation looking at someone who's your wife and not knowing them from Adam.'

'Must be.'

'Know something?'

'What?'

'I don't feel anything at all towards her. You would have thought the photograph would have jolted some emotion at least. But it hasn't.'

Nell was pleased to hear that, although she didn't let it show. Then she became angry with herself for being so selfish.

Later, as she was walking away, she glanced back to see Reith staring at the photograph which he was holding in front of him, looking perplexed.

28

*   *   *

Nell gazed out of a window and watched Reith and another patient strolling in the grounds below. But it wasn't them she was seeing, but the photograph of Irene and the children.

It had been signed To Reith with all her love. Reading that endearment had been like having a knife stuck into her and twisted. Irene loved Reith, and no doubt he'd loved her before losing his memory. And when he went home he would, no doubt, in time, fall in love with her all over again. So what right did she have to interfere, stick her oar in?

What if the positions had been reversed and she'd been Irene waiting dutifully for a husband who'd risked life and limb by going off to war? How would she have felt if her husband had survived only to become entangled with some nurse he'd fallen for and who'd fallen for him? Bitter! She'd certainly be that. And bloody angry. Not to mention completely let down. She'd think that the nurse had taken advantage of the situation which was more or less the case.

If Reith had come to Harrington under different circumstances then nothing would have developed between them. His loyalty and love would have remained with Irene, his lawfully married wife. And then there were the children, Mathew and Agnes. What a blow it would be to them to lose their father now. What a cruel twist of fate that would cause them untold suffering.

Nell knew then that her relationship with Reith mustn't develop any further. Their burgeoning romance, for that's what it was, had to be nipped in the bud. She'd been stupid even to consider the alternative.

Then another thought struck her, a chilling one. What if she had gone off with Reith and his memory had returned one day, as it well could. He might be in love with her, but would also be in love with Irene. What an impossible, and heartbreaking, situation that would be.

Her mind made up, she left the window and went about her duties.

Nell glanced up to find Reith framed in the doorway. He looked smart in the demob suit that had been issued to him and which he was wearing for the first time.

'Can I have a private word?' he requested.

She laid down the dressing she was holding. 'Carry on,' she said

29

to the VAD who was assisting her, and followed Reith outside to the corridor.

'I thought you'd come and see me off. The driver has kindly agreed to wait for a few more minutes,' he said.

Nell didn't reply.

'Goodbye Nell.'

'You know I wish you all the best.'

'Thank you, I'll write . . .'

'No don't,' she interjected.

He stared hard at her. Their relationship had never recovered since Irene's first letter. She'd remained pleasant enough, although cool and distant as if a barrier had come down between them. He'd guessed correctly that it had been the photograph. On the several occasions he'd tried to broach the subject, quickly and expertly she'd channelled the conversation in a different direction. In the end he'd accepted that she didn't want to talk about it.

'Have a safe journey home,' she said.

He smiled wryly, then attempted to peck her on the cheek. But she moved her face at the last minute.

'So long,' he said, and started back the way he'd come.

'Reith!' she called out after he'd gone a few steps.

He stopped, but didn't turn round.

'If things had been different . . .' She trailed off.

When it was obvious she wasn't going to say anything further he continued on his way. Deeply saddened, Nell wiped a single tear from her eye.

Chapter Three

The taxi carved its way through the grey Glasgow streets as Reith sat in the rear staring out. Nell had described the city to him in detail but that hadn't prepared him for the actuality with its lowering, brooding presence. And it was cold, far more cold than it had been at Harrington. He shivered, not sure whether he was cold or afraid. For he wasn't merely apprehensive about meeting Irene and the children, he was scared rigid.

'Back from the war then, Jim?' the female driver queried over her shoulder. She'd taken on this job during the hostilities when so many men had gone off to fight.

He nodded as she watched him in the overhead mirror. 'How did you know?'

'The suit. It's a dead giveaway.'

Reith smiled to himself. Of course, he should have realized.

'Saw action did you?'

'A bit.'

'Where? We can ask questions now there's no secrecy any more.'

'Greece.'

'Oh aye! Was it bad?'

'Bad enough,' he replied, not really wishing to chat.

The driver, realizing this, left him alone, knowing from experience that men were often tight-lipped about the war. She thought momentarily about her Alex who'd bought it on D-Day. There would be no demob suit or homecoming for him.

Reith gazed at the soot-encrusted tenements they passed,

thinking how austere and friendless they seemed. Did he live in a building like that? He'd soon find out. He took out the photograph from his pocket and studied Irene for the umpteenth time. He'd written and told her the time of his arrival and she'd replied saying they'd be waiting for him. Would he like them to meet him at Central Station? He'd penned a brief note saying that wasn't necessary. Besides, trains were often late he'd been told and didn't want her, and the children, hanging around. It was best if he came on by himself.

Finally the taxi turned into Mill Street. He only knew that because he saw a sign on the corner and they drew up outside number twenty-three.

'Here you are, Jim,' the driver declared.

She wouldn't take any money from him, telling him to have this one on her. He waved his appreciation as she drove away.

He looked up at the tall tenement, similar to all those he'd passed *en route*, wondering which of the many windows overlooking the street was his. A middle-aged woman, wearing a shoddy coat and a scarf on her head, hurried by. He noted that her flat shoes were very much down at heel.

Reith entered the tenement through what he later learned was 'the close', a semi-tiled entranceway with dirty white paintwork. He was hit by a strong smell, which forced him to wrinkle his nose. Boiled vegetables, cat urine and something else that eluded him. There were two doors at the end of the entranceway, one said McKenzie, the other McLean. He climbed the well-worn stone stairs till he found what he was after on the third landing: a small brass plate that bore the legend, Douglas.

He paused for a few moments, aware that his heart was hammering, summoning up the courage to tug the bell-pull. When he finally managed there was a loud clang from inside. He heard pattering feet, watched the door being flung open and there was Irene.

He was shocked to discover she had golden-red hair, she'd appeared brunette in the photo. And her face was freckly, he hadn't expected that either.

'Oh Reith darling,' she whispered, and flew into his arms.

So this was her, his wife, in the flesh, he thought in a detached sort of way. She smelled strongly of soap.

'Welcome home.' Her voice sounded muffled against his chest.

The children had come into the lobby to stare at him. Agnes, sticking a thumb into her mouth, burst into tears.

'Aw don't be a big baby,' Mathew admonished her.

'It really is you. After all this time,' Irene said, looking as though she might start crying as well.

Reith kissed her lightly on the lips. 'Hello.'

She reached up and stroked his cheek. 'It's been so long.'

He attempted a smile which came out crooked. 'It's good to see you.'

'And to see you.'

She released him, hooked her arm round his, and bustled him inside, swinging the door shut with her free hand. 'The kettle's just coming to the boil. I'll make some tea. Are you hungry?'

'A little,' he confessed.

'I can do you a sandwich for now and we'll have tea shortly. It's only spam I'm afraid, that's all I could get.'

Spam! He wanted to burst out laughing.

'You like spam, don't you?'

'Love it,' he lied. Well, what else could he say? He could hardly say he loathed it.

'The damn butcher let me down,' Irene went on. 'I explained to him it was a special occasion and he promised me something nice and tasty, then broke his promise. I was furious I can tell you.'

She had a temper to go with her red hair, Reith realized.

They stopped in front of the children. Agnes was still crying. 'There's no need for that, lass,' Reith said softly.

'Mum says you don't remember us. That you got shot in the head and have forgotten everything,' Mathew stated matter of factly.

'I'm afraid that's so, son,' Reith replied.

'Well, I remember you. I was only wee when you went away. But I remember you all the same.'

Kiss the boy? Shake his hand? Reith smiled, holding out his hand. They solemnly shook. But he decided he should kiss Agnes. After all, she was a girl. Bending down, he pecked her on the cheek. 'Hello to you too,' he murmured. They wandered through into the kitchen where Irene told him to sit in what she described as his favourite chair. When he'd done so he glanced round the completely unfamiliar room which he must have once known so well.

'Is that all you've brought with you?' Irene asked, indicating the small suitcase he'd placed to one side.

'That's it. There wasn't much to bring.'

33

She looked him up and down. 'Well your old clothes are in the wardrobe and should still fit. You seem about the same size as when you went away.'

He then spotted something which made him stand up again and cross to the mantelpiece. The photograph was in an ornate brass frame, and was of him and Irene. He was dressed up to the nines, she in a wedding dress.

'Does that . . . ?' she began, and trailed off.

Reith shook his head. 'Sorry. No.'

'Did you kill many Germans?' Mathew demanded.

'I simply don't know, son. It's all gone.'

'Can I see where you were shot? Is there a hole?'

Reith laughed. 'There's a scar and indentation, but no hole. Here, look.' He squatted and inclined his head.

'There,' he said, touching.

'Is it sore?'

'Not any more. Though it is a bit tender at times.'

'Gosh,' Mathew murmured, lightly running a finger over the spot.

'Can I feel too?' Agnes asked.

'Of course you can.'

'The scar is jaggedy,' she declared.

Irene was busy making the tea. 'Don't go bothering Dad. He's probably tired,' she said.

'It's all right,' Reith smiled at her. The terrible fear he'd felt on the way was beginning to subside.

'Have you got any medals?' Mathew enquired.

'I'm afraid not. At least not here. I believe I may be due for a couple.'

'Gosh,' Mathew repeated.

He sat down in his favourite chair, as Mathew and Agnes watched him closely. 'Don't you remember anything at all?' Mathew queried.

Reith shook his head. 'Not before waking up in the hospital.'

'Not even Mum?'

Irene turned to glance sideways at Reith.

'Not even Mum,' he confessed.

'Mathew, lay out a plate for your dad. And stop asking so many questions,' Irene said.

'I want to go for a wee,' Agnes declared.

'Then go silly,' Irene told her.

34

Agnes skipped from the room.

'At least she's stopped crying,' Reith commented to Irene.

'She was just anxious.' Irene hesitated, then added, 'We all were.'

'So was I. It is . . . an odd situation to say the least.'

'Yes.'

She had a good figure, he noted. Trim, not voluptuous like Nell's, and for a moment he wondered how she was getting on. Would she be thinking about him at all? Quickly, he put Nell out of his mind. It was Irene he had to concentrate on now. There were so many questions he wanted to ask her, but that would come later.

'Tell me about school,' he said to Mathew.

Mathew was only too happy to talk to his dad, and Agnes joined them with similar enthusiasm when she returned to the kitchen.

'I think I might like to go for a pint before tea, if you don't mind,' Reith announced later. The truth was, having met his family, he wanted time to mull things over.

Irene looked at him in surprise. 'That's interesting.'

'Why?'

'Because you used to do that several times a week before the war. After work you'd stop in at McTavish's for a couple before tea.'

'McTavish's?'

'A pub just round the corner.'

Reith dismissed it as mere coincidence. 'Is that all right then?'

'Tea can wait a bit. We're in no hurry. Off you go.'

He paused at the door. 'Round which corner?'

'Turn left as you go out, then left again. You can't miss it.'

'Right,' he smiled. 'Won't be long.'

It was a relief to leave the house, to be on his own again. Not that the reunion had been that much of a strain, it could have been far worse. And the children were lovely, he'd taken to them straight away. As for Irene . . . Well, she was nice enough. The golden-red hair and freckles had thrown him somewhat. He'd been convinced she was brunette from the photograph. But it was the weirdest thing to meet someone who was your wife and who'd had your children, but remained a complete and utter stranger to you.

He found McTavish's without any trouble and went inside. There were about half a dozen men standing at the bar, a few others scattered round the tables, but no women. The chap behind the bar looked as if he were in his sixties with thinning grey hair swept straight back from his forehead. His face lit up when he spotted Reith.

'Well, look who's here! Another Johnny come marching home.'

Reith wondered if this was McTavish whom the pub was named after.

One of the blokes round the bar grabbed his hand. 'Reith Douglas, welcome back! When did you blow in?'

'A few hours ago.'

'And more or less straight down to the boozer,' the bloke chuckled. 'Can't say I blame you after what you must have been through.'

'Did you hear about Donny Baxter?' another man asked Reith. 'Didn't make it poor sod. And him with a wife and four weans too.' The man shook his head.

'The first one's on the house,' the barman beamed, extending a beefy hand. 'Welcome home Reith.'

Bewildered, Reith shook his hand. He was clearly well known in the pub.

'Back, and not a scratch on you,' the barman said, picking up a glass and reaching for the pump handle.

'Are you McTavish?' Reith queried.

The barman stared at him in astonishment. 'Is that a joke? I've owned this pub since you were in short pants. I pulled your first ever pint.'

'I'm afraid I don't remember you,' Reith muttered apologetically. Then turning to the others added, 'Or any of you. Sorry.'

'Aw come off it Reith, stop taking the piss. What's all this "don't remember" malarkey? We grew up together for Christ's sake. You and I ran together as boys.' The bloke who'd grabbed his hand frowned.

'I don't remember,' Reith repeated. 'I've lost my memory.'

'Lost your memory? Is this for real?'

Reith nodded. 'I was shot in the head you see. I don't recall anything from before.'

McTavish paused. 'You are serious, aren't you?'

'That's right.'

'You don't know me or anyone else?'

'No. You're all new faces to me.'

'Holy shite!' one of the men round the bar exclaimed, and whistled.

'It happened in Greece apparently,' Reith further explained. 'I didn't even recognize my wife today.'

They all gazed at him in sympathy.

'Aye well, it could be worse,' McTavish declared, placing Reith's drink in front of him.

'That's what I've often told myself. And there's an excellent chance my memory will return. As I'm certain it will.'

'Well I'm Bob McTavish. Bob to you.'

'And I'm Billy Drummond,' said the man with whom Reith had grown up.

Further introductions were made, after which an awkward silence fell among them. Reith sipped his pint, recognizing that it was different to the beer he'd become used to in England during his visits to The Wheatsheaf. It was darker, and stronger too.

'When are you taking up work again?' Billy Drummond asked.

'I've no idea,' Reith replied. 'Soon I suppose. There's no point hanging about.'

'No point,' Billy agreed.

'What do you do?'

'I'm a crane driver in the shipyards. That's how I missed the war, it's a reserved occupation.'

'Ah!' Reith murmured.

'All of us here are in reserved occupations.'

'And I was too old to serve,' Bob McTavish grinned.

The conversation remained stilted until Reith finally excused himself and left.

'Good night then,' Reith said to Agnes, tucking her up in bed.

'Dad?'

'What pet?'

'Will you play with me tomorrow after school?'

His heart warmed to her. She was such a sweet little thing. 'You can count on it.'

'Thanks Dad.'

He kissed her on the forehead. 'Have a good sleep and I'll see you in the morning.'

Her eyes followed him as he turned off the gas mantle.

'Good night again Dad,' she said in the darkness.

'Do you have the door open or shut?'

'Open.'

Once he'd said good night to Mathew, he returned to the kitchen where he found Irene sitting in front of the range. There was a lump in his throat.

'Well, that's that,' he declared, sitting facing her.

'Would you like a cup of tea?'

He shook his head.

'Or coffee? There's some in.'

'No thanks. I know what I would like though.'

'What's that?'

'For you to tell me about myself. Everything you can.'

'That could take a while,' she answered quietly.

'I'm in no rush. Are you?'

'No,' she replied.

He settled himself back in the chair and waited for her to start.

Going to bed with Irene was what Reith had dreaded most. The bed in question was a recessed one in the kitchen. He noticed that she'd already laid out pyjamas for him, and a clean nightie for herself.

The clock on the mantelpiece chimed midnight as he began to undress, acutely aware of Irene, standing a few feet away. She draped her blouse over a chair, then unhooked her bra. Next she tackled the zipper at the side of her skirt. Irene sat down to take off her suspender belt and stockings, but stopped when she noticed his expression. 'Shy?'

'I'm afraid so,' he mumbled.

'That's understandable I suppose,' she smiled.

'And you?'

'Not in the least. We've been to bed oodles of times together, don't forget.'

'True, but—'

'You don't remember any of them,' she interjected.

'I'm sorry,' he apologized.

'Don't be.' She looked thoughtful. 'In a way it's rather nice. A completely fresh beginning you could say. Tonight will be like our honeymoon all over again.'

'For me anyway,' he said.

When her suspender belt and stockings were off she slipped out of her knickers to stand totally nude before him. 'What do you think?' she asked, not in the least embarrassed.

'Lovely,' he pronounced.

She moved over to him and put her hands on his shoulders.

'Don't be scared Reith. I won't bite. At least . . . not enough to harm you.'

He swallowed hard. 'Was it . . . good between us?'

'Very.'

She pulled his head down, because she was so small, brushed her lips against his, then nuzzled him. 'God it's wonderful having you here again. It was so lonely when you were away. I missed you dreadfully.'

Had he missed her the same way before he was shot? He presumed he had.

She kissed him, her tongue flickering inside his mouth, at the same time running a hand up and down his back. 'Hmmh,' she crooned.

He gingerly touched a breast and she crooned again when he rubbed her nipple.

She broke off, eyes gleaming. 'Come on, hurry up. I'm getting cold.'

She crossed to the bed and pulling back the bedclothes she swung herself under them.

Reith removed his underpants and turned off the glowing gas mantles. Then he joined her in bed where she immediately turned and hooked an arm round his chest.

'Irene.'

'What?'

'You must appreciate I . . .' He hesitated.

'Go on,' she urged.

'It's as if I've never made love to a woman. It'll be all new for me.'

She laughed throatily.

'It's not funny.'

'Oh come on! It is in a way.'

'Well I'm glad you think so.' He sounded hurt.

She gently stroked his chest. 'There's nothing to worry about. Honest.'

'But I am worried.'

'And tense,' she commented, feeling the tension in his body.

'Wouldn't you be in my position?'

She agreed. 'Yes, but we'll just take things naturally. There's no rush,' she said, continuing to stroke him.

They kissed again, and gradually he relaxed.

'Oh Reith, darling Reith,' she whispered.

When they were both ready she guided him in.

That hadn't been so bad, in fact it had been downright enjoyable, Reith reflected later. Irene was fast asleep beside him, curled up against his side. He'd wondered what making love would be like, and now he knew. What would it have been like with Nell? he wondered. Different, he supposed, though basically the same.

He was still ruminating on the pleasures of lovemaking when, smiling, he fell asleep.

He woke to hear the clatter of crockery being laid out and Mathew saying, 'I can't find my socks, Mum.'

'You haven't looked properly. Look again.'

'Aw come and help me, Mum.'

'I'm busy. Now on you go.'

Irene was already up and dressed, pausing to wipe a stray wisp of hair from her face.

'Good morning,' he said.

'Good morning,' she smiled. 'Sleep well?'

'Like a top.'

'There's no need for you to get out of bed yet. Stay where you are and I'll bring breakfast over.'

'Are you sure?'

'It's your first *full* day home. Enjoy it.'

Agnes came rushing into the kitchen. 'What's to eat, Mum?'

'Toast and tea.'

'I'd love an egg,' she declared wistfully.

'Wouldn't we all. You'll get one Sunday, if you're lucky.'

Reith noted that Agnes was also in school uniform, as Mathew had been. 'Morning pet,' he said.

She gave him a quick kiss on the cheek. 'Ooh!' she exclaimed, pulling a face. 'You're all bristly.'

He laughed. 'Men are in the morning. It's why they shave.'

She rubbed a palm over his chin. 'Are you going to shave?'

'Later.'

'I kept the children off yesterday because of you,' Irene explained. 'The headmistress was quite understanding when I told her the reason why.'

'And what about you? What are you doing today?' he enquired.

'I'm working. I've got a job at the dairy. I also took the day off yesterday.'

'So when do you get back?'

'A little after half past five. The children let themselves in.'

He frowned. 'Are they old enough to be on their own?'

'They're used to it,' Irene pointed out. 'Anyway it's only for a short while. And one of the neighbours is always in should there be a problem.'

She placed a plate of toast on the table, then poured out a cup of tea.

'I see you found them,' she commented knowingly when Mathew returned. 'All you had to do was look properly.'

He scowled, but didn't reply. Sitting at the table he began to wolf down the toast.

'Take your time Matt! You'll give yourself indigestion,' Irene scolded, wagging a finger at him.

The scowl deepened.

'Guts,' Agnes said, sitting opposite.

'Am not.'

'Are so. Greedy guts.'

'Stop it you two! What will your father think?'

Family life, that was something he was going to have to get to grips with, Reith thought.

Irene brought him his toast. 'There's no jam I'm afraid. That's rationing for you.'

She smiled at him. 'Did you bring your coupon book with you?'

'It's in my jacket pocket.' He'd been issued one before leaving Harrington Manor.

'Good. I'll be needing that.'

'Take it now if you wish.'

'No, I'll get it later.'

Mathew deftly whipped the last slice of toast from the plate and silently leered at Agnes.

'He had more than me,' she complained.

Irene sighed. 'It never changes. They could drive you mental at times. At least they'll have a man round the house now to keep them in better check.'

Reith took his cue. 'Behave you two,' he growled.

Mathew shot him a startled glance.

'Sorry Dad,' he mumbled.

'Sorry Dad,' Agnes echoed.

Irene was delighted. 'Hoo . . . ray!' she said quietly. She then squeezed his shoulder and winked at him without the children seeing.

'Where are those clothes of mine you mentioned last night?' Reith asked.

'In Matt's room. The big wardrobe. Shirts and other things are in the top drawer of the chest of drawers.'

'Right,' he nodded. He'd investigate when they'd gone.

Irene piled the dirty dishes and cutlery at the side of the sink. 'I'll do these when I get home. There's no time now,' she stated.

'I'll do them when I get up,' Reith offered.

'You will not! It isn't a man's job to do housework,' Irene retorted, scandalized. 'What would the neighbours think if they found out?'

That amused Reith. 'Then the children can do them when they get in from school.'

Mathew was horrified. 'I'm not washing dishes!'

'All right, you can dry. Agnes will wash,' Reith informed him.

'Mum!'

'They always make such a fuss when asked to do anything,' Irene said to Reith. 'It just isn't worth the bother.'

'Bother or not, they'll do them,' Reith stated firmly.

Mathew's scowl returned, but he didn't protest any further. He could see life was going to be very different now that Dad was back. He wasn't going to be as easygoing as Mum.

Irene put a key on the table. 'That's for you if you want to go out,' she told Reith, who nodded.

'Now then, let's be off or we'll all be late,' she declared to the children.

When Agnes had put on her coat, she went and kissed Reith. 'See you later Dad.'

Irene also kissed him, but Mathew hung back. When they'd finally departed, Reith thought about his family and hoped he wasn't going to have trouble with his son. Then his mind turned to other things: a lie-in or get up straight away and explore?

He decided on the latter.

A fat woman was puffing up the stairs as he emerged from the house. He automatically smiled.

'Reith, how are you?' the fat woman exclaimed. 'Irene said you were due home.'

'I'm fine, thank you,' Reith replied, wondering who she was.

She halted beside him, a frown creasing her forehead. 'Oh aye, that's right. Irene mentioned you'd eh—'

'Lost my memory,' he completed for her when she trailed off.

'Poor soul. You don't remember a thing?'

'I'm afraid not.'

'Well, I'm Bessie Loudon. Me and my hubby George live directly above you on the next landing up. We've been here since before you and Irene moved in.'

There was going to be a lot of this he thought, running into people like Bessie and the chaps in the pub who knew him whom he'd forgotten. They chatted for a few minutes, and he learned about George and their married daughter Lena who stayed in Maryhill. Outside in the street he was hailed by another neighbour and had to go through the explanatory process yet again.

One thing was certain, he didn't think much of Bridgeton. There was a squalidness about it that repulsed him. Everything was so filthy, and it reeked of unpleasant smells. He wrinkled his nose in disgust as he stepped over a large pool of vomit on the pavement.

And it was so cold! Colder than the previous day. He was glad of the heavy coat he'd found in the wardrobe. He'd have been frozen without it. A tram rattled and swayed by, the destination sign on the front declaring it was bound for Argyle Street which Nell had told him was in the centre of Glasgow. When it halted at a nearby stop he decided to jump on board.

Argyle Street was another disappointment, as were Buchanan Street and Sauchiehall Street. They weren't quite as awful as Bridgeton but hardly what you'd expect for main arteries of a major British city. As for the people themselves, they all looked so ground down, no doubt the result of the war. They appeared to have had the stuffing knocked out of them.

Feeling extremely depressed he went into a bar and ordered a pint to try and cheer himself up a bit.

Later, when Irene arrived home, she found Reith sitting morosely reading an evening newspaper.

'Had a good day?' she asked with a smile.

'Interesting,' he prevaricated.

'What did you do?'

'Had a wander round.'

'And?'

43

'Nothing came back if that's what you mean.'

Her smile widened slightly, then disappeared altogether. 'I worried that you might get lost if you went out.' Her eyes glanced over to the sink where there was no sign of the morning's dishes.

'The children did them,' he informed her.

'Any trouble with that?'

'Matt wasn't too pleased, but did as he was told. I saw to that.'

Irene nodded her approval. 'I know I may have been a bit soft on them, but . . . well, it hasn't been easy since you went away. With Matt in particular, he can be a strong-minded little bugger.'

'I'll soon sort them out, don't worry.'

She crossed and knelt beside his chair. 'It really is so good to have you here again, Reith. I can't tell you.'

The frustration of his memory loss welled up within him. If only he could remember! He felt so . . . inadequate. Reaching down he stroked her hair.

'It's going to take some getting used to,' he said softly.

'I appreciate that.'

'For me in—'

'For *all* of us,' she interjected. 'You were away a long time.'

'Six years,' he breathed.

'Six long, lonely years.'

'And . . . according to you last night I never came home on leave?'

She shook her head. 'Not once.'

'I find that baffling. I know you explained that it was because of my postings. But it's still baffling.'

'It wasn't your fault,' she assured him.

'I still find it hard to believe.'

'But you're here now and that's all that counts.'

Bending over, he kissed the tip of her nose. 'What's for tea? I'm starving.'

Irene laughed. 'Kippers. I was lucky enough to get some. You always adored kippers.'

'Did I?'

'Always,' she declared, rising. 'Where are the children by the way?'

'Gone out to play. I made them do their homework first. Was it all right to let them go? They said they were allowed.'

'Only until the nights draw in and it gets dark early. Then they're not.'

44

'That seems sensible. I've a lot to learn about children. I know nothing,' he confessed.

'You're doing well so far. Common sense goes a long way.'

'I'll remember that.'

He still found it baffling that he'd never once been home on leave during his sojourn in the Army, he thought, returning to his newspaper. But there again, what did he know about the time before Zuwarah? That was a black, impenetrable hole.

Chapter Four

Slowly Reith laid the tool he was holding down on the workbench and stared at it in despair. It was his first morning back at work and he'd hoped . . . oh how he'd hoped, prayed, that all his old skills would somehow have been retained. He slumped over the bench and closed his eyes. He didn't know one tool from another. And as for using them, that was a cruel joke.

After a few minutes he straightened up and went in search of the foreman.

'What's wrong with you, pal? You look as though you've lost a pound and found a tanner,' Billy Drummond said breezily to Reith, joining him at the bar in McTavish's.

Reith had a sip of his 'hauf', the whisky he'd ordered along with his pint. 'Bad day,' he muttered in reply. 'I started back at work this morning.'

'And?'

Reith sipped more whisky. 'I couldn't do the job. I'd forgotten everything.'

'Christ!' Billy sympathized. 'Told Irene?'

'I have. Then came straight down here.'

'What did she say?'

'Not a lot.'

Billy called to Bob McTavish for a pint. 'Let me get you another hauf,' he said to Reith.

'That's kind.'

'And I'll have one myself, I think.'

When their drinks had been placed before them, Billy asked: 'So what are you going to do?'

Reith shrugged. 'Look for something else, I suppose. Though I've no idea what.'

'It's a poser right enough,' Billy mused.

Reith made a fist and gently tapped it against the bar. 'Damn!'

'There was nothing else the firm could offer you?'

'No. All their workers are skilled.' He paused, then added miserably, 'Except for the sweeper-up, and they already have one of those.'

'It'll not come to that!' Billy protested. 'Sweeper-up indeed.'

'You don't need a barman by any chance, do you, Bob?' Reith asked McTavish, who was standing a few feet away serving another customer.

''Fraid not, Reith. Though I'll keep you in mind should a vacancy occur.'

'Thanks.'

Reith finished his first whisky and started on the second. It had been awful waiting for Irene to tell her what had happened. She had taken it well though, commiserating with him and giving him a big hug before he'd left for the pub. She told him to take as long as he wanted, tea could wait.

'Hold on a minute,' said Billy thoughtfully. 'I wonder if there's anything going at Black's.'

'Black's?'

'The yard where I am.'

'Do you think there might be?' Reith asked eagerly.

'There's no harm in finding out.'

Reith's sudden elation died. 'But what could I do? I know nothing about building ships.'

'You wouldn't have to, if you went after what I'm thinking about. It would be a bit of a come-down, mind, you having been a cabinet-maker and all. But it would be better than nothing.'

'So, what's the job?' Reith queried.

'You're all right physically I presume and not adverse to hard graft? For it would certainly be that.'

'What's the job?' Reith queried again.

'You don't need any skills to be a labourer. Just a strong back.'

'A labourer!'

'Tell you what,' Billy went on, 'if you're keen I could meet you outside your close the morn's morn and take you there. Show you where to go, like. Even put in a word for you.'

'You're on,' Reith enthused.

'I got it! Start next Monday,' Reith said to Irene as she entered the kitchen the following evening. Rushing over to her he picked her up and whirled her round. 'Isn't that smashing?'

She hid her disappointment. Reith a common labourer, the lowest of the low on the working-class totem pole. It was a blow.

'Absolutely smashing,' she agreed, pretending to be pleased. 'What's the pay?'

She almost flinched when he told her. It was just over half what he had been earning.

'Now you can give up your job,' he declared. 'I know it was necessary for you to work while I was away, but not now. You can go back to being a proper housewife.'

'Hang on a wee,' she said. 'There are four of us, don't forget. We could manage on those wages, just, but adding on what I bring in would make life an awful lot easier.'

He frowned. 'Are you saying you don't want to stop work?'

'No,' she replied quietly. 'I just don't think it's entirely practical or sensible for me to do so.'

Now it was his turn to be disappointed. 'You'll keep on then?'

They were interrupted by Agnes, blundering into the room, tears streaming down her face. 'Matt pulled my hair,' she sobbed.

Irene immediately gathered her daughter to her. 'There, there, hush.'

'He's a big bully. He hurt me,' Agnes further sobbed.

'What did you do?'

'Nothing.'

'Oh yes you did. You annoyed me,' Matt stated from the kitchen doorway, scowling.

'That's no reason to pull her hair,' Reith admonished sternly.

'She deserved it,' Matt retorted, before striding away.

'Matt, come here this instant!' Reith called out, and a few seconds later a reluctant Mathew reappeared in the doorway.

'I don't know what happened, and don't want to. But never, I repeat, never, lay your hands on your sister again. If you do I'll give you a thrashing, I promise you.'

Matt went white.

Reith rounded on Agnes. 'And the same thing goes for you,

young lady. No more getting at Matt, or annoying him in any way. You'll treat each other with respect or you'll have me to account to.'

He stabbed a finger at Matt. 'Now you go to your room and stay there until I say. You may or may not be getting tea.'

He pointed the same finger at Agnes. 'You also. Bedroom. Now.'

'Aw Dad!' Agnes wailed, crying even harder than before.

'*Now.*'

'Will I have to go without tea?'

'We'll see. Now off with you.'

Reith sighed with exasperation when the children had gone. 'I hope I wasn't too harsh, but I'm not having hair-pulling and face-slapping.'

'I think you frightened the life out of Matt,' Irene smiled thinly.

'As you admitted, you've been too easy on them. Well, that's all changed, which they'll soon learn.'

'They will get tea though, won't they?' Irene pleaded.

'I never really intended they wouldn't. I only wanted them to think they might not.'

He had changed in some ways, Irene thought. He was more aggressive, and certainly more dominant, than he'd been before the war. She didn't know whether that was a result of the war itself or of being shot in the head. It could have been either.

'Tell you what,' she said, 'about the dairy. Why don't I ask Mr McDougall my boss if I can go part-time? Would that suit?'

It didn't really, he hated the idea of his wife working at all, but agreed anyway.

'I'll speak to him tomorrow,' Irene declared, and set about making the tea.

Reith waited till it was on the table before calling Matt and Agnes to come through.

Both children ate in well-mannered silence.

Several weeks later Irene was woken in the middle of the night by Reith talking in his sleep. She stared at him bleary-eyed.

'Billy,' he muttered. 'Billy.'

It puzzled her. Why was he mentioning Billy Drummond?

'Billy,' he said again.

Then she had a devastating thought which made her go icy cold all over. What if it wasn't Billy Drummond, but . . .

Oh my God! she thought in alarm. Had his memory started to come back? Was that it?

'Billy,' he said yet again.

Reith was convinced his memory would return one day, but Irene had been praying it would never happen ever since she'd received that first letter from Harrington Manor. What relief that letter had given her, what joy. And now . . .

'Billy,' he repeated.

Please God, please let it be Billy Drummond. Please! For if it wasn't Billy Drummond, and this *was* the beginning of his memory returning, then . . . 'Oh Reith,' she whispered in the darkness. 'I love you so much. With all my heart, darling.'

Reith grunted and turned onto his side away from her.

Fearful, Irene lay awake for the rest of that night but he didn't speak again.

Billy Boyne, the name thundered through Irene's mind as she stood alone in the dairy waiting to serve a customer. Even after all these years she could still hear his voice, feel his touch, remember all too clearly the intimate things he'd done to her.

Wee Billy whom she'd known at school, who'd grown up to be a thug and gangster. He was still at school when he and his family had moved to another part of Glasgow. Then one awful day he'd reappeared, because he was doing business in the Bridgeton area, he'd explained, and she'd agreed to go with him to a Tally ice-cream shop for coffee. That had been the beginning of it all. She'd been flattered initially by his compliments. What a beautiful woman she'd become, what a lucky sod Reith was to be married to her.

On the second occasion he'd sought her out, waylaying her in the street and insisting they have coffee again. During that meeting he'd told her about himself, boasting of his exploits, how much money he was making, the fancy car he drove, the well-decked-out apartment he owned.

He'd always had a soft spot for her, he'd said. Never forgotten the lassie he'd had a crush on at school – that was news to her! – but apparently it was true.

Was she happy with Reith? She'd informed him she was. She recalled the way his dark eyes had glittered when she'd told him, and remembered that same look when she spoke about the baby Mathew who was her pride and joy and on whom Reith doted. She couldn't believe her ears when he'd asked her out. Slip away from Reith one night, he'd suggested; he'd pick her up in his car and they'd go to a posh restaurant where he'd wine and dine her, money no object. She'd refused of course. She loved Reith, was happy with her husband and had no intention of going out with Billy or any other man.

But Billy had been persistent, waylaying her again and again, pleading with her to have a drink, coffee, anything.

She'd told him to leave her alone, she was a happily married woman and that was that. But Billy had been smitten, and determined with it, and what Billy wanted Billy got.

During this she'd made enquiries about Billy and what she'd learned was disturbing in the extreme. In a city known for its violence, Billy was a byword. He was reputed to have killed at least three men, which the police had never been able to prove. And added to murder there were countless stabbings, razorings and hatchetings. Oh, Billy was a gem all right. Someone to be feared, not someone to cross.

And Billy fancied her rotten.

Then she remembered the day when she'd been out with Mathew in his pram when a car had slid to a stop beside her and Billy, at the wheel, had looked directly at Mathew and smiled that sinister smile of his.

He'd waited a week after that, letting her mull things over, before waylaying her again. He'd spoken quietly, almost apologetically, which was even more frightening. It was simple: either she complied with his wishes and became his girlfriend or else Reith would suffer the consequences. Easy to do, he'd said. He'd break both Reith's legs, badly, and scar him for life. And if that still didn't work, well . . . He hadn't needed to elaborate, she'd known the bastard was referring to Mathew. Hurt a child? Billy was entirely capable of it. That was the sort of animal he was.

So, she'd given in. What else could she do? The alternative was too horrifying to contemplate. It hadn't been difficult to see Billy. Reith worked regular hours, Billy didn't. As for Mathew, she'd left him with neighbours, a common enough occurrence. She'd often looked after other people's children herself while they were off doing their own thing.

She recalled with a shudder the first time she'd gone to Billy's apartment. There had been champagne, which she'd needed to do what was expected of her, then Billy's double bed. By no stretch of the imagination could it be termed lovemaking. He'd used her brutally in all manner of revolting ways, but she'd begged him time and again not to leave any marks on her which Reith might see.

And so it had gone on. She'd hoped and prayed he'd tire of her, let her off the hook, take a fancy to another woman. But Billy, if anything, had become more and more keen.

Then Agnes had been born. She'd been worried sick that Agnes would be Billy's, but something deep inside her had told her that she wasn't. Agnes was Reith's child.

War hadn't been long declared when Reith found out about the affair. A so-called 'pal' had taken him aside one night and told him that he, the pal, had it on good authority that she was sleeping with a chap called Billy Boyne, and had been for a long time.

The ensuing confrontation had been horrendous. To begin with she'd denied it, saying it simply wasn't true. She wasn't having an affair with anyone, far less the notorious Billy Boyne. A mistake. She did know a Billy Boyne then? All she could think about in her hysteria was that she had to protect Reith, Mathew and now Agnes. If Reith was to go seeking out Billy, she knew what would happen. He'd end up in a wheelchair, if not dead. So she'd lied, which she saw as the only course open to her.

At last she'd admitted that she was having an affair and Reith was appalled. That was when she should have told him why she had consented to the affair. Only that was impossible. That would have forced a clash between Reith and Billy with inevitable results. So she'd said, that she was in love with Billy. And how that had cost her!

Reith had been stunned into silence, then started silently to weep. It had been the only time she'd ever seen him cry. The whole affair had broken her heart, but she felt it was better that than to have Reith go up against Billy. She too had cried, long and bitterly as she lay alone later in bed, Reith slumped in his favourite chair. How she'd hated Billy, even more, and she wouldn't have thought that possible, than before. For he'd cost her her marriage and the only man she would ever love.

Reith had stayed off work for three days, walking the streets, getting drunk. Whose baby was Agnes? he'd wanted to know. Irene assured him she was his, but the doubt remained in his eyes.

On the fourth day he informed her he'd enlisted, then gone off to work to tell everyone there. She'd written when he'd gone, but he hadn't answered her letters. Nor ever come home on leave. The cruel irony was that several months after Reith's departure Billy had been caught during a robbery and gone down for a long stretch.

He was in Barlinne Prison, the Bar-L as it was commonly known. If only Billy had been arrested before the confrontation with Reith then all would have been well. She'd have somehow made Reith believe the story was a load of malicious nonsense. For he would have been safe then, as would the children, free of any reprisals from Billy.

She hadn't known what would happen at the end of the war. Would Reith survive? Would he return to Glasgow? Her only hope was that if he did come back she could explain the situation to him, make him understand she'd been protecting him and the children.

The letter from Harrington Manor had taken her breath away. He had survived and she was to be given another chance. As far as he now knew there had been nothing wrong with their marriage. There had been no Billy, no affair – which was how she desperately wanted things to stay. If Reith's memory came back she'd lose everything. She could still explain, of course, and hope that he'd stay on. But how much better it would be if she didn't have to. Things could remain as they were with Reith ignorant of her betrayal, without any knowledge of what had previously occurred.

Her thoughts were interrupted by the loud ting of the doorbell as a customer came into the shop.

'Good morning, Mrs Beattie,' she smiled. 'And what can I do for you today?'

Reith dribbled the old bladder a few yards, having taken it off Agnes who'd insisted on joining in the kickabout. Mathew adored football he'd discovered, which was why he'd brought the family to Glasgow Green that Saturday afternoon. Smiling, Irene stood and watched.

'Oh no you don't,' Reith muttered, warding off a tackle from Matt who immediately tackled again.

Matt's right foot flicked and the ball was magically gone from Reith. Matt laughed as he dribbled it away.

'You're good, son, really good,' Reith called out enthusiastically, which brought a flush of pleasure to Matt's cheeks.

Agnes barged her brother, trying physically to knock him off the ball, but failed to get it for herself. Matt stopped dead, swung round, and taunted her by offering her the bladder. When she dived in to get it he tapped it gently aside, causing her to miss it completely.

Agnes glared at him, feeling she'd been made a fool of.

'Come on,' Matt teased, offering her the ball again. And he tapped it away a second time before her foot made contact. Infuriated, Agnes wanted to swear but didn't because Reith and Irene were within hearing distance.

Matt went off at a run, pursued by Reith. He finally paused to pass the bladder to Reith who then passed it to a delighted Agnes.

'That's more like it,' she said, setting off on a wee dribble of her own.

They played like this until Reith thought they'd had enough and it was time to go home.

'Aw Dad!' Matt protested.

'Think of your poor mother. She must be frozen stiff standing there.'

Obligingly Irene shivered.

Reith ruffled Matt's hair. 'I'm impressed son. You're so good you might even make a professional when you grow up. Play for Rangers. How about that, eh?'

Matt went almost crimson with delight. Be a professional! Play for the Gers! That must be the dream of nearly every Protestant boy in Glasgow. If he'd been Catholic it would have been Celtic. The gaze he gave his father was one of sheer adoration.

'What about me? Am I good too?' Agnes demanded.

'Very,' Reith replied with a straight face.

'As good as Matt?'

'I wouldn't say so. But there again, he's a boy.'

'I can do anything a boy can,' she retorted stoutly. 'You should see me run flat out.'

Whirling on Matt she challenged him. 'Race you to the road?'

'You're on!'

And off they went, Agnes's arms flailing at her sides as she flew over the grass.

Reith picked up the bladder. 'I enjoyed that,' he declared to Irene.

'Nicely done, praising Matt as you did. You've made him into a real fan.'

Reith smiled at her. 'A little praise never hurt anyone. You learn that in the Army.'

'And gets them onto your side?'

'Of course. Helps win them over, which I felt was needed with Matt.'

Irene suddenly frowned. 'You just said you learned that in the

Army. Does that mean you remember. Learning it, I mean?'

He considered the question for a few seconds. 'I suppose I do,' he replied thoughtfully. 'I wouldn't have said it otherwise. But I don't consciously remember it.'

It was another possible indication that his memory was returning, she thought grimly. It quite spoiled the remainder of what had been a marvellous day.

Billy Drummond had certainly been right when he'd said labouring was hard graft and you needed a strong back, Reith reflected as he shovelled sand into a wheelbarrow. But in a perverse way he enjoyed it, and he certainly relished the company. His mates at Black's were all good blokes. There wasn't one of them he didn't like.

It had been six months now since he'd started. The first couple of weeks had been difficult as he'd become soft during his sojourns at Zuwarah and Harrington Manor, but he'd soon toughened up and become used to the work. He still suffered from the occasional bad headache, but none severe enough to keep him home for which he was thankful. As for his memory, or lack of it before Zuwarah, that remained the same, blank, nothing.

'What you got in your piece today?' Jim McIntyre, another labourer, called out to Reith. The 'piece' referred to were the sandwiches he'd brought for the mid-day break.

'Smoked salmon,' Reith joked in reply.

Jim grinned. 'That missus of yours certainly spoils you. It'll be caviar next.'

Reith pulled a face. 'She wouldn't dare. I can't stand the stuff.'

'Sounds fishy to me,' Bob Barr, another mate, commented drily, raising a laugh all round.

The ship they were currently building was one whose capacity was 8,000 tons, commissioned by the Anchor Line. It was a motor vessel which was to be named, so rumour had it, the *Elysia*.

As he worked Reith wondered what actually was in his piece. Cheese probably, but not spam. He'd finally admitted to Irene that he loathed the damn stuff and she'd chided him for not telling her sooner.

Sand flew through the air as he shovelled on.

He felt Irene's hand come to rest on his buttock and gently stroke it. He sighed with weariness; it had been a long hard day and all he wanted was some sleep.

Her hand moved to slip inside his fly.

'Reith?' she whispered. 'Kiss me.'

'I did when we got into bed.'

'I know. But kiss me again.'

He twisted round to face her. 'I really am tired. Dead beat.'

'You always are nowadays,' she pouted.

'That's not true, and you know it.' He kissed her on the lips, pulling away when she tried to thrust her tongue into his mouth.

'I told you I'm too tired,' he said irritably.

She massaged him. 'Are you sure?'

'Absolutely. A shift at that yard would knacker anybody.'

'The knacker's yard, is it?' she teased, and gave a low laugh.

He smiled. 'Oh very good!'

She snuggled up as close to him as she was able. 'I love you so much, Reith, and just keep on wanting to prove it.' When he didn't reply straight away she added, 'And I get so worried.'

'About what?'

'It's stupid, I know. But I keep thinking, suppose you were to go away again?'

'Now why should I do that?'

'I said it's stupid. But it worries me.'

He put an arm round her. 'I've no plans to go anywhere Irene. Unless it's "doon ra watter fur ra Fair".' Down the water was the Clyde, the Fair the Glasgow Fair Fortnight when the city's workers traditionally took their summer holiday. 'And if I do go there then you and the children will be coming along.'

'That would be nice,' she murmured.

'Now can I get some kip. Please?'

He pecked her on the forehead and then turned over.

His leaving wasn't stupid at all, but a real fear for her. She was only too well aware that it could come about should his memory return. Putting a hand to her mouth she worried a nail and was still chewing it when Reith began to snore. Her last thought before drifting off was that he'd never mentioned Billy in his sleep again. At least not that she was aware.

Two nights later the nightmares began. The soldiers, men with no faces, were engaged in hand-to-hand combat. A bayonet flashed, sinking deep into a chest from which spouted a bright red fountain. The dying man's scream changed into a long drawn-out agonized shriek. A grenade exploded blowing someone to smithereens.

56

Pieces of flesh, blood and gore, flew in all directions. A severed hand waggled obscenely on the ground.

A mist rolled in, shrouding everything and everybody. Shapes moved in and out of it, rifles firing, bayonets stabbing. He was going to die, he knew it. They all were. Then he was grabbed from behind, felt strong arms pinioning his own to his sides. A faceless form loomed out of the mist, bayonet at the ready. Now it was his turn to shriek . . .

'For God's sake, Reith, wake up!'

Reith found himself sitting upright in bed, shaking all over. He was covered in sweat. He gulped in a deep breath, then another.

'You were having a nightmare,' Irene explained anxiously, arms wrapped round him. He shrugged free, remembering those other arms, the German's.

'Sorry,' he mumbled, running a hand over his face.

'What was all that about?'

Christ! he thought. That had been awful – and so realistic. It was as though he'd actually been there.

'The war,' he said.

'Oh!' she breathed.

'None of them had faces. Not on our side, nor theirs.'

'Was it a memory?'

'I honestly don't know. It might have been or simply a product of my imagination. I can't say.'

He took another deep breath to try and stop the shaking.

'Is there anything I can do? Anything I can get you?' she asked.

'No.'

A memory, she thought. Was this another sign?

'Wow!' he exclaimed softly. 'That was quite something.'

'Well, it's all over now. You're here with me, safe and sound.'

She wondered then about the children; that shriek of his might have wakened them. 'Won't be a mo,' she said, and slipped out from beneath the covers. But the children, thankfully, hadn't woken up. When she checked them, not needing a candle as there was a full moon, both were still fast asleep.

'They're all right,' she told Reith, getting back into bed.

'That was scary. Really scary,' he said.

'Want to tell me about it?'

He considered it. 'Not right now. Maybe tomorrow.'

It was well over an hour later before he finally dozed off again.

Chapter Five

'Hello Billy, how's it going?' a man said, joining Billy Drummond and Reith *en route* for Black's.

'Not so bad, Roger. And yourself?'

'Can't complain.'

'How's Catie?'

'In the pink. And Bet?' Bet was Billy's wife, Catie was Roger's.

'Same. Oh by the way, do you two know one another?'

'I've seen your pal round Black's. But we've never met.'

'Roger Smith, this is Reith Douglas.'

'Pleased to meet you,' smiled Roger, as he extended his hand which Reith shook.

'Reith joined us after being demobbed,' Billy explained.

'Oh aye, what were you before?'

'I was a cabinet-maker,' Reith replied.

Roger raised an eyebrow. 'And what are you doing for us?'

'I'm a labourer.'

Roger thought that lowering of status peculiar, but neither commented on the fact nor asked Reith why it had come about. That might have appeared rude. The three of them chatted about other things until they reached the yard gates where they split up.

The following day Reith went to the toilet during his morning break and found himself standing beside Roger who greeted him with a broad smile.

'Billy told me about you yesterday. How you were shot and lost your memory as a result. That's terrible,' Roger sympathized.

'Oh, it could have been worse,' Reith said.

'How's that?'

'Better than being dead.'

Roger threw back his head and laughed. 'I like that. You've got a sense of humour.'

Well it was, Reith thought drily.

'Where do you live?' Roger enquired.

'Mill Street.'

'We're not far from there – Muslin Street. Do you know it?'

Reith nodded.

'So, we're kind of neighbours then. Mind you, a lot of us at Black's are that.'

'Anyway,' said Roger, doing up his final button, 'I'm off. See you around, pal.'

'See you around.'

Reith had to hurry as the hooter sounded, ending the break.

'Hey Reith, hold up,' Roger called out to him a few weeks later as they were coming off their shift. Hurrying over he fell in beside Reith.

'I never realized you were with the paras.'

'So I'm told,' Reith smiled.

'My brother was too. My wee brother that is. His name was Ian.'

Reith noted the past tense and knew what to expect.

'He was killed at Arnhem,' Roger stated.

'Sorry to hear it,' Reith commiserated.

'Luckily he wasn't married, but he did leave a fiancée who still drops in on us from time to time.'

Roger offered Reith a cigarette, but Reith shook his head. 'Don't smoke.'

Roger lit up, flicking the spent match into the gutter. 'I'm taking the missus out for a drink this Saturday night and was wondering if you and yours would care to join us? I'd like to buy you a few, you being a para and all. Who knows? You might even have known our Ian. Though you wouldn't remember, would you?'

''Fraid not.'

'So, what do you say? Are you game?'

'I'm all in favour. But I'll have to speak to the wife first. You know how it is.'

Roger laughed. 'Oh, I do that all right.'

'I'll have a word tonight and look out for you tomorrow.'

'Fair enough. I usually take Catie to the lounge bar of the Tron Hotel. It's quite smart there and women seem to like it.'

The Tron Hotel, Reith made a mental note of that. A little further on they parted company and Roger gave Reith a cheery wave goodbye.

'But you must go, they're expecting us,' Irene said to Reith. It was Saturday evening and he'd been suffering from a blinding headache all day that just wouldn't go away. On top of that he'd had another horrific nightmare the night before.

'My head's killing me,' he groaned in reply.

Irene's disappointment showed clearly on her face; she'd been eagerly looking forward to this night out ever since Reith had proposed it. 'Perhaps if you took another couple of tablets?' she suggested.

'It's too soon for that.'

Damn! she thought. Still, if Reith was so unwell then there was nothing she could do. Surely the Smiths, whom she was keen to meet, would understand once the situation was explained? They weren't likely to take offence.

Reith sighed, and glanced up at the mantelpiece clock. If they were going to go then they should leave within the next five or ten minutes.

Agnes came to stand before him, looking concerned. 'If I gave it a kiss would that make it better?' she asked.

Despite the pain, he smiled. 'It would certainly help, angel. I'm sure of that.'

She planted a big smacker on his forehead. 'There.'

'I'll nip up and tell Bessie Loudon that we're staying in after all,' Irene said. Bessie had agreed to pop down every so often to make sure the children were all right.

Reith realized how disappointed Irene was which made him feel guilty. 'No, don't,' he declared reluctantly. 'I'll give it a go.'

Immediately Irene brightened. 'I've heard so much about the Tron Hotel. I've always wanted to see inside.' She paused, then added. 'If the headache persists we can always make our excuses and come home again. At least we'll have shown willing.'

Reith lurched to his feet. 'I'll take some of those tablets with me.'

'I'll put them in my bag,' Irene said.

Reith crossed to the window and looked out over the back court to the shining windows of the tenement building beyond. It was neither the lights nor the building he saw, but visions from the previous night. He shuddered. A few minutes later he and an excited Irene left to catch a tram into town.

The splendid Tron Hotel was adjacent to the Tolbooth, a well-known Glasgow landmark viewed by Daniel Defoe during his visit to the city in the eighteenth century. They went through some glass doors into a thickly carpeted foyer decorated with exotic potted plants. A sign to their left indicated the way to the Skean Dhu lounge bar where they had arranged to meet the Smiths.

'It's very posh,' Irene whispered to Reith, pleased she'd worn her best bottle-green dress and her smart jewellery. She'd pinned a cameo brooch that had belonged to her mother on her lapel, while round her neck she'd hung a gold locket which had been Reith's wedding present.

Irene gazed around her, soaking in the atmosphere. She felt a proper lady in these surroundings, no less. She fought back the urge to giggle at the thought. They went down a passageway lined with gilt-framed oil paintings that led into the lounge which was reasonably busy. Most of the other Glasgow town pubs would have been bursting at the seams, as it was Saturday night.

Reith spotted Roger sitting at a small table on the far side. 'This way,' he said to Irene, taking her by the elbow.

Roger rose at their approach, while the woman at his side smiled at them. Irene noted that Roger was shorter than Reith, stockily built with an open, good-natured face. His wife was blonde and exceptionally attractive, with a pageboy haircut.

'You made it then,' Roger declared, grasping Reith's hand and pumping it.

'Only just, I've got a dreadful headache,' he replied.

'A few haufs will soon see to that,' Roger enthused.

Introductions were made, coats disposed of, then the newcomers sat down while Roger remained on his feet. 'So, what's it to be, you two?' he enquired.

'Whisky and lemonade please,' Irene replied.

Roger leant forward and said quietly to Reith, 'They don't serve pints in here. Only halfs. That's to keep out the riff-raff you understand.'

'I'll have a half of heavy then.'

'And a hauf to go with it. On its own, water or lemonade?'

'Lemonade for me too,' Reith answered. Whisky and lemonade

61

was a great Glasgow drink, favoured by men and women alike.

'It's very grand here,' Irene commented to Catie as Roger went up to the bar.

'Ever so,' Catie agreed.

'And expensive too no doubt.'

Catie ignored that remark and concentrated instead on Roger's back, with a feline expression on her face.

Reith closed his eyes and saw stars. He sank back against the brown leather upholstery, wishing he was at home, tucked up in bed. The pain had eased somewhat, but not a lot. Catie's gaze flicked across to Reith, wondering briefly what it was like to have lost your memory. He had a sad face, she thought.

'Have you got children?' Catie asked Irene. And as it turned out that the Smiths also had a boy and a girl, the two women proceeded to talk about their offspring until Roger returned with the drinks.

'Here, get those down. They'll help the head,' Roger beamed at Reith, placing his whisky and beer in front of him.

'I've got something to show you,' Roger announced once he was settled. From an inside pocket he produced a photograph and handed it to Reith. 'My brother Ian.'

Reith stared at the picture of a young man in his early twenties who bore a distinct resemblance to Roger.

'Taken during his last leave,' Roger said.

'Hmmh,' Reith murmured.

'I don't suppose . . .' Roger trailed off and raised an eyebrow.

'Never seen him before. Sorry,' Reith apologized, returning the photograph.

'He's hardly likely to remember your brother when he didn't even remember me, his own wife,' Irene declared, and laughed slightly shrilly. The laugh grated on Reith.

'Aye well, worth a try,' stated Roger, lifting his whisky. 'Slainthe!'

'Slainthe!' the other three responded, and drank.

That was good, Reith thought, as the whisky burned its way down his throat. Another swig and the glass was empty.

'You are dry,' Roger commented, staring at the empty glass.

'It's been that kind of day,' Reith replied, and shrugged.

Roger had a natural, easygoing charm about him, Irene thought, warming to the man. She wasn't so sure of Catie however. She seemed aloof and a little off-putting. Aloof and . . . rather cold, Irene decided.

'Here, I've got a story for you,' Roger said, and launched into a very funny account of an incident that had happened recently at Black's. In the middle of this Catie glanced at Reith and saw that, although he appeared to be listening, his mind was really elsewhere, which annoyed her. Even if he did have a headache he should have better manners. She set a high store on good manners.

As he was telling the story Roger was thinking how pretty Irene was – not much in the chest department, mind, and he'd never been mad on gingers, but pretty nonetheless. He couldn't help but wonder what she'd be like between the sheets.

Catie noted his interest. But then that was nothing new, she thought wearily. Roger always showed interest when in the company of an attractive woman. Why should it be any different with Irene Douglas?

'Oh very good!' Irene complimented him when Roger came to the end of his story.

'Funny eh?'

'Hysterical,' she nodded.

Reith grunted.

Roger pulled out his cigarettes. 'Do you smoke?' he asked Irene.

'No.'

He lit up, and blew a perfect smoke ring at the ceiling.

'You're quite a performer,' Irene commented.

Catie smiled inwardly. Many a true word . . .

'How are the drinks?' Reith frowned, wanting a refill.

Irene and Catie both replied they were fine, but Roger saw off what remained in his glass. 'Let me,' Roger offered, starting to rise.

'No you don't. It's my shout,' Reith said, and left the table.

At the bar, he positioned himself in a discreet corner, ordered three large ones, then threw one down his throat before returning with the remaining two. Roger was in the middle of a joke which seemed to be directed at Irene. She let out a tinkling laugh when he delivered the punch line while Catie smiled thinly.

'How are you getting on at Black's?' Catie asked Reith.

'All right.'

She waited for him to elaborate, but he didn't, lapsing instead into a withdrawn silence.

Bugger you! Catie thought, and turned her attention again to Roger and Irene.

The whisky was working, Reith thought, feeling a little woozy. At last, the headache was easing. Thank God! Something stirred in his mind, a picture trying to form. Not of the war, he was certain, something else. He knitted his brows in concentration, oblivious to the rest of the party. Roger began another joke.

Again the soldiers were without faces. Again rifles were firing, bayonets flashing. A body lay thrashing in agony, a large, gaping hole in its back. Unholy fear held him in a vicelike grip. He wanted to run away, but his feet were rooted to the spot. Try as he would he couldn't move. A bullet zinged past. Then everything turned red, the colour of newly spilt blood.

'Reith!' a voice shouted. 'Where are you, Reith?'

'Over here,' he croaked.

'They've got me, Reith. The swines have got me.'

'I'm coming! Hang on, I'm coming.'

But he couldn't, because he was still unable to move.

Suddenly there were German uniforms everywhere. Hundreds of them, thousands, swarming round him, closing in. Then, with a great triumphant roar, they were on him.

He'd forgotten to pick up his evening paper on his way home so had decided to nip out before tea to get one. He was returning from the newsagent's when a female figure loomed out of the swirling fog walking in the opposite direction. There was something familiar about her, he thought. A neighbour? And, by George, the female now only feet away was beautiful. Absolutely gorgeous, a real cracker.

The woman smiled at him, and nodded. Quickly he returned the smile.

She was about to pass him when he suddenly realized who she was.

'Hello, Catie. How are you?'

She stopped. 'I'm fine. And you?'

'Don't be offended, but for a moment there I didn't recognize you.'

She'd thought he'd been wearing a puzzled expression. 'I must have made a big impression,' she replied coldly.

That embarrassed him. 'I'm afraid I wasn't really with it the other evening.'

'You certainly kept quiet. We'd hardly have known you were there. At the time I wondered if we were boring you.'

'No, no, no,' he replied quickly, upset to think she might have imagined that. 'It was the headache. I should never have gone out, but Irene would have been terribly disappointed if I hadn't.'

That mollified Catie a little.

'Irene thoroughly enjoyed herself at the Tron. We must do it again,' he said.

'When you *don't* have a headache,' she jibed.

He decided to explain himself further. 'I get them as a result of my wound. Headaches and nightmares. Hopefully both will disappear in time.'

Perhaps she'd misjudged him, she thought, been too harsh. The poor man had been shot in the head, after all.

'And the headache I had that evening was a blinder. When I closed my eyes I saw stars.'

She touched him gently on the arm. 'In that case it was good of you to make the effort to come at all.'

'As I said, Irene would have been terribly disappointed if I hadn't. She was dying to meet you and Roger and to see the inside of the Tron Hotel.'

What a kind man, Catie thought. Many, her Roger included, wouldn't have put themselves out like that. She was impressed.

'Well, it was nice bumping into you,' Catie said, treating him to another smile.

'And you.'

'I'll mention us having another night out to Roger. I'm sure he'll agree, he likes you and Irene.'

'And I'll mention it to Irene.'

'Goodbye then.'

'Goodbye.'

She continued on her way, but he stood and watched her till she was swallowed up in the thick fog.

What a stunner, Reith thought yet again. And what a very likeable personality to go with it.

She'd got Reith Douglas all wrong, Catie reflected as she carved her way through the fog. The chap she'd just spoken to was quite different to the morose, monosyllabic individual who'd been in the lounge bar. She hadn't been at all keen to pursue a friendship with the Douglases, dead against it actually, but now she'd changed her mind. Something told her that Reith could be fun, although she'd have to keep her eyes on Roger with Irene.

Roger by name, roger by inclination she thought bitterly. He was off to another so-called Masonic meeting later on, which she imagined was an excuse. The trouble with him was that he was such a gifted liar, he had a natural flair for it. Oh, she'd caught him out a number of times, but never on the one thing that mattered. And that was the frequency of his affairs.

She knew in her heart he was being unfaithful, but proving it was something else. He was so damned careful, that was the problem. There was never anything concrete she could lay her hands on, no hard evidence. There had been the occasional giveaway over the years, a hint of scent that wasn't hers on his clothes, a trace of lipstick in a shade she never used. And then there were the persistent rumours which he always denied. Whispers that came back to her. But never a whisper attached to a name. Never that.

Bastard, she thought. And to think how she'd once loved him, doted on him, done anything he wanted, indulged his every whim, sexual and otherwise. And how had he repaid that love? By screwing around. Why? she'd asked herself a thousand times. She was sure there wasn't anything his fancy women would do that she wouldn't. It wasn't as if she was plain, or ugly. She was neither. And she made the best of herself. Not like some who let themselves go after having children, putting on weight or simply not taking care of themselves. So why?

One day, though, she'd get the proof she needed and then there would be a reckoning. One day.

Linda Brasil wiped sodden hair away from her face and gazed tenderly down at Roger, who was grinning up at her.

'Well?' he asked.

'Do I have to tell you?' she almost purred in reply. 'You make me feel things that Andy never did.' Andy was her dead husband who'd been killed serving with the Seventh Royal Tank Regiment during the offensive in the western desert against the Italian Tenth Army. It was after his death that, lonely and bereft, she'd taken up with Roger who'd known Andy.

Roger's grin became a smug leer.

Linda wiped away some of the sweat streaming down her fulsome breasts. 'Why don't you get rid of that wife of yours?' she said. 'You don't love her.'

'How do you know?' Roger queried softly, placing his hands behind his head and studying her.

'I know. Besides, you'd hardly be here shagging me rotten if you did.'

His grin returned. Roger loved it when women spoke dirty, he found it titillating, something Linda was only too well aware of.

'I have the children to consider,' Roger replied. 'They're still young, only seven and four. It's just not in me to walk out on them. How would Catie cope?'

'She'd cope all right,' Linda assured him. 'Women always do.'

Roger had no intention of leaving Catie for Linda whom he merely considered a piece of fun. She certainly wasn't as good-looking as Catie whom he was always proud to be seen having on his arm.

'And I'm better in bed,' Linda went on. 'You've often told me that.'

What Linda didn't know was that was what Roger told all his lady friends. It was part of his seduction technique to complain that Catie was an unenthusiastic bed partner who didn't really like sex all that much. Nothing could have been further from the truth.

Linda sat back on her haunches and stroked Roger's hairy thigh. 'I want you here every night Roger, not just the occasional visit.'

'I come whenever it's possible,' he lied.

'I appreciate that, but I want more.'

She was becoming a problem, he thought. Mind you, he'd seen it coming for a while. He was going to miss his little romps with Linda Brasil. But in the circumstances, pulling the plug was the best, and safest, thing to do. Problems like this could only get worse, never better, in his experience. Anyway, he was beginning to tire of her. They'd had a fair old run for their money. But nothing went on for ever. Time for new conquests, fresh blood.

'More isn't on, Linda. I'm sorry,' he stated.

'Surely you can get away more often?'

'It's difficult. I don't want Catie becoming suspicious.'

'Damn Catie!' Linda exclaimed in a burst of anger. 'I'm thinking about me, *us*.'

Definitely time to say ta-ra, Roger thought, wondering whether to do it that night or leave it for a little while.

'I'll have to go,' he said.

'So soon?' she wailed.

'I'd stay longer if I could, but I can't.'

Annoyance creased her face. She'd hoped they could do it again. 'If you have to, then I suppose you have to,' she conceded reluctantly.

He stroked her left nipple causing her to draw in her breath. God, she responded to him, he thought. All he had to do was touch her and she melted.

'Oohh!' Linda moaned when he brushed it a second time.

Roger made up his mind. It was a pity, but had to be done. He began marshalling his thoughts on how best to extricate himself. Later, when he left, Linda, thinking her heart would surely break, wept copiously into a large white linen handkerchief that had belonged to Andy.

'Would you like a twirl round the floor?' Roger asked Irene who quickly replied that she'd love to. The four of them were back at the Tron Hotel, but on this occasion they were attending a dinner-dance held in an upstairs room. It had been Roger's idea, as he had read about it in the newspaper.

'And you?' Reith enquired, turning to Catie.

'Would you mind if I left it for a bit? I'd like my meal to settle first.'

'Of course,' he replied understandingly.

He leant back in his chair and regarded Catie thoughtfully. Since they'd met up that evening, he'd hardly been able to take his eyes off her.

'The food was good,' she commented.

'Mine certainly was.'

'And plenty of it which surprised me with rationing on.'

He glanced down at her hands, which were long and slim, tapering to red varnished nails. They were exceptionally attractive, like the rest of her. 'So, what have you been up to since I saw you last?' he asked.

'This and that. Not a lot. I read quite a bit in the evenings. Especially when Roger's gone out and the children are in bed.'

'Really? I read a great deal myself. Books I get from the library.' He laughed lightly. 'I'm trying to re-educate myself on what I've forgotten. World events, that kind of thing.'

'It must be difficult for you,' she sympathized.

How often had that been said to him, he wondered. 'You come to terms with it. Though it can be bloody annoying. What type of books do you go in for?'

She shrugged. 'All sorts. Novels mainly. As long as it's something I can lose myself in. If I have a preference it's for novels with a strong romantic story line to them. Daphne du Maurier, for example, she's terrific.'

Reith smiled at her enthusiasm.

'Have you seen the film of *Rebecca*? I was spellbound when I watched that, Laurence Olivier was just out of this world.'

'No, I haven't,' Reith admitted.

'Then you must! Next time it comes round, go.'

'What about *Gone With The Wind*?'

'Aahhh!' Catie breathed. 'That's another I could sit through time and again. It was wonderful.'

'I enjoy films too,' he informed her.

'Do you go often?'

'Not as much as I'd like to. What with work and the children, you understand?'

'It's the same with me. Before I got married I'd go two, three times a week. I was a real fan.' She giggled. 'Charlie Chaplin was my favourite when I was younger, he always made me laugh.'

'Does Roger like the pictures?' Reith asked.

'He puts up with going, but usually gets restless halfway through. He thought *Gone With The Wind* a right old load of sentimental tripe. But there again, I suppose it is a woman's film.'

'Oh, I wouldn't say that,' Reith mused. 'I certainly enjoyed it.'

Catie's eyes sparkled. 'Good for you.'

'Now tell me about the books you've read recently.'

They were still chatting when they were rejoined by Roger and Irene.

'Irene's discovered I've got two left feet unfortunately,' Roger declared, pulling a face.

'Not at all!'

'Well, I'm hardly Fred Astaire.'

'Now that I will grant you,' Irene retorted, which made Roger laugh.

'You two seem to be getting on like a house on fire,' Roger said to Reith and Catie when he'd stopped laughing.

'We've discovered things in common,' Reith explained.

'Books and films,' Catie elaborated, 'though Reith reads heavier stuff than I do.'

Roger picked up the bottle of red wine they'd ordered with their meal and poured out the remainder. He then gestured to a passing waiter that they wanted another.

'It was Catie who introduced me to wine,' Roger informed Reith.

'Up until then I always thought it was a strict Frenchy and nancy boy drink.' He beamed at his wife. 'She's got class, my Catie. One in a million.'

Reith silently agreed.

Shortly after that Catie announced that her meal had settled and she'd now take up Reith on his offer for a dance. As they walked onto the floor, the number introduced was a slow waltz. Reith couldn't help but think she fitted into his arms as if she'd been made for them. They moved together fluidly and gracefully, natural partners.

'Roger wasn't joking when he said he had two left feet,' Catie smiled. 'He's a terrible dancer.'

'Which you're not.'

'You're not so bad yourself,' she replied, returning the compliment.

She suddenly frowned. 'How do you remember the steps if you've lost your memory?'

'A mystery,' he teased.

'Oh?'

'Not really. Towards the end of my stay at Harrington Manor, where I was sent to recuperate, I went to a number of dances. Some of the nurses I knew there were kind enough to instruct me.'

She'd totally changed her mind about Reith, she thought. She found him charming company, and so easy to be with. It really was amazing that this was the same man she'd first encountered at the Tron.

Why didn't Irene generate this excitement in him? Reith wondered. With Catie he felt charged full of electricity which never happened with Irene. He felt truly alive, as if walking on air, dancing on a cloud. He was a happily married man, he reminded himself abruptly. He shouldn't be having such thoughts. And he almost blushed when he realized precisely what those thoughts were.

Happily married, he reminded himself again. And yet . . . there was a slight niggle in the back of his mind. Something he couldn't put his finger on, something from the past.

When the number finished they both applauded. 'Shall we stay up?' he proposed, willing her to agree.

Inwardly, he sighed with relief when she nodded.

'You must tell me all about this Harrington Manor sometime,' Catie said as they broke into a polka.

'You wouldn't be interested, surely?'

'But I would. And the place you were before that. Roger mentioned some name which I can't remember.'

'Zuwarah, in Libya. I was taken directly there from Greece.'

He gazed into her eyes, and the electricity surged within him. 'I'll tell you all about it,' he husked, 'sometime.'

When they returned to their table Irene was rocking with laughter, Roger having just delivered the punchline of an excruciatingly funny, and rather risque, joke.

The next time Reith got up to dance was with Irene. Every so often, while she prattled on about how much she was enjoying herself and how entertaining Roger was, he found himself glancing over at Catie dancing with Roger, wishing he held her in his arms.

Chapter Six

Catie glanced up from her book at the clock ticking above the sideboard. Twenty past midnight and still no Roger. She was coldly furious, a state she'd been in since early that afternoon. A few minutes later there was the scrape of a key in the outside door, followed by the sound of Roger hanging up his coat and cloth cap.

'Not in bed yet?' he queried breezily as he entered the kitchen, rubbing his hands to warm them.

She regarded him steadily. 'How was the meeting?'

'Fine.'

'You're later than usual.'

'Aye well, it did go on a bit.'

She closed her book and laid it by her chair. 'Who was there?'

'The regulars. You know.'

She raised an eyebrow and didn't reply.

'Something wrong, Catie?'

'Should there be?'

He frowned. 'You've got a face like fizz.' Then, changing the subject he asked, 'Would you like a cup of tea before we turn in?'

'No, thank you.'

'I wouldn't mind one.'

'Then make it.'

He stared at her in consternation. 'Now I know there's something wrong. Come on, what is it?'

'Who is she?' Catie demanded in a tight voice.

'Who's who?'

'The woman you've been with.'

Roger laughed. 'So, that's it. More suspicions, accusations. Honestly, you're obsessed.'

'Who is she?' Catie repeated.

Roger filled the kettle at the sink and plonked it on the still-burning range. 'I told you, I was at the meeting. And there were no women present. There never are as they aren't allowed.' He was smiling which belied his inner turmoil. Luckily, on this occasion, he was telling the truth, thank God.

Catie silently fumed. Wasn't he plausible? she thought. Looked as though butter wouldn't melt in his mouth. Well, she knew better, she'd been married to the sod long enough.

'I overheard a conversation in the "steamie" today,' she stated. The steamie was the local wash-house.

'Oh aye?'

'They were talking about you.'

'That's interesting. What did these . . . gossips have to say?'

Catie noted the scorn and contempt he put into the word 'gossips', but didn't let it deter her. 'That you have a ladyfriend staying in Camlachie.'

Roger's stomach knotted, but his smile never wavered. Camlachie was where Linda Brasil lived. 'And who is this supposed ladyfriend?' he questioned.

'No-one mentioned a name.'

'Hah!' he barked out. 'I'm not surprised. For there isn't any such person. She's pure invention.' He busied himself with the teapot and caddy. 'Sure you won't have a cup?'

'I said, no thank you.'

'Suit yourself.'

A few seconds ticked by. 'Well?' she demanded. 'I'm waiting for an explanation.'

'How the hell can I give you that!' he suddenly exploded. 'There isn't one. How can I be held responsible for what some evil old biddies yap about in the steamie? They're making it up, that's all.'

'Why should they do that?'

'Because they've nothing better to do.'

How believable he was, she thought, outraged innocence. 'Funny, it's always your name gets mentioned, no-one else's.'

He looked her squarely in the eye. 'I swear to you, Catie, on all that's holy. On the life of my children. I do not have a ladyfriend.' Which was true enough, he congratulated himself. He'd already given Linda the boot.

73

'On the life of your children?' she queried softly.

'On the life of my children,' he repeated, and crossed his heart.

A hint of doubt crept into Catie's mind. Was it merely malicious gossip? Some of the women round about did have vicious tongues. But why was it always Roger? That was the point.

'It's a case of give a dog a bad name,' Roger went on. 'I don't know how all these rumours get started about me, the ones you throw in my face from time to time. It's beyond me.'

'So, who was there tonight?' Catie further probed.

He reeled off a list of fellow Masons. 'Go and ask any one of them if you want. They'll all give you the same story. I was at the meeting.'

It could be a bluff, she thought, or they could all be in cahoots. Masons did stick together, after all. Wasn't that what being a Mason was all about?

'Maybe I will,' she murmured.

'You do that!'

She could ask as many of those he'd mentioned, or their wives, and the answer would be the same, Roger smirked inwardly. He'd been at the meeting. On other occasions he wouldn't have been so fortunate.

Catie dropped her head into her hands. If only she could find proof, but that had always evaded her. Yet in her heart of hearts she knew he was deceiving her. But how did she know? Apart from the small giveaways, female intuition told her. That little voice in her head whispered that he was screwing around. She was suddenly exhausted, her eyelids drooping.

'Tell you what,' said Roger, 'why don't we go to the pictures one night soon? You'll enjoy that, it'll cheer you up, make you forget all this blithering nonsense. Reith and Irene can come with us, we'll make it a foursome with fish supper afterwards.'

Reith, she thought. That would be nice.

'This Friday or Saturday if you like?' he further proposed.

Catie rose and ran a hand over her face. 'I'll leave you if I ever do catch you out,' she stated. 'I swear I will.'

His smile returned. 'Then I don't have to worry. For you'll never catch me out, because you can't.'

As she left the room Catie wished that she could believe him.

Catie was on the point of dropping off when Roger slid into bed beside her, his hands immediately fumbling for her breasts.

'Good night,' she mumbled.

'Catie love,' he breathed, caressing a nipple.

'No,' she said firmly.

'It grieves me that you're so upset over nothing, gossip. I worry about you,' he whispered into her hair. He then blew into her ear, knowing how she would respond.

'Stop it!'

'Why? You like it.' He blew again.

'Roger!' she admonished with a shiver.

He knew his wife only too well. Within seconds her reluctant body was responding to him. A wolfish grin curled his lips upwards when he heard her breathing become faster.

'I would be stupid to become involved with another woman when I have you to come home to,' he murmured. 'And I may be many things, but I'm not stupid. I'd never risk losing you. You mean far too much to me.'

She squirmed when a hand slipped between her thighs. Make him stop this, she told herself, at the same time knowing she was already lost. He'd always had that effect on her.

'Here,' he said, turning her onto her back. 'Let me show you how much I love you, Catie darling. Do you think I'd be like this so quickly if I didn't? If I didn't find you the most attractive woman in the whole wide world?'

Oh Christ, she thought a little later, writhing beneath him, glorious sensations rippling through her. It was so good, so good. All doubts, suspicions were temporarily forgotten.

'I love you, Catie,' he groaned.

'And I love you, Roger.'

The trouble was, she thought despairingly, it was at moments like this, as he moved within her, that she knew, deep down, she still did. As she climaxed she threw her arms around him, drawing him into her, driving him in as deeply as he could go.

How the hell did these rumours get about anyway! he fumed afterwards when she was asleep. He was always so meticulously careful, never mentioning what he was doing to a soul, never confiding in anyone. Thank the Lord he'd ditched Linda when he had, for if he hadn't that's where he would have been. But he had left her, and had gone to the meeting. That was all that mattered. His story was foolproof.

Bloody gossips, why couldn't they mind their own business. Nothing more than interfering, meddlesome bitches!

Reith absentmindedly picked up the wedding photograph that stood encased in its ornate brass frame on their mantelpiece and studied it. They'd both aged considerably since then, but that was hardly surprising. He'd fought a war, while she'd had to cope with the war years and the worry about him.

'Penny for them?' Irene said from the sink where she was peeling potatoes.

'I was just thinking how much we've both aged since then.'

'Oh, thank you very much!' she replied sarcastically.

He smiled. 'Well, it is only natural. We've both had a lot to contend with in the meantime.'

In her case more than he realized, she thought grimly.

He replaced the photograph on the mantelpiece. 'It was a pity it rained that day though. Rotten luck for June.'

Irene went very still. 'It did, didn't it?'

'You were worried about ruining your dress. You were furious in the car as we left the church when you noticed a couple of spots of mud on the hem.'

She closed her eyes. Dear God, no!

'But the mud was sponged out all right and no harm was done.'

'Yes,' she agreed hoarsely.

He continued staring at the picture, lost in thought. 'I was so nervous that day, literally shaking in my shoes when you walked down the aisle.'

She laid the knife and potato she was peeling on the draining board and turned to face him, eyes sparkling with moisture. 'We got some lovely presents, didn't we?'

'We did indeed. Folks were extremely generous.'

'The tea set which I still use.'

'And the cutlery. Expensive stuff too.'

She crossed to the table and sat heavily on the nearest chair. 'Reith?'

He glanced at her. 'What?'

'You're remembering.'

He sucked in a short breath. 'So I am.'

'Your memory . . . it's starting to come back.'

He could remember their wedding day. Not totally clearly, but in patches. Getting dressed, arriving at the church, going inside. The minister marrying them. Flashes from the reception. Faces, faces with names to them. He swallowed hard. 'Oh Irene, I am remembering!' he exclaimed.

Matt and Agnes, also in the kitchen, were gazing at him in wonder, Agnes's expression one of sheer delight.

'I *am* remembering,' he repeated, voice trembling.

Irene had prayed so hard that this wouldn't happen. She felt sick, her senses reeling. How long would it be before he remembered Billy Boyne?

'I can't wait to tell McAllister,' Reith enthused. McAllister was the specialist he saw at the Royal Infirmary once a month who was monitoring his progress.

Agnes went over to Reith and took his hand in hers, positively beaming up at him.

Furrowing his brow in concentration, Reith went on. 'And I remember that as we left the reception you . . .' Irene felt she was dying inside.

'Well, I thoroughly enjoyed that picture. It was tremendous,' Catie said to Reith as the four of them walked slowly down the street eating their fish and chips. Irene and Roger were a little in front, she and Reith bringing up the rear. Reith gazed at her, thinking yet again how gorgeous she was. 'You look a bit like Ingrid Bergman you know,' he declared.

That thrilled her. 'Get away! You're pulling my leg.'

He laughed. 'I am nothing of the sort. You look like her. I can see the similarity.'

Did she really? Catie wondered, delighted to think she might.

'One thing's for certain,' he chuckled, 'neither Roger nor I look in the least like Gary Cooper.' They'd just been to see *For Whom the Bell Tolls*, based on the novel by Ernest Hemingway.

Catie glanced ahead at Roger. 'Well, that's true enough in his case,' she murmured.

'It was a sad ending though.'

'I cried,' Catie admitted.

Although Roger was talking to Irene, she was listening to Reith and Catie chattering away, the pair of them engrossed in one another and their mutual interest in films. All she could think about was the fact that Reith had remembered their wedding and what that could mean for the future.

'Pardon?' she blinked, focusing again on Roger who she'd just realized had asked her a question.

77

'I said, it's good fish, eh?'

'Lovely.'

She'd hardly touched hers as she had lost her appetite. And what little she'd eaten hadn't registered at all. When they finally disposed of the newspapers that their suppers had come wrapped in, Irene's ball of paper still contained most of her fish and chips, though none of the others were aware of this.

Reith and Catie continued talking together animatedly until it was time for the two couples to say good night and go their separate ways.

Reith paused to take a well-earned breather. He leant on his shovel, thinking about Catie as he had been all that morning. He just couldn't get the woman out of his mind, an ongoing situation that was beginning to make him feel guilty. Mind you, it wasn't as if he had done anything wrong, he and Catie were simply good friends. There was no harm in that, none at all.

On the other hand he knew he wasn't thinking of Catie in a purely platonic way. Truth was, he fancied her. There was something about Catie which was getting under his skin. It was silly, he told himself. She was happily married to Roger, a good bloke if ever there was one, and he was married to Irene.

Perhaps they shouldn't see so much of the Smiths, he mused, for they had been doing a lot together lately. The two families had become closer and closer. Astrid and Andrew, the Smiths' children, were now firm chums with Matt and Agnes.

'Hmmh,' he murmured.

The only problem was that he didn't want to see less of the Smiths, or Catie to be precise. He enjoyed the time they spent together, continually looking forward to their next meeting.

He thought about Irene. Did he love her? Had he loved her? He must have done, surely. But at the moment all he felt was . . . affection. Yes, that was it, affection. Reith shook his head. It was very confusing. He could only presume the love he'd had for her, the awareness of it, would return with his memory. He sighed, hefted his shovel, and got back to the task in hand, the image of Catie remaining with him.

He was sitting in the shared landing toilet, the 'cludgie' as everyone called it, when a scene from the past burst with brilliant clarity into his mind.

'How many you caught so far?' Cammy Sanderson asked.

The young Reith glanced at his schoolfriend. 'Seven, all of them docs.' Docs, short for doctors, although no-one knew why they were called that, were red-breasted minnows highly prized by the boys who fished the river and thought to be better than 'ordinary' minnows, who were the same colour all over.

Cammy whistled his appreciation.

'Have a dekko.'

Both lads bent over the pool Reith had scooped out in the shale of the riverbank and filled with water.

'Look at the size of that beauty, it's a beezer,' Cammy said admiringly, pointing at the largest.

'I wish I could take them home with me,' Reith commented. They both knew from experience that this was impossible as the fish would only die.

Reith straightened up and went to his line which was tied to a stick shoved into the shale. He pulled in the jam jar at the other end of the line. Their method of catching minnows was to spike a hole in the jar lid, drop in some bread, tie string round the neck of the jar and heave it out into the river. Fish would then manage to get into the jar but not out again.

He let out a whoop when he discovered two more minnows trapped in the jar, both of which were docs.

'Incredible luck so it is,' Cammy said, shaking his head in wonderment.

'Nine out of nine, amazing,' Reith agreed.

Cammy glanced up at the threatening grey sky. 'It's going to rain soon. Probably bucket down.'

'Is that why you didn't bring a jar yourself?'

Cammy nodded.

'Do you want to have a go with mine?'

'Oh yes please!'

Cammy did, but was bitterly disappointed when it transpired his catch was only a tiny ordinary minnow.

Reith caught eighteen fish in all, twelve of them docs, before the heavens opened. On the way home Reith commented to Cammy that it had been the best day's fishing he'd ever had. When they joined a knot of pals sheltering from the downpour in a closemouth he boasted about the number of docs he'd caught, and Cammy was able to verify this spectacular deed. For the rest of that holiday afternoon Reith was regarded by the others as something of a hero.

It had become a living nightmare, Irene thought, busy restocking shelves at the dairy. Every day, or every couple of days, Reith remembered something else from his past; and when he did he couldn't wait to regale her with his new-found memory. She'd become a bag of nerves, lost weight to the point where she was scrawny, while her face had developed lines where none had been before. It could only be a matter of time till he remembered about Billy Boyne, and then what?

'Damn Billy Boyne,' she muttered angrily to herself. Damn the bastard to hell where she hoped he'd roast for evermore.

It had been working so well for her and Reith since he'd come home from the war. Just like the old days before Billy. They had fun together, a good laugh. They were a couple. A couple that would be split asunder when, if, Reith finally remembered about her relationship with Billy.

She shuddered, recalling the innumerable times she'd been to bed with Billy and the horrible, sometimes despicable, things he'd done to her, and made her do to him. Reith and Billy were chalk and cheese. The one kind, tender, loving, the other a filthy degenerate animal who'd used her like a whore.

She closed her eyes. Please God, she prayed. Don't let Reith remember about Billy. I love that man and don't want to lose him. You've seen fit to give me a second chance which I've grabbed with both hands. Don't take that chance away from me again, that would be too cruel. Let me keep Reith, he's everything to me. Only the children mean as much. I would never have cheated on him if it hadn't been for Billy's threats, you know that. I was in an impossible situation, unable to refuse Billy, as the sod well knew. Please God, I ask again. Don't let Reith remember about Billy. Keep that part of his memory blank till his dying day.

'You all right Mrs Douglas?'

Irene snapped open her eyes to smile weakly at Mr McDougall, her boss, gazing down at her. 'Just got something on my mind that's all,' she answered. And with that she hastily resumed restocking.

When Reith returned from Black's that evening he'd remembered something else which he gleefully recounted to her.

The Smiths had left after an evening playing whist and now Reith and Irene were preparing for bed.

'Catie was in fine form tonight,' Reith remarked with a smile, thinking Catie had looked knockout, as usual. She'd been wearing a new Coty scent which he'd thought wonderful. He'd complimented her on it, asking if it was a present from Roger. It turned out that she'd bought it herself.

Irene stripped down to a pale pink brassière and matching French knickers, glancing sideways at Reith to see if he was watching her. Sadly he was wrapped in thought. It hadn't escaped her how taken Reith was with Catie. You only had to witness the way his eyes followed her every move when they were in company. 'Fine form,' Irene agreed, tight-lipped.

'Roger too,' Reith added as an afterthought.

Irene frowned, recalling how earlier Roger had kept accidentally, or so she'd presumed, touching her leg with his under the table. And once, when he'd dropped a card on the floor, his hand had brushed her calf. She couldn't believe that Roger had been trying it on, making overtures. Surely not! He and Catie were as thick as thieves, that was as plain as day and was the main reason Reith's little infatuation didn't bother her. Well, that wasn't entirely true. It might not bother her but it did hurt nonetheless. She wanted Reith to be interested in her, his gaze following her every move.

Reith was tying the cord of his pyjama bottoms when Irene's arms curled round his chest.

'What's all this then?' he joked.

'I just want to hold you. There's nothing wrong in that, is there?'

'Nothing at all.'

She slipped a hand inside his top and fondled him. 'I do love you Reith. You know that?'

'Of course I do.'

He made to move away. 'Irene, it's late,' he said softly.

'So? It's Sunday tomorrow, we can have a lie-in.'

He knew what this was leading to, and groaned inwardly. The last thing he felt like was lovemaking.

'Kiss me Reith.'

He turned to her and smiled. 'You're insatiable.' He kissed her lightly on the forehead. 'How's that?'

'It'll do for starters.' Then, suddenly, she began to cry.

'Irene, what is it?'

'Just hold me, Reith, hold me tight.'

Perplexed, Reith ran a hand over her hair as she wept onto his chest.

'I wish I could stay like this forever. That you'd never let me go,' she choked.

'What's wrong, Irene?'

'Oh, just being a woman I suppose.'

He didn't understand. How could being a woman cause her to suddenly burst into tears? Had she noticed the way he'd been looking at Catie earlier? Was that it? He made a mental note to be more circumspect in future. It was hardly fair on her after all for him to show so much interest in another man's wife.

'I'm being daft, sorry,' she apologized, wiping her face. 'I couldn't bear to lose you again Reith.'

'You won't lose me a second time, I promise you.'

But she might if he remembered about Billy Boyne, that awful secret she carried about with her, forever gnawing at her insides.

'You're a good man Reith, the best,' she told him.

'Thank you.'

'No need for thanks, it's true.'

'Shall we go to bed?'

Irene sighed. Bed, where she had him all to herself, where they could be as one. 'Yes.'

Once he'd turned off the gaslight she snuggled up to his back and clung onto him as though for dear life. He was filled with affection for this woman who was his wife and who clearly loved him so very much.

Catie picked up the battered brown leather bag she used when she went shopping, or going the messages as Glaswegians called it. She paused to mentally tick off the items she had to buy before heading for the outside door. She was just about to open it when their bell rang.

'Mrs Smith?' the well-dressed woman asked.

'Yes.'

'I'm Mrs Brasil. Linda. A friend of your husband's. I wonder if I could come in and have a word?'

Chapter Seven

'She did what?' Roger exclaimed. He'd only just arrived in from work to find Catie waiting in ambush.

'Came here, to this house, *my* house, and told me all about you and her.'

'Jesus Christ!' Roger muttered, unable to believe his ears. How could he possibly deny this?

'Well?' Catie demanded, coldly.

He glanced about. 'Where are the children?'

'Upstairs with the Loudons, out of the way. They've already been fed.'

Roger fumbled for his cigarettes. 'What exactly did she say?'

Catie wanted to shriek her reply, but instead kept her voice at its normal level. 'That you've been fucking her for quite some time. That she loves you and wants you for herself.'

'I, eh . . . eh . . .' Roger trailed off, lost for words.

'Stood right where you are now, bold as brass. And out it all came.'

Roger lit up, his mind racing, trying desperately to think of an excuse, some sort of acceptable explanation.

'Well?' she demanded again, her voice still icy.

'It's not what you think Catie, honest.'

'No? What is it then?'

'I never meant it to become physical. Her husband had been killed, Andy, a fellow Mason, and I was sent round to see what we could do. Offer help, financial and otherwise. She was in a terrible state, well, you can imagine. Losing her husband and all . . .'

'So you saw a perfect opportunity and took advantage of it,' Catie interjected.

'No, it wasn't like that.'

'What was it like then?'

'I don't know, one thing just led to another. I never meant it to happen,' he lied.

'No? Convince me.'

'I didn't, Catie. I only meant to comfort her. Give her some solace.'

'Oh, you're good at that,' Catie said sarcastically.

'It didn't mean anything. Not on my part anyway. But once . . . that had happened it was difficult to bail out again. It put me in a dreadful situation, I can tell you.'

Catie didn't believe a word of this. He was lying. Not about being sent by the Masons, that would be true enough, but the rest of it. Linda Brasil had been an opportunity he hadn't been able to resist. After all, as a grieving widow, she was a perfect victim. She could just imagine it.

'How many others have there been?' Catie demanded. 'I know she isn't the first.'

'None.'

'Liar!' she hissed.

He made the signs of the cross over his heart. 'Let me be struck down dead if I'm lying. Linda was the one and only.'

He went over to Catie and tried to envelop her in his arms but she shrugged away. 'Don't touch me.'

'It's all a mistake.'

'Damn right it is. On your part.'

'It's over, Catie, done with.'

'So she said. You broke it off. The mistake you made was in not realizing she couldn't accept that. She's convinced you love her as much as she loves you.'

'Why should she believe that, for Christ's sake?' Roger exploded.

'She thinks you left her because of your duty to me and the children. Your responsibilities to us. But that your heart and feelings are with her.'

Catie pointed to a suitcase which Roger now noticed for the first time. 'I've packed for you. Get out.'

'Get out?' he breathed.

'You heard me. Get out. I don't care where you go as long as it's away from here.'

Roger took a deep breath, then another. This was ridiculous, getting all out of proportion. He couldn't leave Catie. She was everything to him, his life.

'Don't do this to me,' he pleaded.

She didn't reply, staring contemptuously at him instead, as if he was something foul and nasty she'd discovered under a stone.

'Catie, please?'

She turned her back on him.

Next thing Catie knew he was behind her, on his knees, tugging at her skirt. 'Please, Catie? I'm sorry, it'll never happen again.' Tears welled up in his eyes.

'What could she give you that I couldn't? Or was it just another conquest for you? Another notch to your tally?'

'You've got me all wrong, Catie. Sure I flirt a bit, always have. I enjoy it. But that's as far as it's ever gone until Linda. And that was an accident.'

How convincing he sounded, she thought bitterly. 'You missed your occupation sonny Jim,' she said. 'You should have been an actor.'

'I'm not acting.' He pulled her skirt tight to his chest. 'Give me another chance Catie. Forgive me.'

She fought back the impulse to smack his tear-stained face. 'I'll never forgive you.'

Roger sobbed, a pitiful sound. 'You must. My life will be ruined if you don't.'

How pathetic he was, she thought, the contempt she felt for him deepening. He then did something that amazed her. He let go of her skirt and collapsed to the floor where he drummed his fists. 'You should have thought of that before you shagged Linda Brasil,' she stated.

He glanced up at her, his face racked with emotion. 'One rotten mistake, that was all. One.'

My arse, she thought. All these long years she'd wanted proof, well now she had it. Irrefutable proof at that, straight from the horse's mouth.

'But I love you!' he wailed. 'And you love me. I know you do.'

She turned away again so he wouldn't see her expression. Her heart was pounding, her chest heaving. He was right, that was the trouble.

'Don't destroy what we've got together, Catie. If nothing else, think of the children.'

'They'll stay with me. I'll look after them.'

He decided to change tack. Sitting up he wiped away his tears. 'How?' he asked craftily.

'What do you mean?'

'If I go how will you look after them?'

'I'll get a job.'

'Doing what?'

'I don't know. Just a job.'

'Easy during the war, but difficult now with the men back home.'

She hadn't thought of that. 'I'll manage.'

'And what if you don't? What then?'

Her resolve faltered. He had a point.

'You need my money coming in,' he went on. 'You'll need it for the rent on this house and for most other things as well. A woman gets paid a pittance compared to a man.'

Catie bit her lip.

'Besides, I'm staying put. Wild horses wouldn't get me out of here, and that's that.'

She regarded him frostily. 'Then I'll go.'

'Where?'

'To my mother's.'

He barked out a scornful laugh. 'Oh yes! To your parents' single end? A one-room flat. They'd welcome you and the children with open arms.'

'To my sister's then.'

'And her with five children of her own. They haven't enough space to swing a cat as it is.'

Damn him! she inwardly raged. He was quite right on both counts.

Roger came to his feet and grinned. 'Buggered, aren't you?'

'I'll find a way. You'll see.'

He knew then he'd won, that the crisis was over. He became contrite again. 'I said I'm sorry. I can't say more than that. I'll never be unfaithful to you again. You can count on it.'

'If you were a man you'd leave.'

'I'm a man all right, as you well know. I've never had any complaints in that department.'

'There's more to being a man than sex,' she retorted.

Roger shrugged.

'Now I'm asking you for the last time. For all our sakes, if you really care, go.'

'No,' he stated emphatically. 'My place is here. And here's where I stay.'

Catie crossed to a chair and slumped into it. She was beaten. Buggered, as he so tastefully put it.

Roger lit another cigarette, gazing at her through the smoke curling upwards in front of him. 'I'll make it up to you, lass. I promise.'

She felt empty, defeated, defiled. How often had he come to her straight from Linda Brasil's bed? Made love to her directly afterwards without even a bath or decent wash in between. That thought made her skin crawl. She hated the lies, deceptions, deceits.

'I'll put the kettle on,' he proposed. 'A nice cup of tea is what we both need.'

She stared at his back as he filled the kettle. If looks could kill he'd have dropped dead on the spot.

Catie stood looking out over the Kilpatrick Hills thinking the scenery was breathtaking. It had been a long tram ride to get there, but she'd wanted to go somewhere where she'd be completely alone. Away from Bridgeton and the city in general. Someplace totally quiet and peaceful. The air here was fresh and sharp, a tonic after the dirt and soot-filled atmosphere of Bridgeton. She turned up the lapels of her camel-haired coat, then pushed her hands into her pockets. Overhead a large black bird, a hawk of some kind, glided past, its eyes riveted on the ground beneath.

Imagine Roger actually crying! That had stunned her. She'd never seen him cry before – or any grown man come to that. Glaswegian males simply didn't cry. Well, they might, in a very dignified way, at funerals. The odd tear quickly hidden behind a handkerchief. But to break down and almost blubber like a wean – that had been remarkable. It was put on of course, she had no doubt about that. She'd meant it when she'd accused him of acting. It was quite some performance! One that Laurence Olivier would have been proud of.

She'd always sworn to herself that she'd leave him if she got proof of his infidelity, but hadn't thought it through properly. As Roger had pointed out it wasn't practical for her to do so. At least not at present. She had the children to think about, their welfare to consider. If she'd been on her own she'd have been off like a shot. But she wasn't. Irene Douglas had coped on her own during the war, but then Irene had had Reith's Army pay coming in. And jobs for women had been plentiful then, no trouble at all in landing one. Now it was different.

Roger and Linda Brasil, the picture of them together in her mind made her want to vomit. And what had he said about her? They were bound to have shared confidences, which was the most galling thing of all. Loathing for Roger filled her and anger towards him. No, more than anger, fury.

'Bastard,' she hissed.

It had been so good between them in the early days. They'd lived for one another. She certainly had for him, worshipping the ground he walked on, idolizing the swine. Where had it gone wrong? She didn't know. Perhaps . . . Self-doubt nagged at her. Except how could she be to blame? She'd done everything she humanly could to keep their marriage alive and well. Their sex life had certainly never been a problem, far from it. They'd both thoroughly enjoyed what went on in bed. So why had he felt the need to go elsewhere? It was a complete mystery to her. Maybe what it all boiled down to was that Roger was one of those men who could never be satisfied with a single partner. He needed to prove himself, again and again. If so, all she felt for him was pity.

Her thoughts were halted when the black bird wheeled, then screamed. She watched in fascination as its outstretched talons raked the ground, grasping a small animal which the bird then triumphantly carried aloft. Catie shivered. That's what she was, a victim of Roger, of circumstances. She was unable to escape as that poor creature imprisoned by the predator's talons. At least, that was true for now, she thought, but not always. She swore that to herself.

She watched as the bird receded into the distance until, finally, it vanished from sight. An hour later, feeling a lot better for her solitary walk in the hills, she returned to find the tram that would take her home again to Bridgeton.

Roger paid Linda Brasil a visit at the first available opportunity. Her welcoming smile disappeared when she saw his expression. Linda hastily backed down the hallway as he advanced on her, his hands clenched into fists at his sides, their knuckles glowing white.

'You stupid, stupid bitch,' he snarled.

Linda's progress was stopped by a wall which she pressed into, eyes starting in their sockets.

'I know you love me. I know it,' she choked.

'I never loved you. You were simply a leg over, a bit of nookie on the side,' he thundered in reply, shoving his face almost into hers.

'But I thought—'

'Well, you thought wrong. You mean nothing to me. You hear? Nothing.'

'Oh Roger!' Her face crumpled while her body shook.

He wanted to hit her, knock her from one end of the house to the other. 'How dare you do what you did? How dare you?'

She tried to speak, but all that emerged was a gargling sound.

He mustn't hit her, he told himself. If the police were to become involved, that would only make matters worse with Catie. But how he was tempted. 'Don't ever come near me or Catie again, understand?'

Linda frantically nodded.

''Cause if you do I won't be responsible for my actions.'

She gulped and nodded again.

A hint of her personal scent wafted up his nostrils instantly arousing him. For a brief moment he considered . . . But that was far too risky, quite out of the question. Whirling round, he strode from the house, banging the door shut behind him.

A leg over! Bit of nookie on the side! Linda slid to the floor where she curled into a foetal ball. How she'd misjudged him and their relationship which she'd set such great store by and had had such high hopes of. She'd never felt so cheap, or humiliated. How could she have been so wrong? Why hadn't she seen through him?

'Oh Andy,' she whimpered, the name catching in her throat. If he was watching what must he think? The pain was almost unbearable.

'A pint, please, Bob,' Roger said, plonking a brown paper parcel on the bar.

'Coming up.'

'And what about you, Reith?'

Reith indicated his three-quarters full glass. 'I'm fine for now.'

'We don't often see you in here,' Billy Drummond commented. Roger normally favoured a pub closer to home.

'Aye well, just felt like a change.'

When his pint arrived Roger had a quick gulp, then another. 'That's better,' he declared, wiping froth from his mouth.

'You look like you've had a hard day,' Reith observed.

'Hard enough.' Roger made up his mind there and then to get drunk. Between Catie and that idiot Linda Brasil, it had been quite a week. He didn't want another like it in a hurry.

To think how close he'd come to losing Catie. That would have been a disaster, a bloody disaster. What would folk have thought? He could well imagine the sniggers, the quiet, snide remarks, the fingers pointing at him, the man who couldn't keep his woman.

Besides, Catie was a real looker. He wouldn't find another like her in a hurry. She was a cut above the rest which was why he'd married her in the first place, a right bobby dazzler. Mind you, her figure wasn't quite what it had been, but that was hardly surprising after having had two children. She wasn't as slim as she'd once been. She could certainly do with loosing a few pounds off her bottom, but it was still nice though, if plumper than he preferred. Now Irene Douglas had a lovely bum. It was one of the first things he'd noticed about her.

He thought of Catie with pride. His wife and only *his*. It had been his lucky day when he'd met her. She'd looked spectacular when they'd married – radiant in her white dress and orange blossom. He'd felt like royalty walking her back down the aisle when the ceremony was over.

As for the honeymoon, that had been an eye-opener. She'd been putty in his hands, as compliant and eager to please as any man could have wished. She'd been a virgin too, but he wouldn't have expected otherwise of Catie. She might have come from a very poor family, but she was a nice girl, one who wouldn't have dreamt of doing anything without that gold band on her finger. God alone knew how her da had afforded the wedding, but somehow the old geezer had managed it, borrowing – had to have been that – the money from somewhere. It had meant a lot to him.

'You and Catie going out tonight?'

Roger blinked himself out of his reverie, turning to Reith who'd spoken.

'No, we've no plans to do so. How about you and Irene?'

Reith shook his head.

'Women,' Roger mused into his glass. 'Can't live with them and can't live without them. It's true enough.'

Reith wondered what had brought that on. He waited for Roger to elaborate, but Roger kept quiet.

When he left shortly after that Roger was ordering up another pint, this time with a chaser.

'Not my fault, not my fault, angel!' Roger declared, staggering into the kitchen clutching his brown paper parcel. 'I only stopped in for a quickie but that bugger Reith wouldn't let me go. You can blame him.'

Catie glanced at the clock; she'd been expecting Roger home hours ago. Now here he was, paralytic. 'I've thrown your tea out, it was ruined,' she stated. 'Waste of good food.'

'I've brought you a present,' Roger smiled, waving the parcel at her. 'At enormous expense too.' He winked salaciously. 'To make up for the wee misunderstanding.'

Wee misunderstanding! Hardly the word she would have used. And there was no misunderstanding. Linda Brasil had been no figment of her imagination.

'There you are. Open it,' Roger said, thrusting the parcel into Catie's hands.

'Did you get anything for me?' Astrid asked.

Roger rubbed the top of her head. 'Not this time, darling.'

'Aw!' Astrid complained, pouting.

'Know something?'

'What?'

He squatted in front of her. 'You're going to be as pretty as your mother when you grow up. And that's a fact.'

'People say I look like her.'

'And you do. You do.'

Andrew, on the other hand, took after him.

Catie laid the parcel on the table and began undoing the string binding it. A peace offering, she thought. Well, even if it were diamonds, and it would hardly be that, it would take a lot more than a present to get round her.

Astrid squealed when Catie pulled out a large box of chocolates. 'Oh yummy!' she exclaimed.

'How did you manage to get this?' Catie questioned. 'We've only got a few sweet coupons left.'

Roger winked again, this time conspiratorially. 'You don't need coupons where those came from; a pal of mine, a dockie.'

Catie knew what that meant, the chocolates were stolen.

'It costs mind,' Roger went on. 'But you don't need coupons.'

He went to Catie and threw an arm round her shoulders. 'Pleased?'

'They're very nice. Thank you.'

'Then give us a kiss.' He puckered his lips and planted them wetly on hers.

'Can I have a chockie, please?' Astrid begged.

'Of course you can,' Catie informed her.

'And me,' said Andrew, joining the others at the table.

'Happy families. That's what I like to see, happy families,' Roger beamed.

'I suppose I'd better make you something else to eat. It'll have to be bread and scrape though, I've nothing else in,' Catie said to him.

'That'll be fine, darling. Anything you like.'

Roger crossed unsteadily to a chair and slumped into it. Very satisfactory, he congratulated himself. The chocolates had gone down a treat, just as he'd known they would. It was something he must do more often, spoil his lovely Catie. He gazed blearily across the room at her. If the children hadn't been present he'd have dragged her off to bed, showed her what she meant to him.

Catie was slicing the loaf when Roger's head dropped onto his chest.

'Mine, all mine,' he muttered, referring to Catie, then started to snore.

'Hello,' Reith smiled.

Catie glanced round in surprise to find Reith standing beside her. 'Why hello,' she replied, matching his smile.

He tapped the book she was holding, as they were in the local library. 'Anything interesting?'

'Not really. All the good ones seem to be out. But no doubt I'll find something. What about you?'

'A history of the Great War.'

'Oh! I would have thought you'd had enough of war.'

'How can I when I don't remember a damn thing about the last one? I am recalling all sorts now, but nothing about the war. At least not so far.'

'I'm sure it will all come back to you eventually,' she said sympathetically. 'And how about the headaches?'

He held up a hand with two fingers crossed. 'Haven't had one for over a fortnight.'

'Good for you.'

'And not so many nightmares either, which is a huge relief.'

An assistant paused at the head of their aisle to glare at them, as their voices had been overheard.

'Ooops!' Reith whispered, which made Catie grin.

He then had an idea. 'Fancy a coffee when you're done here?' he further whispered.

Why not? she thought. She wasn't in any great rush. 'All right.'

He waited for her in the marble-floored hall outside the main library room. 'There's a cafe just down the road,' he said, the pair of them falling into step together.

The cafe wasn't busy so they had a choice of seats, opting for a table near the window. Reith ordered the coffees and had a brief natter with the woman who served him. He was known in the cafe, often popping in after a visit to the library. When he got back to their table he noted Catie's melancholic expression. She was staring out of the window, rapt in thought.

'Here we are,' he declared, setting a cup and saucer before her.

'Thanks.'

'It can't be that bad, surely?'

She frowned. 'I'm not with you?'

'You looked sad staring out of the window. Or worried, possibly both.'

'Did I?'

'Something bothering you?'

She'd been thinking about Roger and their relationship. Smiling thinly, she spooned sugar into her cup.

'I'll understand if you don't want to talk about it, if it's too personal. On the other hand, I'm all yours if you do.'

Not for the first time she thought what a kind man Reith was, one whom she'd come to like very much indeed. What was more, she sensed he was someone who could be trusted with confidences, not a person to gossip. And she did so want to unburden herself, discuss the matter of Roger and Linda Brasil. She had considered her sister Daisy, then decided against it, as she and Daisy were not really that close. Anyway, Daisy would only crow exultantly, though not to her face, to learn of Roger's infidelity; Daisy had always been jealous of her better looks. And Daisy would no doubt tell her husband Alan and who knew where it would go from there.

'You mustn't breathe a word, to *anyone*. And I mean that, not even Irene,' she said slowly.

'I promise.'

She gazed into his eyes and believed he'd keep that promise. 'We only met a relatively short while ago and yet I feel as though I've known you for years,' she said.

Reith nodded. 'Same for me.'

'Strange, isn't it?'

Reith reflected on that. 'It's being comfortable together for want of a better way of putting it. At ease if you like.'

'Do you have that with Irene?'

Reith glanced away. 'Not quite,' he answered quietly.

'Nor me with Roger.'

'Not that there's anything wrong between Irene and me,' Reith went on in the same quiet tone. 'Simply that that special ease I mentioned is missing.'

'Perhaps it was there before you were shot?' she speculated.

He shrugged. 'Perhaps.'

'Roger's been having an affair,' Catie stated baldly.

That startled Reith. 'Are you sure?'

'Certain. The woman in question came round to the house and told me.'

'Dear me,' Reith murmured, thoughts racing. 'Actually came to the house?'

'Bold as brass. She's convinced Roger loves her, which he doesn't.'

The man was mad, Reith thought. Imagine cheating on Catie. 'Does he know that—'

'I had it out with him,' Catie interrupted, and proceeded to tell Reith everything – the gossip, her suspicions, the giveaways over the years. Reith listened, fascinated.

'Well, well,' he breathed when Catie was finally finished. 'I never put Roger down for a womanizer.'

'I can't prove the others of course. But in my heart of hearts I'm convinced they've existed.'

'I am truly sorry,' Reith said gently. Reaching across he briefly placed his hand over Catie's. 'Is there anything I can do?'

She shook her head. 'Not really. If there was I'd ask.'

'Any time, Catie, all you have to do is say.'

She smiled at him in gratitude, knowing that he was being sincere. Reith wasn't the type to make such offers lightly.

'Do you think I was wrong to stay?'

'I don't see what else you could have done in the circumstances. Roger's right. Where would you go? How would you support the children on your own?'

'If only I had some skills to fall back on,' she mused. 'But I haven't. Before getting married I had a silly job that anyone could have done and which paid very little.'

Reith felt for Catie, wanting to take her into his arms and comfort her. He longed to protect her from harm and further suffering, be her knight, her champion.

'I'll leave him one day though, I swear I will,' Catie stated vehemently.

'I can't say I'd blame you. If he'd only strayed once, well, you could excuse that, put it down to an aberration. But to do it repeatedly, that's unforgivable.'

'Exactly.'

They continued to talk until Catie declared she should make a move, which disappointed Reith who didn't want her to leave. He was amazed when he glanced at his watch to see how quickly the time had flown by. What had seemed only a few minutes was in reality almost an hour. They parted outside the cafe, shaking hands. Hers felt warm and delicate in his.

'Thanks for being a true friend. And remember, not a word,' she said.

'About what? I've already forgotten the conversation.'

That made her laugh. 'Bye then, Reith.'

'Bye, Catie.'

The sound of her laughter rang in his ears like sweet music all the way home.

Chapter Eight

Afterwards, he often wondered if it was Catie telling him about Roger's infidelity that made him remember Irene's. If that had been the trigger, he'd never know.

'Cammy, how are you! Long time no see.'

It was a Saturday night and Reith had met up with a few pals in McTavish's for a couple of pints. A couple was a Glaswegian euphemism for a right old bevy.

Cammy shook Reith's hand and the hands of the other men present. 'Hello lads, how's it going?'

'Fine,' they all replied in unison.

'Let me get you a drink,' Reith offered.

'No, I'll do the honours.'

Charlie Nevis whistled when Cammy pulled out a thick wad of folded fivers. 'Holy shite, look at that! Enough there to choke a whole herd of bloody horses.'

'You're rolling in it, man,' Billy Drummond declared enviously.

'I'm doing well. Can't complain.'

Reith regarded Cammy over the rim of his glass as he drank. Cammy had moved out of Bridgeton some years previously to an address somewhere in town. No-one knew precisely what he was doing now, only that it was shady. He certainly didn't have a regular nine to five like the rest of them.

Reith took in the smart suit, expensive shirt, tie and shoes, plus the gold cuff-links. Whatever Cammy's occupation it was obviously extremely profitable.

'How are things at Abercrombie & Jess?' Cammy asked Reith when he'd ordered a round. That was the name of the firm where Reith worked as a cabinet-maker.

'So so.'

'Just so so?'

Reith made a face. 'We could do with more orders. It's been slack recently.'

'You're not going to be laid off, I hope?'

'It hasn't come to that yet. But it could if things don't pick up.' Reith looked thoughtful. 'Not that it might matter in the long run.'

'You mean Germany?' War had been declared the previous month.

A sombre mood fell over the group as they contemplated what awfulness might lie ahead. Many of them were thinking about the sinking of the battleship, *Royal Oak*, a week earlier with the loss of over eight hundred lives.

'That Hitler's an effing maniac,' Mo Durrant said. 'Somebody should have shot the bastard before it came to this. God alone knows how it'll all end.'

'Are you married yet?' Reith enquired, changing the subject.

Cammy shook his head. 'Still playing the field.'

'Lucky sod,' commented Don McStay, which raised a laugh because, apart from Cammy, they were all married men with families.

'Can I speak to you in private, Reith? A wee word?'

'Aye, of course,' Reith replied.

They glanced round, but there were no empty tables. So they took themselves off into a corner instead.

'What can I do for you?' Reith smiled.

'It's more like what I can do for you.'

'Oh?'

Cammy was suddenly uncomfortable, unsure of himself. 'You and I have known each other a long time. Been best mates, right?'

'Right.'

Cammy fidgeted. 'Look, I don't know if I should be doing this. I've turned it over in my mind again and again before coming here tonight.'

Reith frowned. What on earth was this leading up to?

'It's simply that I've heard something that you should know about.' He paused, then added softly, 'Something, coming from the source it did, I have every reason to believe is true.'

He cleared his throat. 'Christ, this is hard.'

'Go on,' Reith urged, now mystified and intrigued.

'There's this chap called Billy Boyne . . .'

Reith leant against his front door and sucked in a deep breath. Cammy had to be mistaken. Not his Irene. Please, not Irene! He'd wanted to rush off home directly after he'd spoken to Cammy, but had waited till he was sure the children would be asleep. By now they would be, leaving Irene alone in the kitchen. Inserting his key into the lock he twisted it and went inside.

'Had a good night?' Irene enquired, glancing up from her ironing.

He stared at her, his expression stony. 'I had an interesting chat.'

'Who with?'

'An old chum.'

'About what?' she asked when he didn't elaborate but continued to stare at her.

'A chum of *yours*. Billy Boyne.'

Irene went rigid with shock, having been caught totally unawares. Oh my God! she thought. Luckily she was looking down at the ironing so he couldn't see her face. Making a supreme effort she somehow managed to compose herself. 'Billy Boyne, who's he?'

'As I said, a chum of yours.'

'No chum of mine, Reith.'

'Is that so?' he queried softly. 'Surprising that, when you're sleeping with him.'

Panic threatened to engulf her and she felt sick to the very core of her being. She contrived what she hoped was a look of outraged incredulousness. 'Is this a joke?'

'I wish it was.'

She was babbling now. 'Well, if it is I think it in very poor taste. How would I know such a villain?'

Reith grunted, and slowly smiled a terrible smile. 'A villain?'

She realized then what she'd said, that she'd given the game away.

'I never mentioned he was a villain. But he is,' Reith stated, eyeing her venomously.

She opened her mouth, only to shut it again with a snap.

'Why?' he asked, aware that he might cry at any moment.

Hysteria mounted rapidly within her. She was trying to think, but couldn't. Her mind had seized, gone numb. She bit her lip.

'Why?' he repeated.

'I, eh . . . I . . .'

'Don't try to deny it further, Irene. You have been sleeping with him. This *villain*.'

'We were at school together,' she heard herself say in a cracked voice.

'So?'

'I remet him. I—' She trailed off.

'And that's when it started?'

'Oh Reith,' she wailed. 'It's not what you think.'

'Isn't it? What is it then?'

How could she explain, justify her actions? If she did the consequences would be horrendous. Reith would go up against Billy with inevitable results. And there was Mathew and Agnes to consider, she had to protect them at any cost. Reith in a wheelchair, a cripple. Or worse still, Reith dead. Anything was better than that. And the children . . . the children.

'Do you love him, Irene?'

It was her only hope. For she knew Reith, if she admitted to that he wouldn't bother with Billy. It would remain between the pair of them. And maybe something could be salvaged, somehow.

She nodded. Reith turned his back to her, and shook. Then the tears came.

After tea that evening Reith had announced he was going out for a walk, the second evening in succession that he'd done so. Irene had been curious as it wasn't one of his normal habits, but accepted the explanation that he wanted some fresh air.

He now stood on Glasgow Green, staring at the People's Palace in the distance. What should he do? This question had been consuming him since he'd remembered about Irene and Billy Boyne, a man he'd never met. Tell her he knew about her past, bring it all up again?

If she loved Billy Boyne, or had done, why had she stayed in their house after he'd left for the Army? The only explanation he could think of was that this Billy Boyne character had broken with her.

Fortunately he'd arranged for money to be sent home while he was away, but that had been for the children more than her. To take care of them, see them all right.

He ran a hand across his tortured face. What a fool he felt. To come back and believe her burblings about loving him, knowing he couldn't remember her affair with Boyne, or the fact she'd loved Boyne, and maybe even still did. All that passion in bed, the demands. It made his skin crawl now to think of it.

And he, unsuspecting chump that he was, had gone along with the charade, thinking that he simply didn't feel love for her because he'd been shot in the head. Well, he knew better now. That love had gone, evaporated long before Greece. It had started to wither and die the night she'd confessed to her feelings for Boyne.

As for Agnes, was she his or Boyne's? Irene had sworn before he left that Agnes was his daughter, but how could he be sure that she was telling the truth? It wasn't as though Agnes looked particularly like him, she didn't. If anything she took after Irene. And somebody else? Or was that merely his imagination playing tricks?

He needed a drink, he decided. But not McTavish's, he wanted to be alone, to think. And then he had another idea. It wasn't a drink he needed, but Catie. Yes, Catie. She was the only person who could help. He hurried on his way.

'Reith! Come in,' Roger cried, ebulliently. Reith's heart sank. He'd hoped to find Catie alone even though he knew that would be unlikely.

'So, what brings you here?'

Reith carefully wiped off his work boots which were muddy from Glasgow Green. 'I was passing and just thought I'd drop in. If you're busy though . . .'

'Not at all. Not at all.'

Roger called over his shoulder. 'Catie, we've got a visitor. Reith.'

She was drying her hands on her pinny as he entered the kitchen. 'This is a nice surprise,' she declared.

'A spur of the moment thing.'

'I'll put the kettle on,' she said.

'Don't bother on my account.'

'I wouldn't mind a cup myself,' Roger smiled, ushering Reith to a chair.

He shouldn't have come, Reith told himself as he sat down. But he'd wanted to see Catie so badly, to talk to her.

'Sorry we've nothing stronger in. You know how it is,' Roger apologized.

'Not to worry. We rarely keep it in either unless it's for a special occasion.'

'And how's Irene?' Roger queried, sitting opposite.

She's a lying bitch, lying by default that was, not saying anything and an adulteress, Reith wanted to reply. Instead he answered, 'Same as usual.'

'And the children?'

'Fine.'

'I made some scones earlier. Will you have one?' Catie asked Reith.

'That would be nice.'

'She's a marvellous baker, my Catie. And cook too,' Roger enthused.

Reith gazed at Roger, wondering how many married women Roger had slept with. How many husbands he'd done the dirty on? He was suddenly seeing Roger in a new light, as another Billy Boyne.

Shortly after that Catie told Astrid and Andrew to go and get into their pyjamas, and they said good night to Reith before they left the kitchen. He was finishing his second cup of tea and discussing football with Roger when Catie went through to tuck in the children.

'Your turn,' she said to Roger on her return.

'Won't be a mo, pal,' he grinned to Reith, jumping to his feet and disappearing out of the doorway.

At last Reith had the chance he'd been waiting for. 'Listen, I've got to talk to you,' he whispered to Catie. 'Can you meet me in the cafe, same day and time as before?'

She frowned at the urgency in his voice, and secrecy of his tone. 'The one just down from the library?'

He nodded.

Her eyes flicked to the doorway, then back to Reith. 'I suppose so. What's it all about?'

'I'll explain then.'

Seconds later Roger breezed back into the room. 'Now where were we?'

Having arranged the rendezvous, Reith excused himself a little later and went.

'No!' Catie exclaimed when Reith came to the end of his tale.

'I'm afraid so.'

Catie shook her head in amazement. 'I would never have imagined that of Irene. Never!'

'Just goes to show, doesn't it?'

She placed a hand over his, and squeezed it. 'I really am sorry. Truly I am.'

'Something else you and I have in common other than films and books,' he declared ruefully.

'What a shock it must have been for you.'

'It was that.' He paused, then went on reflectively, 'Mind you, I've felt for some while that there was something funny. Nothing I could ever put my finger on, till now.'

'So what are you going to do?'

'That's what I've been asking myself. Certainly nothing for the moment. She doesn't know that I've remembered about it and that's how it'll stay until I decide otherwise.'

Catie stared at him, her expression a combination of sympathy and pity. 'It hurts, doesn't it?'

'Like buggery.'

'I know,' she stated softly.

He twisted his hand round so that her palm was in his, curling his fingers over hers. 'You were the obvious one to confide in, being in the same boat.'

'I understand.'

He knew she would. 'There's more,' he stated, sighing.

'More?'

'About the war. Memories of that have also started coming back.' He paused to swallow hard. 'After I left Irene I didn't care what happened, to me that is. I was completely shattered, bereft you might say. Nothing seemed worthwhile anymore. I didn't even know if Irene would be there when and if I returned, or whether I wanted her to be there. As the war went on I began to almost invite being killed.'

'Oh Reith,' she murmured.

'And a number of times I nearly was. Taking risks that were downright stupid. Putting myself directly in the firing line so to speak. I think that's what happened in Greece.'

'But you did survive, that's all that matters,' she said. 'And there's your children.'

'Yes, true enough.'

'How do you get on with them?'

He smiled wryly. 'I'm not sure Agnes is mine. She could well have been Billy Boyne's. Irene swore before I left that Agnes wasn't, but . . .' He broke off and shrugged.

'But Mathew is?'

'Definitely. No doubt about it. You only have to look at him. Anyway, he was conceived before she took up with Boyne. Or at least so I believe.'

'And what happened to Boyne, any idea?'

Reith shook his head. 'No, but I'll find out.'

'Is it possible Irene is still seeing him?'

'If she was then why make such a big fuss over me?'

Catie considered that. 'What if Boyne's a married man with a family of his own? It could be he refused to leave them, but has continued with Irene.'

Reith hadn't thought of that.

'There are all sorts of possibilities when you think about it,' Catie went on.

'Whatever the truth of the matter, I'll find out,' Reith declared emphatically.

'And Irene?'

'We're through, although that doesn't mean I'll leave her. Not for the present anyhow. As I said, I've yet to decide what I'll do.'

'I'll help in any way I can,' Catie stated.

Reith smiled at Catie echoing his own words to her when she'd told him about Roger. 'Thank you.'

'Now can I have another cup of coffee please? This one's gone stone cold.'

'Of course.' Before rising he said, 'Can we do this again next week? Meet here and chat.'

'If you like.'

'I'd like it very much.'

She would too, she thought.

'Reith, what's wrong?' Irene asked, the two of them were lying in bed.

'Nothing,' he replied in the darkness.

'You won't make love anymore. You don't want to know.'

He winced when her hand moved onto his thigh, as he had his back to her. 'I just don't feel like it,' he said.

'But you haven't for over three weeks now.'

'Sorry.'

She rubbed his leg. 'Is it me? Have I done something to upset you?'

'No,' he lied.

'Then what is it?'

'I told you, I haven't been feeling in the mood. Now go to sleep.'

'How about a cuddle first?'

'Irene, I'm dog-tired. All I want to do is sleep.'

She removed her hand and twisted away from him. It wasn't only the lack of lovemaking that was disturbing her, it was his recent coldness towards her. Nor had it escaped her notice that he'd stopped recounting memory returns. When she'd asked him about that he replied they seemed to have stopped for the time being. Was he lying? She didn't know. What she did know was that she was scared stiff he'd remembered, even partially, about Billy Boyne. If he had she'd have explained to him why she'd had the affair and she was sure that he would understand and forgive her. But she didn't want to launch into an explanation if he hadn't remembered. That would be cutting off her nose to spite her face.

Perhaps he was ill? But he hadn't mentioned it and he seemed fit enough. Unless the headaches were back and he wasn't saying anything because he didn't want to worry her.

No, it couldn't be that, she told herself. She would have known. There was no mistaking the pain he was in when he had one of those headaches. Maybe there was trouble at work, she speculated. Was something going on there? She decided to have a word with Roger next time she saw him.

The Roxburgh was, even by Glasgow standards, an appalling pub, the atmosphere inside rank with stale sweat and cigarette smoke. Reith gazed round, finally spotting who he was looking for at the far end of the bar.

'Hello, Cammy,' he said quietly.

Cammy Sanderson, his old boyhood chum, had changed dramatically over the years. His eyes were sunken, his skin blotchy, and there was several days' stubble on his cheeks and chin. Cammy peered at Reith, trying to place him. Then the penny dropped. 'Well, I'll be . . .' He thrust out a bony hand and grasped Reith's. 'How are you, china?'

'Not too bad,' Reith replied, trying not to recoil from the fetid breath that washed over him. Cammy had gone down in the world, a lot.

'What brings you into a dump like this?' Cammy inquired.

'Looking for you.'

'Me!'

Reith nodded.

Cammy was suddenly wary. 'I don't owe you money or anything. I'm sure of it.'

'No, nothing like that. I thought I'd buy you a drink and have a natter.'

Cammy's face brightened. A free drink, it was his lucky day.

'A pint?' Reith queried.

Cammy laughed, a low husky, hoarse sound. 'You've got the wrong boozer for that, Reith. No beer or spirits here, only wine and cider.' He winked. 'We usually buy one of each. More effect that way if you get my meaning.'

Reith saw now that there weren't any beer pumps behind the bar, or optics on display. 'Then that's what we'll have.'

There were several barmen on duty, one of whom bustled over when Reith gestured to him. Reith placed their order and turned again to Cammy.

'You weren't easy to find. I had to do a lot of asking.'

'Aye well, I haven't been around Bridgeton in a long time. Sort of lost touch with the place.'

Reith paid for their drinks when they arrived. Two tumblerfuls of red wine and the same of cloudy cider. He decided to try the wine first.

'Jesus Christ!' he choked. 'This is rot-gut.'

'But does the necessary. Believe me.'

Reith watched as the entire contents of Cammy's wine tumbler vanished down his throat. 'Sheer nectar,' Cammy beamed.

'Listen, can we talk privately. Go somewhere quiet.'

Cammy studied Reith for a few moments, then said, 'There's a room out the back. It should be empty this early on.' Cammy led the way into a small room, furnished with rickety wooden tables and chairs.

'Have you got a fag on you?' Cammy asked when they were settled.

'Sorry, don't smoke.'

'Oh aye, I remember now. Still, you might have taken it up in the meantime.'

'No.'

Cammy sipped his cider, wondering if Reith was good for another round and a tap before he went. 'Things have been tough for me,' he said.

'So I see.'

'Down on my luck, you know?'

'Last time I saw you you were wearing expensive gear including gold cuff-links.'

Cammy gave a heartfelt sigh. 'Those were the days, Reith. Aye, right enough. I was flush then.'

'What happened?'

Cammy regarded Reith through bleary eyes. 'The Bar-L happened.'

'Barlinne?'

'That's it. That hell-hole of a prison. I got three years for a job I was nicked on.'

He shuddered. 'When I came out of there I swore I'd never go back in again. And I won't. I'd top myself first.'

'That bad, eh?'

'It's not just the Bar-L itself, it's what goes on inside. I thought I knew some hard men until I went in there.'

Cammy had another sip of cider, his eyes darkly reflective. 'And I fell foul of one of them, God help me.'

'Why was that?'

'I had something he wanted which I didn't want to give.'

Reith remained silent, waiting for his friend to go on, which Cammy eventually did. 'There aren't any women in there don't forget, and I was quite a handsome sod then,' he said in a tight, strangulated voice. It dawned on Reith what Cammy was getting at. 'And?'

'He and a few of his cronies beat the living daylights out of me, honestly, I came within an ace of dying. I was laid up in the infirmary for months. Broken this, broken that, internal injuries. They made a real mess of me. When I was finally returned to my cell I was given the option, comply willingly, or be beaten again plus have my face razored to shreds.'

Reith didn't have to ask what Cammy's decision had been, there weren't any razor marks on his face.

Cammy shook his head. 'As I said, I'll never go in that place again – or any other prison come to that. Which is why I went straight on my release and have stayed that way since.'

'So what are you doing for a living?'

'I'm not exactly qualified for much. This and that, wherever I can get a start, usually on a casual basis. I can't really do any hard physical work though, I'm just not up to that anymore.' The rest of the cider in his glass vanished down Cammy's throat. 'That was terrific.'

'Have mine,' said Reith, pushing his two tumblers across the table. 'I don't want either.'

'So,' exhaled Cammy, 'have you dropped by to see me for old times' sake, or is it more than that?'

'More than that.'

Cammy raised an eyebrow.

'Billy Boyne.'

'Ah! Your wife Irene. I'd forgotten about that.'

'It was you who told me about her and him, at the beginning of the war in McTavish's.'

'Not long before he got sent down.'

'Sent down?'

'The Bar-L again. He's still there and will be for a good long time to come. Evil swine that he is.'

That answered one question; Irene wasn't still involved with Boyne. And probably explained other things as well, such as why she'd never left the house, and why she'd been so pleased to have him home from the war.

'Thanks Cammy, you've told me what I wanted to know.'

'Glad I could help.'

They spoke a while longer, mainly reminiscing about their childhood. Reith learned a great deal as Cammy did most of the talking. As he was about to leave Reith gave Cammy a ten shilling note for his trouble.

'I don't like taking it, but . . .' Cammy shrugged. 'You can see how things are with me.'

Reith could only agree.

Chapter Nine

On the stroke of midnight all the church bells in the neighbourhood began to ring out.

'Happy New Year, darling!' Roger declared to Catie, sweeping her into his arms and hugging her tight.

'Happy New Year, Reith,' Irene smiled to her husband whose reply was to give her a perfunctory peck on the cheek.

'Is that all?' she queried. 'Surely you can do better than that.'

He responded by kissing her lightly on the lips, much to her disappointment. Things continued to be strained between them, though Reith had never actually said why. Irene turned away to be promptly kissed by another reveller at the Smiths' hogmanay party. He was a neighbour called Tom McGloan, a great bear of a man boasting a black bushy beard and moustache.

'Here, get that down you,' Roger said to Reith, topping up his glass with whisky.

Everywhere hands were being shaken, backs pounded, lips kissed, for it was *the* night in the Scottish calendar. It was far more important than Christmas which, by tradition, was considered no more than a children's holiday.

Roger was grabbed by his fat cousin Joan who crushed him to her ample bosom. He didn't mind at all, as he had fond memories of her bosom when it hadn't been quite so large. Joan, who was already drunk, swayed dangerously on her feet. 'Come on, a big kiss then, you gorgeous man you,' she slurred, homing in on Roger's mouth.

Reith had a sip of whisky, and laid his glass aside. It was going to be a long night and he intended to pace himself. He looked round the room for Catie, wanting to wish her the best for the year ahead, but she'd temporarily vanished.

Roger eventually managed to pull himself free from Joan, and clouted her playfully on the bottom as she squealed with delight.

'That's right, you sort her out, Roger,' Sammy, Joan's husband, called from where he was standing by the range and laughed. He was as thin as his wife was fat.

Someone put another record on the gramophone and Irene found herself dancing with another of the Smiths' neighbours, an elderly chap who declared he may be past his best but there was still life in the old dog yet, by jingo!

There was a loud rapping on the outside door. 'A first foot!' Catie announced to the gathering, appearing in the kitchen doorway, eyes bright with excitement and alcohol.

'I'll get it!' Roger replied, and hastened to the door which he threw open. The Baxters lived across the landing.

'Happy New Year!' said Roy Baxter who had the obligatory bottle in one hand, while his wife Elspeth was carrying the obligatory piece of coal and shortbread. Roy was dark haired, again a necessary requisite in a first foot.

'Come away in,' declared Roger, shaking hands with Roy, and then kissing Elspeth. He was having the time of his life.

Reith returned to his drink and had another sip, watching Irene dancing with the elderly chap who'd earlier been introduced to him as Bert. Irene was wearing an emerald-green dress that contrasted favourably with her golden red hair, and although it dated from pre-war days, she still looked attractive. New clothes had been difficult to come by during the war which was why so many women had simply had to make-do. The same was true for the men, with the exception of those now sporting a demob suit. His gaze switched to Catie who was moving amongst her guests. He'd never seen her look more beautiful or alluring, and he wondered yet again what on earth had possessed Roger to stray.

'Are you all right Dad?' Roger asked his father, sitting in a comfy chair.

Davey Smith glanced up at his son and nodded.

'Can I get you a sandwich or sausage roll maybe?'

A flicker of irritation swept over Davey's face. 'If I want something I'm quite capable of getting it myself.'

'I know that, I was only trying to be a good host.'

'Well I'm fine.'

Roger left his father to it, thinking no matter how hard he tried with the old bugger he never seemed to do the right thing. But then that was nothing new, it had always been the same. He idolized his father, loving him dearly. But Davey, to his ongoing dismay, never returned the affection; he had always been cold towards him. He'd never known why. It was the same story with his mother, Beryl; she'd always been cold as well. He couldn't remember many cuddles and kisses from her as a child; those given were few and far between.

Joan, getting drunker by the minute, threw back her head and roared with gutsy laughter at something Roy had said to her. It was something filthy no doubt, Roger speculated, knowing that his cousin and Roy both had minds like sewers. He was pleased that Joan had come, she was one of his favourite people. She might be plain, and fat now, but she still exuded a raw sexuality he found appealing. She'd been quite a girl when younger which he knew only too well from experience. He smiled, thinking back to that evening years ago when he and Davey had had a monumental barney.

'Roger, what's wrong? You look awful.'

'It's my dad. We had a fight.'

The eighteen-year-old Joan ran a hand through her long hair that was unpinned and hung to her shoulders. She was naked underneath her dressing gown, as she'd been about to have an uppy and downy at the sink.

'You'd better come ben and tell me about it then.'

Roger was aware of Joan's nakedness beneath the clinging cotton gown as she went ahead of him, and he was transfixed by the movement of her buttocks swaying provocatively from side to side.

'I'll put the kettle on,' Joan declared as they entered the kitchen.

Roger glanced around. 'Where are your folks?'

'Gone to a whist drive at the Labour Hall. They won't be home for hours.'

As Joan's sister Marion was married that meant they had the house to themselves.

'So what happened?' Joan queried, placing the kettle on the range.

'That's the funny thing. I don't really know. It all sort of blew up out of nothing.'

110

Roger stared at the linoleum underfoot. 'They just . . . they just don't seem to care for me. Neither of them.'

'I'm sure that's not true.'

'He's hard that dad of mine, never lets you off with anything. Always criticizing. And Mum's not much better. She always takes his side against me.'

Joan rearranged her front so that her breasts weren't so much on display. Roger had changed a lot in the last couple of years she realized. He'd grown up considerably. How old was he now? Fourteen if her memory served her right. Young, but mature with it. He was turning into quite an attractive young man.

'It's not unusual,' Joan said. 'We all have trouble with our parents. I certainly have in the past. I've often thought that's why our Marion got married when she did, to get away from here.'

'I wish they liked me more,' Roger said quietly.

Joan felt sorry for her cousin who was clearly distraught, feeling unwanted and unloved. She didn't have much time for her Uncle Davey and Aunt Beryl herself. Uncle Davey was totally different to her mother, his sister, who was bright and bubbly. He'd always made her think of a dour church elder, sanctimonious and holier than thou.

'Well I like you Roger.'

'I know that Joan,' he smiled thinly. 'That's why I came here. You've aye been a great pal.'

She went and placed a hand on his cheek. Already shaving, she noted.

His gaze strayed to her cleavage and he wondered how it would be to hold her naked breasts. The breath caught in his throat, he'd never seen naked breasts, far less held any. He found himself becoming aroused at the thought. Joan guessed what was going through his mind, she'd seen that look too often before. And she also started to become excited.

'I get awfully lonely sometimes,' Roger husked.

'Lonely?'

'I have my friends and that, but I still get lonely.'

'Maybe you need a girlfriend?'

He flushed.

'Or perhaps you've already got one?'

'Not at the moment.'

'So you have had in the past?'

'Oh aye, lots.'

111

He was lying, she could tell. He was completely inexperienced, a thought which made her even more excited.

She then thought of Bob, the lad she'd been going out with for over six months, and the secluded spot they'd often gone to in Rouken Glen to make love. She desperately missed Bob and his lovemaking. In fact, to be honest, she missed the lovemaking more than Bob, especially as currently she didn't have a man in her life. She was dreadful, she further thought. A born tart through and through. In the last few weeks she'd been so randy she'd have gone to bed with anyone who was available and willing. But a fourteen-year-old cousin? That was going a bit far, even for her. But he was quite capable, she was certain of that. And he'd enjoy the experience, she could guarantee that. Fortunately, she reflected with an inward smile, she had a packet of three hidden safely away.

'The kettle's boiling,' Roger commented.

She removed the kettle, placed it to the side, then turned again to him. 'Shall I make you forget all about your row?' she husked.

'How?'

She smiled slowly, enticingly. Reaching for the bow on her belt she tugged one end, and her dressing gown fell open.

Roger couldn't believe it. He stared in fascination at the large dark patch between her legs, then up at the voluptuous swell of her breasts.

Joan pulled her dressing gown further apart revealing her nipples. 'Well?' she queried.

Roger was speechless.

'Come here.'

She took him in her arms and drew his head down to her breasts. The warm, heady scent of them made his senses reel. He felt he'd suddenly arrived in heaven.

'Shall we go to bed?'

There was nothing he wanted more. 'Oh Joanie,' he croaked.

Taking his hand she led him to her room.

Roger was on top of the world as he strolled away from Joan's. It had been a simply wonderful experience, heightened, if anything, by the sheer unexpectedness of it all. It was like discovering sweeties for the first time, and he wanted more. As much as he could get. To gorge himself again and again. He'd been so proud when she'd told him how good he was, how manly he'd been. She'd stroked him when it was over, stopping every so often to cuddle and hold him tight.

He hadn't wanted to leave, longed to stay in that bed forever. For he'd found in that bed something he'd never had before, not just sexual love, but emotional security as well. He felt ten feet tall as he continued down the road.

He saw everything through different eyes now. He'd been rather scared of girls up until then. But that was now a thing of the past; Joan had seen to that. Girls were no longer a mystery, but creatures of hidden delights, transporters to ecstatic pleasures. All the same, yet different Joan had said. No two girls were quite alike, each a variation on a common theme. That thought fascinated him.

The party had begun to thin out, some people had gone home, others moved on elsewhere. Roy Baxter, who'd been dancing with Irene, now held up his hands and called for attention.

'I'd like to invite everyone next door to our house for a wee drink. I've got something special in.'

Roger liked the idea of that. Besides, Roy had been their first foot, and it was only polite to respond to his generosity.

'Tom, you're to be the first across the door,' Roy declared, pointing at Tom McGloan who was suitably dark.

Tom beamed back. 'I'm pished.'

Everyone laughed.

'That doesn't matter a damn,' Roy replied. 'Pished or not, just as long as you're the first one in.'

Irene left Roy and joined Reith. 'Enjoying yourself?'

He nodded. 'You?'

'I'm having a whale of a time.' She regarded him steadily. 'You haven't danced with me yet. I'm beginning to think you don't want to.'

'You don't dance with your wife on these occasions,' he answered glibly.

'Roger has with Catie.'

And he hadn't so far, Reith thought bitterly. Every time she'd been free and he'd made a move in her direction she'd been snapped up before he could get there.

Reith shrugged. 'That's up to him.'

Irene turned away so that he couldn't see her expression, one of disappointment, sadness and anger. She felt a failure, yes that was

113

it, a total failure of late. Why was he treating her so indifferently? Half the time she might have been a complete stranger. She put a hand to her mouth and worried a nail. *Had* he remembered? If so, surely he would have said something?

A noisy exodus began to take place as the revellers headed across the landing. 'Shall we?' Reith queried.

When she hooked an arm round his she thought for a moment he was going to shrug it off, but he didn't.

'Oh, there you are, I wondered what had become of you,' Reith said to Catie. Once Reith had noticed she was missing, he'd gone back into the Smiths' flat to find her.

'I wanted to check that the children were all right, and also take a couple of tablets. I've got a bit of a headache.'

'Well, it's been quite a night.'

'And far too much booze. My head was whirling at one point.'

'Anything I can do?'

'You can get me some water while I hunt out those tablets.'

He rinsed out a glass, then filled it from the tap. 'There you are,' he said, handing it to her.

'Ta.'

When she'd finished with the glass she placed it on the draining board. 'If I was you I'd sit down for a few minutes to let those tablets take effect,' he counselled.

'Maybe you're right. Anyway, they'll hardly miss me for a while. It's bedlam through there.'

'They are having a fair old time,' Reith agreed.

'I could murder a cup of tea,' Catie sighed when she'd settled herself in a chair.

'I'll make you one.'

She regarded him with affection. 'That's kind of you. But then, you're a kind chap.'

'For you, Catie, anything.'

'*Anything?*' she queried softly.

'Anything that's in my power to provide.' He hesitated, then added, 'You must know that?'

They gazed deep into each other's eyes. 'Oh Catie,' he breathed.

'What?'

He was unsure whether or not to confess how he felt. Suddenly he decided he would. 'I think it happened that day in the fog when we bumped into one another.'

Her heart began to beat faster. She'd known this would come about at some point, that he'd reveal his feelings. If she had any sense she'd stop him now before it went any further, she told herself. Except, she wanted him to speak out. She remained silent.

'I didn't realize it at the time, but on reflection I think that's when it happened. You and I, together, in that fog.' He crossed over and squatted beside her. 'Catie, I'm in love with you.'

She reached up and flicked a long slender finger through his hair. 'I know. I've known for ages.'

'And?'

'What about Irene?'

'I was in love with her once, but her affair with Boyne destroyed that.'

She thought of Roger and his affair with Linda Brasil, among others. There were occasions when she could cheerfully have clawed his eyes out for what he'd done. Had he any real idea of how profoundly he'd hurt her? She doubted it. Sensitivity and insight weren't exactly strong points with Roger. They were, however, with Reith as she'd come to realize during the blossoming of their friendship. He wasn't a man to betray the woman he loved. Oh, he would deceive Irene, but as he said, he didn't love her anymore. And who could blame him after she'd carried on as she had.

'How do you feel about me?' Reith asked, his voice strained.

'I like you. A lot.'

'And love?'

'Perhaps I could come to, I don't know. But not yet.'

He knew he'd have to settle for that for the time being. But it was a start, gave him hope. She hadn't ruled it out altogether.

'Can I kiss you Catie?'

The first step, to what? she wondered. 'It's hogmanay,' she replied levelly. 'Everyone's been kissing everyone else, so why not?'

Again, it wasn't the answer he'd wanted, but one he'd settle for. He leant forward, and their lips met. Then, after a few moments, their tongues intertwined, hers as eagerly as his.

'God, you're beautiful,' he breathed when the kiss was over.

'Am I?'

'You know you are. There isn't a man here tonight who doesn't fancy you.'

That bolstered her ego. She was never quite convinced about her looks. 'My nose is too long, and slightly crooked,' she said.

'I hadn't noticed.'

'Liar!' she teased.

'All right, I had. But it doesn't matter, honest. It gives your face a little bit of character.'

'And my bottom's too big.'

'Who told you that?'

'Roger.'

'Then he's daft. I think it's perfect.'

It was too big, she thought. Reith was being kind again. He took her hand in his and kissed her knuckles, each one in turn. She glanced nervously at the doorway. 'What if Roger comes searching for me?'

Bugger Roger, he thought. 'I'm listening. I'd hear.'

He couldn't resist kissing her again, especially as she fitted naturally and snugly into his arms. He'd have given anything to take her home later instead of Irene. Catie was enjoying the danger of the situation. There would be hell to pay if Roger did suddenly appear and surprise them like this. She smiled inwardly at the thought. This was a tiny revenge on her part for everything he'd made her go through.

'You smell incredible,' Reith whispered into her ear. 'But then you always do.'

'It's the scent I'm wearing.'

'That's only part of it. The nicest part is you.'

Catie stiffened when his hand came to rest on her breast. That was going too far.

'Enough!' she declared, pushing him away and wiping a stray wisp of hair from her face.

He gazed adoringly at her. 'Next week, the usual time and place?'

'I can't.'

His face fell. 'Why not?'

'I'm busy that afternoon.'

'The following Saturday then?'

His eagerness was almost childlike, she thought. It was touching. 'I'll do my best to be there. I can't promise mind. Something might come up.'

'Well I'll be there, waiting. Hoping.'

She smiled, a feline smile. 'How about that cup of tea you promised me?'

'I'd forgotten,' he said, rising to his feet.

Suddenly he bent again and kissed her lightly on the lips. 'I do love you, Catie. With all my heart.'

'Tea,' she smiled again.

When they returned to the Baxters Catie went straight over to Roger whom she quickly realized had been oblivious to her absence.

'You've left that bloody wardrobe door open again!' Irene complained loudly, storming into the kitchen. Matt and Agnes gaped at her.

'Have I indeed?' Reith responded, glancing up from his book.

'It's just not good enough.'

'Hardly a capital crime though?'

'It's annoying, that's what it is. Damned annoying!' Irene went to the sink where she clattered dishes into a bowl.

Reith knew he shouldn't rise to this, but did anyway. 'You're hardly one to criticize considering how untidy you are.'

Irene glared. 'I am nothing of the sort.'

'Oh come on! I'm forever picking up after you.'

Irene knew precisely why she was in such a filthy mood. The frustration of living with a man who refused to be a proper husband was beginning to take its toll. It had been one thing when he'd been away during the war, but it was quite another to share a bed night after night with someone who wouldn't make love to her. How she craved a cuddle, a proper kiss, to be caressed.

'That's a lie,' she retorted.

It wasn't, as she was well aware. 'And while we're on the subject, one of the pots you used this evening hadn't been properly cleaned. It was all crusty inside. I've told you time and again, you must soak them first.'

Irene snorted. 'What have you turned into, some sort of expert on household chores? By God! You sound like a Crossmyloof.' Reith's own anger began to mount.

'Stop it Mum, Dad,' Matt beseeched them.

'And you shut up! Be seen and not heard,' Irene screeched at him.

'There's no need to take it out on the boy,' Reith chided her.

'He's my son and I'll treat him as I see fit,' Irene fumed, feeling tears coming on. Standing beside Reith, Agnes clutched at his trouser leg, but wisely didn't speak.

Irene's face had gone all red and blotchy, Reith noted, thinking how unattractive it made her look. And her hair could have done with a good wash. You'd never have caught Catie with hair in such a state, not in a thousand years. He decided he needed some fresh air, to get away from there and their squabbling. The sight of Irene in her present mood depressed him. He rose, having first patted Agnes on the hand.

'I'm going out,' he announced.

'Where?' Irene hissed. 'The pub I suppose. Spending money we can ill afford. You're not earning as much as you used to, you know. If it wasn't for what I brought in from the dairy I don't know where we'd be.'

'I'm not going to the pub,' he replied, as calmly as he could.

'Don't be long, Dad,' Agnes pleaded.

He bent and kissed her on the forehead. 'I won't be, angel. And when I get back we'll play a game of snakes and ladders. How about that?'

'Oh yes please!'

'Well shut the wardrobe door before you go. I'm damned if I'm doing it,' Irene said.

When he'd gone Irene burst into floods of tears, knowing she'd been quite unreasonable about the wardrobe. She simply hadn't been able to help herself. Something had snapped. What was happening between them? She loved Reith and there she'd been treating him so badly. She was so confused, bewildered. If she hadn't known better she might have suspected she was pregnant. She'd make it up to him when he got back, she promised herself. And she'd be tidier round the house in future, take more care with the dishes. The emptiness inside her was a chasm as she continued to sit in front of the range, hands covering her face.

Outside Reith walked aimlessly along the road, hands thrust deep into his pockets. It was dark; the street gas lamps, which were glowing brightly, were reflected in puddles of water because it had been raining heavily earlier. He came to McTavish's and for a moment was tempted to go inside, sod what he'd said to Irene. But he decided to continue on his way.

These days he couldn't bear to be with Irene, her very presence irritated him. Had she guessed that he'd remembered about Boyne? He wasn't sure. She might have done. But so far he hadn't let on, nor would he until, and if, it suited his purposes.

His memory hadn't fully returned, there were still large gaps, particularly of the war years. But with every passing month more and more pieces of the jigsaw were fitting into place. Unfortunately his skills as a cabinet-maker remained a mystery which meant he had to stay on at Black's in the humble position of labourer.

It hadn't been his intention to go to Catie's street, at least not consciously anyway, but that's where he now found himself. He stopped to gaze up at their windows, neither of which were lit. They'd still be in the kitchen, he realized, which faced the rear. Going through their close he emerged into the back court from where he could see the window in question. It was lit as he'd known it would be. So near, and yet so far. Catie. She was behind that window, doing her chores. Tea would be long over so she could be ironing, mending, dealing with the children. It didn't matter, all he was worried about was that she was there.

This was ridiculous, he suddenly thought. He was a grown man acting like some love-sick kid. And what if she glanced out the window and saw him. Worse, what if Roger did?

He hurried back through the close and out again into the street. On his return home he did call into McTavish's after all and there he propped up the bar for a while, thinking of that window with Catie behind it.

Chapter Ten

'With the school holidays coming up I thought I might take the children down to Dunoon for a few days to visit my folks. What do you think?' Irene said. Her parents had moved to this popular resort on the Clyde the previous year shortly after her father had retired.

Agnes's eyes grew wide. 'Oh please Dad, please?' she pleaded, running to Reith and giving him her most winning smile.

'Can we go on a paddle steamer?' Matt asked eagerly. These ships were a popular feature on the Clyde, adored by Glaswegians, young and old alike.

'I don't see why not, if we go,' Irene replied.

Reith was careful not to let the delight he felt show on his face. This was the opportunity he'd been waiting for.

'McDougall at the dairy won't mind?' he queried.

'I've already sounded him out and he says it'll be all right. In fact he told me I could have a whole week if I wanted.'

A whole week! Better still Reith thought.

'I take it you wouldn't be able to get off work?'

''Fraid not,' Reith said. 'That's completely out of the question.'

'So it would just be the three of us.' Irene ran a hand across her face. 'I must admit I could use a break. I've been feeling awfully tired recently. The sea air, I'm sure, would do wonders.' She had been looking tired and haggard of late, Reith thought. Not at all her usual bright self.

'Well?' Irene demanded.

'It's fine by me.'

Agnes squealed and clapped her hands. She couldn't wait to get going.

'That's settled then,' Irene declared.

Terrific, Reith thought, absolutely terrific.

'I don't know,' Catie prevaricated. This latest development had taken her completely by surprise. 'What if the neighbours saw me?'

'You pop in from time to time, so who would see it as being strange?'

'But Irene won't be there.'

'You're not to know that. Or anyway, they're not to know that you weren't to know.'

Catie gave a low laugh. 'Very confusing.'

'Not really.' He fought back the impulse, as they were in public, to take her hand. 'So what do you say?'

She wasn't at all sure that she wanted their relationship to go so far. It was great fun meeting Reith secretly, the pair of them snatching the occasional kiss, talking intimately the way they did. But to actually go to bed with him? That was something else entirely. She'd never have entertained the idea before Linda Brasil, just in case she'd been wrong about Roger all these years. Now things were different.

'I love you Catie,' he stated earnestly.

'I know, you tell me every time we meet.'

He raised an eyebrow. 'I hope I'm not boring you?'

She laughed again. 'Not at all.'

'And I'm convinced that deep down you love me.'

Did she? She didn't really know the answer to that. Reith had become a tremendous friend, probably the best friend she'd ever had. She felt completely at ease with him, and they had so much in common. But love him?

'It's a golden opportunity Catie, God knows how long it will be before we get another.'

'It would be difficult getting away from Roger.'

'Surely you can think of some excuse for going out by yourself one evening? Or if that wasn't on there's always Saturday afternoon, like now.'

She bit her lip. 'I'll have to think about this Reith. It's such a big step.'

Suddenly he panicked that she wouldn't come. That would be dreadful. He'd built up such high hopes since Irene's proposal about going away. He dropped his gaze to the table. 'If nothing else it would be nice to be alone with you in a private place. Nor would it mean you actually had to . . . I wouldn't presume that was necessarily on.'

'Promise?'

'Promise,' he assured her.

'I still don't know,' she muttered.

He didn't want to beg, but was shameless enough where she was concerned to do so. 'Please?'

That single word, and the emotion with which it was said, pierced her heart. 'What would the dates be then?'

He told her. She thought of Roger and his many betrayals. How little he must respect her to sleep with so many other women. Oh, he swore he still loved her, but how could he? And there was that saying about sauce for the goose and gander. Well her gander had certainly had his sauce so why shouldn't she?

But she wouldn't commit herself, not yet. She knew herself so well that she could imagine getting cold feet when the actual moment arose.

'Let's leave it open, shall we?' she suggested.

'Open?'

'For now. I don't want to be pushed, backed into a corner, Reith. That's important to me.'

'All right,' he agreed reluctantly.

'Thank you.'

He gave her a brave smile that came out all crooked and lop-sided.

Reith couldn't sit still, had been jumping up and down like a yo-yo for the past hour. He glanced again at the clock, there was still ten minutes or so to go. If she came at all, that was. He began pacing the kitchen floor, willing the seconds, minutes to fly by. What a state to be in! he thought, he was reverting back to that love-sick kid again. He stopped to stare at his and Irene's wedding photograph on the mantelpiece, wondering if he should remove it, hide it in a drawer. It seemed inappropriate somehow having it on full view. He decided to leave it where it was.

He flashed another glance at the clock. Damn! The hands must be moving through glue. He rubbed his wound which was aching slightly, no doubt the result of his anxiety, then he resumed pacing.

Finally, he heard the knock he'd been waiting for. He hurried to the outside door. She was wearing her camel coat and looking as nervous as he felt. 'I can only stay for a short while,' she declared, stepping inside.

'Why?'

'Things,' she muttered unconvincingly.

Well, it didn't matter. She was here, that was all that counted.

'I don't think anyone saw me,' she said.

'So what if they did? As long as you were acting normally.' He took her coat. 'You didn't skulk down the street and up the stairs, did you? Looking like some sort of furtive burglar or undercover agent?'

Despite herself she laughed. 'No.'

'Thank goodness. There's nothing more suspicious than a person behaving like that.'

'You sound as if you've done this before,' she teased, relaxing slightly.

'Oh hundreds of times. Whenever Irene's away I have a procession of women coming in and out.'

'Really?' she queried, pretending to believe him.

'They call me Don Juan, and sometimes Lothario.'

'Idiot!'

He drew her towards him. 'But a nice idiot. Don't you agree?'

'Fishing for compliments?'

'Why not?'

He kissed her. At first she was resistant, then gradually she melted against him. 'Oh Catie,' he breathed. 'I'm so glad you made it.'

'I'm still not sure about this.'

'I am. Nothing could feel more right than you and me together.'

'We're both married, Reith.'

'To partners who haven't been exactly faithful themselves.'

'That doesn't mean to say we should copy them,' she countered.

'I told you, you don't have to go that far. I gave my word.'

She relaxed even further. 'Did Irene and the children get away OK?'

'I saw them to the train myself. And watched it pull out of the station. They'll be in Dunoon by now.'

He kissed her on the neck, drinking in her intoxicating smell which he found so wonderfully exciting.

'Roger's gone to a football match,' she stated.

'Which gives us hours.'

'Hardly that,' she replied quickly.

He decided to change the subject. Taking her by the hand he led her into the kitchen. 'Would you like a cup of tea or coffee? Or how about a glass of wine?'

'Wine!'

'I thought it might be a bit early for whisky or gin.'

'Where were you able to buy wine round here?'

'I was in town don't forget. I picked it up there.'

'Wine would be lovely,' she said.

She watched him as he moved about, arranging the glasses and opening the bottle, and noticed that his figure was quite different to Roger's. He was leaner and taller. Then she glanced around, feeling uneasy, an intruder in another woman's domain, an usurper in the nest.

'A naughty little claret,' Reith declared, handing her a glass.

'Naughty?'

'I thought it was appropriate.'

Catie laughed. She laughed a lot with Reith, it was one of the things about him that attracted her. 'And where did you learn that highfalutin jargon?'

He winked at her. 'From a book, where else?'

He clinked his glass against hers. 'To us. You and I, Catie.'

They both drank to that.

'What if someone knocks on the door or rings the bell while I'm here?' she queried.

'We'll ignore them.'

'They might hear our voices?'

'You do worry, don't you,' he teased.

'You can't be too careful. Not in a situation like this anyway.'

'Easily remedied,' he declared, and closed the kitchen door. 'Now our voices can't be heard out on the landing. Satisfied?'

She nodded.

He laid his glass aside and took her in his arms again. 'Have I ever told you you're beautiful?'

'Only a thousand times or so.'

'Well you are.'

He kissed her neck, her cheek, the tip of her nose as she closed her eyes and sighed. Then his mouth was once more on hers, their tongues entwining.

She hadn't intended to go to bed with him, had convinced herself that she wouldn't. And yet she had succumbed. But she'd been unable to relax completely, give herself the way she did with Roger. Echoing in her mind was the word naughty which Reith had used earlier about the wine.

'Oh Catie,' Reith whispered, moving within her. 'My darling.'

She knew she wasn't going to climax, which rarely happened with Roger. She put it down to nerves. It was their first time, after all. And she was in a strange bed with a different man. She smiled when he groaned and convulsed, clutching him tightly to her. For Reith was struck by a sense of peace and tranquillity such as he'd never known – or if he had he couldn't remember it.

'I can't tell you how good that was,' he exhaled, lying beside her. 'Thank you.'

He gently squeezed one of her breasts. He was obsessed by this woman, and didn't think he ever would recover. Moving his other hand he smoothed his fingertips over her naval. Catie watched him through partially slitted eyes, and he recognized that feline expression of hers he'd come to know so well. 'That's nice,' she murmured. He was so tender, Catie thought dreamily, so caring and considerate. She ran a hand over his shoulder and down his back as far as she could reach. Other fingers snaked through his hair, although he flinched slightly when she accidentally touched his wound.

'Sorry,' she apologized, realizing what she'd done.

'That's all right.'

'Have I hurt you?'

'Not really. Forget it.'

This was more like it, she thought. Initially they'd been hurried, too eager, Reith in particular. Now he was taking his time, getting to know her body, making her respond from within herself.

'I love you,' he whispered. 'God, how I love you.'

Lovemaking had never been like this with Irene, Reith was thinking. At least not since returning home. She gasped when a loving finger found its mark, then writhed to his touch. The climax she'd thought was to be denied her began to build. 'Oh yes,' she moaned. Now it was her turn to convulse as waves of sensation exploded outwards from her core making her cry out several times in succession.

'Enough,' she declared eventually. 'Enough!'

He moved up the bed again to lie beside her, stroking her slick forehead and smiling. 'I love you,' he repeated.

Catie slipped an arm round his neck and drew his head to her bosom, his cheek resting against one of her breasts.

They lay for a while in silence, each lost in thought. 'Catie,' he said, voice muffled by flesh.

'What?'

'Marry me.'

She stiffened, and held her breath. Then she slowly exhaled. 'What did you say?'

He propped himself up on an elbow to stare directly into her eyes. 'Marry me.'

'But we're already married. I mean, you to Irene, me to Roger.'

Reith gazed intently at her. 'There's such a thing as divorce, you know.'

Get married? Divorce! Her thoughts were suddenly whirling. She pulled herself up so that she was sitting opposite him. 'You mean it, don't you?'

'I've never meant anything more.'

'But . . . I can't,' she protested.

'Why not?'

'There are a dozen reasons.'

'Name them,' he challenged.

'I don't know. The children for a start.'

'We'll sort something out.'

'And the expense of a divorce. Do you know how much it would cost?'

He had an idea. 'A lot.'

'Well then. And what about Roger? He'd go mental if I even tried to leave him for another man.'

'Let me bother about Roger,' Reith stated quietly.

What had she got herself into? Catie panicked. 'You don't really know Roger,' she babbled. 'He's got a terrible temper when roused. He'd murder you.'

'He could try.'

'And me into the bargain. If he ever found out about today he'd batter me all round the house. And then come looking for you.' There was a pause during which Catie regarded Reith steadily. 'And what about your own children? You don't think Irene would give them up, do you?'

'As I said, we could sort something out.'

'You're not being practical, Reith. You haven't thought this through properly.'

'It would be difficult, I grant you. But not impossible, surely?'

'Think of the hurt all round,' she pointed out.

'And what about the hurt Irene and Roger have caused us?' he retorted quickly.

That was true enough, she thought. But divorce, to marry Reith? It was unthinkable.

'You told me you tried to throw Roger out after that Linda Brasil,' Reith went on.

'But as Roger said at the time, how could I manage without his money coming in? Even going on the Parish I couldn't. I couldn't manage without a decent job which is almost impossible for an untrained woman to find nowadays.'

'You'd have my wages . . .'

'For a start you earn less than Roger. Secondly, what about Irene and your children. What would they exist on?'

'Irene would have to go back full-time at the dairy.'

'Would that be enough for the three of them? Don't forget, she had your Army pay during the war.'

Reith closed his eyes and sagged in despair. He was sure there had to be a way round this one. 'I don't even know that Agnes is mine,' he stated quietly.

'But you dote on that lass. I've seen you with her.'

He nodded. 'She's come to mean an awful lot to me. And Matt.'

Catie placed a hand on his arm. 'I'm sorry.'

'But you love me, Catie.'

'I've never said that, Reith. You know I haven't.'

'I know you do. And don't say I'm deluding myself, I'm not. I know that deep down you do.'

He seemed more convinced than she was, but she didn't contradict him. 'I must go,' she declared instead.

'Stay a little longer. Please?' he pleaded.

'I'm all muddled, Reith, and confused. I should never have come.'

He swept her to him, and held her tight, feeling her heart beating against his own. 'I will see you again?'

'Of course.'

'You and I together, alone. Not merely socializing as families.'

'Do you think that wise Reith?'

'Bugger being wise!' he exclaimed vehemently, 'I have to see you again, just the pair of us. I have to.'

'Then you will,' she promised reluctantly.

Relief surged through him. For a few awful moments he'd thought it was all over between them and that he'd scared her off. He cursed his stupidity for proposing marriage so early on. She was right, he hadn't thought matters through sufficiently, having been blinded by emotion and the sheer longing to have her as his wife in place of Irene.

Catie detached herself from him and swung out of bed. Silently she began to dress. Reith watched her, savouring her every move and gesture.

'Aren't you going to get up as well?' she queried.

'As I'm going to be on my own for a week, why don't you and Roger ask me over for tea one night?' he suggested hopefully.

'Roger isn't aware that Irene's away.'

'I'll mention it to him on Monday.'

'If you like then.'

'And . . .' He hesitated. 'What are the chances of you coming back here again before she returns?'

Catie smiled at him in a wall mirror, as she ran a comb through her hair. 'Don't you think that's pushing it a bit far?'

He shook his head.

'Well I do.'

'Have I upset you dreadfully Catie?' he asked.

The comb stopped moving and she regarded him in the mirror. 'Not upset, alarmed I'd say.'

'Too much too soon?'

She shrugged and didn't reply.

Reith cursed himself again for his stupidity at rushing fences. He should have been content, for the time being, that she'd gone to bed with him.

'I couldn't bear to lose you, Catie. I . . . well, I don't know what I'd do.'

And if the truth be known, she didn't want to lose him. He'd come to mean so much to her – friend, confidant, and now lover. 'Tell you what,' she said, 'when Roger gets in from the match I'll say I ran into you and have invited you over for Sunday dinner. How about that?'

His face brightened. 'Terrific!'

'It's a date then.'

He leapt from the bed and embraced her, she remaining neither stiff nor yielding in his arms.

'Now I must get on,' she declared.

'What time tomorrow?'

'Half twelve.'

'I'll be there on the dot.'

In fact, he was early.

'I've been thinking—' Catie began saying.

'Well, that makes a change,' Roger quipped, and grinned.

Typical of the man, she thought, absolutely typical. She took a deep breath and continued, 'that I'd like to go to night school. Perhaps learn shorthand and typing.' She'd also enquired about day courses, but there weren't any available for adults, only school leavers.

He regarded her blankly. 'What for?'

'To become qualified at something. Then I might be able to land myself a job.'

'You don't need a job,' he retorted irritably.

'But I'd like one.'

He lit a cigarette, blowing a perfect smoke ring at the ceiling. 'It's quite unnecessary for you to work.'

'You mean you don't want me to.'

'No I don't!' he snapped in reply.

'Isn't that just a teensy bit selfish?'

'How do you mean?'

'You're not thinking about me, my wants and desires.'

'Oh, desires is it?' he laughed. 'I believe I'm well acquainted with those Catie dear.'

She flushed; he was being deliberately crude. 'Don't be rude.'

'That wasn't what you said to me last night. Oh no, you were keen and eager enough then. Thrashing all over—'

'Stop it!' she hissed, embarrassed. She glanced at the open doorway. The children were home and she hoped they hadn't overheard any of that.

'Well you were,' he persevered with a salacious leer.

She could have slapped him for that leer alone. 'When the children are at school I'm at home all day on my own. It isn't enough,' she stated.

'It was enough for my ma, so why not you?'

'Things have changed, Roger. Women want more out of life nowadays.'

'You know your trouble,' he declared, pointing a nicotine-stained finger at her. 'I've been too good to you. Spoilt you. A

129

backhander now and again would have done you the world of good.'

She glared at him. 'Don't you ever hit me. I know you're quite capable of it, but don't even think about it.'

'See, you're spoilt.'

She retreated further into her chair, fuming inside. She'd expected resistance, and hadn't been proved wrong. 'I've enquired. There's a course starting in September—'

'Drop it, Catie. I'm warning you,' he growled.

'You might at least consider it,' she said.

'I don't have to. There'll be no course for you, my girl.' He waved the hand holding the cigarette at her. 'Who do you think would have looked after the children in the evenings anyhow?'

'You.'

'Me!' He was incredulous. 'You must be joking, out of your skull. I'm not baby-sitting God knows how many nights a bloody week. What would my chinas say if they found out? I'd be the laughing stock.'

'Are you so small a person that you care what others think?' she taunted.

'Damn right I do!'

'It's not that you're doing much. Most nights you're only sitting around.'

'What about my Masonic meetings?' he riposted. 'I couldn't miss those.'

'We could ask a neighbour to pop in from time to time when that happened.'

'No, no, no,' he declared emphatically, shaking his head. 'That would be too much to ask.'

'Can't miss your Masonic meetings?' she sneered. 'How many did you miss for that tart Brasil?'

Now it was his turn to flush. 'No more of that. She's past and finished with.'

'You just do what suits you. No consideration for me.'

'You're talking soft. Of course I have consideration for you.'

'Then prove it. Let me go to night school.'

He smashed a fist down on the wing of his chair. 'I said no, and that's that. Understand?'

Bastard, she thought bitterly. Well, he needn't try to come crawling all over her later on. He was going to be right out of luck.

Roger took another puff from his Senior Service. He'd never

130

heard such nonsense. Night school indeed! She should realize just how fortunate she was. He prided himself on being a good provider. She always got a decent wad of money in her hand at the end of the week, and it wasn't every Glasgow housewife could say that. A lot of wage packets went straight into the boozer and never came out again. Then he had a thought.

'Who was it put such a daft notion into your head anyway? Was it Reith Douglas? You and he seem to have become as thick as thieves since we met. Whenever the four of us are together you and he are always yapping. Inseparable.'

Alarm flared up in Catie. 'It has nothing to do with Reith.'

'Are you sure?'

'Positive. I swear.'

'Hmmh. For I'd be upset if I thought it had. That's interfering in another man's marriage, that is.'

Roger stubbed out his cigarette. 'I'm beginning to think we're seeing too much of the Douglases anyway,' he went on.

Was he suspicious? she wondered. To be on the safe side she and Reith would have to be more careful in future, not showing such an interest in one another. She'd have to speak to Reith about that.

'I thought you enjoyed their company,' she said lightly.

'Aye well, familiarity breeds contempt and all that.'

'Suit yourself,' she declared. 'I'm easy, one way or the other. Now how about a cup of tea?'

He wouldn't give Catie the opportunity to earn her own money, Roger thought craftily. That was a key to open a door that he had no intention she should ever go through.

Catie was smiling to herself as she spooned tea from the caddy. She could have wiped that smug smile from his face in an instant by telling him she and Reith had slept together. There and then she decided she'd sleep with Reith again, to spite Roger if nothing else.

Chapter Eleven

'Snap!' Mathew exclaimed exitedly. 'Mine.'

Agnes glowered across the table at him. 'Not fair. He's winning.'

'Then you'll just have to concentrate more my darling,' Irene commented.

Matt gathered in his trick and threw down a king which Reith topped with an eight. The clock on the mantelpiece chimed the hour.

'Almost time for bed, you two,' Irene said.

'Snap!' Agnes shrieked, delighted with herself.

Reith smiled at Irene who'd allowed the wean that trick, as had he. Both of them had spotted it before she'd spoken.

'Well done,' Reith congratulated Agnes. 'It's all down to concentration as your mum says.'

They continued to play for a few more minutes before they were interrupted by a ring at the door.

'I'll get it,' Agnes declared, slipping quickly from her chair.

Irene raised an eyebrow to Reith.

'Probably one of the neighbours come to borrow something,' Reith speculated. He was tired, it had been an exceptionally hard day. Life as a labourer was no joke, even when you were used to it.

'It's a man to see you Dad,' Agnes announced, reappearing in the room.

A man? Reith rose and went to the door himself where a well-dressed elderly gent stood clutching a brown hat.

'Can I help you?'

'Are you Reith Douglas?'

'I am.'

'I'm Charlie McCall, Jack's father.'

The name meant nothing to Reith who frowned. 'I'm sorry?'

Charlie McCall frowned in turn. 'Maybe I've got the wrong Reith Douglas. I was looking for one who was in the paras.'

'That's me.'

'Then you must remember my son Jack. You and he were the best of friends.'

'I see,' Reith murmured. 'You'd better come in, Mr McCall.'

'Charlie please, everyone calls me that.'

In the kitchen Reith introduced Irene and the children, briefly explaining why Charlie had called.

'Would you care for some tea or coffee?' Irene enquired.

'I took the liberty of bringing along something stronger. I hope that's all right.' And with that he produced a bottle of fine malt whisky.

'Well, that's always welcome. It's kind of you,' Reith smiled, accepting the bottle, thinking it was a magnanimous gesture from a complete stranger.

'I'll get this pair off to bed while you chat,' Irene declared.

'Aw Mum!' Agnes protested, wanting to stay up as they had company, liking the look of this kindly old man.

Charlie chuckled; Agnes's protest brought back fond memories. 'Tell you what, maybe this will make it easier young lady,' he said, delving into a trouser pocket. From a fistful of change he extracted two half-crowns, giving one to a wide-eyed Agnes and the other to Matt. 'There you are.'

'Say thank you,' Irene instructed the delighted children.

'Thank you Mr McCall,' Agnes and Matt chorused, unable to believe this unbelievable stroke of luck. They were both already planning how they'd spend their windfall.

'You're welcome. More than welcome,' Charlie beamed back.

'Bonnie children, Reith. May I call you that?' he said after Irene had ushered them from the room.

'Of course.'

Charlie glanced round the kitchen as Reith poured out the whisky. It was more or less what he would have expected – working-class Glasgow, the usual decor and knick-knacks.

Charlie accepted his glass and raised it in front of him in a toast. 'To Jack. Do you mind?'

'Not at all. To Jack.'

'May he rest in peace.'

So Jack was dead, Reith thought as he sipped the malt. He and this Jack had been the best of friends?

'Sit down Charlie,' he said, gesturing towards a chair. Positioning himself on the chair opposite, he asked, 'Where was Jack killed?'

Charlie blinked. 'You know where. You were there. At Patra, in Greece.'

'The same battle in which I was wounded,' Reith mused.

'Wounded? I didn't know anything about that.'

Reith studied Charlie for a few moments, then inquired, 'Why are you here?'

Charlie's expression became one of infinite sadness. 'I wanted . . . well, I wondered if you could tell me exactly what happened to Jack. The only information I was given was that he was killed, but without any of the details.'

He paused in thought, then went on, 'It's taken me a long time to look you up, Reith, once I'd established you were still alive. On a dozen occasions I've nearly come to your door, then found I couldn't because it was still all too painful and raw. Can you understand that?'

Reith nodded.

'Jack was our only child you see, much loved by his mother and me. She was stricken when we got the news, absolutely stricken. Three months later she died. It was just too much for her to bear.' He paused to take a gulp of whisky. 'I, eh . . . well, first Jack, then Fanny. How I coped I don't know. Not that I coped very well, I didn't. But somehow I muddled along. Missing them both like hell. I'll be honest about that, they were everything to me. My wife, and then Jack, he my son and heir.' Charlie gulped more whisky. By this time his face had gone grey. Then he shook his head. 'Jack often spoke of you in his letters home. The pair of you were great mates according to him. Always doing things together. More than he let on I'm sure. How we praised you when you saved his life.'

'Where was that?' Reith asked.

Charlie stared at him in astonishment. 'Don't you remember?'

'I'll explain in a minute. Remind me.'

'During a training exercise. His parachute didn't fully open. Somehow you managed to grab hold of him and saved his life in the process. That was eighteen months before Patra.'

Reith had no recollection of the incident whatever. Just as he had no recollection of Jack McCall.

Charlie cleared his throat, then said matter of factly, 'Now, can you tell me about his death. I'd like to know. It may sound a bit morbid, wanting the details like, but it would help, I assure you. Did he suffer or was it outright?'

'I don't know,' Reith replied with a sigh.

'But if you weren't actually there when it happened you must have heard about it from your mates?'

'I mentioned I was wounded,' Reith said.

'That's right.'

'I see,' Charlie murmured when Reith finally came to the end of his tale. Irene had rejoined them in the meanwhile.

'I can recall only flashes of the war, and nothing at all about a Jack McCall and Patra. I really am terribly sorry.'

Charlie sat for a little while in brooding silence, digesting what he'd been told. He was disappointed that he would learn no further details about Jack's death, especially as he'd imagined Reith would be able to fill in the missing facts.

'How awful for you,' Charlie commented at last.

Reith shrugged. 'It's liveable with. And at least I'm here, all in one piece so to speak. Which is more than can be said for your Jack and many others like him.'

'True,' Charlie nodded.

Irene refilled their glasses.

'I'd like to read those letters that mention me sometime,' Reith requested. 'Unless you feel they're too personal, that is.'

'No, I'd be delighted to let you read them. I have every one he sent in a box. Fanny used to go through them again and again until—' He trailed off.

A few minutes later Charlie straightened in his chair. 'How does it feel being in civvy street again? You're back working as a cabinet-maker, I take it?'

Reith gave the older man a rueful smile. 'My old job was there waiting for me, but unfortunately I couldn't do it any more. I'd forgotten all my skills which have never returned.'

'So what are you doing now?'

'I'm a labourer with Black's the shipbuilders.'

'A labourer!'

'A real come-down,' Irene muttered.

'And less pay too I should think?'

135

'We get by,' Reith said. 'It does mean Irene has to work part-time, but between us we manage.'

'Hmmh,' Charlie murmured. 'And you didn't remember your wife or children?'

'I'd have walked past them in the street if it hadn't been for a photograph Irene sent me. They were completely wiped out.'

'But you say you're remembering some things now?'

Irene tensed, and averted her face so that Reith wouldn't see her expression.

'Here and there, bits and pieces. Though that seems to have stopped for the present,' Reith replied, although he was lying. He was continuing to remember but never told Irene. Most of them were pre-war memories though, hence his genuine inability to recall Jack McCall.

Charlie glanced at the clock. 'I've taken up enough of your time. I'd better get along.'

He rose, and Reith and Irene followed suit. 'I'd like to take you both out for a meal one night, a sort of thank you for being such a good pal to Jack. What do you say?'

'That would be lovely.'

'No trouble with the kids?'

'We'll arrange something.'

'Fine, then I'll be in touch.'

Reith and Irene saw Charlie to the door where they all shook hands. 'I'm sorry I can't help,' Reith apologized to Charlie. 'Perhaps there's someone else who can, another para who was at Patra?'

'Maybe. I might look into that.'

They said goodbye, and then Charlie was off down the stairs while Reith closed the door behind him and Irene.

'Nice man,' he commented.

'I liked him too. He clearly idolized his son.'

Thoughtful, Reith returned to the kitchen and drank a few more glasses of whisky.

Reith was impressed, as indeed was Irene. Charlie McCall had asked them to join him at His Lordship's Larder, arguably the smartest restaurant in Glasgow.

Reith studied the menu, wondering what on earth he should order from the selection of gourmet dishes.

'Have you ever tried oysters?' Charlie enquired with a smile.

Reith shrugged. 'If I have I can't remember.'

'Of course. Sorry.'

'I haven't. Aren't they slimy?' Irene queried.

Charlie chuckled. 'I've never found them so. Why don't you have a go?'

Irene considered them, and decided against them. She plumped instead for prawns fried in a hot butter sauce. Reith declared he'd have the oysters. For their main course Reith chose venison, Irene lamb, while Charlie selected fillet steak with new baby potatoes and various vegetables. They left the choice of pudding till later.

When they had placed their order, Charlie glanced round, making sure they couldn't be overheard, then said to Reith in a low voice, 'How honest are you?'

Reith was taken aback. 'I beg your pardon?'

'How honest are you?'

He thought about that. 'I don't know. Fairly, I suppose. I wouldn't steal if that's what you're getting at.'

'Good answer,' Charlie nodded.

Reith wondered what this was all about. What a strange question.

'I never mentioned what I did,' Charlie went on. 'I'm an off-track bookie which, as you know, is strictly illegal.'

'Oh?' Reith was fascinated.

'Do you gamble yourself?'

''Fraid not.'

'That's an advantage,' Charlie approved.

'A few of the lads I know at the yard bet,' Reith informed him. 'But it doesn't really appeal to me. I think it's a mug's game.'

'Depends which end you're at,' Charlie said. 'Punter or bookie. The bookie never loses, not overall that is, not if he's smart.'

Reith could believe that.

'The thing is,' Charlie continued, 'I've been mulling things over and it grieves me that you're reduced to working as a labourer.'

'Not as much as it grieves me,' Irene muttered.

'Therefore I was wondering whether you'd like to come and work for me as a runner?'

'A runner,' Reith repeated.

'You know what that is, don't you?'

Reith nodded. 'The chap who collects the bets and pays out.'

'That's right. What do you earn now?'

Reith glanced at Irene, who was hanging on Charlie's every word, and then back to Charlie. He told him.

'I'll double that to begin with. And we'll see how you go from there.'

Reith was speechless. 'You'll *double* it?' he managed to say at last.

Charlie grinned. 'I just said so, didn't I?'

'And what happens if I'm caught?'

Charlie winked at him. 'You won't be.'

'How can you be so certain?'

'Because that's taken care of, if you understand my meaning.'

'You bribe the police?' Irene queried, wanting it spelt out.

'Have been doing so for years. A backhander all round and there's never any trouble. So, you've no worries on that score, Reith.'

Reith considered the offer. It would certainly be a lot easier than the back-breaking graft he put in at Black's. And tremendously lucrative. 'Are there any problems connected to the job?' he asked.

Charlie shrugged. 'Occasionally some idiot tries to rob a runner, so it's best if you know how to take care of yourself. Which I believe you could do. However, if a runner is robbed the thief is invariably found and dealt with. It's a well-known fact which is why it doesn't happen very often.'

'Dealt with?'

'Either by the police or by my own men. I have several blokes who specialize in that department.'

Reith was bemused; it was all so unexpected.

Charlie reached across the table and grasped Reith by the wrist. 'Take it lad. Let me repay a little of your friendship with Jack and the fact you once saved his life. It would mean a lot to me.'

'A doubled wage would mean a lot to us,' Irene commented enthusiastically.

'When would I start?' Reith queried.

'As soon as you can. Hand in your notice at Black's then report straight to me. You'll be on my payroll from the day you leave Black's.' Charlie paused, then added, 'The one quality I look for, demand, above all else, is honesty. I want people I can trust, and I know I can trust you. So, how about it?'

'Reith,' Irene urged, eyes glistening. 'You must do it. It's too good an opportunity to turn down.'

'She's right,' Charlie said.

Reith took a deep breath. Why the hell not! He nodded. 'You're on.'

'That's my boy,' declared Charlie, patting Reith's hand. 'Welcome aboard.'

What had he let himself in for? Reith wondered. Well, only time would tell.

It was a doddle once he learned the ropes, Reith reflected. The punters came to him and placed their bets. He then wrote it up in his book, gave them a slip noting the bet and off they toddled. Later he returned and paid off the winners. And what a racket! The profits were huge. When he multiplied the profit he personally took by all the other runners Charlie employed, the figure he arrived at was eyebrow-raising.

He glanced at his watch. Another five minutes at this spot and then he was due to move on to another. A figure slipped out of the shadow to approach him. She was one of his regulars who called herself – all the punters used pseudonyms – by the exotic name of Pocahontas. Anyone less like an Indian princess would have been hard to imagine. The woman in question was ancient and gnarled, with her head and shoulders covered by a grey woollen shawl. 'There you are son,' she said, acknowledging him. 'I want two bob to win on . . .'

Reith took down the details, wrote out the slip and handed it to her.

'See you later then,' she declared optimistically, convinced she'd win.

Reith smiled when she was gone, swallowed up again in shadow. Pocahontas hadn't a snowball's hope in hell with that particular dog. She wouldn't be coming back as she anticipated, not that night anyway. He took three more bets before moving on.

Reith was fidgety with impatience. It was a fortnight since he'd seen Catie and it had seemed like an eternity. He glanced again at the cafe door, willing her to appear. At long last, she turned up.

'I was beginning to think you weren't coming,' he said in relief as she sat facing him.

'I got held up at home.'

'Problems?'

'Nothing important. Just Astrid being difficult. You know what children are.'

He smiled in agreement.

'How are you?' he asked.

139

'Fine. You?'

'A lot better now you're here. I've missed you.' He stared into her eyes, thinking how gorgeous she was, and how different he always felt in her presence. Much more calm and at peace.

'I'd like some coffee please,' she said.

He started. 'Sorry, I was forgetting my manners.' He rose reluctantly and left her, regretting every moment during their brief time together when they were parted.

'There you are,' he declared on his return, setting a cup and saucer before her. A thrill coursed through him when their hands accidentally brushed against one another.

'How's the new job going?' she enquired.

'Great. Couldn't be better.'

'Roger's green that you're now earning more than him. It seems rather mean spirited to me. But there you are, that's Roger.'

'Talking of me earning more, I can now afford to keep your children as well as pay for my own. You, too, of course.'

So, it was back to that, she thought. She should have anticipated it.

'Leave Roger,' Reith urged.

'And marry you?'

'I'd give anything for that Catie.'

She sighed. 'You know what the divorce laws are like in Scotland. A divorce could take years. And what happens in the meantime?'

'We could live together.'

She stared at him. 'You mean in sin?'

'It would have to be that until we got married. There isn't any way round it.'

'But think of my children,' she pointed out. 'Think of the shame and humiliation. I couldn't ask them to go through that.'

'We'd move away, move completely out of Bridgeton,' he argued desperately. 'Someplace we're not known and start afresh.'

'That wouldn't work. You know it wouldn't—'

'Yes, it would,' he cut in.

Catie shook her head. 'Reith, be reasonable, see sense. How long would it be before people, neighbours, found out? If we were on our own it might be possible, but not where our children are involved. School for a start, they'd have to be registered as Smith, not Douglas. And then there are ration books and all sorts. We couldn't keep it a secret.'

'I don't give a damn what people would think,' he retorted. 'All that would be important is that you and I would be together.'

'You're being selfish,' she chided him. 'And again I say, what about the children, their feelings on the matter? I'm their mother, Reith, I won't do anything that might lose me their love and respect. That counts more to me than anything else.'

Despite himself, he could see the sense of her argument, knew she was right. It filled him with despondency and black despair.

'It would be one thing chucking Roger out, or leaving him to set up by myself with the children. But quite another entirely to leave him for someone else. That's simply not acceptable. Not to me anyway.'

He dropped his head to gaze at the white linen tablecloth. He must have been insane to think she'd agree. Emotion welled up within him, clogging his throat.

'Perhaps I was wrong in allowing this to happen between us,' she said softly.

'No! Don't say that, Catie. Don't ever say that.' He hesitated, then added, 'You've become everything to me, my whole life.'

She felt sorry for him, wanting to hold him close like a babe, to stroke and soothe him. Give him comfort and solace against the pain he was going through. In her heart of hearts she knew that if she'd loved him the way he loved her she'd have left Roger and damn the consequences.

'I've brought you something,' he mumbled.

'What?'

'A present.'

She brightened. 'That's nice. Kind of you.'

He fumbled in a pocket to produce an envelope which he pushed across the table. He watched in eager anticipation as she opened it.

'A gold pendant,' Catie breathed.

'Like it?'

'Oh Reith, it's lovely.'

She didn't extract the pendant because there were other people in the cafe, but she fingered it inside the envelope instead.

'It's an antique I spotted in a shop in Sauchiehall Street. I could just see you wearing it.'

'It must have cost a packet.'

'Not really, considering what it is. It's eighteen-carat gold.'

'I, eh . . . don't know what to say.'

'Thank you would be all right.'

141

'Thank you, Reith,' she smiled. Then, reluctantly, she added, 'The only thing is I can't accept it.'

'Why not?'

'How on earth would I explain to Roger? I don't have the money to go out and buy a pendant like this. Not just off my own bat anyway. Not without a reason.'

'Ahh! I've already thought of that. You tell him you found it in the street. You could say that the clasp couldn't have been securely fastened, which caused it to fall from someone's neck. He'd believe that surely?'

'If I'd found it then I should hand it in to the police?' she prevaricated.

Reith pulled a face. 'Come on Catie, this is Glasgow. Who would hand anything of value in to the police? That's most unlikely.'

She knew that was true, particularly folks from where they lived. 'I might get away with that,' she relented.

'Of course you will.'

She thought of Roger. She'd tell him she found it and *suggest* handing it in. Knowing him he'd reply that she shouldn't be so daft, finders keepers and all that. That way it would be Roger's idea to hold onto the pendant.

'What are you laughing at?'

Reith smiled when she explained to him. 'Women,' he declared, shaking his head, 'devious as all get out.'

'But you mustn't buy me anything else,' she said. 'You can't go spending your money on me.'

'Why ever not? I enjoy it.'

'Because it's not right.'

'Let me be the judge of that, Catie.'

She couldn't remember the last time Roger had bought her anything decent, miserable sod, which made her wonder if his tightness was due to the fact they were married. Why spoil a wife after all! She was there all the time, on tap, willy-nilly. These thoughts made her wonder if he bought gifts for his various girlfriends. Probably, she decided. That would impress them, keep them sweet. And they, of course, would repay him in the way he wanted – with gratitude and enthusiasm.

'I wish we could get together again,' Reith said.

'But we *are* together,' she replied, teasing him.

'Not the way I mean.'

She slipped the envelope into her handbag, deciding to put the

142

'found it' story to Roger later on. 'Thank you again,' she said.

'My pleasure.'

How would it be being married to Reith? she mused. Certainly different to Roger. She'd be appreciated a lot more, looked after, not taken so much for granted as she now was.

'What are you thinking?'

'Nothing,' she lied.

'You looked as though you were.'

'How's Irene?' she asked, changing the subject.

'Same as usual.'

'Are you two . . . sleeping together again yet?' Reith had confided this fact to her some while previously. He shook his head.

'Doesn't she complain?'

'Like billy-oh. At least she did, but she seems to have given up recently.'

Poor Irene, Catie thought. It must be awful going to bed with a husband who didn't want to know. Mind you, there must be lots of women who'd be delighted not to be bothered.

'Will you reconsider the business of us living together?' Reith implored.

She could hardly deny him that, not after he'd gone and bought her such a lovely present. She nodded. 'But I doubt I'll change my mind for the reasons I've already given,' she added hastily.

At least there was still a chance, Reith thought. All wasn't lost. 'I suppose I'll have to settle for that,' he declared, putting on a brave smile. God, he loved her so much, it hurt.

'Now I'd better go,' Catie said.

'So soon! Stay a bit longer, please?'

She heaved a sigh. 'Five minutes then. No more.'

By some swift talking, keeping her engrossed in conversation, he managed to stretch the five minutes to ten.

Chapter Twelve

'No no, when you're with me I pay,' admonished Charlie McCall, throwing a crisp white fiver onto the bar.

Reith picked up his pint of heavy and had a sip, having a quick glance round the pub. He'd never been here before, but he liked its friendly atmosphere. Someone called out to Charlie, and waved; Charlie acknowledged the wave. 'Scrap metal merchant I know. Biggest crook unhung,' Charlie explained to Reith with a thin smile.

'Lots of money in that game I believe,' Reith said, making conversation.

'Oh there is, as Doug over there could tell you. Another one who came from nowhere to make his pile.'

Reith interpreted that to mean that Charlie had also come from nowhere, probably the Glasgow backstreets. He didn't comment or probe, believing that if Charlie wanted to expand on his background then he would, but it wasn't his place to pry.

'So,' smiled Charlie, having seen off most of a double whisky, 'are you wondering why I asked you for this meeting?'

Reith nodded. 'I presumed there was a reason.'

'Indeed there is.' He studied Reith, eyes gleaming. 'You've done well, lad, very well. I couldn't be more pleased.'

'Thank you.'

'Are you enjoying the work?'

'It certainly beats labouring at Black's.'

Charlie gave a low laugh. 'I imagine most things would do that.' He knocked back the rest of his whisky and turned to his chaser. 'How would you fancy promotion?'

'Promotion?'

'You're intelligent, Reith, capable of being far more than a runner. And you've proved your honesty, which I never really questioned. But you've confirmed it nonetheless. Now I think it's time you moved up a step.'

Reith had learnt that Charlie was not only a bookie but ran a sizeable organization of which betting was merely a sideline. 'What do you have in mind?'

'I want you to be in charge of all the runners, they will report directly to you.'

Reith frowned. 'Les McIlwham does that.'

'Did Reith, did. I'm moving him elsewhere.'

'I see,' Reith murmured, excited at the prospect. It would mean more money, of course, and more responsibility, but he wasn't afraid of that.

'Well?'

'Fine, if you think I'm up to it.'

'I know you're up to it, Reith. I wouldn't be offering otherwise.'

Reith was pleased, and flattered. 'I must say I'm a bit surprised. I haven't been with you all that long.'

'I admit I wouldn't normally promote someone so quickly. But you're a special case, Reith. I owe you.' Charlie chuckled. 'Besides, this isn't the civil service. There's none of that time-serving nonsense with me.'

'When would you like me to take over from Les?'

'The sooner the better, eh?' He extended a hand, and they shook. 'I've got big things planned for you, Reith. Big things.'

Reith couldn't wait to tell Catie the news.

'That's wonderful,' Irene beamed. 'What's the pay?' Her look was one of sheer amazement when he told her. 'Charlie's being very generous,' he added.

'And how!' she exclaimed.

'We'll be quite well off. Regular toffs.'

Irene took off her pinny and threw it over the back of a chair. 'It means we can move away from here. Get a better house,' she declared.

Reith hadn't foreseen that reaction. 'Move away?' he queried.

'Of course. I want a house with an inside toilet and bath. I've dreamed about this for years. I hate sharing that cludgie on the landing. It might be what I was brought up to but it's still so demeaning.' She snapped her fingers. 'I read in the paper recently that they're building new houses out at Battlefield. We should go and have a dekko at those.'

Battlefield was miles away, Reith thought with a sinking heart. Miles from Bridgeton, and Catie. He didn't fancy that at all. 'I don't know,' he said hesitantly.

'What do you mean, you don't know?'

'I rather like it round here.'

'Like it! You told me when you came home you thought Bridgeton was a dump, which it is. This is our chance to better ourselves, Reith, go up in the world. And think about the children. Battlefield would be a far nicer place for them to grow up than round here.'

He thought furiously. 'It might be too far from the job,' he pointed out.

'There are trams and buses, aren't there?'

'It would still be difficult,' he said, continuing to prevaricate.

'And taxis too. You'd be able to afford as many of those as you needed.'

She had another idea. 'Or a wee car. You can learn to drive.'

'Why not a bloody Rolls Royce?' he replied sarcastically. 'And why learn to drive when I could hire a chauffeur?'

'All right, keep your hair on,' she snapped, not understanding his sudden bad humour. 'I'm only trying to help.'

'If you want to help then forget Battlefield and the like. For now anyway.'

Snatching up his jacket he strode from the house, heading for McTavish's. He was damned if he'd leave Bridgeton. He wanted to remain near Catie, know she wasn't far away. There was such comfort in that.

Irene was in a sulk when he returned home and she refused to reply when he spoke. The atmosphere in the kitchen was frosty.

'Let's see how I do in the new job before we discuss upping sticks,' he said in a placatory tone. He'd decided this was the line to take with her.

Irene softened a little. At least that made sense.

'You just caught me unprepared, that's all.'

She softened further. 'It wouldn't do any harm to have a look at those houses. See what's what.'

'I'll think about it,' he conceded. 'But not for a while, OK?'

She turned to him. 'I'm sorry, Reith, I didn't mean to upset you.' She wanted to go to him, throw her arms round his neck and kiss him. But she knew better than to try, he'd only shrug off her advances.

'Tell you what,' he smiled. 'The school holidays are coming up again. Why don't you take the children for another trip to Dunoon? They loved the last one.'

'I couldn't get away from the dairy this time.'

'Bugger the dairy! You don't have to work there any more, we don't need the money now.' He paused, then added, 'Unless of course you want to stay on, that is?'

Did she? The answer was no. 'I'll speak to Mr McDougall tomorrow,' she declared. 'He shouldn't have any trouble replacing me.'

'That way you can stay away for a fortnight, make a proper holiday of it. I'll ensure you have plenty of cash to enjoy yourselves.'

He smiled with satisfaction. He hadn't slept with Catie since the last time his family had gone to Dunoon, as there just had not been the opportunity. Now he'd have the house to himself for an entire two weeks. He prayed Catie wouldn't let him down.

He shut the door behind her and pulled her into his arms. 'God you smell good,' he breathed.

Catie gave him that feline smile of hers. 'How are you?'

'How do you think with you here? Us alone together.'

She laughed throatily.

'I've got a present for you.'

'Reith! You promised . . .'

'No I didn't,' he interjected.

'You're very naughty,' she admonished.

'I know. Completely round the bend. But only where you're concerned.'

He brushed his lips over hers, but she pulled back a little, teasing him.

'How long have we got?' he asked.

'Ten minutes.'

'Catie!'

She laughed again. 'An hour, hour and a half at most.'

'Where's Roger?'

147

'At home. At least he was when I left. I'm supposed to be in town shopping.'

'And what'll he say when you don't take anything back with you?'

She shrugged. 'I didn't find what I was after. Happens to us women all the time.'

He took her by the hand and led her through to the kitchen. Sitting on the table was a brown paper bag which he handed her.

'Nylons!' Catie almost squealed. They were like gold dust. 'Where did you get them?'

'Through Charlie's contacts. I've discovered I can get almost anything, including unlimited coupons.'

'You mean the black market?'

'That's it.'

'Six pairs,' she said, counting them. 'I don't know how to thank you.'

'Oh, I can think of a way.'

She arched an eyebrow.

'How will you explain them to Roger?'

'I'll find a way, don't you worry about that. I'm not going to turn down nylons when offered.'

He kissed the tip of her nose, then each cheek in turn. His senses were reeling from her closeness.

'When I'm with you I feel as though I've died and gone to heaven,' he said.

'Well I'm no angel,' she grinned.

'I should hope not. Me neither.'

Afterwards they talked about a new film they'd both recently seen, comparing opinions, laughing, joking, teasing one another. Before she left, Catie promised she'd come again before Irene and the children returned from Dunoon.

Reith watched Roger dancing with Irene, as he sat alone at their table while Catie went to the toilet. They were in The Cocoa Club, a small private club owned by Charlie McCall where Reith had brought the four of them to celebrate his birthday.

The more he knew about Roger the more he disliked him, Reith reflected. If it hadn't been for Catie he'd have discontinued his friendship with the man. There was something sleazy and uncouth about Roger, particularly when he'd had a drink, that Reith found repellent. He smiled, thinking of the previous Saturday when he and Catie had gone to bed together. They'd had three hours in all, three glorious, delightful hours that had whizzed by, as time always did when he was with Catie.

It depressed him to think it might be months before he could go to bed with her again. He had suggested that they book into a hotel, but she'd turned that down, saying that for a large city Glasgow was in reality quite small. There was too big a risk of them being seen, or someone on the hotel staff recognizing her and reporting back to Roger. Although this was unlikely, nonetheless it was a possibility. And Catie was terrified of Roger's reaction should he ever find out about the pair of them.

When she'd left him on Saturday it had been galling to know she was returning to Roger, and his bed. How many times since then had Roger . . . No, no, he mustn't think about that. Madness lay in that direction. Roger making love to Catie was something he had to shut completely out of his mind.

Reith shook his head and reached for his glass. So far it had been an enjoyable evening, but then it always was when Catie was present. She was like a light being switched on in a darkened room, the mere sight of her making his heart leap.

One thing was certain, he would marry her. He was absolutely determined about that. He would make her his wife in place of Irene.

On the dance floor Irene glanced over at Reith, brooding at their table, and wondered what he was thinking about. He hadn't danced with her yet, though he had taken the floor several times with Catie. It just wasn't fair, she thought bitterly. If only he knew the sacrifices she'd made for him and the children. Going to bed with the repulsive Billy Boyne, suffering the horrors that had entailed. And all for Reith's sake, to keep him out of a wheelchair. And why? Because she'd loved him as she still did.

How long was it since they'd had sex? So long she couldn't even remember. But worse than that was his treatment of her, his cold indifference. He looked at her sometimes as though she wasn't even there. How that hurt, deeply and profoundly.

If only she could explain to him about Boyne, tell him her reasons for the affair. But that was out the question because she didn't know whether he'd remembered about Boyne or not.

'Good band, eh?' Roger smiled.

'Very.'

The number ended and they applauded. 'Will you stay up?' he asked.

149

'I would have thought you'd had enough for the moment. I'm not exactly the best dancer in the world.'

'Who told you that malarkey?' he protested. 'You're a wonderful dancer. And I don't lie.'

'You really think so?'

He made a quick gesture over his chest. 'Cross my heart.'

Roger was sweet, she thought. Just what she needed to help bolster her ego, which had taken such a terrible battering of late. Well, what spurned female wouldn't feel as she did? Rejected by a husband who could hardly bear to touch her, a husband she craved with every fibre of her being.

The band started up again, playing a slow waltz, and Roger gathered her to him.

'This is quite a place, I've never been here before,' Roger commented.

'You have to be a member.' Reith and their party had been waved through as Reith was well known.

'A member!' Roger repeated caustically. 'My my, we are posh all of a sudden. But then I suppose you can afford to be when you're earning the money Reith is nowadays.'

'It's certainly a big jump from Black's. We've been lucky.'

'I'm surprised the pair of you are still talking to the likes of us,' he jibed.

'Oh come on Roger! Neither Reith nor I are like that. Although I have to admit I did want us to move to a better area, but Reith wouldn't entertain the idea. At least not for now.'

'Where did you have in mind?'

'Battlefield,' she replied. 'They're building some lovely houses there. Ones with inside toilets and bathrooms.'

Jealousy gnawed at Roger who'd have given his eye teeth for a house with such amenities. 'And he's not interested?'

'Says he wants to wait and see how the job pans out before moving.'

Roger spotted Catie threading her way back to their table. Reith jumped to his feet and helped her with her chair.

'Nice dress you're wearing. Is it new?' he queried, turning his attention again to Irene. Her dress was navy blue, tight fitting with a scalloped neckline, which accentuated her cleavage.

Irene relished the compliment. 'I bought it especially for tonight.' She added in a conspiratorial whisper, 'Reith can get all the coupons he wants now. I just have to ask and they turn up.'

150

Roger gritted his teeth. 'It must have been expensive.'

'Terribly. I swear my hands were shaking when I handed over the money.'

Lucky bastard, Roger thought, meaning Reith. What he would have given to be in such a position.

Irene prattled on making Roger more and more envious.

'Close your eyes for a moment,' Reith smiled to Catie.

'What for?'

'Just do it.'

She did. 'Now what?'

'Think back.'

'To when?'

'Last Saturday. You and I.'

Her eyes flew open again. 'Stop it, you'll embarrass me.'

'I love you, Catie.'

He was like a big puppy dog at times, she thought, all soft and endearing which made you want to pat him on the head. She giggled.

'What brought that on?'

'I'm not telling.' She giggled again.

'I think you're drunk.'

'I'm nothing of the sort. I'm just enjoying myself, that's all.'

'Want to dance?'

'You should get Irene up.'

He pulled a face. 'I don't want to dance with her. I want to dance with you.'

'Nonetheless, you should get her up. If for no other reason than I don't want Roger commenting on the fact you didn't dance with your wife.'

'Later then. You now.'

'No,' she said firmly.

'Catie?'

'No,' she repeated, revelling in the power she had over him. It had never been like this with Roger, he'd always been the dominant partner. But she held Reith in the palm of her hand. She knew he was so besotted that he'd do anything she asked. A shiver ran up her back.

Later, she was startled, though managed to mask it, when, having danced with Irene, Reith began playing footsie with her, rubbing his leg up and down hers. Roger and Irene remained, to Catie's amusement, blissfully unaware of what was happening.

'For me!' Catie exclaimed in amazement.

'Who else?'

She accepted the bunch of flowers from Roger. It was the first time he'd ever brought flowers home. 'What's the occasion?'

'There isn't one. I simply thought you'd like them.'

She kissed him on the mouth. 'Why thank you.'

'I also thought we might go out for a drink later. Just the two of us.'

'That would be nice.'

'We could go to The Beresford.'

Catie smiled. That was where he'd taken her during their courting days. It was years since they'd been there. 'Lovely.'

'Right then.'

Surprise followed surprise. Roger helped her on and off the tram, opened the door for her when they reached The Beresford, not only opening the door but opening it with a flourish, standing aside and waving her in, telling her repeatedly how wonderful she looked, asking her about this and that, questioning her views on everything. Her head was whirling when they returned home. They hadn't behaved like a married couple who'd grown slightly bored with one another; but like two people out on what the Americans call a first date. He'd chatted her up, flirted with her, romanced her!

Catie lay back, aglow with sexual satisfaction, her body satiated. Roger had always been an excellent lover, but that had been extraordinary, way beyond anything they'd ever achieved before.

'Can I cuddle you?'

She smiled lazily. 'Of course.'

He snuggled up, draping an arm over her bosoms which created a feeling of warm intimacy quite different to their coupling. Kissing each other one last time, they then both drifted off into sleep, a loving couple in every sense.

The scenery surrounding the Kilpatrick Hills was as breathtaking as ever. Catie, hands deep in the pockets of her camel coat, strode along, lost in thought. Roger was a changed man since the night he'd taken her to The Beresford. She didn't know what had inspired the change, only that it had taken place. He loved her, showing that love in a hundred different ways. And her love for him, which she thought had been chipped away over the years, had blossomed again, returning to its former passion.

All the suspicions and memories of Linda Brasil had blown away; he'd never be unfaithful again. She knew that with total certainty. He was, once more, completely hers. Roger, the man she'd married and loved, husband of her children, her life's companion and friend. That was perhaps the nicest thing, they'd become friends in a way they'd never been before.

She paused to stare out over the bracken and heather, smiling as she remembered the first time she'd met Roger. As was often the case in Glasgow, it had been at a dance.

'You're the prettiest girl in the hall. And that isn't flannel either,' the lad who'd got her up declared, introducing himself as Roger Smith.

Catie blushed.

'Honestly you are.'

She stared into a beaming, open face that radiated friendliness and admiration. 'Get away with you,' she stammered in reply.

'A real corker in my book.'

'You're some patter merchant. I'll bet you say that to all the lassies.'

'I do nothing of the sort. I swear to you.'

Catie glanced around. Prettiest girl in the hall? She could hardly believe that was true.

'Where do you live?'

She told him.

'That's not too far from me. Can I walk you home afterwards?'

That astonished her. They'd only been up a few minutes and there were hours to go before the dance was over. To commit himself so soon!

'I don't know,' she prevaricated.

He suddenly frowned. 'You're not here with someone, are you?'

She nodded.

'Who is he?'

'I didn't say it was a he.'

'Ah!' Roger exclaimed. 'A china then?'

'Kirsty. We're great pals.'

'Well, you'll just have to tell Kirsty you've been lumbered and that from here on in she's on her tod.' Lumbered was the Glaswegian word which meant to have been picked up.

'You are confident, aren't you? I might not fancy you.'

'Yes you do. I can see it in your face.'

She laughed, because he was right. She did fancy him. There was something about Roger that had instantly appealed.

'We're fated,' he declared.

She laughed again, he really was going too far. 'We've only just met.'

'Doesn't matter. We're fated. I knew it the moment I spotted you. Roger my old son, I said to myself, she's the one for you. So get straight over there and state your claim before some smooth-talking bugger whips in ahead of you.' He shrugged. 'Even if one had I'd simply have bided my time.'

'And what if this smooth-talker had lumbered me?' she teased.

'There would be other nights, other dances. I'd be bound to run into you again. But that's something I don't have to worry about now, do I?'

He had a gorgeous smile, she thought, like a ray of sunshine. And there was no doubt about his charm, he oozed that. Could he be right and they were fated? An electric thrill coursed through her as she imagined that he might be right.

'Now tell me all about yourself?' he urged. 'And when you've done that I'll tell you about me.'

After a while she excused herself to go to the ladies, and there she peered at her reflection in a mirror. She'd never considered herself to be particularly pretty, not exactly a plain jane, but nothing startling either. Perhaps she'd been wrong. It certainly made her feel good to be so complimented.

She remembered asking her mother, that cold, austere woman, when she was little if she'd be pretty when she grew up and her mother replied that she shouldn't be so soft and that looks weren't everything. She recalled crying after that, convinced she was ugly, which of course, with hindsight, she hadn't been. But the incident had remained with her, badly denting her confidence, making her unsure of her physical attraction to the opposite sex.

Now this chap had happened along telling her she was the prettiest girl in the hall and lumbering her after only a few minutes. Someone who'd declared that the pair of them were fated. She couldn't wait to get back into his company, and arms. Or for the kissing that would surely take place later in her back close.

'Roger Smith,' she whispered to the mirror. He was already her hero.

154

Catie halted a few yards from the cafe entrance and took a deep breath. She wasn't looking forward to this at all, but it had to be done, her mind was made up. She was sorry for the pain she was going to cause.

Reith glanced across in expectation and smiled when the bell tinged announcing her arrival. She felt like Judas as she walked towards him.

Chapter Thirteen

Irene woke to the muted sound of crying. Reith was sitting slumped in a chair, his head cradled in his hands, an almost empty bottle of whisky by his side. She stared at him in consternation. She had gone to bed before he'd arrived home from work, so she'd had no inkling that he was upset. There again, she thought, he had been acting strangely during the past couple of days.

Billy Boyne! Was that it? Had he finally remembered and that's what had brought this on? Cold fear clutched her heart.

'Reith?' she queried.

He didn't reply, not having heard her, lost in a great black hole of despair. He felt as if he was coming apart, that his mind was disintegrating. His body was one large pulsating raw nerve.

'Reith?' she tried again, more loudly this time.

He glanced up at her, his face awash with tears, eyes bloodshot. His expression was reminiscent of a man in hell.

'Go back to sleep,' he croaked.

'What's wrong? What's the matter?' she asked, fearing his answer. It had to be Billy, surely? What else could produce such an effect?

He groped for the bottle and splashed the remaining contents into a glass which he threw down his throat. Catie! he wanted to scream at the top of his voice. Catie!

Slipping from the bed Irene shrugged into her dressing gown and went over to him. 'Reith, what's wrong?' she asked again.

He shook his head, unable to tell her. How could he say to his wife that his mistress, the woman he loved profoundly, had broken up with him, shattered his dream and life? He felt paralysed.

'What's brought this on? Something at work?'

He shuddered from head to toe.

Then she had a terrible thought. 'You're not ill, are you? Has the doctor diagnosed something awful?'

'No,' he husked.

She steeled herself. 'Is is to do with me?'

He knew why she'd asked that, she felt guilty about Billy bloody Boyne. Well, he didn't give a shit about Boyne any more, he didn't give a shit about anything. The only thing that mattered was the fact that Catie had left him. The pain was almost unbearable, mental anguish was ripping him to shreds. He wished he was dead, that he'd never met Catie Smith, that the bullet which had hit his head had killed him.

Irene squatted by his side, not knowing what to do. At least it wasn't Boyne, she thought in relief. If Reith wasn't lying, that was. But why should he lie?

'I'm sorry,' he whimpered.

'There must be some reason, Reith. Can't you tell me?'

'Go back to bed, Irene. Leave me be.'

'But you're in such a state, my darling.'

He wasn't her darling, he inwardly raged. He was Catie's. Catie whom he hoped he'd never see again. Catie who'd done this to him. Catie who was even now inside his head, smiling, laughing, standing naked. Catie whose imagined smell was strong in his nostrils. Catie, whom he worshipped, who'd chosen that sleazy oaf over him. Catie!

Irene bit her lip as she watched Reith grope for the empty whisky bottle, his hand shaking in desperation. Had he drunk the whole bottle? she wondered. He'd obviously brought the bottle in with him so she had no way of knowing whether it had been full or not. One thing was certain, he'd had more than enough.

'Shall I put the kettle on?'

'Fuck the kettle,' he snarled.

He saw himself in the cafe after Catie had left, her words ringing in his ears. He'd just sat there, stunned with disbelief. God knows what he'd looked like for the person serving behind the counter had come over and enquired if he was all right. He must have replied, but couldn't remember doing so, for she'd gone away again. How long had he sat there? Five minutes? Half an hour? Longer? He had no idea. But at some point he'd got up and stumbled from the cafe.

157

Things had been hazy for a while after that. Confused images, distorted voices. He'd walked on and on, through familiar streets, strange streets and alleyways, in one of which he'd vomited.

She wouldn't change her mind, Catie had told him. He mustn't hold out any hope of that. It had been a mistake on her part. Although she didn't regret it, it had been a mistake nonetheless. And as she'd spoken she'd smiled, an outward manifestation, he'd numbly realized, of her nervousness.

He'd died at that table, spiritually and emotionally if not physically. His body might remain, but the rest of him had gone forever. If only his body had died, given him the peace that would never again be his. Relieve him of this living torment.

'Is it connected with the war?' Irene queried quietly. 'Have you remembered something about that?'

He wished she would shut up, fighting back the urge to lash out at her. The war? That was as good an explanation as any. He nodded.

'I see.'

She saw bugger all. But no matter. He craved more whisky but it was all gone. He knew there was nowhere he could find another bottle at this time of the morning.

'Come to bed Reith. Try and sleep,' she pleaded.

'No.'

'Please?'

He didn't reply.

'It might help if you could talk about it.'

He shook his head.

'Do you want—'

'I want to be fucking well left alone. That's what I *want*,' he hissed.

The venom in his voice rocked her back on her heels. If that's what he wished, so be it. Rising, she returned to bed and got back underneath the sheet from where she lay watching him, pitying him.

Catie! Reith thought, wallowing now in self pity, relishing the misery which had engulfed him since the cafe.

'Sit down Reith,' said Charlie, waving to the chair that stood in front of his desk. They were in Charlie's office.

'You look dreadful,' Charlie stated quietly once Reith was seated.

Reith ran a hand over his face and didn't reply. He was tired beyond belief, having only slept in fits and starts during the previous fortnight. He felt completely drained, wrung out.

'Like a drink?'

Reith nodded. 'Thanks.'

Charlie poured two large whiskies, noting when he gave Reith his glass Reith's hand was trembling. So what he'd heard was true, Reith had been hitting the bottle.

'You've been falling down on the job recently,' Charlie said. 'Is there a reason?'

So that was it, Reith thought dully. That explained why he'd been summoned. 'Are you going to sack me?'

'That depends. I repeat, is there a reason?'

Reith closed his eyes. He could lie to Charlie, tell him he was haunted by memories of the war. But that wouldn't be fair to someone who'd treated him so well. No, he couldn't lie to Charlie.

He opened his eyes again. 'It's a longish story.'

'I'm in no hurry to be anywhere.'

Reith started at the beginning, with Irene and Billy Boyne.

Outside the hotel room the sun was streaming down over Euston, but Reith's world was grey, devoid of colour. He didn't think he'd ever see colour again. He told himself he should get up and shave, have a bath, eat, possibly go for a walk, but he didn't have the energy to do any of those things. He'd been in London now for a week. Charlie had suggested the trip so he could get away from everything and be on his own to try and come to terms with the situation. He had told Irene that he was on a business trip.

Charlie couldn't have been more understanding or sympathetic, only asking one question when he'd come to the end of his sorry tale. Did he now remember Jack? The answer had been no. How he'd wished it could have been otherwise.

He stretched out on the bed and rasped a hand over his stubbly chin. Then he reached for the whisky bottle. When that was finished he'd pick up the phone and ring down for more. Thank heavens he'd chosen a decent hotel with room service. Charlie, bless him, was funding the trip.

'Catie,' he murmured, wondering where she was at that moment, what she was doing. At least she wasn't with that bugger Roger for it was the middle of the day which meant Roger would be at Black's.

The nights were worst. For some time then, nine? ten? eleven?

they'd been going to bed, making love. Roger and Catie, the woman he'd literally have cut off an arm to get back.

A mistake, she'd said, but she had no regrets. Did he? Sometimes yes, sometimes no. And yet he still wished he'd never met her, never walked down that street and seen her looming out of the fog, never stopped to talk.

He pulled himself round to sit on the edge of the bed, drinking straight from the whisky bottle, not bothering with a glass. Whisky helped. It dulled the pain and gave him long stretches of restless oblivion.

Common sense told him to remain in London, get a job there. Stay away from Glasgow and Catie. Put distance between her and him. But there were the children to consider, he couldn't abandon them. Not even Agnes whom he still wasn't certain was his. There again, he could get the family to come down and join him once he'd found a place to live. That was a possibility. But why cut off his nose to spite his face by leaving Charlie and going back to something like labouring. And then Reith smiled, knowing he was kidding himself. He wouldn't leave Glasgow because that's where Catie was. She'd told him not to hope, that she'd never change her mind. But he would always hope which was why he'd be on hand should she ever have a change of heart.

'You're a bloody fool,' he chided himself. She never would change. But maybe . . . maybe . . . It was a lifeline he had to cling to, because without it he'd go completely out of his mind.

Nine o'clock that night found him staring at the clock, watching the minutes tick by, visualizing.

Charlie rose as Reith entered his office. 'Better?'

'I'll never be that Charlie. But I'm in control again.'

'Drinking?'

'Some. But not like I was.'

Charlie nodded. 'Ready to start back?'

'That's why I'm here.'

'Good.'

'I eh . . .' He looked Charlie straight in the eye. 'I want to thank you. For understanding, the break, the money . . .'

'I know what it's like to lose someone you love,' Charlie interjected softly. 'It's not easy.'

'No,' Reith agreed.

Charlie extended a hand. 'Welcome home, son.'

160

Roger was humming as he climbed the stairs. Catie thought he was at a Masonic meeting, or on his way to one. The reality was quite different. He smiled, thinking about her. Things between them were brilliant again and he was determined they would continue to be so. But he still needed some excitement.

He stopped humming when he knocked at a familiar door. He grinned from ear to ear when he heard the tread of approaching feet. Feet that belonged to a war widow, as Linda Brasil had been.

'It's the first time you've been here, isn't it?' Charlie said to Reith, ushering him into the drawing room.

Reith gazed round him in awe. The room was magnificent, as was the house, situated in Newton Mearns, an extremely smart area. The house was a veritable mansion.

'That's right.'

Charlie shrugged. 'I lost the habit of entertaining when Fanny died, and conduct all my business, with the exception of some phone calls, from the office.'

He removed a crystal decanter from a silver tantalus. 'Drink?'

'Please.'

He poured the whisky into crystal glasses that matched the decanter. 'Water?'

'Neat.'

Charlie handed Reith a glass. 'Like the house?'

'I'll say. It's breathtaking.'

Charlie laughed. 'I'm glad you like it because it's going to be yours. I'm giving it to you.'

Reith gaped at him, then also laughed. It was obviously a leg-pull. 'Oh yeah!'

'I'm serious,' Charlie stated.

Reith stared at him. 'You're giving me this house?'

'And everything else. The business, what's in the bank. The whole kit and caboodle. Congratulations.'

Holy Christ! Reith thought. He *was* serious. 'Why?'

Charlie crossed over to a white marble mantelpiece and gazed up at the portrait hanging over it. 'Fanny, my wife,' he explained.

'Handsome looking woman.'

Charlie's eyes misted. 'She was that.' He paused, then added, 'A day doesn't go by when I don't think of her, and miss her.'

He turned to Reith. 'Do you believe in God?'

Reith considered that, still stunned by what Charlie had told him. The whole kit and caboodle! 'I don't know,' he answered truthfully. 'I'd like to.'

'Well I do,' Charlie declared. 'Just as I believe you meet up again with loved ones in the afterlife. That's why I'm not bothered about dying. In fact, I'm quite looking forward to it. It means I'll be reunited with Fanny and Jack.'

The penny began to drop for Reith. 'What's happened, Charlie?'

Charlie had a sip of whisky. 'Fine stuff Macallan, my favourite.'

'Charlie?'

'I've got cancer, Reith. It's been confirmed by a second specialist. Apparently it's pretty advanced. I've got six months at most.'

Reith was stunned a second time by this new thunderbolt. He didn't know what to say. Charlie had just pronounced his own death sentence. 'I'm sorry. Really I am.'

'The joke is, I've never felt better in my life.'

'Then maybe there's been a mistake?' Reith suggested hopefully.

Charlie shook his head. 'No mistake Reith. The two specialists I saw are the top men in their field. I could pop off any day.'

'Is there anything I can do?'

'There's nothing anyone can do.'

Reith went to Charlie and affectionately squeezed his arm. 'I'll miss you. You've been a good friend.'

'I've seen you for some time as more than a friend Reith. You could never replace my own flesh and blood of course, never that. But you've become the next best thing. A sort of adopted son. That's why I'm leaving you everything.'

'But surely there's someone more entitled. A relative?'

'No-one Reith. No-one immediate that is. Besides, I want you to inherit. That'll please me.'

'It's . . . a bit hard to take in all at once. Coming completely out of the blue as it has.'

Charlie laughed. 'It's an ill wind, eh? Now, let's top up these glasses, we've a lot to discuss. I want you to take over the reins right away, so that I can help and advise for as long as I'm around.'

Irene fainted when he told her, but luckily Reith managed to grab her before she hit the floor.

'I still can't believe it,' Irene said in the darkness.

'I know. It's incredible.'

'A mansion in Newton Mearns!'

'Well, you've wanted to move away from Bridgeton for a long while. Now you can.'

'Charlie must be worth a fortune.'

'I don't know the exact figures yet, but there's a lot of money involved. There has to be.'

'I feel sorry for Charlie though. What an awful thing to happen.'

'He believes he'll meet up with his wife and Jack again, he has that as a consolation.'

'I hope he's right, Reith. He deserves it.'

Reith silently agreed.

Her hand moved under the bedclothes to grasp his. 'This is going to be a new beginning for us, Reith. Can we both see it like that?'

He didn't reply.

'Please?'

He thought about Catie, whom he hadn't seen since he'd returned from London, then Billy Boyne. Wasn't it hypocritical to continue condemning Irene for having had an affair when he'd had one himself? Irene had loved Boyne after all, as he'd loved Catie.

'Reith?'

A new beginning, she'd said. It made sense, he decided reluctantly, especially in the circumstances. Turning to her, he took her into his arms, banishing Catie from his mind.

Chapter Fourteen

To commemorate the anniversary of Charlie's death Reith poured himself a large Macallan. Going to the large window of his office he stared down on the busy street below, thinking about Charlie, remembering.

He'd come a long way in those six years since Charlie's passing, expanding the organization on all fronts, adding new assets, all of which were proving extremely lucrative. One of the first moves he'd made was to 'persuade' the rest of Glasgow's bookies to come in under his protective umbrella. In other words, they worked for him and he took a percentage of their profits. He smiled grimly recalling the difficulties of that little operation, for what man with his own business wanted to be 'creamed' by another? He'd hired new staff, the most effective of whom was Jameson who acted as his personal chauffeur and bodyguard. An ex-commando who'd been down on his luck, Jameson had soon gained a reputation for terrifying ruthlessness.

Once the bookie situation had been sorted out he'd opened a new club, Fanny's, named after Charlie's wife, which was the largest and swankiest in the city. It boasted two French chefs and the prettiest hostesses and waitresses to be hired locally. The club was situated on three floors, the ground consisting of the bars and restaurant, the second for gambling, the third administration. He'd followed up the success of Fanny's by opening five other clubs, these smaller, each catering for different types of clientele.

He also owned three brothels, having opened two over and above the one he'd inherited from Charlie. He wasn't particularly proud of these, but business was business, after all. And he partially justified owning them, confident that his girls were well looked after and cared for. He'd insisted on that.

Then there was the Whiteinch Dog Track, Ibrox Speedway, a scattering of pubs supplied by a small brewery that he also owned, a construction firm and printing works. Last, but not least, he was a sleeping partner in a prestigious insurance brokers.

Yes, he'd come a long way since that night Charlie had first called at their house in Bridgeton. Who'd have believed that he'd have become the powerful and affluent, not to mention influential, figure he now was? Certainly not him.

'To you Charlie!' he toasted, raising his glass.

His thoughts were interrupted by the intercom buzzing. 'Yes, Milla?' he said, answering his secretary who worked in an outer office.

'Your wife's on the line, Mr Douglas.'

'Thank you. Put her through.'

He lifted his telephone. 'How are you, darling. What's the problem?'

'Nothing really. I just wanted to remind you about the dinner party this evening in case you'd forgotten. I should have mentioned it before you left home but it slipped my mind.'

Lucky she had rung, Reith reflected, for he had forgotten. It wouldn't do, or be in his interest, to forget the Chief Constable. 'Anything I can bring with me?'

'No, everything's arranged. Just bring yourself.'

He smiled. 'Right, I'll see you then.'

'Bye.'

'Bye Irene.'

He hung up and pressed the intercom. 'Milla.'

'Yes Mr Douglas?'

'Find Jameson and tell him I want him.'

'Straight away sir.'

He finished his drink and returned the glass to the small bar built into one wall. He was glancing through some paperwork when Jameson arrived.

'We're going for a spin,' Reith stated.

'I'll bring the car round to the front. Which one do you want?'

Reith considered that, then smiled. 'As we're off to the country I'll have the Riley.' He'd bought the two and a half litre Roadster the previous year and absolutely adored it. He kept it privately garaged nearby with his Daimler.

'OK Reith, give me ten minutes and she'll be waiting.' Jameson was the only one of Reith's employees who called him by his Christian name.

When Jameson had gone Reith put on his black crombie and hat. He then spent several minutes talking to Milla, instructing her on various things he wanted doing, after which he slowly sauntered downstairs thinking about McNeice. He purposely hadn't telephoned, wanting his visit to be a surprise, but hoped the damn man was going to be in and this wouldn't be a wasted visit. Leaving the club he crossed the pavement and climbed into the Roadster.

'Where to?' Jameson enquired.

Reith told him, then settled back to enjoy the journey. As they drove Reith thought about Mathew and Agnes, the latter now attending a secretarial college in London. She was still undecided about her future, whether to stay on in London or return to Glasgow. He of course hoped she'd return, but that was entirely up to her. If she decided it would be better to stay in London, he would respect her decision.

As for Mathew, and here Reith's heart swelled with pride, he was reading English at St Andrews' University and hoped to become a journalist when he graduated. A son of his at university! Reith marvelled at that. Thanks to Charlie he'd been able to put both children through private school which had proved a resounding success, particularly in Mathew's case. And Reith felt he didn't need to worry about Agnes who wasn't nearly as academically bright as her brother. She was a delightful girl and he presumed she would marry in the not too distant future. University, Reith mused, thinking again about Mathew. What he'd have given for that chance! He was delighted that he'd been able to give Mathew such a good start in life.

'We're here,' Jameson announced forty minutes later, turning the Riley into a long winding drive.

The house at the end of the drive was centuries old with turrets protruding from each corner of the building. Reith reflected that it looked as if it could have jumped straight out of a history book, a place where William Wallace or Robert the Bruce might have slept. They rapped on the front door, using the cast iron lion's head knocker. A butler answered.

'I've called to see Sir Ewan,' Reith declared.

166

'Do you have an appointment, sir?'

'I'm afraid not.'

'Then I—'

'Is he about?' Reith interrupted.

The butler frowned at this rudeness. 'He is, sir, but—'

Reith nodded to Jameson who pushed the apoplectic butler aside.

'Tell him he has guests,' Reith said, stepping into an oak-panelled hallway lined with ancient oils.

The butler was about to protest until he saw the look on Jameson's face which swiftly changed his mind. 'If you gentlemen will follow me please,' he requested, and led them down the hallway. They were ushered into a study, also oak lined, and were asked to wait.

'Who shall I say is calling sir?' the butler enquired.

'A Mr Douglas and Mr Jameson. You might also mention Fanny's.'

'Fanny's,' the butler repeated, wondering who or what that was. Reith didn't enlighten him.

A few minutes later Sir Ewan McNeice appeared, scowling. In his early fifties he had thinning sandy hair and a high complexion.

'What's the meaning of this outrage?' he demanded.

'You owe me ten thousand pounds,' Reith replied quietly.

Sir Ewan harumphed. 'Of course I do. But that doesn't give you the right to come storming into a chap's home. Impertinence I call it.'

'And I call it impertinent to take me for a mug,' Reith answered. 'You were supposed to pay a fortnight ago, and haven't.'

'You'll get your money Douglas when I get round to paying it. As it so happens I'm rather short at the moment. Nothing to be concerned about, it's merely temporary.'

'And yet you were able to buy yourself a rather expensive horse only a few days ago,' Reith smiled thinly.

'How did you know that?'

'I hear things,' Reith informed him, still smiling. 'You'd be surprised.'

'That deal was supposed to be on the quiet. Someone will get a rocket for speaking out of turn.'

'How's Lady McNeice?' Reith enquired.

Sir Ewan's brow furrowed, as far as he knew Reith had never met his wife. 'She's tiptop,' he answered slowly. 'Why do you ask?'

'I was just wondering how she'd react to finding out about the mistress you keep in town. Hyndland to be precise.'

Sir Ewan went white. That, or so he'd believed, was a closely guarded secret.

'I told you I hear things.'

'You can't . . . you mustn't . . .' Sir Ewan spluttered.

'A week from today. Don't fail me,' Reith said, and jerked his head at Jameson who went and opened the study door.

Thoroughly shaken, Sir Ewan watched Reith stride from the room. God help him if Pamela were to learn of Cissie, or his gambling. She'd murder him.

'What a charming dress,' Jane Ogilvie, the Chief Constable's wife, commented to Irene. The dress in question was made of green crushed velvet, had a heart-shaped neckline and plunged in a V at the back to end in a bow.

'A little creation I picked up during my last visit to London,' Irene declared. 'It's a Dior.'

Typical, Jane thought acidly. Talk about flaunting it! The dress itself might be in good taste which could hardly be said for the woman wearing it. Why oh why had Simon insisted they come to the Douglases? The pair of them were no more than a couple of jumped-up peasants.

'It certainly suits you,' said Lena Dewar. She was married to Harry Dewar, a Glasgow MP.

'Why, thank you, Lena,' Irene gushed, which made Jane groan inwardly.

Lena was as green as the dress with envy. She would have loved a Dior and the diamond bracelet Irene was wearing. That alone must have cost a small fortune. But then the Douglases could afford such things, they were rolling in it.

'Do you often go to London?' Jane enquired of Irene, forcing herself to make conversation.

'Usually twice a year on shopping trips. And of course I now combine that with seeing our daughter Agnes who's at college there, doing awfully well.'

Jane arched an eyebrow. 'College?'

'Training to be a secretary.'

'How interesting,' Jane replied with only the vaguest trace of sarcasm in her voice.

Lena was trying hard not to stare at the diamond bracelet which she coveted with all her heart. Lucky woman, she thought, visualizing the bracelet on her own wrist. Jane risked a glance at a nearby clock, groaning inwardly again at how slowly the time was passing.

While this exchange was taking place Simon Ogilvie was managing to have a private word with Reith, one of the reasons for his accepting the dinner invitation. He had been no more enthusiastic than his wife. 'I have some colleagues coming up from England shortly and was wondering if you could, discreetly of course, lay on a corresponding number of your girls for them?'

'Consider it arranged. Just let me know where, when and how many and they'll be there,' Reith replied.

'I'll naturally ensure they're paid the going rate.'

Reith held up a hand. 'No need for that, Simon. It'll be my pleasure to attend to the matter.'

Simon Ogilvie beamed at Reith, knowing he would say that, but he felt it necessary to make the gesture.

'And if there's any other way I can help entertain your colleagues you only have to mention it.'

'Thanks Reith. That's most kind of you. And you will make certain the girls are the sort to be discreet. If this were ever to leak out, well!'

'They won't talk. You have my assurance of that. I'll have Jameson personally instruct them. That'll do the trick.'

Simon nodded his approval, reflecting that Reith did have his uses, although having to socialize with the man was a big price to pay. Now it was his turn to glance at the clock his wife had looked at only moments before, his train of thought exactly as hers had been.

Meanwhile Reith was staring over Simon's shoulder to where Harry Dewar was deep in conversation with Mathilda McPherson, who was the wife of one of Glasgow's leading industrialists. He had heard on the grapevine that Harry was having financial problems. He'd offer his services before the night was out, another politician in his pocket would be no bad thing. As he and Simon continued to chat Reith thought of how much it cost him per month for police protection. It was a hefty sum that increased every year, but it was worth every penny. He idly wondered if Jane Ogilvie, who had a face and figure like the back end of a bus, knew her husband was on the take. If he'd asked Simon he was sure the answer would have been no.

A little later dinner was announced and they all trooped through to a sumptuous meal.

Irene sank onto her bed having just returned from a shopping expedition into town. She'd bumped into an old school chum with whom she'd exchanged reminiscenses.

'Do you remember . . .' And with that the friend had casually dropped a bombshell that had caused Irene to feel sick ever since.

Billy Boyne had been released from Barlinne thanks to earning time off for good behaviour. Released! The news sent cold shivers coursing up and down her spine. Surely he wouldn't try to contact her? The very thought was a nightmare. But what if he did? What if he wanted to take up with her again? There was no worry about Reith and the children now, Reith would take care of Boyne as easy as pie. But that would mean Reith would find out about her previous affair with Boyne and all that entailed.

Irene worried a thumbnail. She still didn't know whether Reith had remembered about the affair or not; that remained a mystery and a subject she never broached. If he had remembered he'd kept quiet about it. But deep down she believed he hadn't, the episode remaining one of the many gaps in his pre-wound memory. How desperately she wanted it to stay that way.

What would happen if he now found out about her and the odious Boyne? What would his reaction be? She dreaded to think. Their marriage had been on an even keel since the night Charlie had told Reith about his cancer and announced Reith his successor, but this could blow it apart. Billy Boyne was the fuse to a God-almighty explosion that would hurt both her and Reith.

She gazed round their ornately decorated bedroom, the word divorce thundering in her mind. Reith would have just cause, after all, for hadn't he been betrayed, irrespective of the reasons? He might understand when she explained, he might even forgive her. But what if he didn't? And the last thing she wanted was to have to explain, wishing with all her heart to maintain the status quo.

The thought of losing Reith filled her with horror, for she loved him as much as she always had. He, and the children, were everything to her. She stood to lose not only Reith but the lifestyle they now enjoyed. The house, the money, the clothes, all these would be snatched away from her if he threw her out. She accepted that material possessions weren't everything, but for a woman from Bridgeton brought up in a tenement they'd come to mean an awful lot. Their present life was the fairy tale that had come true, the dream that had become reality. It was only human of her to want to hang on to what she had.

But more important than the material possessions was Reith. He'd be devastated to find out about her and Boyne, hurt to the quick. And even if he didn't chuck her out their relationship would be severely damaged, if not irreparable.

'Oh Reith!' she whispered. Life had been so good of late, so very very good and now this.

She prayed with all her heart that Boyne stayed well away.

'Laid off!' Catie repeated, appalled. Roger had just arrived home with the dreadful news.

He lit a Senior Service, then crossed to the mantelpiece and leant against it. 'Things have been going from bad to worse since the end of the war, we all knew that. But, maybe stupidly, we never believed it would come to this.' He swore viciously, and dragged heavily on his cigarette.

'Is it a temporary thing, or what?'

He shrugged. 'No-one knows. Apparently management thought they'd secured a new order, only it has fallen through. I've been given a week's notice, others a little longer.'

Catie's mind was numb. Roger had never had a day off since they were married, now this. At least Astrid was working, she thought. That was something. Their daughter was currently a live-in chambermaid at the St Enoch's Hotel. She glanced across at Andrew, who was still at school, as he gaped at his father. Three mouths to feed and after next week no wage packet coming in. They'd have to go on the Parish of course, but what they doled out was laughable.

'What are we going to do?' she asked tremulously.

Roger barked out a laugh. 'How the fuck do I know woman! I'll have to look for another job I suppose. And I won't be wasting time with any of the other yards either, none of them are taking people on.'

Catie went to the range where the mince and tats were merrily bubbling away. She tested the tats with a fork and decided to give them another couple of minutes. Using a wooden spoon she stirred the mince.

Roger stubbed out his cigarette. 'No more of those when this packet's finished,' he said darkly. He adored his fags, having been

171

smoking since he was twelve. No more of many things until he was employed again, Catie thought, bustling to the table which she finished laying.

Roger formed a fist and smacked it into the palm of his other hand. He wasn't simply angry, he was bloody furious. He'd never felt so helpless in his life.

'It's a shock right enough,' Catie stated quietly.

'A shock! You can say that again. Usually the lads are laughing and joking as they leave the yard, but not tonight. It was like a funeral procession. I've never seen so many long faces.'

'Can I help in any way Dad?' Andrew queried.

Roger regarded his son with a small smile. The offer was genuine enough, but what could the boy do? Any boy in the area with a paper round would be holding on to it like grim death after this. 'Thanks Andy, I appreciate that but I doubt it. It's your dad's problem.'

'And mine,' declared Catie. 'I'll start looking tomorrow. Who knows? I might get lucky.'

'I don't want you to work . . .'

'It isn't a case of want, but necessity,' she cut in. 'No matter how low the pay, or what's entailed, I'll grab it and be thankful.'

'Come here you,' Roger said, beckoning her over. When she reached him he pecked her on the cheek. 'You're the best, lass. And I'm sorry, truly I am, that it's come to this.'

'Hardly your fault Roger.'

'Aye, I know, but still . . .' He trailed off.

Catie was suddenly all business. 'Right you two, if you'll sit I'll dish up.'

As she drained the tats, there was a hint of tears in her eyes, which she managed to blink away.

As he strolled down Sauchiehall Street, Billy Boyne was amazed. He still wasn't used to walking where he wanted, doing as he liked. On his first day out he'd gone straight into his local boozer and got paralytic to the extent he'd had to be helped home by two of the regulars who knew him from old. And that was how it had continued since, booze, fags and nookie he'd had to pay for, but what the hell! Now it was time to sober up and think about the future. He'd no doubt about that, as he intended to take up where he'd left off. No straight and narrow for him, no hard graft and the like. It was back to the trade he'd grown up in, that of dyed in the wool villain.

But first he had to sniff around a bit, find out how things had changed. Well they were bound to have done after all! He needed to see who was about, what they were up to, what was going on. He thought of his ma's place with distaste, it was almost as stinking as that cell in the Bar-L. Well, he wouldn't be there for long and it was convenient in the meantime. At least his ma's scoff was better than what he'd been getting in prison. That stuff was diabolical, not fit for pigs.

He smiled as he reached the Caley Snooker Hall to see that it was still up and running. It had been one of his favourite haunts in the past. There were bound to be some cronies here he could chaff to, who'd bring him up to date. He ducked inside.

'Come on Cliff, hurry up for Christ's sake. We haven't got all sodding night,' Billy whispered. This was his first job since getting out and he was surprised at how nervous he was. His palms and armpits were sweating, his breathing laboured. He'd be glad when it was all over.

'It's a harder lock than I thought,' Cliff Kelman whispered back, concentrating.

'But you can open it?'

'Oh, do me a favour. It's only a matter of patience, that's all.'

Cliff grunted when there was a loud click. 'Got you, you bastard.'

If it had taken Cliff that long with a door lock how long would it take him to open the safe inside? Billy wondered as they stepped into the offices of the Blue Diamond Shipping Line. Forever at this rate.

Billy shielded his torch from the windows as they moved forward, going through one office into another where they knew the safe was kept. Their information was that it contained the wages of a ship docking that night whose crew were due to be paid off in the morning. Cliff knelt and laid out his tools in front of the safe. 'No bother at all!' he declared quietly, pursing his lips and staring hard at the metal box. Billy focused the torchlight while Cliff worked, shifting slightly from time to time to ease the cramp that developed in his legs. They both froze when a police car bell clanged on the street outside.

Billy snapped off the torch. 'Christ!' he muttered.

'Want to scarper?'

'Hang on a bit.'

Billy relaxed when the bell went past and receded into the

distance. 'Some other poor bugger they're after,' he whispered, flicking the torch back on.

Cliff grinned up at him. 'You shitting yourself?'

Anger flared up in Billy, for it had been true. The last thing he wanted was a return to the Bar-L. 'Get on with it and less lip,' he snarled. Cliff, remembering Billy's reputation for violence, bent again to his task.

An excellent Saturday night, Reith thought as he moved amongst the members and their guests. Occasionally he halted to have a word with a regular, congratulating the person when they were winning or had won, commiserating if they were losing or had lost.

He scanned the tables where games of blackjack, poker, roulette and dice were in progress, the croupiers and dealers female in the main. He preferred females as he believed they encouraged the male punters. The prettier the better, though in this case that wasn't a necessity. He ran honest games; his philosophy was that his profits were high enough without having to resort to cheating. Also he knew that it paid better in the long run.

He spotted Sir Ewan McNeice who scowled at him. That debt had been paid on the specified day after his, and Jameson's, visit to the bugger's house. The threat of exposure had worked wonders which pleased him. He hated having to resort to violence, only using it these days as a last resort.

He glanced at his watch, time for a quick tour of the other clubs. There was nothing like a personal appearance to keep his various managers and their staff on their toes. He stopped a passing hostess and asked her to find Jameson.

'There they are,' Cliff Kelman said to Billy.

Billy, who'd turned away and hunched slightly to light a cigarette, glanced across at the house they'd been watching for over an hour now. He smiled to see the elderly man close the door behind him and his wife, then assist her down the steps to where their car was parked. The man was a prosperous city jeweller who took his wife out to a restaurant every Saturday night without fail.

'Let's go,' said Billy as the car drove off.

Five minutes later they were inside the house, Billy ransacking it while Cliff worked on the safe. The valuables from the safe and all other stolen items had already been sold on when the elderly couple returned to discover they'd been burgled.

Catie knew from Roger's face as he entered the kitchen that it had been another unfruitful day. 'I'll put the kettle on,' she declared.

'Can we afford to?' he queried bitterly.

'It isn't as bad as that yet.'

'But damn well nearly so.'

With a sigh, he dropped into a chair. 'I swear there's nothing doing out there. Or if there is I can't find it.'

'It's early days yet Roger.'

'Early days! It's been three months Catie. I hardly call that "early days".'

She'd only been trying to cheer him up. She hated seeing him down like this. 'Astrid called in,' she said.

'Oh aye?'

'Left me thirty bob, God bless her. Also some food she'd managed to scrounge from the hotel kitchens.'

'Leftovers, no doubt,' Roger said cynically.

'No it isn't. There are six lovely slices of ham, a few tomatoes and a wedge of cheese. They'll do nicely for tea.'

Three months without a smoke, he thought, and still the craving hadn't left him. Forget the luxury of a Senior Service, he'd have sold his soul for a Willy Woodbine, a fag he'd always despised in the past. How times had changed.

'If only the Masons could help more,' Catie commented.

'They're doing their best, but there are so many of us unemployed right now.'

That line of conversation was interrupted by Andrew, who was thankfully getting free dinners at school, breezing in. 'I'm starving Mum,' he declared. Not half as much as your Dad or I, she thought. Not half as much.

Reith stopped at one of the perfume counters in Daly's, a large department store, and studied the display. He was after a present for Ena, Jameson's wife, whose birthday was the following week. The trouble was, he mused, he had no idea what sort of scent she liked. He decided, before the assistant homed in on him, to continue strolling round the store to see if anything special caught his eye. Handbags were a possibility, or lingerie? No, he dismissed that thought, it was too personal and might offend. How about . . .

He recognized her instantly. She was standing staring at a selection of scarves. His heart raced into his mouth. She was thinner than she'd been, and pasty faced. He'd so often dreamed about that face during the years since they'd last met.

Should he turn round and walk away? But even as he considered that he knew he wouldn't do it. He was only kidding himself to think that he might.

Walking over he halted beside her. 'Hello Catie,' he smiled.

Chapter Fifteen

'Well,' declared Reith, placing a cup of coffee and a sticky bun in front of Catie. 'Just like old times, eh?'

She fought back the impulse to snatch up the bun and cram it into her mouth. She was ravenous. Giving him a weak smile instead, she said, 'I must say you look smart, Reith, that suit is very impressive.'

He fingered a lapel. 'It is rather. Even impresses me.'

They both laughed.

'So tell me, how long have you worked at Daly's?'

'A fortnight now. It's only part-time but better than nothing.'

'And what do you do there?'

'I'm a packer.'

'Hmmh,' he murmured, sipping his coffee. He watched as she started on the bun, noting how quickly she chewed. 'How's Roger?'

'He's all right, though finding things difficult at the moment.'

Reith knew the men at Black's had been laid off. 'What's he doing?'

She shook her head. 'Nothing. Though not from the lack of trying, I can assure you.'

'And the children?'

Catie explained that Astrid was working at the St Enoch Hotel and Andrew was still at school. Reith had the picture. Catie's money was all that was going into their house. No wonder she was thin and pasty faced, poor woman. If he'd realized sooner he'd have suggested lunch instead of this. He wondered if it was too late to do so.

'Still living in the same house?' he asked, heart aching for her.

'Yes. Where are you now?'

'Newton Mearns.'

She glanced again at the expensive suit he was wearing, then took in the quality shirt and silk tie. 'We'd heard on the grapevine that you'd gone up in the world. But Newton Mearns! That really is posh.'

He shrugged dismissively. 'What of you and Roger? Are the pair of you still making a go of it?' He found himself holding his breath waiting for her reply.

'Oh yes, we couldn't be happier. If it wasn't for the work situation that is. Or lack of it.'

He dropped his gaze so that she didn't see his disappointment. Oh Catie, he thought. A few minutes back in her company and it was as though they'd never been apart.

'How about you and Irene?'

He picked up his spoon and, although he'd already done so, stirred his coffee again. 'We muddle along. In fact, we get on quite well nowadays.'

'That's good.'

'Both children are away at college. We're very proud of them.'

'I'm pleased.'

'Do you still like books and going to the pictures?' he queried.

'Well I haven't been to the pictures for a while. Can't afford to. But the library's free.'

It had been insensitive to mention the pictures, he thought, chiding himself. Of course she couldn't afford to go with Roger out of work and her part-time.

'Do you?'

He wanted to reach out and take her hand, hold it, cup it as if it were something precious, which to him it was. Or *had been*, he quickly reminded himself. All that was in the past, however. Catie had made her choice, Roger over him. 'I don't get much time for pictures anymore,' he informed her. 'Too busy unfortunately. Same with books. I usually have one by the bedside but it's rare that I pick it up. I think the same one's been there for the last six months, if not longer.'

'You look well, Reith,' she said.

It was a compliment he couldn't honestly return. He'd never lied to Catie and wasn't about to start now.

Suddenly it was all too much for him. He had to leave, get away from her. He glanced at his watch. 'I'm afraid I have an appointment.'

'I understand,' she replied.

'Finish your coffee first though.' The bun had long gone.

'Funny us bumping into one another after all this while.'

'Glasgow isn't such a big city. I'm surprised we haven't before.'

'I don't suppose you get to Bridgeton all that often these days,' she laughed. That was a statement, not a question.

'No.'

'And I've never been to Newton Mearns. A bit rarefied for my blood.'

He didn't know how to reply to that, so didn't.

She drained her cup. 'Right then.' And with that she started to rise.

'Catie!'

She hesitated.

'Sit down again.'

'We were very close friends you and I,' he said softly when she had.

Catie nodded.

'Now promise me you won't take offence at this? I mean, that's the last thing I want you to do.'

He'd changed she now realized. She wasn't sure how, only that he had. There was a certain toughness about him, mentally speaking, that hadn't been there before. And a number of other puzzling things, too. 'Depends on what it is,' she replied.

'You and Roger are clearly having a rough time, while I . . . well let's just say I'm not short of a few bob. Let me give you some cash to help you get by.'

Now it was she who dropped her gaze. 'I couldn't possibly Reith.'

'Of course you can.' He thought of Ena Jameson. 'Call it a birthday present if you like, yours isn't that far off.'

She could certainly use some cash, there was no doubt about that. But how could she accept money from Reith of all people. After what she'd done, the awful hurt and pain she must have caused him.

'No false pride Catie. Please.'

As though trying to remind her she'd hardly eaten in the past few days, her stomach rumbled loudly. 'You were always kind Reith,' she whispered.

He pulled out his wallet, held it in his lap and extracted all the notes inside which he folded in half.

'Here,' he said, slipping them to her, overwhelmed to be able to touch her hand as she took them.

'I can't take this amount!' she gasped.

'I can easily afford it, honestly.'

'But how will I explain all this to Roger? He'd hit the roof if he knew I'd accepted charity from you.'

'It isn't charity Catie, it's a birthday present, remember? And why tell Roger? He doesn't have to know. Hide it and use it piecemeal. A bit at a time.'

Emotion welled up inside her. He'd given her a small fortune, enough to keep them going, if eked out, for ages.

'I wish it was more, but that's all I have on me,' he said.

She bit her lip, not trusting herself to speak at that moment. 'I don't know what to say,' she mumbled eventually.

'There's nothing to say. Now stick that in your pocket and we'll go.'

'It was good to see you again,' he said when they were standing outside on the pavement.

'And you Reith.'

'Take care now.'

'You too.'

On impulse she kissed him on the cheek, then turned and hurried away.

He watched her go, elated yet despondent at the same time. Catie, after all these years. The woman who'd broken his heart. And very nearly him.

'You all right Reith?' Jameson asked, having left the Daimler which was parked across the street. On leaving Daly's Reith had discreetly gestured for him to follow but not join him and Catie.

'I just met an old friend,' Reith answered.

Jameson knew when to keep his mouth shut. If Reith wanted to elaborate on that, he would. As Jameson guessed, he didn't.

Reith sucked in a deep breath. 'Tell you what, let's go for a drive.'

'Anywhere particular in mind?'

'No,' Reith replied quietly. 'It doesn't matter. Just a long drive.'

They went to Loch Lomond where Reith spent nearly an hour standing on the bank throwing pebbles into the water.

*　　*　　*

180

Billy Boyne gazed round the rented furnished accommodation he'd acquired, thinking it would do for the present. It was certainly a big improvement on his ma's, but then nearly anything would be that. He wouldn't be here long, not if he had his way. For he had plans, big plans. Plans that had been hatched in, and seen him through the long years at, Barlinne. He nodded with satisfaction. So far so good. The next step was to buy a motor.

Reith had pulled his chair over to the window in his office and was now, sitting in darkness, staring out over Glasgow. Since bumping into Catie again he couldn't get her out of his mind. She was haunting him just as she had before. Ever present in his thoughts. From the moment he woke up to the moment he fell asleep, and sometimes beyond, she was there. Catie whom he'd never ceased loving. Catie whom he would have laid down and died for. Catie, Catie, Catie . . .

There was a tap on the door which then opened and Jameson entered. 'Why are you sitting in the dark Reith?' he frowned.

'Just resting my eyes,' Reith lied in reply.

'Do you know the time? We shut up ages ago.'

'Did we?' Reith ran a hand over his chin. 'Will you have a dram with me?'

Jameson wasn't much of a drinker, but decided he would. 'Aye, all right.'

'Will you pour? I'll have a Macallan.'

'Can I put the light on?'

'Go ahead.'

Reith blinked when several bulbs burst into life. He was tired, it had been a long day. But then all his working days were. It was something he enjoyed.

'How's Ian?' he asked. Jameson and Ena had one child, a boy called Ian who'd been born a mongol. He was now three years old and the apple of Jameson's eye.

'He's fine, the lad. Ena took him to the zoo the other day.'

'And what did he make of that?'

Jameson, who rarely smiled, was beaming as he handed Reith a glass. 'He thought it was terrific. Particularly the reptile house. He adored the snakes.'

Reith laughed. 'He's welcome to them. I loathe the slimy buggers. Give me the creeps.'

'They're not my favourite either, I have to admit.'

Reith swirled his whisky round. 'Do you know any private dicks, à la Philip Marlowe?'

Jameson's forehead creased in thought. 'I have heard of one bloke who's supposed to be good. Name of Cairns I seem to recall.'

'Get in touch with him tomorrow. Tell him I'd like a word.'

'Right.'

'He's to ring me here, not at home.'

Jameson nodded that he understood.

'Aye, quite a few of these clubs have opened in the past few years. Pretty snazzy, eh,' Cliff Kelman said to Billy; the pair of them were having a night out together, on the lookout for birds to pick up. Cliff was also a bachelor.

Billy gazed round Club America which was done out in the style of 1920s Chicago and New York. Al Capone, Billy couldn't help but think, would have felt quite at home here.

'Is that a tommy-gun on the wall?' he queried, pointing.

Cliff laughed. 'Don't get any ideas of pinching it. It's a fake.'

A waitress wearing a hoodlum outfit walked by carrying a tray of drinks. Billy thought she was as sexy as hell and wondered if he could get off with her. She'd suit him a treat.

'I like it here. A lot,' he commented.

'Great fun. Expensive mind, but great fun all the same.'

The club was busy, Billy noted, even though it was only a Wednesday night, not a traditional night in Glasgow for drinking. 'And you say there's gambling?'

'Upstairs. Do you want a go?'

'Maybe later.' Billy smiled. 'There have been some changes in Glasgow since I went up the road.'

'Not that many. It's still the same old Glasgow. But these new clubs have made a difference. They're very popular.'

'I can imagine.'

'You should see Fanny's.' Cliff whistled. 'Now that is something. At least so I'm told. I've never been there.'

'Why not?'

'It's fairly exclusive, for the nobs and such. They wouldn't let the likes of me in.'

'And where is it?'

Cliff told him.

'Big?'

'About three times the size of this. A lot of money changes hands at the tables there. It's real Monte Carlo land.'

A lot of money? That interested Billy. 'Who owns it?'

'The same guy who owns all these clubs. A chap called Reith Douglas. Quite an operator by all accounts.'

Billy went very still. It couldn't be! But the Christian name was unusual, he'd only ever heard of one Reith. And for the surname to be the same, well that just couldn't be coincidental. Irene's husband. It had to be. 'Well, well, well,' he murmured. Now that was a turn-up for the book.

'Has he got a wife?' Billy asked.

Cliff shrugged. 'Search me. I'm not exactly on nodding terms with the man.'

'Reith Douglas,' Billy repeated. How in Christ's name had a cabinet-maker turned into a club owner? 'Is he a villain?'

'How can he own clubs and not be?' Cliff leant forward conspiratorially. 'And he's got more irons in the fire than that. He runs all the betting in Glasgow. And more I'm led to understand, though I couldn't tell you what "more" is.'

Billy was intrigued. 'What else can you tell me about him?'

He listened attentively as Cliff spoke.

Reith's intercom buzzed. 'Yes, Milla?'

'A Mr Cairns to see you.'

'Send him right in.'

The man who entered Reith's office was short, balding, and looked rather like a somewhat down at heel insurance clerk. He would never have stood out in a crowd which seemed to Reith an ideal quality for his profession.

Reith extended a hand. 'Thank you for coming Mr Cairns.'

'My pleasure Mr Douglas.'

'Please sit down. Drink?'

Cairns shook his head. 'Not during working hours, thank you very much.'

Reith approved of that. 'Are you busy at the moment?'

Cairns cleared his throat. 'I'd be a liar if I pretended I was. Things have been slack recently.'

Reith was delighted by the man's honesty. 'Then perhaps you'd consider doing a job for me?'

'I'm listening Mr Douglas,' Cairns replied, not committing himself until he heard what this was all about.

Reith explained what he wanted done.

'Holy shit!' Billy exclaimed as he and Cliff drove slowly past the Douglases' house. 'Would you look at that. It's the size of a sodding castle.'

Cliff nodded his agreement.

'Let's have another dekko,' Billy said. He was driving, as they were in his car. He went to the end of the road where he turned round.

He thought of Irene. Now she'd been quite a bird, and he wondered what she was now like. Was she still a looker or had the years taken their toll?

He soon found out, for as they were approaching the Douglases' driveway for the second time, a Jaguar with Irene at the wheel poked its bonnet out into the street. Billy recognized her instantly. So it was the same Irene Douglas, there could be no question of that now, Billy told himself. As for Irene, from what he could see she was extremely smartly turned out. She was an elegant, coiffeured figure compared to the working-class housewife he remembered.

He put his hand to the side of his face so that she wouldn't spot him, then she was off, driving in the opposite direction.

'I wonder if that was his wife?' Cliff mused.

'It was.'

Cliff glanced at him. 'How can you be so sure?'

Billy's smile was thin and vicious. 'Because I used to know her once.'

'Really! And him?'

'We've never met.'

The house and Irene had given Billy lots to think about as they drove back into town.

'What the . . . !' Alasdair Spence broke off to stare at Billy and Cliff in shocked amazement. He'd left home ten minutes previously to visit his wife who was in hospital having an operation. When he realized he'd left behind the small bag he'd packed up consisting of things she wanted taking in he'd swung his car round to go back for it. Only to surprise two burglars red-handed. At forty-three, Spence wasn't as fit as he'd been in his rugby playing days, but still considered himself in good enough shape to take care of a pair like this.

'Oh no you don't!' he declared firmly, striding towards Cliff who was closest.

Cliff tried to bolt, but was caught by Spence who grappled with him. Billy snatched up an iron poker from the hearth and smashed it into the back of Spence's head. Spence, dazed and in excruciating pain, released Cliff and swung on his attacker. 'You little . . .'

He never finished the sentence as the poker thunked sickeningly across his face. There was a crunching sound as his nose broke, blood spurting in all directions. Still conscious, Spence threw his arms in front of his face in a desperate attempt to ward off any further blows, but to no avail. The poker flashed through the air again and again till he was lying crumpled on the floor in a bloody heap. But watched by a wide-eyed Cliff, Billy kept hitting Spence in a maniacal frenzy till at last he came out of the red haze that had enveloped him. Panting, he stood over his victim, clothes spattered with blood and gore.

'You've killed him,' Cliff whispered, for there couldn't be any doubt about that.

'Of course I've fucking killed him!' Billy retorted tightly. 'Even if we'd got away the bastard could have identified us which would have meant another long trip up the road.'

He fixed Cliff with a baleful look that made Cliff shiver. 'And they'll never get me in the Bar-L again. Never! Understand?'

Cliff nodded. Billy's shoulders suddenly drooped. 'Never,' he croaked. Cliff turned away and threw up.

'So,' said Reith coming to the end of Cairn's meticulously typed report. 'Smith is definitely seeing a woman.'

Cairns nodded. 'Seeing her, yes. That is definite. But I have no way of knowing whether or not he's actually sleeping with her.'

Reith laid the report on his desk and stared at it. With Roger's past track record it seemed to Reith highly unlikely that Roger's relationship with this Mrs McDonald was platonic. Her husband was a commercial traveller, away for longish spells at a time and Roger only called on her when he was away. Roger was sleeping with her all right, Reith would have bet money on it.

Sadness filled him as he thought about Catie being cheated on yet again, and that she was oblivious to the fact. She totally believed that she and Roger were happy together, Roger long since reformed. How many had there been over the years? Reith dreaded to think. And all the while, Catie, his dear sweet Catie, was convinced the rat was being faithful. What should he do?

'Satisfied Mr Douglas?' Cairns enquired. Reith looked as though he'd just been kicked in the stomach, a reaction Cairns often encountered from his clients in cases like these.

'Very,' Reith murmured in reply. 'You've done a first-class job.'

'Thank you.' It pleased Cairns to be complimented, he wasn't always. It wasn't uncommon for his clients to turn against him as the bearer of bad news.

'How much do I owe you?'

When Cairns had gone Reith reread the report, then placed it in a desk drawer. What they said about leopards and spots was only too true, he reflected, sincerely wishing for Catie's sake that it could be otherwise.

Reith smiled at a blank-faced Andrew Smith who'd answered his ring. 'You don't remember me, do you?'

Andrew shook his head.

'Is your mother or father in?'

'Yes, they both are.'

'Then tell them an old friend's at the door.'

Reith waited patiently as Andrew disappeared off into the kitchen. He still wasn't sure he was doing the right thing, but it was too late to turn back now. He smiled again when, frowning, Roger stepped into the hallway.

'Guess who?' he said.

Roger stared at him in astonishment. 'Reith Douglas! Where did you spring from?'

'I had to visit someone nearby,' he lied. 'And thought I'd see how you were.'

'Well, I'll be . . .' Roger, uncertain whether he was pleased to see Reith or not, shook his hand. 'Come away in pal.' Placing an arm round Reith's shoulders he ushered him through. Catie, who'd just taken off her pinny, fluffed her hair. She, too, was surprised that Reith had called.

'Catie!' Reith declared. 'How good to see you again after all this time.'

The relief in her eyes confirmed that she hadn't mentioned her bumping into him in Daly's, as he'd imagined.

'Reith, how are you?'

'Never better,' he replied, kissing her on the cheek.

He handed Roger the tissue-wrapped bottle he was carrying. 'I thought we might have a dram, eh?'

'Haven't had a drink in ages,' Roger said, unwrapping the bottle. 'I was laid off, you know.'

'Aye, I heard about Black's. I'm sorry. I take it then you haven't had any luck in finding another job?'

Roger shook his head. 'Thankfully Catie got herself some part-time work which helps keep the wolf from the door. If only just.'

Reith put on a sympathetic face.

'But I must say you look well and prosperous,' Roger declared, enviously eyeing Reith's clothes.

'I'm doing all right. I've been fortunate.'

'And where are you and Irene staying now?'

'Newton Mearns.'

'Newton!' Roger gave a soft whistle. 'You must be really coining it to live there. I'm impressed.'

'How are you Catie?' Reith enquired, steering the conversation away from himself.

'Can't complain. You know how it is.'

'Are you having a dram darling?' Roger asked, placing several glasses on the table. Newton Mearns, he thought. Bloody hell! Reith was doing even better than he'd been led to believe.

'Why not? Just a little one though.'

Her voice was slightly tremulous, Reith noted. It always was when she was nervous. She was still painfully thin, but her complexion was healthier than previously. He wondered if he'd get the opportunity to slip her some more money, as he'd come prepared with a wad of notes in his jacket pocket.

'Here, let me take your coat,' Catie said. When he'd removed it she gave it to Andrew instructing him to hang it in the hallway.

'He's grown,' Reith commented. Then laughed. 'Hardly surprising, it's been over six years after all.'

'Sit down,' smiled Catie, indicating one of the chairs by the range.

'As I said I was nearby and thought I'd look you up. Hope I'm not intruding,' Reith said once he'd sat down.

'Not at all,' Roger replied in a tone that wasn't entirely convincing. 'How about Irene? Is she well?'

Reith accepted a dram from Roger. 'In the pink. As are Mathew and Agnes.'

There then followed twenty minutes of catching up and reminiscing. Reith remained vague about what he now did, merely saying he was in business and leaving it at that.

187

'Well, I'd better go,' Reith declared eventually, standing up. 'I was just thinking, how about the four of us going out for a meal one night? My treat, of course.'

Roger glanced at Catie. He didn't really want to go out with Reith and Irene, but a free meal! It was just too tempting to refuse, even if it did go against the grain to accept 'charity' from Reith. 'What do you think, Catie?'

She couldn't remember the last time she'd had a night out. 'That would be smashing.'

'Good,' Reith smiled. 'How about this Saturday?'

'Fine,' Roger agreed.

'I'll pick you up at seven.'

Reith was disappointed as he went down the stairs because he hadn't had the chance to slip Catie the wad of notes. Perhaps he'd manage on Saturday though. Then he smiled, having had a better idea.

Chapter Sixteen

Irene was furious with Reith for bringing them to Fanny's. Poor Catie's frock – the best in her wardrobe as Irene rightly guessed – would look so dowdy compared to those worn by the other female clientele. As for Catie's hair, it couldn't have been near scissors for goodness knows how long. But Catie wasn't thinking about her frock or her hair as she gazed in awe round Fanny's; the place simply oozed taste, money and class. Roger was still bemused by the Daimler that had brought them there, driven by Reith's own chauffeur no less. He'd had no idea Reith was so wealthy. Well off, yes, Newton Mearns had told him that, but a Daimler! Reith escorted them to a bar which was done out predominately in gold and black marble, the stools at the bar, chairs and sofas covered with black leather.

'Wow!' Catie whispered to Roger, who swallowed hard.

Reith rubbed his hands together. 'Now, what's everyone having? Or will you leave that to me?'

'I'll leave it to you,' Roger replied, wondering how much a single round would come to. It was bound to be more than he liked to think about.

A waitress came over as they were sitting. 'Good evening, Mr Douglas,' she beamed.

'Good evening, Claire.'

'Good evening, Mrs Douglas.'

Irene nodded.

'I think we'll have champagne. A bottle of vintage Billecart-Salmon,' Reith said to Claire.

'Certainly, sir.' And with that she moved away.

Another waitress appeared at their table to place several bowls of crisps in front of them.

'Good evening Maria,' Reith smiled.

'Good evening sir. Anything else I can get for you?'

Reith raised an enquiring eyebrow. 'Irene? Catie?'

'These will be fine,' Irene stated, while Catie shook her head.

'You're certainly well known here,' Roger commented when Maria had left them.

'He should be. He's the owner,' Irene informed Roger.

Roger and Catie were both dumbstruck. 'Owner!' Roger choked.

'That's right,' Reith casually declared, relishing Catie's expression which was a combination of incredulity and disbelief.

'All by yourself?' queried Roger, pop-eyed.

'I beg your pardon?'

'I mean, do you own this, all by yourself? Sole owner like?'

'Sole owner,' Reith confirmed.

Roger almost involuntarily swore, but somehow managed to stop himself. 'How did that come about?' he queried.

'My old boss Charlie McCall died leaving me everything. I was his heir. I just took things on from there.'

'Was he the bookie you worked for?'

'That's right,' Reith nodded.

'So you inherited the bookmaking side of things as well?'

'That too,' Reith further confirmed.

This time Roger couldn't help himself. 'Christ!' he muttered.

'Would you like a crisp, Catie?' Irene enquired, pushing the bowl in Catie's direction.

Claire arrived back with the champagne in a silver ice bucket and four flutes. 'Will you open it or shall I, Mr Douglas?' she asked.

'You can Claire.'

They all watched as she removed the bottle from the bucket, tore off the foil round its neck, removed the metal web covering the cork, then popped the cork.

The wine frothed satisfactorily into the glasses which Reith handed round. 'Here's to the four of us,' he toasted. Catie eyed Reith speculatively as she sipped, her mind reeling from the turn of events. Who would have thought it? Without realizing what she was doing, she reached out and placed her hand on Roger's thigh.

'I don't know about anyone else, but I'm starving,' Irene

declared gaily. Then she immediately regretted it, considering it tasteless in the Smiths' present circumstances.

'Ah Maurice!' Reith said to a man approaching their table. 'How are you this evening?'

'Fine Mr Douglas, thank you. I heard you were in the bar and wondered if you'd care to order now. Or perhaps you'd prefer to wait?'

'Maurice is the *maître d'*,' Reith explained to Roger and Catie. 'And I think we'll order now. That suit everyone?'

Roger and Catie nodded.

Maurice passed round the menus, after which he produced a small pad and pencil.

'What would you recommend?' Reith asked him, studying his menu.

'The smoked salmon would be my choice as a starter,' the *maître d'* replied.

'And main course?'

'The fillet steak with mushroom sauce is excellent.'

'Catie?'

'I'll have the salmon please.'

Maurice wrote that down.

'Irene?'

'The lobster thermidor.' That had been absolutely delicious when she'd had it previously.

'Same for me,' Roger declared. Most of the menu was gibberish to him. He would happily have settled for a nice plate of fish and chips, or better still, black pudding.

When they'd decided on their main courses they all studied the sweets, Catie's mouth watering at the superb choice.

'I'd like the treacle tart,' she finally elected.

'And I'll have the steamed orange pudding,' Irene stated, which was another of her favourites.

When Maurice had taken their order, Reith topped up their flutes.

'You don't get many lobster thermiwhatsits in Bridgeton,' Roger commented drily, raising a laugh all round. Reith studied him, wondering when he'd last been to see Mrs McDonald. According to Cairns's report he contrived to visit her most weeks, sometimes twice, depending on the husband's whereabouts. And there was Catie blissfully unaware of what was going on. Jealously, he'd noticed the way she'd been continually touching Roger, as if to

191

reassure herself, or was it to reassure Roger? He'd have given anything for it to have been him she kept touching.

Roger was thinking that Irene had improved with age. She had enormous dignity now that she'd lacked before. She was certainly well turned out and cared for. Beside her Catie looked almost plain.

Catie was entranced by the dress Irene was wearing which was made from ruby velvet. The dress was basically a sheath, supported at the V shaped bosom by two thin straps, which snaked over Irene's bare shoulders. Catie thought Irene looked stunning.

'Bumped into an old pal of yours the other day,' Roger said to Reith.

'Oh. Who's that?'

'Billy Drummond.'

'How is he?'

Roger shrugged. 'Like a lot of blokes in Bridgeton, having a hard time. He hasn't found another job either.'

Reith remembered that Billy had once done him a great favour and had helped him to get a start at Black's. Perhaps he could repay the compliment. He'd give it some thought later.

They were just finishing the champagne when Maurice reappeared to say their starters were ready if they'd care to move through to the restaurant. Once seated Reith ordered another bottle of champagne. The meal was a huge success, even Roger grudgingly admitting to himself that he enjoyed the 'fancy French muck'. He was fulsome in its praise to Reith.

Catie wasn't drunk, but the champagne had certainly gone to her head. She felt like Cinderella who'd suddenly and unexpectedly ended up at the ball. She was having a wonderful time.

Irene had also mellowed and had chatted away nineteen to the dozen with the Smiths, mostly about Bridgeton and the old days before she and Reith moved to Newton Mearns. The Smiths were further astonished to learn that Reith owned other clubs besides Fanny's, some of which they'd vaguely heard of, others not.

Once Reith was called away from the table on a matter that required his personal attention, but soon returned, not wanting to be out of Catie's company a second more than was absolutely necessary. In his mind he fantasized about taking her to Paris, staying together at the Georges Cinque, decking her out in haute couture gowns, buying her expensive lingerie, showing her the sights, the Left Bank, the Folies Bergère. And the nights they'd have had. Taking her to bed, making love, waking beside her in the morning. Perhaps sitting up and watching her still sleeping figure.

'Shall we go up and do a little gambling?' Reith suggested as they neared the end of their coffee and brandy.

Roger reacted to that with embarrassment. 'I'm afraid I can't . . .'

'There's no need to worry about that,' Reith smiled, cutting him off. 'You and Catie are guests of mine and it's a tradition of this establishment that my special guests get a stake on the house. Isn't that so Irene?'

'Yes,' she confirmed, though this tradition was news to her. Now that was kind and thoughtful of him, she thought approvingly.

Catie slipped an arm through one of Roger's as they left the table. 'Roger adores gambling, don't you darling?' she gushed.

'When younger I played quite a bit of pontoon,' Roger explained to Reith.

'You can play that here, only we call it blackjack.'

'And you were always lucky, weren't you?' Catie smiled at her husband.

Roger this, Roger that, they'd had rather a lot of that through the meal, Reith reflected wryly. And then there had been all that touching. She was rattled, he thought, no doubt about it. Which amused him on the one hand, and saddened him on the other. Well she wouldn't have been so effusive about 'darling' Roger if she knew about Mrs McDonald. Oh no, she'd be singing a different tune then.

He surreptitiously eyed Roger with distaste. What was it about the man that made Catie love him? Reith knew Roger to be particularly good in bed, Catie had told him that long ago, but surely there was more to it than that? Chemistry he supposed, the same chemistry he felt for Catie. On the surface the Smiths presented to the world a happy marriage. And he had it in his power to break that marriage. All he had to do was show Catie Cairns's report, and bang! But would she necessarily come to him? What was it Cairns had said? It wasn't uncommon for his clients to turn against him as the bearer of bad news. That made him extremely wary about taking that particular risk with Catie.

In the gaming room Catie, Roger and Irene were each given chips to the value of twenty pounds, after which they went straight to a blackjack table.

Roger gambled, and lost quickly. Catie abstained as did Irene.

'Too bad,' Reith commiserated at the end of Roger's final hand.

193

'Easy come, easy go,' Roger declared, trying to put a bright face on it.

'I want to try the roulette wheel,' Irene stated, which Reith had expected. Roulette was Irene's game.

Irene played numbers while Catie, on Reith's advice, played colours. Again and again Catie won till she'd amassed fifty pounds in all.

'I think you should call it a night,' Reith further advised. She then tried to return her stake which Reith refused to accept, so she'd made fifty pounds clear profit.

Roger was ecstatic. Fifty quid! What they couldn't do with that.

Catie grasped Reith by the arm. 'Thank you for this evening. I've thoroughly enjoyed myself.'

'You're welcome,' he replied, an amused gleam in his eyes.

She knew then, with a dead certainty, that she'd been allowed to win, that it had been fixed.

'For *everything*,' she added meaningfully.

He nodded, realizing she was aware of what had happened. The smile she gave him brought a lump to his throat.

'Patronizing bastard!' Roger spat as they entered their kitchen. Crossing to the gas mantle he quickly lit it. Catie didn't reply. She certainly wasn't going to make matters worse by informing Roger that her win had been rigged.

'And jammy sod. Imagine that geezer dying and leaving him a fortune. How jammy can you get for Christ's sake!'

'I thought it was nice of him and Irene to take us out for the evening,' she stated quietly.

'Nice! Like hell it was. Reith only suggested the evening so he could rub our noses in it, so he could show off. That's what tonight was really all about. Him the big man while I'm unemployed, grubbing round for pennies and ha'pennies.'

'At least we came out of it with fifty quid. That's something.'

'Fifty quid! That's pocket money to him nowadays. Nothing at all.'

Envious, Catie thought sadly. She was, too, if she were honest. But she didn't for one moment think Reith had been rubbing their noses in it.

'Swanky car, swanky clothes, swanky fucking club. Or should I say *clubs*,' Roger further raged. 'And him no more than a common labourer not that long ago. He wasn't so high and mighty then. Nor Irene the grand madam she's become.'

'I thought her extremely pleasant. Clothes and make-up apart, the Irene we used to know.'

'He was treating me like a peasant. Some sort of low life.'

'Oh come on Roger, he wasn't.'

'He damn well was. Lording it over us with his champagne and exotic scoff. One bottle of that champagne alone probably cost enough to keep us comfortably off for a month.'

Roger threw himself into a chair.

'You're just green,' Catie teased, trying to lighten his mood.

'Am not.'

'Oh yes you are. Green through and through.'

Roger harumphed, knowing that was true.

'Anyway, let's forget it. It's over and done with.' She took a deep breath. 'Now how about a cup of tea?'

'Not for me, but you go ahead if you want.'

He continued to brood on the injustice of life as she filled the kettle.

Later, Catie was ferociously demanding in bed till at last even the libidinous Roger had to cry enough. Only then was she satisfied.

'Reith Douglas, now there's a name to conjure with,' mused Plookie John, sliding a dirty, gnarled hand with chipped and broken fingernails up and down the sides of his pint of Guinness. Plook was the Glasgow word for pimple and John had suffered dreadful acne all his adult life.

'So what do you know about him, apart from the clubs and betting, that is?'

Plookie glanced at Billy Boyne out of yellow-rimmed, rheumy eyes. 'Why are you asking?'

'I just am, that's all.'

Plookie considered that. 'You're no thinking of tangling with him, are you? That would be a big mistake.'

'Who said anything about tangling with him? I'm just interested. He's someone who's come up since I went inside, and I like to know what's what.'

Plookie wasn't deceived, Billy was lying. 'How long I known you son?'

'Since I was a wean and you used to rake the midgies.' A midgie was the dustbin area behind each tenement.

195

Plookie laughed. 'That's going back some. I haven't done that in a long time now.'

Billy laid a ten shilling note on the table between them. 'I'm listening you old goat, get on with it.'

'No need to be insulting.'

Plookie hesitated. He'd always had a soft spot for Billy. 'Are you sure about this?'

'Dead sure.'

Plookie tried to snatch the note but Billy's hand, faster than his, stopped him from doing so.

'You're a mine of information, Plookie, always have been. There's not much goes on that you don't get to hear about. Who's who, up to what. So cough.'

Plookie sighed. If Billy chose to cross Douglas that was his business. He couldn't say he hadn't been warned. 'Make it a quid?'

'Up your kilt with a wire brush, Plookie. Cough.'

'See's a fag then.'

Billy took out his packet and threw it on the table, waiting patiently while Plookie lit up.

'Do you know the Whiteinch Dog Track?'

Billy nodded.

'His. And the Ibrox Speedway. His as well. The man's an octopus, tentacles everywhere.'

'Anything else?'

'Oh aye, lots. For example, him and the *polis*.' Plookie, enjoying himself, waited to be prompted.

'What about him and the polis?'

Plookie crossed two fingers and waggled them in front of Billy's face. 'Like that they are. The whisper has it that even Ogilvie, the Chief Constable, dances to his tune.'

Billy couldn't believe it. 'The Chief Constable?'

'So the whisper says. A wee arrangement the pair of them have, if you get my meaning. And not only the Chief Constable but many other boys in blue besides.'

Plookie had a gulp of Guinness while Billy digested that. 'I've also heard he's got the same arrangement with several politicians and leading members of the Corporation. He bought a large patch of land recently, what for I've no idea, but got it at a rock bottom price. Land sold by the Corporation.'

Billy was staggered. This Douglas was something else. 'Anymore?'

'I told you it was worth a quid,' Plookie said slyly.

'Aye, OK, a quid. What else?'

'Then there's . . .'

He should forget her, Reith counselled himself, sitting in the back of the Daimler as it purred its way through the city streets. Consign her to history. Pretend he'd never bumped into her again. There was Irene to consider after all. These last years hadn't been so bad, there were certainly plenty of worse marriages around. And Irene was the mother of his children whom he adored.

If only Catie hadn't reappeared in his life. But she had, like a damn genie released from a bottle where she'd been tucked away out of sight, if not out of mind. She believed she and Roger were happy, but how could they be when Roger was seeing someone else? No, no, she was wrong to think things were hunky-dory between them.

Reith knew then he was going to go after Catie again, that he had to. He remained far too obsessed with her not to press his suit a second time.

Billy told himself he had to admire Douglas. That was one very smart cookie. What a set-up. Jesus! He'd thought he'd come up with some big plans in the Bar-L, but they were nothing compared to what Douglas had achieved. Kid's play. And the beauty was so much of what Douglas did and had was legal and above board. Not all of it mind, but much of it.

And to think he'd once been knocking off his wife and threatened to kill the bugger! He laughed. Oh that was rich. Yes indeed, he admired Douglas. You had to give him credit, credit where it was certainly due.

If only he could get into a similar position, now that would be something. In his mind's eye he saw himself as owner of the Whiteinch Dog Track, the Ibrox Speedway and Club America. He could have anything he wanted then. Cars, women, a snap of his fingers and it would be there. That would almost be worth the years in Barlinne. Those rotten, stinking years that on more than one occasion had nearly driven him up the wall, made him consider suicide.

He thought of Irene in the Jag, the old lust for her surging hot within him, smiling as he remembered the 'seeing tos' he'd given her. The way she'd squealed. He had a hold over Douglas which he doubted Douglas knew about. He'd been screwing the big man's wife. It was a trick he didn't yet know how to play. But that would come to him in time. And when it did he'd play the trick for all it was worth. And he hoped to have a little fun into the bargain.

For three days now Reith had missed Catie coming off shift at Daly's, but on the fourth attempt he was successful.

'Reith!' she exclaimed, paling.

'I want a word. How about I buy you lunch?'

'I . . . eh . . .'

'It's to your benefit, Catie. I promise you.'

She shrugged. 'Why not.'

'Right.' He took her by the elbow. 'Any suggestions?'

'There's a nice cafeteria upstairs. We could go there.'

He'd have preferred something a bit more intimate and sophisticated than Daly's cafeteria. There again it would be convenient, and it was Catie's choice. 'OK.'

Luckily the cafeteria wasn't crowded and they managed to get a table to themselves in a quiet corner. 'So what's all this about?' she queried nervously when they'd settled down with their meal in front of them.

'I've come up with an idea.'

'Oh?'

He smiled at her. 'How would you like to work for me as a croupier and dealer? The money's good.'

She stared at him in astonishment. 'But I know nothing about that sort of thing.'

'Don't worry, you'd be trained. So that's not a problem.'

He continued smiling at her, thinking that the magic of her presence never changed. He felt totally complete when he was with her, and absurdly happy. He'd already dangled half his carrot, now for the remainder.

'Are you worried about Roger?'

She nodded. 'I doubt he'd like me working for you, Reith. He's bound to kick up a hell of a stink if I propose it.'

'I imagined he might, which is why I'll offer him a job as well. I need a new night-watchman for the Midnight Rooms, my second largest club.'

'Night-watchman,' she repeated with a frown.

'More of a security guard really. I have one in all my clubs.'

'I see,' she murmured.

'How's the steak and kidney pudding?'

'Fine. Well, it's filling anyway. The ones I make are a lot better. And your fish?'

'Not too bad. Quite tasty actually. Your pay would be thirty pounds a week.'

She gawped at him. 'Say that again?'

'Thirty pounds.'

'Is that . . . what the others get?'

'Yup.'

Good grief! she thought. Thirty pounds *a week*. It was a fortune. She'd be mad to pass this up.

'I don't normally pay the full whack during training, but as you're a personal friend, and if you keep your mouth shut, I will to you. So there's an added bonus.'

'And Roger?'

'A tenner.'

She thought about the thirty pounds. 'The work must be harder than it looks?'

'It is. But nothing you can't handle. With the right training behind you that is, which you'll have. So, what's the verdict?'

'I'm . . .' She made a gesture with her hands. 'I'm speechless.'

Reith laughed, knowing he had caught her.

'Roger wouldn't appreciate the idea of you waylaying me. Do you think you could come to the house and make the offer again, as if for the first time?'

'Of course. I take it you want the job then?'

'What do you think?' She reached across and laid a hand on his, sending a shiver up and down his spine. 'You're a good friend, Reith. The very best.'

'Anything for you, Catie. You know that.'

She averted her eyes.

'It's my pleasure to help the pair of you. When shall I call round?'

'Tonight?'

'I'll be there.'

'Bloody night-watchman!' Roger raged when Reith was gone.

'It's a job,' Catie pointed out. 'And you're desperately in need of one.'

'Even though.' He bit his lip, then added, 'I just hate being beholden to him. The fact that he's doing us a favour is difficult.'

'You should be thankful that he is. In one fell swoop he's solved all our problems.'

'I know . . . I know but . . .' Roger broke off and angrily shrugged. Reith Douglas his boss, that was a bitter pill to swallow. Apart from anything else, hadn't the bastard always fancied Catie? He'd been certain Reith had which was a large part of the reason he'd disengaged their friendship in the first place. If he ever thought . . .

'Beggars can't be choosers, and that's exactly what we are,' Catie declared.

He glared at her. 'There's no need to rub it in.'

'Anyway, it's settled. We both start at the beginning of the month, me in training, you at the Midnight Rooms.'

Roger still didn't like it. Not at all. But what could he do? Nothing. He'd had to agree.

'Tell you what, why don't I go out and get fish and chips and a bottle of whisky to celebrate?' she proposed.

That prospect cheered him a little, though only a little.

Chapter Seventeen

'Christ!' Billy swore as an alarm bell began clanging. That wasn't supposed to happen.

'I'm off pal,' said Cliff, and raced off down the street, away from the licensed grocer's they'd been breaking into.

Somewhere a police whistle shrilled as Billy hared after his friend.

Cliff ducked into a dingy gas-lit close and Billy followed, shooting out the rear entrance and across the back courts to the tenements opposite. Once there would have been palings to climb but they had been dismantled for use in the war effort. They raced through a second close and over the street, only to dive into yet another close. Five minutes later they judged themselves to be far enough away from the scene of the attempted crime to slow down to a leisurely walk. Cliff's chest was heaving from a combination of exertion and fright while Billy, far fitter despite his long incarceration in prison, was merely breathing heavily.

'I didn't know it had an alarm, honest,' puffed Cliff.

'Of course you didn't, you silly sod. You'd hardly have suggested the place if you had.'

'We turned it over a couple of years ago and it was dead easy then. The alarm must have been installed since.'

Billy was furious. A totally wasted night with not a penny piece to show for profit. It just wasn't good enough, he told himself. Not at all what he'd planned when in the Bar-L. He swore viciously and kicked a wall they were passing.

'I know how you feel,' Cliff commiserated, feeling dejected.

'Do you?' Billy spat in reply.

'I said I'm sorry.'

Not half as sorry as he was, Billy thought. 'You know what we need don't you?'

'What?'

'A reliable source of information so we don't just blindly go about things, trusting to chance.'

He thought of Plookie John, then dismissed the idea. To trust someone like Plookie with the knowledge of what they were up to was far too dangerous. As was trusting any third party come to that, no matter what the arrangement. And then, right out of the blue, like the proverbial bolt of lightning, it hit Billy. Coming to a sudden halt he threw back his head and roared with laughter while Cliff stared at him in amazement.

'Oh sweet,' Billy declared, still laughing. 'Sweet as sugar candy!' thinking there was an exception to every rule. Or in this case, never trusting a third party.

'Do you mind sharing the joke?'

Billy didn't reply. Instead, lurching on his way, he continued laughing.

Reith stopped talking to Jameson as they approached the table where Catie was being instructed by Marlene, the most able croupier and dealer in his employment. Marlene had learned her trade and skills at the legendary Las Vegas. Marlene glanced up and smiled at his approach. Like most of his employees Marlene had enormous respect and affection for Reith.

'Good afternoon Mr Douglas,' she said.

'Good afternoon Marlene. And how's your latest pupil progressing?'

'She's coming along just fine sir.'

Reith nodded his approval. 'When can she face the punters?'

'Not quite yet sir, but soon. Another week perhaps.'

Reith turned his attention to Catie. 'How will you feel about that?'

'Nervous,' she answered truthfully.

He laughed. 'Well that's to be expected. But the nerves won't last for long, eh Marlene?'

'After the first hour she'll feel like she's been doing it all her life. That's the usual experience.'

Reith glanced at his watch. 'Come up and see me in half an hour, Catie. I want to speak to you.'

'Yes, sir.' She too called him sir or mister in public, it was only when they were alone she referred to him as Reith.

'Now Jameson . . .' Reith said, and moved away, Jameson by his side.

'Come in!' Reith called out when there was a knock on his office door. It was Catie as he'd presumed it would be. He gestured for her to close the door behind her.

'Is something wrong?' she asked anxiously.

'Not at all. I just wondered how you felt things were going?' He'd purposely not had much personal contact with her since she'd started training.

'Well, I'm actually quite enjoying it.'

That delighted him. 'No problems of any sort?'

'None.'

He rose from his chair and crossed to the small bar. 'Would you like a drink? I'm going to have one.'

'Are you testing me, Reith?' she teased. 'You know it's a rule that employees aren't allowed to drink.'

'Ah!' he grinned. 'So it is. But then it's my rule and I can bend it if I wish. Besides, you're only training, not on duty with the public.'

'I still won't. It's rather early for me. But thank you very much.'

'You don't mind if I indulge, do you?'

'Not at all.' Then, teasing again, she added, 'Anyway, it's hardly my place to mind.'

He poured himself a small whisky. 'I thought you'd like to know, so you can pass it on, that the word on Roger is favourable. He seems to have settled in all right and is doing a good job.'

'I'll tell him.'

Reith regarded her over the rim of his glass. 'Everything hunky-dory at home?'

Catie frowned. 'How do you mean?'

'Oh, I don't know, generally I suppose.' He gave her a hooded smile that she found puzzling.

'Andrew's in good health, as is Astrid. Roger's finding it strange having to sleep days, but that's something he'll just have to get used to.'

'I shouldn't care to do it myself, but there we are.'

Catie waited for him to go on, which he didn't. The hooded smile remained in place. 'Anything else? If not I'd better get back.'

'Nothing Catie, on you go.'

Outside Reith's office Catie frowned again. How odd, what a peculiarly stilted conversation that had been. And why ask about home the way he had? It was as if he knew something she didn't. Could he?

Inside the office Reith was sitting once more at his desk having accomplished what he'd set out to do. He had wanted to sow a little seed of doubt. He knew his line of enquiry had puzzled Catie and would make her wonder. It was a process he'd work on. If Roger was still seeing the McDonald woman then he might just make a slip that would otherwise have gone unnoticed by an unsuspecting Catie.

A little seed here, another there. Nothing obvious, but subtle. Who knew what the result might be. Nothing perhaps, but there again . . .

Irene, on the recommendation of a friend, had just tried out a new hairdresser and was delighted with the result. From there on in she'd insist that Henry would look after her.

She was inserting her key into the door of the Jag when a voice behind her said, 'Hello Irene, long time.'

She froze with horror, remembering that voice only too well. The nightmare had become reality.

'You're looking great,' Billy Boyne added.

She turned to face him, shivering involuntarily. He'd aged and lost weight but his eyes retained that sinister glitter that had always made her think she was being stared at by a reptile.

'What do you want?' she demanded.

'Dear me, is that the way to speak to an old friend?'

'You're no friend of mine. Now get away and never come near me again.'

'All right,' he drawled. 'If that's what you want.'

'It is.'

He made as if to move off, then hesitated. 'But I'll be dropping your husband a wee note concerning you and I, telling him about our relationship before I went inside.' He smiled to hear her sharp intake of breath. So, it was as he'd thought. Douglas didn't know about the pair of them.

204

'Do that and he'll kill you,' she declared.

Billy shrugged. 'Possibly, I know he's a very powerful man nowadays. Owns clubs and all sorts. But even if he did have me killed the damage would have already been done between the pair of you. And from what I hear I doubt he's the forgiving type.'

Irene started to shake which amused Billy. He was thoroughly enjoying this. 'Except why cause trouble when there needn't be any? All I want is a bit of co-operation from you, that's all.'

'What kind of co-operation?'

He glanced about. 'Not here Irene, not in the street. Why don't I buy you a drink and we can talk civilized like?'

She didn't see what else she could do. 'Where?'

'There's a boozer with a quiet little snug not far from here. We'll walk.'

'Together? What if we're seen.'

'OK. I'll go ahead, you follow. That suit?'

'Yes,' she husked.

He sauntered off and she reluctantly followed. God, how she hated him.

Irene sat hunched in front of her dressing-room mirror. Billy had backed her into a corner from which there was no escape. She had to comply with his wishes as the alternative was too dreadful to contemplate. What cruel irony she thought. She'd initially lost Reith when he'd found out about her affair with Billy, only to regain him miraculously when he'd returned home from the war with amnesia. She'd lived in fear ever since that that part of his memory would return, which it presumably never had. He remained blissfully unaware of her and Billy. Now Billy was out of prison threatening to tell Reith unless she did what he wanted. She'd have to comply or possibly lose Reith a second time.

She ached with love for her husband. Oh they'd had their bad patches, the worst that long period before Charlie McCall died. But things had been more or less fine ever since. Now this, a bomb that could blow her marriage sky-high. She could explain to Reith why she'd slept with Billy in the first place, he would surely accept and understand that. But still the damage would have been done, perhaps irreparably so.

She squeezed her hands till the knuckles shone white. Billy had promised to leave her alone if she only provided the information he was after. Could she trust him to do that? She didn't know and could only hope and pray he'd keep his word.

'Oh Reith,' she sobbed. What a position to be in. What an awful, bloody position. Damn Billy Boyne to everlasting perdition. And the sooner he got there the better.

Catie's initial nervousness had quickly vanished just as Reith and Marlene had predicted. Several hours into her first night at the blackjack table and she felt like an old hand. She glanced up and saw Reith staring at her, smiling. He winked, and she winked back. He gave her a swift thumbs up sign before turning to engage a portly punter in conversation.

'Do you do this for all your new staff?' Catie asked as Reith undid the foil round the neck of a bottle of champagne.

'What do you think?'

'I'm privileged then.'

'You could say that.'

He twisted the bottom of the bottle in one direction, the cork in the other. The cork popped almost immediately and went sailing across the office.

Catie laughed and lightly clapped her hands. 'Quite the professional.'

'Just as you were down there tonight,' he complimented her in return, pouring the bubbling wine into some glasses. He gave her a glass, then clinked his against hers. 'Here's to a successful début. Good for you Catie.'

They both drank. 'I was proud of you tonight,' he stated.

'It was so much fun. Not like work at all.'

'That's what I like to hear,' he smiled.

'I can't thank you enough for the job Reith. And Roger's. They're life-savers.'

He wanted to touch her, stroke her, take her into his arms. But none of that showed on his face. 'Don't worry about getting back, Jameson and I will drop you off.'

'Now you are spoiling me!'

Not nearly as much as he would have liked to, he thought. God, she was stunning in the new outfit he'd provided. She'd filled out again, thanks to regular diet and was no longer the painfully thin woman he'd encountered in Daly's.

'So what are you going to do with your days now they're completely free again?' he queried.

'Believe it or not, after what we've been through recently, with this sudden upturn in our fortunes we're considering moving, so I shall be looking at houses.'

'Oh? Anywhere in mind?'

She smiled. 'Remember Irene wanted to go to Battlefield? Well we thought of going there.'

'A big improvement on Bridgeton, that's for sure.'

'A big improvement,' she agreed.

'How about Newton Mearns?' he teased.

'We're not quite in that category yet thank you very much.'

'Who knows about the future though?' he said, making it sound like another tease. What he was really thinking about was her installed in his house as his wife. If only he could win her, winkle her away from Roger. Patience, he counselled himself.

'What's drawing dead?' he abruptly asked.

'Drawing to a hand that can't win,' she promptly answered. 'Is this another test?'

'In the dark?'

'To check or to bet blind without looking at your cards.'

'Belly hit?'

'To fit an inside straight.'

'Very good,' he nodded. 'You know your stuff. But then Marlene wouldn't let you face the punters unless you did.'

'She's an excellent teacher.'

'You'd better believe it. Hungry? We could stop off in the kitchens and see what we could find. I do that sometimes.'

She shook her head. 'I'm not hungry in the least. Sorry.'

Pity, he thought, that would have given them more time together. 'Let me top you up. Can't let this go to waste, eh?'

As her glass was being refilled she noticed a large set of plans spread across his desk. 'They look interesting,' she said, gesturing towards them. 'You're not thinking of going into the building trade, are you?'

'In a way. Come and have a look, tell me what you think.'

They crossed over to the desk where he turned the plans round to face them. 'I bought a piece of land a while back and this is what I'm thinking of doing with it.'

The plans meant nothing to Catie, simply lots of lines, boxes and figures. 'What does it all represent?'

'A building complex of new shops. There's a housing estate going to be built in the vicinity which these would service.'

She frowned. 'I haven't heard of any new estate going up around there.'

He gave her a thin, mysterious smile. 'Few people have. But it'll happen, I assure you.'

'Few people know, and yet you're one of them?'

'That's right.'

Curiosity got the better of good manners. 'Will you make a lot of money out of this complex?'

'A considerable amount. I have to get planning permission first of course, but I don't envisage any problems there. I think we can take that as read.'

She glanced sideways at him. 'You sound very certain.'

'I am,' he replied, repeating the mysterious, knowing smile.

A shiver of something went through her and she suddenly found herself sexually aroused. Now why had that happened? she wondered. She'd been relaxed in his company up until then, now she was on edge. No, more than that, though she couldn't have explained what.

'I'd better be going,' she declared.

He heard the tremulousness in her voice that was always there when she was nervous. He too had appreciated that the atmosphere between them had changed.

'I'll get my coat, then take you down for your things,' he said, and drained his glass.

As they went downstairs Catie moved ever so slightly away from him, which he didn't fail to notice. Nor did he take offence. He understood.

McKendrick, the night-watchman at Fanny's, never knew what hit him. One moment he was sitting with his feet up reading the paper, next he was on the floor out cold. Billy, who'd coshed McKendrick, put the cosh away and produced a length of thin rope with which he proceeded to tie McKendrick's hands behind his back, and feet. That done he gagged McKendrick.

'So far so good,' commented Cliff.

'Right, come on.'

When they entered Reith's office Billy went straight to the window and closed the curtains. Meanwhile Cliff, torch in hand, had opened two wooden doors behind which lay the safe.

'Exactly as she said,' Billy declared with approval. If she was right about everything else, and she had been so far, then this wasn't only going to be a doddle but an extremely lucrative one as well.

Cliff concentrated on his task of opening the safe, swiftly dialling the combination.

'Wow!' he breathed when the door swung open to reveal stacks of notes.

Five minutes later they were back in the street heading for Billy's place.

In the small hours of the following morning, Reith was roused from sleep by the insistent ringing of his bedside telephone. 'Hello?' he queried into the receiver. He listened intently to what was being said on the other end, the signs of sleep quickly vanishing from his face.

'No, don't call the police, McKendrick. I will. And yes, you were quite right to ring me first.'

Reith hung up and stared thoughtfully at the telephone.

'Something wrong?' Irene asked, having sat up in bed.

Reith grunted and turned to her. 'Fanny's was broken into late last night. That was McKendrick, he was knocked out and tied up. He's only just managed to free himself a few moments ago.'

'Was much taken?'

'They cracked the safe and got away with the entire Saturday night's takings.' Reith swung himself out of bed, then reached again for the phone. 'I've a few calls to make, then I'd better get straight there.'

Irene's heart was pounding wildly, her emotions a combination of extreme anxiety and guilt. For she knew only too well who'd done the break-in.

Chief Inspector Dodd was a dour Scot with a lugubrious face. In his early fifties he was one of the top officers in his field. 'It's a highly professional and competent job, I have to give him or them that,' he admitted, rubbing a hand over a bristly chin. He had been summoned directly from bed as well. He moved aside to allow the finger-printing expert, who was dusting the office for prints, past.

He pointed a stubby finger at Reith's safe. 'There are less than a handful of villains in Scotland, far less Glasgow, who could open that without blowing it. So that narrows the field considerably.' He rounded on Reith. 'Do you know how much was taken?'

Reith went to his desk, opened a drawer and extracted a ledger. He was able to inform Dodd of the precise amount. Dodd raised an eyebrow in surprise. 'Is it wise to keep so much money on the premises Mr Douglas?'

'Normally the takings are only here for a few hours before being transferred to the bank. But on Saturday night the takings, which are invariably the largest of the week, have to remain there till Monday morning, over twenty-four hours.'

'And night safes. What about those?'

Reith shrugged. 'You're right. It's a mistake I won't let happen in future.' He smiled cynically. 'A touch of arrogance, Mungo. I just never imagined anyone would be stupid or mad enough to rob me.'

Mungo Dodd nodded. He quite understood that having his own arrangement with Reith. Robbing Reith was tantamount to walking into a lion's den.

'Anything else in your safe apart from cash?' he queried.

'Some jewellery held as collateral. A couple of pieces worth in the region of five thousand.'

'The thieves certainly had a successful night,' Dodd commented drily.

'All finished here sir,' the finger-printing expert announced.

'You get along then.' Turning to Reith he said, 'I doubt there will be any prints. These were real pros.' Dodd took a deep breath. 'Now let's talk this through further. I want all the information you can give me.'

'Why did you ring? You promised—'

Billy held up a hand to silence Irene. 'I lied,' he stated simply.

Oh God! she thought. This was getting worse.

He glanced round the pub, the same one he'd taken her to previously, and smiled darkly. He'd already put the word out that the job at Fanny's had been done by a London team. It was a red herring to confuse the police and Douglas. He'd also warned Cliff not to breathe a single syllable to anyone that it had been them, *or else*. Cliff had known only too well what Billy meant.

'I want something more,' Billy stated.

Irene's heart sank even further.

'This is the last, I swear, on my mother's life.'

'How can I trust you?' she queried harshly.

He shrugged. 'You can't, Irene. But there again, have you a choice?' He paused, then added, 'I don't think you have.'

She dropped her gaze to the table and covered her face. 'What do you want?'

She would dance to his tune as long as he wished her to, Billy congratulated himself, thinking yet again how attractive she was. She was built rather like a boy, the way he liked his women.

'Tell me about the bookie set-up? Collections, and other such details.'

Irene sighed. 'I don't know everything. Only what I've picked up over the years.'

'That'll do for starters. The rest you can find out.'

Irene felt like someone who'd stepped into quicksand and was slowly sinking deeper and deeper. She began to speak.

'A London team,' Reith mused into the phone. That made sense.

'I've been in touch with Scotland Yard, pulled a few strings. They're putting out some feelers,' Dodd said from the other end.

'Good,' Reith nodded.

Dodd hesitated, then added, 'We're doing all that can be done. I hope you appreciate that.'

'I wouldn't expect less,' Reith replied matter-of-factly.

'I'll ring again when I've something to tell you.'

'Or if you haven't,' Reith said, a slight hardness creeping into his voice.

'Or if I haven't. You'll be kept fully informed.'

Reith hung up. He wanted whoever had done this. It wasn't merely the money, though that had been substantial, it was the principle involved. And his reputation. And that's what worried him most of all.

'Will you do me a favour, Catie?' Reith asked.

'Of course. If I can.'

He glanced at his watch. It was minutes before they opened. There was time for a quick coffee.

'So what is it?' she queried while they waited for their coffees to be brought to them.

'It's our anniversary next week and I have to buy Irene a present. I've a couple of ideas but I'm not certain which would please her most. Would you come into town with me tomorrow or the day after and help me choose something?'

'Why don't you just tell me and . . .'

211

'Not as easy as that,' he interjected. 'I'd prefer you to be there in person to help me decide.'

'If that's what you want. It'll be my pleasure.'

He smiled at her. 'Thank you. Shall I pick you up at home?'

She thought about that. 'No, better if we meet in town. I don't want Roger getting any funny notions. You know what he's like.'

Only too well, Reith thought, only too well. 'So, tomorrow or the next day?'

'Tomorrow would be fine.'

'Good.'

He hesitated, appearing to be reluctant when he asked, 'And Roger himself, everything still all right there?'

There it was again, that inference that he knew something she didn't. Or was it merely her imagination? 'Couldn't be better.'

Reith changed the subject to enquire how her house-hunting was coming along.

Later, in the ladies toilet, Catie frowned into the mirror. *Did* Reith know something? A man in his position was liable to know all sorts. Hear things, pick up stray pieces of information. No, she only half convinced herself. He was simply being polite, concerned. There was no more to it than that.

Chapter Eighteen

'Have you read *Forever Amber*?'

Catie shook her head. 'Strangely, I haven't. It's a book I've been meaning to read for ages but never got round to.'

Reith plucked a copy from the shelf. 'Then you will now. It's marvellous. You'll love every page of it. Real romantic stuff.'

He gazed round the bookshop he'd brought Catie to in Union Street after they'd finished buying the gift for Irene. That had only been of minimal interest to him, he could easily have chosen something by himself. The real reason for meeting up with Catie in town was that they could spend some time alone together away from work.

'Anything else take your fancy?'

It was good being with him like this, she thought. They always had such fun. He made her laugh. 'Not really.'

'Are you sure?'

She picked up a J.B. Priestley book and flicked through the pages. 'This looks interesting.'

'Then have that as well.'

She laughed. 'You're spoiling me again.'

'You deserve to be spoiled Catie. Anyway, indulge me. They say it's better to give than receive, which I wholeheartedly agree with. Certainly in your case.'

She was filled with a warm glow as he took the book from her hands and added it to the other.

'What about yourself?' she asked. 'Aren't you going to buy anything?'

'I explained before, I haven't got much time to read nowadays. More's the pity. No, I just like to come into bookshops and browse. It takes my mind off other things.'

She could understand that. She adored browsing in bookshops too. 'I should be getting back,' she declared.

'What's the rush?'

'I've got the ironing to do.'

'Can't it wait?'

She thought with a sinking heart of the stack of ironing waiting at home. Ironing was a chore which, if she didn't loathe it, wasn't exactly something she enjoyed.

'I thought we might have some lunch?' he proposed.

Now that was tempting.

'Anywhere you like. Just name it.'

'I don't know,' she prevaricated.

'I fancy a bit of fish myself,' he said. 'And there's none better to be found in Glasgow than at Rogano's. Their plaice is out of this world. Particularly if drunk with a glass of decent Chablis.'

His eyes twinkled. 'Besides, you have to have lunch with me, because I have a surprise for you.'

That intrigued her. 'What kind of surprise?'

'Ah! Only over lunch. No plaice and Chablis, no surprise.'

Catie laughed. 'That's blackmail.'

'I do believe it is,' he admitted in a teasing tone.

It must be something to do with Fanny's, she decided. But what? For the life of her she couldn't think.

'Of course if the ironing is more attractive . . .' He broke off and shrugged.

'You know it isn't.'

'Well then.' He grasped her lightly by the elbow. 'Shall we?'

She watched him as he paid for the books. As she'd thought a few moments ago, he could be such fun, never dull or boring. Not that Roger was either, but with Reith there was another element, an added spice. One thing was certain, the position he'd achieved in life gave him an authority that hadn't been there before. And that was exciting.

He carried the books to the Daimler where Jameson was waiting. 'Rogano's,' he instructed, settling himself into the backseat, having already helped Catie inside.

Jameson's eyes flicked to the overhead mirror. He couldn't make out what was happening between Reith and this Catie Smith, but

214

there was something all right. But he would never have dreamt of asking Reith, that wasn't his place.

When they arrived at Rogano's Catie was miffed to discover that Reith had already ordered a table, but was quickly placated when he explained that he hadn't presumed she'd come with him but had intended lunching there anyway. It was, however, a lie on his part, he'd only have turned up if she had agreed to accompany him.

'So, what's the surprise?' she asked eagerly, once they were settled and their orders taken.

He regarded her mockingly. 'I hope you won't be angry?'

'Do you think I will be?'

'I don't know.'

'Well, I will if you don't hurry up and tell me what it is. I'm dying of curiosity.'

'Hardly *dying*,' he teased.

'You know what I mean.'

'Do I?'

He was stretching this out, she realized, tantalizing her. 'Perhaps I'm not really all that interested,' she declared, pretending indifference.

'All right then. We'll forget it. Plaice and Chablis and no surprise.'

'Reith!' she exclaimed.

Why did her company always make him feel so happy? He wanted to stay at that table with her forever. Well not quite that, what he wanted was to be with her forever. Every waking moment, every sleeping one. He reached into his pocket and took out a velvet-type covered box which he placed in front of her.

'For you,' he declared.

She stared at it.

'Remember in the shop you went to the toilet?'

Catie nodded.

'And before that there was something you admired?'

That rocked her. 'You didn't?'

'You liked it. I bought it. Why not?'

'But it was so incredibly expensive!'

'One of the nice things about being so well off is you can afford such luxury items.'

She reached out and stroked the box.

'Of course,' he further teased. 'The bloody thing could be empty.'

215

She knew better than that. Slowly she picked up the box and opened it, gasping slightly when the watch was revealed. 'This cost a fortune,' she breathed.

'Fortunes are relative,' he said drily, as he gently touched her hand. 'Try it on.'

She fumbled with the catch until it snicked shut round her wrist.

'It's beautiful,' she declared.

Light caught the gold which caused it to glint. He'd have bought her a hundred such watches if only . . .

'But I can't accept it,' she said. 'How would I explain it to Roger?'

'I've already thought of that. Tell him you got it through the club for a fraction of the price as it's knocked off. He'll buy that story, believe me.'

Reith was right, Catie thought, Roger would accept that. 'It really is beautiful,' she repeated.

Not half as much as you, he wanted to tell her, but didn't. 'I'm glad you're pleased.'

'But *why?*'

'For helping me choose Irene's present,' he lied.

'That wasn't so much,' she protested.

Dare he? he wondered. Just a little step, not too much he decided. 'You know I've always been very fond of you, Catie, so let's just say it's a gift from one good friend to another.'

She coloured slightly and averted her gaze.

'Well, that's what we are, aren't we? Good friends?'

She nodded.

Their conversation was interrupted by the arrival of the wine. Once it was poured out, he began talking about something else altogether.

Catie stretched out on a chair in front of the range and reached for the cup of tea she'd just poured herself. Sod the ironing, she decided, she'd do it later. Perhaps she'd even leave it till tomorrow.

She thought of her lunch with Reith as she sipped the tea, and smiled. The whole outing had been thoroughly enjoyable. As for the watch! She glanced at it and smiled again, as she turned her wrist first one way, then the other, causing the gold to catch the light and sparkle. She sighed with contentment. Imagine him buying her such a gift, especially after what she'd done to him. She recalled how much he'd been in love with her. Up until now she'd presumed he'd got over it, now she wasn't so sure.

What was it he'd said? 'One good friend to another.' Was that all it was, or was he still holding a torch for her? It was gratifying to think he might be, a boost to her ego which she'd always considered to be fragile. Oh sure she was reasonable looking, a glance in any mirror would confirm that. But deep down she'd always felt she was somehow lacking. That was where Roger was so marvellous, complimented her so very well. He was strong in comparison to her, someone who believed in himself 100 per cent. He was perhaps a little too strong, over dominant perhaps, she reflected. Yes, maybe to her detriment. Whereas with Reith, that had always seemed more a meeting of equals.

She glanced admiringly at her watch again and couldn't help but wonder what life would have been like for her if she had gone off with Reith, eventually marrying him one day. The Daimler, house in Newton Mearns, the clothes, jewellery, money. She shivered at the thought of being so pampered and cosseted. Imagine her husband owning Fanny's and all those other clubs, a husband as immaculately turned out, refined almost, as Reith. Not that there was anything wrong with the way Roger dressed and behaved, he was a working man after all, and one who, until recently, had been badly out of work. But refined! She silently laughed. That was the last thing you could call Roger. He was a Glasgow keelie through and through. And they were hardly poor now either. What with their combined wages, they were extremely well off by working-class standards. Many would have labelled them rich, though hardly in Reith's league.

There again, they owed it all to Reith. He employed both of them. If it wasn't for him they'd still be starving. It must be wonderful to have such power, she further reflected, to control the lives and destinies of so many, which was precisely what Reith did. How many people depended on him as a source of income, to put food on their families' tables?

And was such a man still as much in love with her as he'd once been? It was . . . thrilling, yes that was it, thrilling to think he might be. But if so, he'd never admit it knowing she was in love with Roger. Why jeopardize his own marriage, after all?

She pictured herself standing outside a mansion, wearing an ankle-length mink coat, dripping jewels, climbing into the Daimler and telling Jameson to take her here, there, wherever. She visualized being driven along Sauchiehall Street looking like Lady Muck. She laughed aloud at that vision. Lady Muck indeed! Well, a girl could dream, couldn't she? For it was only a load of baloney. She was quite content being Mrs Roger Smith – more than content.

During a lull in the proceedings Catie spotted Reith deep in conversation with a well-known Scottish newspaper proprietor. It never failed to impress her that so many famous, wealthy and influential people patronized Fanny's. Why only the previous week an extremely popular comedian had called in, while a few days before that a local football hero had graced them with his presence. And Reith was on a friendly basis with them all, sometimes dining with them in the restaurant, on other occasions escorting them round the tables. And to think this was the same chap who not that long ago had been a labourer at Black's.

She watched Reith now, perfectly at ease with the newspaper proprietor, who was rumoured to be a multi-millionaire, just as he'd been relaxed with the comedian and football hero. She shook her head in wonder. You had to admire and respect the man. What he'd become was simply incredible. As if sensing she was staring at him Reith suddenly glanced across at her, and smiled. She found herself instantly smiling back. Then her attention was reclaimed by the blackjack table she was working.

Irene picked up the sherry decanter, considered it for a moment, then replaced it on the sideboard. She opted for the gin bottle instead, pouring herself a generous measure.

'Bit early for the spirits, isn't it?' Reith commented casually from where he was sitting. He was worried about Irene who hadn't been at all herself recently. She'd become edgy, preoccupied and extremely nervous. Earlier she'd nearly jumped out of her skin when he'd silently walked into the room and pecked her on the cheek. She'd claimed it was because she hadn't heard his approach, but he thought it was more than that. She'd never jumped in the past.

'Do you mind?' she queried.

'Not in the least. Just thought it a bit early, that's all.'

She topped her glass up with tonic and added a slice of lemon. 'What about you?'

'No thanks.'

'I'd prefer the company,' she said, giving him a strained smile.

'All right then. What the heck! I'll have the same as you, only a weak one.'

Were her hands trembling as she poured? He wasn't certain at that distance, but they could be.

'Are you all right? You appear poorly of late,' he said.

'I'm fine. Fit as a flea.'

'Perhaps you're ill and don't realize it. Maybe you should see the doctor for a check-up.'

'I'm fine I tell you,' she snapped back, clearly irritated.

'Sorry.'

'Why, don't I look it?' That worried her.

'Not really.'

She took him his drink. Her hands were trembling he noted as she gave it to him. 'So why don't you see the doctor just to be on the safe side,' he urged.

She shrugged. 'I'll think about it. Now can we leave it at that.'

Over their Sunday lunch he further noted that she drank far more wine than usual, gulping rather than sipping it as she normally did. When he tried to engage her in light conversation her replies were often as not monosyllabic. In the end he gave up and simply concentrated on his meal.

Catie had never seen Reith look so angry. His expression was positively thunderous as he strode past. He halted briefly beside Jameson, had a quick word, then abruptly turned and headed back the way he'd come with Jameson in tow.

'Finlay was robbed tonight,' Reith harshly informed Jameson when they were alone in his office and the door firmly closed behind them. Finlay had Reith's old job, in charge of the runners with whom the street punters made their bets.

Jameson's expression remained impassive. 'How did it happen?'

'He was starting to unload the night's takings from the boot of his car when he was coshed from behind. He's in the Western Infirmary being operated on now for a smashed skull. Apparently it's touch and go.'

Reith went to the bar and poured himself a whisky. '*Coshed* I said, ring a bell?'

'You mean McKendrick?'

'That's right. Two jobs pulled against me, a cosh used on both occasions. Think it's a coincidence?'

'Possibly,' Jameson mused.

219

'Well, I find it hard to believe.'

'The rumour was that Fanny's was done by a London team. Perhaps it wasn't.'

'Scotland Yard haven't come up with anything to substantiate that it was London people. Or person as the case may be.'

Jameson rubbed a hand across his chin while Reith drank some of the whisky. 'Therefore it's local.'

'Beginning to look that way.'

A few moments of contemplative silence ticked by. 'So what are you going to do?' Jameson queried.

'Speak to Dodd and others for a start. But I also want you out on the streets trying to find out who's done this. And when we do find out, you've to sort them.'

Jameson nodded his understanding and approval.

'You'd better take a couple of lads with you to help with the legwork.' Reith sipped some more whisky and thought. 'Make it Watt and Heraghty, unless you've any objections?'

'None,' Jameson stated.

'Shit!' Reith exploded. 'Finlay's a good man with a wife and three small kids. They're going to be devastated if he pegs it.' Reith took a deep breath. 'I'll see they're all right whatever happens, but that's hardly the point.'

Jameson crossed over and sat on the edge of Reith's desk. 'Could they both be inside jobs?'

'The thought had crossed my mind,' Reith replied softly.

'I don't know why, but I was never totally happy about the Fanny's business. The ease with which they got in, took out McKendrick and cracked the safe bothered me. It was as if they knew beforehand precisely what was what.'

Jameson paused, then went on. 'Now Finlay. How would an outsider know where to find him and at the right time? The only constant in Finlay's routine was when he arrived home and unloaded. And how many folk know that Finlay keeps the takings overnight in the safe you had installed in his home? Precious few.'

Because the takings were illegally earned they never went directly into a bank but were disposed of, and absorbed into, various outlets belonging to Reith.

Reith stared hard at the man who was virtually his lieutenant and whose abilities and opinion he respected enormously. 'You get started on the streets while I look into that side of things.'

'Tonight or tomorrow?'

Reith considered that. 'Tomorrow. It's too soon to begin now.'

'Right. Anything else?'

'Yes.' Reith returned his empty glass to the bar. 'You can drive me to the Western. Margie Finlay is already there and was in a terrible state when she rang me.'

Both men were grim faced as they left the office and made their way downstairs.

Irene woke to the sound of Reith moving quietly about their bedroom. She'd been sleeping fitfully over recent weeks which was why she'd been so easily roused. 'What time is it?' she blinked.

'Just after seven.'

She noticed he was still wearing his evening clothes. 'You're late.'

'Finlay got robbed last night. I've just come from the Western where he's critical.'

The news, which she'd been expecting, was even more awful than she'd anticipated. 'What happened?'

'Some bastard coshed him, badly, then made off with the entire night's takings.'

She quailed inside. Trust Billy to be so brutal. There had been no need for that. 'Doesn't Finlay have three children?'

Reith threw his tie aside. He was as coldly furious as he'd been since talking to Jameson in his office. 'All girls, the youngest only two. Margie Finlay was beside herself so they had to give her a sedative to calm her down.' Reith went to the bed and stared down at Irene, his eyes so hard and penetrating that she was sure he could read her guilt. 'God help whoever did this when Jameson gets hold of him or them, that's all I can say.'

Irene cringed.

A little over an hour later Reith was informed by telephone that Finlay had died.

Irene gazed at her reflection in her dressing-table mirror. She looked and felt a wreck. She was appalled that Finlay was dead, shaken to the very core. This business with Billy had gone far enough she decided. No matter what the consequences to her marriage she had to come clean with Reith, tell him everything. One death was bad enough, but what if there were a succession of others. What then? No no, it had to be a full confession.

221

Having made that decision she immediately felt a little better. By rights she should go to court along with Billy, but doubted Reith would allow that to happen. Billy wouldn't go to court either, Reith's retaliation for Finlay's murder would be personal, and terminal.

She shook her head. A widow with three small children. A woman who'd still have her husband, and her children their father, if it hadn't been for her. She groaned at the thought. The sooner she told Reith the better. She'd go to Fanny's and . . .

Irene caught her breath. Perhaps, just perhaps she wouldn't have to tell Reith. She'd meet Billy and tell him what she intended to do which would negate the threat of Billy's letter. His hold over her would then be broken and if he was wise he'd make himself scarce, leave Glasgow altogether before Reith's men got hold of him. If that happened she wouldn't have to tell Reith after all. The threat of doing so would be enough. It might work, she thought. But if it didn't then Reith would have to be told. She owed Finlay and Finlay's family that.

She shuddered, thinking of the confrontation with Billy. God alone knew how he would react. And then she had another idea.

Billy's eyes glittered venomously as Irene finished speaking. Moving quickly, he grabbed her by the throat. 'You bitch,' he snarled.

She tried to pull herself free, but couldn't. All she managed to do was to make a choking sound as the fingers round her neck tightened even further.

'I should kill you here and now,' he declared, his expression truly frightening.

'No,' she managed to gasp. 'Letter.'

'What letter?'

She was tugging at his hands which he now slightly relaxed. 'What fucking letter?'

'My insurance. A letter to Reith telling him everything. I've arranged for it to be delivered should anything happen to me.'

She staggered backwards when he abruptly released her, drawing air deep into her lungs.

'Very clever,' he hissed.

Irene massaged her neck, wondering if it would bruise. 'You're not the only one who can write you know. Kill me and Reith will hunt you down like a dog.'

Billy strode across the room, picked up a bottle of whisky and poured himself a drink. As he did it he reflected on what Irene had said.

'Your mistake was murdering Finlay. You should never have done that,' Irene stated, a new hardness in her voice.

He didn't reply. Instead he sipped his drink and studied her. 'You might be bluffing about wanting to tell Douglas,' he said eventually.

'I'm not. Believe me.'

'Or this letter.'

'I'm not lying about that either. You'd better believe it.'

A smile crept onto his face. 'And I'm to hightail it, right?'

'You can stay of course and face the consequences, which wouldn't be a very bright thing to do.'

He nodded. 'Shall I tell you what'll happen if I do go?'

'What?'

'Agnes.'

That shook Irene. 'What about Agnes?'

His smile widened. 'Your and Douglas's beloved daughter.'

Irene had been frightened ever since she'd set out for Billy's apartment. Now she was downright terrified. She swallowed hard.

'I'll razor her,' Billy declared.

Irene started to shake, her inner resolve crumbling with that statement.

'So badly no man would ever look at her again,' Billy qualified.

'You . . . you . . .' She fought back the bile that had suddenly risen into her throat. A picture of Agnes, mutilated, flashed through her mind causing her to whimper.

'I know where she is, you see. The college she's at . . .' Billy broke off and shrugged. 'It wouldn't be difficult.'

'I'd warn her,' Irene gasped. 'I'd telephone, get her out of there. I'd . . .'

Billy laughed. 'Not as simple as that, Irene. I could disappear some place where even Douglas would never find me. Then, one day, quite out of the blue, pop up again and . . .' He made several flicking motions with his right hand. 'Zzztt, zzztt!'

Irene turned and vomited on the floor.

'It hurts,' Irene sobbed. 'It hurts.'

Of course it was hurting, Billy thought gleefully. That's why he

223

was doing what he was. Inflicting pain during the sexual act gave him added pleasure. As he gazed down at Irene's perspiring, rounded flesh he imagined it wasn't her he was screwing, but *the big man* himself. In more ways than one.

For a few moments the face puzzled Reith, as it was somehow familiar, then the penny dropped, and he realized who she was. He strolled across to the roulette table where she and her male companion were watching.

'Hello Nell,' he said.

She turned to stare at him.

'Remember me?'

Astonishment blossomed on her face. 'Reith! Reith Douglas!'

'The very same, Sister McIntosh.' He extended a hand. 'It's good to see you.'

She ignored the hand and threw her arms round him, kissing him on the cheek. 'You look wonderful.'

'You look rather wonderful yourself. Being out of uniform suits you.'

She laughed while her companion looked on. 'Let me introduce you. Reith Douglas, ex-patient at Harrington Manor, this is my husband Peter Wiley, another ex-patient.'

The two men shook hands. 'Congratulations on marrying the prettiest nurse at Harrington,' Reith smiled.

'She was too,' Peter agreed.

'Flatterer,' Nell giggled, waving an admonishing finger at Reith.

'Not at all. What I said was perfectly true. You were.'

'How's . . . your wife and family?'

'In the pink, all three.'

'And the headaches?'

'What headaches?' he teased.

She laughed again. 'That's good. Brilliant in fact.' To Peter she explained. 'Reith was shot in the head while in Greece. He suffered blinding headaches as a result, and loss of memory. How's that coming along by the way?'

'There are still blank patches, particularly about the war, but a lot of my memory has returned.'

Nell beamed at him. 'I can't tell you how pleased I am to hear that. Did you go back to being a cabinet-maker?'

She'd remembered his former occupation, Reith thought. That pleased him. 'No, not quite.'

She raised an enquiring eyebrow.

'It's a long story. I own this club now.'

'*Own* it!' she exclaimed.

'Lock, stock and roulette wheels.'

'You wouldn't be pulling my leg by any chance?' she queried suspiciously.

'Not in the least.' Using an index finger he made several gestures over his chest. 'Cross my heart. Honest Injun.'

'Well I never,' she breathed.

'And you?'

'Gave up nursing to have children. We've got a little boy called Dallas.'

'Congratulations again,' Reith said. She was happy in her marriage, and with life in general, he could see that. 'And have you settled in Glasgow?'

'Aberfeldy actually. We're here visiting my parents. As today is our anniversary Peter decided to take me out on the town. So here we are.'

'Are you gambling?'

'Later,' Peter said. 'We're going to eat first.'

An open, honest face and roughly the same age as Nell. He liked Peter Wiley, Reith decided. 'Then I'll tell you what. Tonight your meal is on the house, a gift and thank you to Nell from me.'

'We couldn't . . .' Peter started to protest.

Reith held up a hand. 'It's the least I can do. Simply order whatever takes your fancy and that's that.'

Nell recalled how fond she'd been of Reith, and how things might have turned out differently if he hadn't already been married. There again, she'd only thought she could love him, whereas with Peter there had never been any doubt. No, the fates had been right, it had turned out for the best. She wouldn't have swopped her Peter for anything or anybody.

'I'll take you to the restaurant to ensure you get a good table,' Reith declared, 'And what if I join you for coffee and liqueurs later? We've a great deal of catching up to do, Sister McIntosh.' This last remark addressed to Nell.

'We'd be delighted,' Peter stated.

Nell again kissed Reith on the cheek. 'I can't wait to hear all about you and your family.'

'Or I about you and yours.'

As he was escorting Nell and Peter to the restaurant Reith saw

Catie staring at them, her expression one of . . . Could it be jealousy? For Nell was clutching onto his arm and chatting away to him like the old friend she was. Now that was interesting, Reith thought with satisfaction.

Chapter Nineteen

'You certainly haven't lost any of your ability with a cue considering you were inside for so long,' Desperate Dan Henderson commented wryly to Billy who'd just thrashed him. Billy grinned as he plonked himself into a well-worn leather bench-type seat. 'If you have it, you have it, sunshine. So, envy.'

Billy took out his cigarettes and lit up, not offering the packet round as was the custom. He inhaled deeply, gazing out over Caley Snooker Hall which comprised eighteen tables, all currently in use.

'I'm going to get a coffee,' Cliff Kelman said, and left their group to head for the glory-hole where coffee, tea and soft drinks were served.

Mikey Sullivan sniffed, then pulled out a far from clean handkerchief which he honked into. 'Effing cold,' he grumbled.

'You want to give yourself a holiday and get away from bloody Glasgow,' his china Mo Drysdale advised. 'Away "doon ra watter" for a fortnight.' 'Doon ra watter' was the Clyde coast.

'Can't afford it. I'm dead skint,' Mikey replied.

'As bad as that?' Billy queried.

Mikey shook his head. 'Worse. I've had no luck at all recently. Did a house the other night that was a right loser. Nothing in it worth a toss.'

Billy pulled a sympathetic face.

'But you seem to be doing OK. That's a real flash suit you're wearing,' Mikey remarked.

Billy fingered a lapel. He wanted to boast about how much the suit had cost, and that it had been privately tailored, but refrained. 'Things haven't been too bad of late,' he said vaguely instead.

'Better than that I'd say from the roll of fivers I saw you with earlier.'

Billy fastened him with a hostile look. 'You've always had a big mouth, Mikey. You'd better watch someone doesn't shut it for good one day.'

Mikey was instantly apologetic, for like all of them he was terrified of Billy whom they all knew to be a total headcase. 'Sorry pal, no offence. And we're among friends after all.'

Cliff returned with his coffee. He was sporting an expensive suit as well. 'Don't look now but bad news just walked in,' he stated quietly.

Billy's eyes instantly flashed towards the doorway where a man he didn't recognize stood framed. 'Who is he?'

'Someone you don't want to know, believe me,' Desperate Dan informed him.

Billy was intrigued. 'Villain?'

'The hardest bastard in Glasgow, which is saying something. A commando during the war who won all sorts of sodding medals. The real hero type.'

'Oh aye?'

Cliff had become fidgety. 'Works for Douglas, who owns all the clubs.'

Billy got the message and imperceptibly nodded to Cliff. He composed his face, wiping it of all expression as Jameson walked towards them.

'Shite, he's coming over,' Mo Drysdale breathed.

'Hello lads,' Jameson said pleasantly when he reached them.

'Hello Jameson,' Mo smiled.

'How's it going?'

Mo shrugged. 'Could be better. You know.'

Jameson's gaze flicked to Billy who was unknown to him. 'Hello,' he said directly to Billy, who nodded back.

'New in Glasgow?'

'Nope.'

'My name's Jameson.'

Billy nodded again.

'And yours?'

Billy considered not answering, but thought, why be difficult? That was hardly in his interests in the circumstances. 'Billy Boyne.'

The name meant nothing to Jameson who hadn't been involved with villains before Billy went into prison.

'Pleased to meet you Billy.'

'And you Jameson.'

Billy was sizing Jameson up. The man wasn't particularly tall, or broad. Yet there was something about him which, even without the warning, would have made Billy wary.

'What can we do for you, pal?' Mikey asked, lounging back in his seat and lighting up.

'I'm looking for a name.'

'Uh-huh?'

'It's worth a hundred nicker.'

That caught Mikey's attention. Like many Glaswegians he would have sold his granny for such a sum. 'Whose name?'

'Or names,' Jameson qualified. 'Who did Fanny's and robbed Finlay who also works for Mr Douglas?'

Mikey shook his head. 'Can't help you, I'm afraid. Anyway, I heard Fanny's was done by a London team.'

'We don't think so,' Jameson said softly. 'We believe it was local.'

'If they were they're off their chump,' Desperate Dan commented. 'No-one takes on Douglas and gets away with it.'

'Mr Douglas,' Jameson corrected him with such a chilling smile it made Desperate Dan catch his breath.

'Aye, that's right. Slip of the tongue. Sorry. *Mr* Douglas.'

Billy noted that Cliff was sweating and hoped Jameson wouldn't notice or, if he did, he'd put it down to his presence.

'What about the rest of you? There's a hundred quid going begging,' Jameson queried.

With the exceptions of Billy and Mikey, they all shook their heads.

Jameson refocused on Billy. 'And what about you?'

'I've been out of circulation for a long time. I'm clueless about what's going on in Glasgow nowadays. Apart from my chinas here that is.'

That seemed to satisfy Jameson. 'All right lads. If you do hear anything I'm sure you'll get in touch. Mr Douglas would take it amiss if he thought anyone was holding out on him.' His tone became steely. 'This is important to Mr Douglas, understand?'

'Aye. Aye, we do,' several chorused in unison.

'See you then.'

And with that Jameson turned and walked away, crossing the hall to engage another person in conversation.

'If it is local, I wonder who the bampot is?' Mo Drysdale mused.

'Thank Christ it's not me,' Cliff declared, a little too enthusiastically for Billy's liking. He shot Cliff a warning look.

'So how about another game?' Mikey asked, seeing a table had come free.

He and Mo decided to play together, and up they went. Billy waited till Jameson had gone then jerked his head to Cliff that they should also leave.

'I should never have let you talk me into this,' Cliff complained bitterly, when he and Billy were alone together later. 'I should have known better.'

'Losing your nerve, son?' Billy queried contemptuously.

'You don't know that Jameson. He's sheer bloody poison, I'm telling you.'

'He can't be that good.'

'He sodding well is. Desperate Dan called him the hardest man in Glasgow which I wouldn't dispute. He's a professional you see, unarmed combat and all that malarkey. I saw him myself in action once, he was devastating. And as cool as ice throughout. He might have been some damned civil service chappie going about his daily business. He frightened the hell out of me and no mistake.'

Did he still need Cliff? Billy asked himself. The answer had to be no. At least where Douglas was concerned. So he'd let him off the hook. And looking on the bright side, it meant more money for him.

'All right Cliff, I'll work on my own from here on in.'

Cliff sagged with relief.

'But just remember this, breathe a word about what we've done, or I plan to do, and you're dead meat. You'd better believe I mean that.'

'Oh I do Billy, I do. And don't you worry, I'll stay stum. I don't want either you or Jameson coming after me.'

'Right then. I'll see you around.'

Cliff scampered away.

Perhaps he should play it really safe and 'do' for Cliff anyway, Billy reflected. That way the cat couldn't possibly be let out of the bag. He decided to give it some thought before finally making up his mind.

★   ★   ★

'I hardly ever see you anymore,' Moira McDonald complained to Roger, whom she'd let into her home moments before.

Roger sighed. 'I've told you, it's this new job of mine. It's playing havoc with my life all round.'

He ran a hand over his face. He was dog tired, as he'd come straight to Moira's from his shift at the Midnight Rooms. All he wanted was a bed and some kip.

He slumped into a chair. 'I could murder a cup of tea.'

'I'll put the kettle on.'

He stared at her backside as she filled the kettle at the sink. He'd always thought that was her best feature. Her gorgeous backside.

'How long can you stay for?' Moira asked, turning round.

'Half an hour.'

'Is that all?'

'It's hard to come up with excuses at this time of day. I can hardly say I've been to a Masonic meeting now, can I?'

Moira swore.

'And it's going to be worse when we move to Battlefield.'

She regarded him grimly, seeing their relationship rapidly disappearing down the pan. 'Do you have to flit there?'

'Catie insists, wants to better herself like,' he replied, which was only a half truth. It was his wish as much as Catie's, but that was something he wasn't letting on to Moira.

'I'll bet she's a real stuck-up cow, that wife of yours,' Moira bitched, tight-lipped with jealousy.

'She has become a little grand of late. It's hobnobbing with all those swells I suppose,' Roger reflected. He hated her working full-time when he was too. He was the man, he should be supporting his family. But what he hated most of all was the fact that she was earning three times as much as him. That really riled him. A woman earning three times as much as a man, it was obscene! But what could he do? It would be sheer lunacy to insist she stop and lose that income.

Then he thought about his own job which he'd come to loathe. It was so lonely being on your own all that time. He did have a wireless for company, but that was hardly enough. He missed the mateyness and general camaraderies of Black's, and also being out and about in the fresh air rather than stuck indoors. He ground his teeth in frustration. Reith Douglas was to blame for all this. He might have been their saviour but he'd gladly have seen the bastard in hell. Him and his swanky cars and all the rest of it.

231

'You look done in,' Moira sympathized.

'It's boredom more than hard graft, I can tell you. I'm nearly driven demented with it sometimes.'

'Maybe you can find something else?'

He barked out a laugh. 'Fat chance! You know what things are like. I'll just have to stay where I am and be grateful.'

'I've got a drop of whisky in if you'd prefer that to tea?'

He shook his head. 'A single dram and I'd nod right off in this chair.'

When the tea was made she brought him a cup, squatting and stroking the inside of his thigh as he sipped it. After a few moments, her hand strayed to his crotch.

'I haven't got the energy Moira. Honest. I'm sorry. Perhaps I shouldn't have come, but I didn't want to let you down having said that I would.'

She smiled up at him. 'We don't have to go to bed.'

That was a relief, he thought. Nor did she appear too upset about it either.

'You just lie back in that chair,' she crooned. 'And leave it all to me.'

He realized what she intended when she began undoing the buttons of his flies. He did as instructed and leant back.

Irene had had more than she should to drink, but thankfully Reith was so preoccupied he hadn't so far noticed.

'We're getting nowhere at all,' he declared, pouring himself a whisky which he topped up with soda. 'Jameson and the two men helping him have been everywhere, asking everyone, without any joy. They've even been round the gangs, the Cumbie, Tongs and the like with no luck there either.'

'Perhaps it was a London team on both occasions,' Irene suggested, hoping he might buy that.

Reith slowly shook his head. 'I just don't believe it.'

'And, eh . . .' she swallowed hard, 'how are you getting on with your investigations?'

'Nothing there either. Not so far anyway. I've still a few people left to see. Ex-runners who're proving difficult to get hold of.'

'Someone could be lying of course,' she said.

'I'm aware of that. But if they are they'll trip themselves up eventually.'

'How?'

He gazed over at her. 'A lot of money has been taken and if they're supplying inside information then they must be getting a substantial cut, cash they'll want to spend. Understand?'

'You mean someone spending more than normal?'

'Exactly. And if and when they do I'll hear about it.'

That wouldn't happen, Irene thought. He was barking up the wrong tree there. 'Can I have another g and t?' she asked sweetly, holding her glass out to him. 'Just a small one.'

Reith sighed. 'I saw Margie Finlay again today.'

'How is she?'

He took Irene's glass. 'Dreadful. It'll take her a long time to get over what happened, if she ever does. Those two were very, very close.'

Irene shut her eyes and shuddered inwardly. She hadn't been able to face the funeral or Margie Finlay knowing she was indirectly responsible for her husband's death. Her presence would have been sheer hypocrisy. So she'd pretended to be ill to get out of it, an excuse that Reith had accepted without question. He'd been somewhat preoccupied, but had paid for Finlay to have a grand send-off, poor bugger.

'More lemon?' Reith queried.

'Please.'

'By the way, did you ever see the doctor? You never mentioned it.'

'Yes, I did. He said I was run down and gave me a tonic.'

'Are you feeling better for it?'

Visiting the doctor had only been a smokescreen, the tonic her suggestion. 'Lots. Doesn't it show?'

'You're still looking below par,' he said, returning her glass to her. 'Perhaps a holiday?'

'Maybe later on in the year,' she prevaricated with a smile. She daren't leave Glasgow, Billy would have a fit. Reminded of Billy her stomach knotted in terror at the thought of what he'd threatened to do to Agnes, and for the umpteenth time since the threat had been made she had a mental picture of Agnes with her face slashed to shreds. She bowed her head so that Reith couldn't see her expression. What if Billy didn't keep his word and razored Agnes anyway out of sheer spite? The bastard was capable of it, being evil through and through. The idea that he might terrified her.

Oh Reith! she wailed inside her head. What had she done to deserve this? Things had been so good between them until Billy had appeared. How very different it could have been otherwise. If only she could tell Reith everything, confess, explain. But she daren't take that risk. Oh God help me, she prayed, please, please help me.

Reith, driving himself as Jameson was busy elsewhere, drew up outside number eighteen Speanside Road in Battlefield, the very road Irene had once wanted them to move into. The houses, on two floors, were recently built and semi-detached with pebble-dashed exterior walls. Each had a neat, if small, garden in front.

He picked up the gaily wrapped box from the passenger seat beside him and got out. Dishevelled, Catie answered his knock.

'Surprise!' he declared. 'I come bearing gifts.' And with that he handed her the box, kissing her chastely on the cheek at the same time.

'Who is it?' Roger called out from upstairs where he was wallpapering.

'Reith,' Catie called back.

Roger paused in what he was doing and cursed under his breath. What did *he* want?

'How's it going?' Reith smiled at Catie.

'A shambles. Stuff stacked everywhere. But we'll get it sorted out.' She returned his smile. 'Thank you again for giving Roger and myself time off for the move. It makes things all that much easier.'

'My pleasure.'

She gazed down at the box. 'And what's this?'

'The best way to find out is to open it.'

She laughed with pleasure. 'How exciting. I love surprises.'

And I love you, he thought.

Roger appeared. 'Hello, Reith. I didn't expect you to drop by.'

'I had a couple of free hours,' he lied. 'And thought I'd call in. Hope that's all right?'

'Of course,' Catie replied. 'Especially when you bring us presents.' She showed the box to Roger. 'From Reith.'

'Just a little house-warming thing. Nothing much,' Reith said.

Catie perched herself on a tea chest and began unwrapping the box, gasping in delight when she discovered six crystal spirit glasses. 'They're beautiful!'

Reith reached into the inside pocket of his coat which he hadn't yet taken off and pulled out a bottle of whisky. 'This is to go with them so we can all have a dram.'

Roger looked on sourly. He didn't want a drink but wouldn't

refuse in case he offended Reith whom he couldn't afford to offend. 'It's all very kind of you,' he declared, forcing a smile onto his face. The two men stared at one another, and for a brief moment their true feelings towards one another flowed between them. Then they were gone, masked again.

Catie extracted three of the glasses and placed them on the tea chest. Just for devilment Reith gave Roger the bottle and said, 'I'll let you pour.'

Roger realized the gesture hadn't been made out of politeness. He was being reminded, as if he needed to be, of how much lower on the totem pole he was to Reith. He could cheerfully have brained Reith with the bloody bottle. Nor had any of this interplay been lost on Catie who found herself reddening. She hastily took herself off to the kitchen for some water so that neither man would notice. When she rejoined the men carrying a small jug her complexion was back to normal.

'To your new house. May you find all the happiness in it you deserve!' Reith toasted.

It didn't strike Roger, who had no idea that Reith knew about him and his affairs, that that was a jibe directed straight at him.

They all drank.

'I've got some news for you, Catie,' Reith announced. 'Another present you could say.'

She looked expectantly at him, while Roger's face clouded over.

'I'm afraid we're losing Marlene to the bright lights of London. I'm sorry to see her go but can hardly stand in her way if that's what she wants.'

He paused, then went on softly, 'So I'm promoting you to her job, supervising the tables. It means an extra ten quid a week.'

Roger, who'd been about to have another gulp of whisky, nearly choked, while Catie's eyes widened in disbelief.

'Me?'

'You,' Reith confirmed.

'But there are others there with far more experience.'

'True. But you're quite capable and the one I've chosen for the job. You'll take over in a fortnight's time.'

'Oh Reith,' Catie whispered.

'Congratulations, darling,' Roger said and, getting a little of his own back on Reith whom he'd always strongly suspected fancied Catie, kissed her lustily on the lips. Reith's smile never wavered, but suddenly it was no longer as warm as it had been. As had happened so often in the past a picture of Roger and Catie in bed together flashed through his mind making him cringe inside.

'I can't thank you enough Reith. Honestly I can't.'

'I wouldn't give you the job if I didn't think you were up to it,' he declared, which was true enough.

'What if the others object?'

'They'd be wise not to,' he replied, meaning they'd get short shrift if they did.

'Forty pounds a week,' Catie breathed, shaking her head in bewilderment. 'Isn't it fantastic, Roger?'

'Fantastic,' he agreed. Now she was earning *four* times as much as him. How much did a man have to bear!

Reith, watching Roger's face, guessed what was going through his mind. Suffer you little shit, he thought. Catie's promotion had been arranged for more than her advancement. Reith knew the Glaswegian male ego only too well, being a Glaswegian male himself.

After a short while Roger made his excuses and returned to his wallpapering leaving Catie and Reith to chat. They talked books and he promised to pick up a copy for her of a book that she'd read a particularly good review of in the newspaper.

As he drove away Reith reflected on his love for Catie. He hoped that one day she would come to him of her own accord.

Billy swore with amazement as he studied the lists of names Irene had provided him with. It was a comprehensive run-down of who was on the take from Reith. Was there anyone in authority who wasn't? Of course, there were many, but from the number of names on the lists it didn't seem that way. Billy gave a thin smile. And someone who took from one source would take from another, namely him. The point was he now knew precisely who he could approach without making mistakes. Naturally, until he built himself up, he'd have to start in a small way. But that would grow and grow as he prospered, he promised himself.

One thing was certain, Douglas was inviolate. Any thoughts he'd had of killing the man had to be put from his mind, at least for the present. To do so would bring the wrath of God down on his head.

He leant back in his seat and mentally figured out how much he had stashed away. It was almost enough for his first legitimate move, he decided. And the amusing thing was that it would be funded by Reith's own money. He didn't only like that, he revelled in it.

Catie gaped at the full-length beaver-lamb coat Reith was holding. They were in his office and Milla had been issued with strict instructions that they weren't to be interrupted.

'For me? You must be joking!'

'No joke, I assure you.'

She reached out and stroked the front. 'It must have cost a fortune.'

'What's money between friends?' he smiled.

'I've always wanted . . . dreamt . . . but never thought . . .' She trailed off to stare at the coat in awe.

'Why don't you try it on?'

'Can I?'

'Of course.'

He continued to hold the coat as she slipped into it, immediately hugging the lapels to her face. 'It's a perfect fit,' she declared. Reith, who'd personally gone down to the female staff changing-room to find out what size she took, would have been upset if it hadn't been.

She twirled round, eyes ablaze with excitement.

'It looks good on you,' he commented.

'I feel . . . like royalty!'

He laughed.

'Or a Hollywood film star.'

'If you don't like it I can always change it?'

'No no, it's simply wonderful.'

He thought of all the things he'd have liked to buy her, shower her with. The coat was just the first.

She gazed at Reith in sudden consternation. 'But Roger . . .'

'Sod Roger,' he interjected. 'Or there again . . .' He paused dramatically for several seconds. 'I could always return it.'

'No!' she squealed. 'I can't let this go. I couldn't.'

That's what he'd thought.

'But I still have to explain it to Roger.'

'How about the story you used before about getting it cheap through the club? Tell him it fell off the back of a lorry. Or better still, tell him it was left here one night months ago and has never been reclaimed. And that when you mentioned it I gave it to you.'

Now it was Catie's turn to laugh. 'That's preposterous. No woman would leave a coat like this behind, far less not come back and reclaim it.'

'Then say it fell off the back of a lorry and you got it dirt cheap. You can always embellish the story by saying several girls in the club bought ones just like it. He'll never know that isn't true.'

She hugged the lapels to her face again. 'Why did you buy it for me, Reith?' she asked, suddenly deadly serious.

He held her gaze. 'Call it an early Christmas present. Or a bonus for doing so well in your new job.'

He turned away. 'I saw it in a shop window and instantly thought it would suit you. Do I need more reason than that?'

She didn't answer.

'And in case you're feeling guilty, remember the giver gets more pleasure from these things than the receiver. So humour me.'

'Reith?'

He turned again to face her.

'I don't want there to be any misunderstandings between us.'

'Like what?'

'You know,' she said softly.

'Do I?'

'Oh yes, I think so.'

'Catie I . . .' He trailed off. Much as he wanted to declare himself he knew the moment wasn't yet right. 'I understand,' he stated instead.

'I don't want you to be under any illusions?'

Like she was about Roger, he thought bitterly. That little shit was still cheating on her, betraying her. And yet she was totally unaware.

'I was thinking,' he said, changing the subject, 'you and Roger have never been out to Newton Mearns. How about coming this Sunday for lunch?'

Her face lit up. She'd adore to see his house and what was inside. Nor would Roger decline such an invitation. He could hardly do that after all Reith had done for them.

'Sounds great,' she replied.

'Fine. Be ready for twelve and I'll pick you up.'

He had a thought. 'I wouldn't wear the coat if I were you. We don't want Irene asking awkward questions.'

She thanked him and gave him a peck on the cheek before leaving his office. Reith smiled thinly when she was gone. He knew that he would do anything if only Catie would agree to become his wife.

Chapter Twenty

Catie was dumbstruck. The house in Newton Mearns was even more lavish and sumptuous than her wildest imaginings. It screamed of exquisite taste, and money.

'That's an impressive picture,' she commented to Irene, pointing to a canvas hanging in splendid isolation on one wall.

'It's a Pepoe,' Irene declared airily. 'Reith bought it in Edinburgh.'

'Is he famous?'

'Very,' Irene nodded. 'And Scottish.'

Roger stared about him, green with jealousy, thinking what all this must be worth. It made their house in Battlefield, which he was so proud of, look like a dog kennel.

'How's your glass?' Reith interrupted his thoughts. 'Need topping up?' They were drinking champagne.

'Please.'

Reith crossed over to where the bottle stood in a silver-plated ice bucket. 'And you ladies?'

Roger was ill at ease with his surroundings, half expecting the Queen and bloody Prince Philip to come strolling in. It just wasn't the sort of place for him. Reith tended to Irene and Catie, then refilled Roger's glass. 'Drink up, there's plenty more where that came from,' he smiled.

Catie glanced down at a green table ornament displayed on a finely worked, filigree coffee table. She knew it was rude to ask, but her curiosity got the better of her. 'Is that jade?'

'Beautiful, isn't it?' Irene gushed, thoroughly enjoying herself. 'And yes it is.'

A maid in traditional black and white appeared. 'Lunch is served, madam,' she informed Irene.

'Thank you, Catriona.' Turning to the others she said, 'Shall we all go through?'

Catie's eyes widened with disbelief when they entered the dining-room which made Reith smile to himself. It could all be yours, my darling, he thought. Think about that. All you have to do is leave Roger and come to me.

When Catie and Roger got home all she could do was talk about the Douglases' fabulous house, much to Roger's intense annoyance and irritation.

The young Reith took his mother's hand as they headed down the path that led to his father's grave. Reith didn't remember his father as John Douglas had died when he was only two years old leaving his mum to bring him up. He and his mother were very close as a result.

When they reached the grave Martha Douglas stared sadly down at it, Reith still holding her hand. How she missed her man, as much now as the day he'd died. In her mind's eye she saw again the pitiful figure he'd become, thin to the point of being skeletal, the once handsome face now deeply lined and haggard, the spectre of death already in his haunted eyes. He'd coughed again and again into his hanky, his body shaking from effort and agony. Then he'd lain back gasping in air, apologizing as he always did after a coughing attack. He'd worried about Reith. How was she going to manage all on her own? She would somehow, she'd assured him for the umpteenth time. Everything would be all right. For her and Reith she'd thought, but not him. It would never be all right for him ever again.

'Can I put the flowers in the pot, Ma?' young Reith asked.

She nodded and handed him the bunch of early daffs she'd bought.

Reith walked up the side of the grave to the headstone and laid the daffs beside the pot from which he now removed the withered blooms placed there on the last occasion they'd visited. He then placed the daffs in the pot, arranging them nicely as his ma would have done.

'I'll throw these in the bin,' he said to his mother and went off to where the bin was located some yards distant.

Martha watched him go, thinking how like his da he'd become.

240

There was a lot of her in him, too, but physically, and especially facially, he looked more like John. He was a good and intelligent lad whom John would have been proud of, she thought, just as she was. Her 'wee man' as she often referred to him. And he was doing well at school, top of the class recently, for once beating that brainy Lawrence Sands which was quite an achievement. University material his teacher had once said, but of course that was out of the question. No, it would be a trade for him when he was old enough. A pity, but that was how it would have to be.

She turned her attention once more to the grave, seeing John, as he'd been before consumption had taken its toll, lying sleeping under the earth. Consumption, she thought bitterly. How many had that killed in Glasgow? A legion. But then what could you expect considering the conditions under which they lived and worked. So much of Glasgow was a vast, sprawling, stinking slum where people often didn't have enough to eat and the sanitary arrangements were a grisly joke. Glasgow, she hated and loved it at the same time. But it was all she knew, and all she ever would know.

Reith wondered if his ma was going to cry, she sometimes did when they visited the grave. It always upset him dreadfully to witness those tears, making him want to take her in his arms and comfort her as though he were a grown man. He'd have done anything for his ma, walked over broken glass in his bare feet if that had been required.

She looked so tired he thought, but then she worked extremely hard and such long hours too. When he was big enough he'd see she stopped and never grafted again. A promise he fully intended to keep. He stared at her, adoration showing clearly on his face. He was a lucky boy because he had a ma in a million.

He wondered again what his da had been like. His ma had told him about his father often enough, but that wasn't the same as actually knowing his da, being in his company, hearing him speak, watching him doing things.

Reith glanced up at the sky. 'It's going to rain soon,' he said, recognizing the signs.

'Aye,' Martha agreed, glancing up as well.

As always, she was reluctant to leave but didn't want either Reith or herself to get soaked in a downpour.

'We'll come again soon,' she declared.

Reith slipped his hand back into hers and, together, they walked silently away.

241

Reith stared down at the same grave which now contained both his parents, Martha eventually succumbing to the same consumption that had killed her husband. It had been her strict instruction that she was to be buried with her beloved John, reunited at last in death. Consumption, tuberculosis as it was now called, Reith loathed those two words for the disease which had robbed him of his parents. What would his mother have thought of him now? he wondered. She'd have been amazed to say the least.

He wiped a tear from the corner of his eye. 'I'm sorry I forgot you for a long time Ma,' he whispered. 'But there was nothing I could do about that. You're back inside my head now, in my memory. And I'll never forget you again. I only wished you'd lived Ma, there's so much I could now give you to make up a little for the hard times. So much.'

Reith straightened his hunched shoulders and took a deep breath. 'Goodbye Ma, goodbye Da. I'll come again soon.'

He put on his hat, turned up the lapels of his crombie against the cruel, biting wind that was blowing through the cemetery, then, as he and Martha had done so often in the past, he walked silently away.

Roger stared hard at Catie, angry with her, angry with himself. She even held herself differently nowadays, he brooded. There was a poise and self-assurance about her that hadn't been there before. It was as though she was turning into a different woman from the Catie he'd married. And all thanks to that bloody job at Fanny's and the fabulous money she was earning. Forty pounds a week! It was ludicrous. And shaming for him earning only ten. It was as if – he struggled with the idea – their roles had become reversed. Which in a way they had as she was now the main bread-winner.

'You look like a fucking tart,' he suddenly snarled.

Catie stopped what she was doing and stared at him in astonishment. 'I beg your pardon?'

'You heard me. You look like a fucking tart all dolled up as you are. A painted Jezebel.'

Had she put on too much make-up? Catie wondered. Overdone it? She didn't think so. As for the dress she was wearing, there was nothing tartish about it. Why only the previous week Reith had said how becoming it was.

'What's wrong with you today? You've had a face on you ever since you got up.'

'There's nothing wrong with me,' he snarled in reply.

She raised an elegantly shaped eyebrow. 'There is from where I'm standing.'

He fought back the impulse to leap from his chair and slap her. Talk about cheek!

Andrew entered the room, immediately sensed the atmosphere, glanced quickly from Catie to Roger, and left again.

'Did you have a bad night?' Catie queried sympathetically.

'Why ask? All you care about nowadays is that job of yours. It's all we ever hear about round this house.'

'I find my work interesting and exciting, so it's natural to talk about it,' she protested.

'Not boring like mine,' he snapped back.

She regarded him in consternation, sorry that he found his job boring, but there was nothing she could do about it. Besides, he should be thankful to be in work even if it did have its shortcomings. Without Reith's help he might still have been idle.

Then she had a thought. 'I could speak to Reith,' she proposed hesitantly. 'Perhaps he might be able to find you something out at Whiteinch Dog Track or the Ibrox Speedway? You'd have plenty of company in either place. Or maybe he can suggest somewhere else. He has his finger in so many pies as you know.'

That infuriated Roger. 'I won't go crawling on my hands and knees to him. And you won't either. So forget it. I'll stay put, thank you very much.'

'Suit yourself,' Catie replied, thinking he was being totally unreasonable.

'I will!'

It was funny, he thought. Moira McDonald didn't hold a candle to Catie, and yet he kept on seeing her. If it had come to a straight choice Catie would have won without question. There again, variety was the spice of life. It was like having a favourite boozer, just because you went there regularly didn't mean you didn't get the urge to pop into others. Roger yawned. Thinking of boozers made him fancy a pint and a natter with whoever might be there. He lurched to his feet and announced his intentions.

'I'll be gone when you get back. I'm going into town as I have a hairdressing appointment,' Catie said.

'There's nothing wrong with your hair the way it is. Waste of good money if you ask me,' he grumbled.

'It's my money to . . .' She hastily broke off, knowing that was a red rag to a bull.

He glared at her. That's right, he thought, rub it in. 'I'll see you when I see you,' he declared, and strode from the room.

She stared after him in dismay. He could be so bad tempered at times, often quite unjustifiably so. Reith on the other hand . . . She stopped herself thinking along that tack. Reith was Reith, Roger Roger. Chalk and cheese, the pair of them. And it was Roger she loved, whom she married and who was the father of her children. And things weren't easy for him, she knew only too well how mortified he was that she was earning more than he. His pride was injured which was perfectly understandable.

She winced when the outside door slammed shut.

Irene sat staring into space, wondering what on earth the outcome of the mess she was in was going to be. Try as she might she just couldn't get Billy, and all the problems related thereto, out of her mind. She sighed, a long drawn-out sound that whistled mournfully from her mouth. Reith glanced across at her, noting her abstracted expression, and the haunted look in her eyes. His own mind flew back to the days when they'd first met, and courted. How he'd loved her then, the slip of a girl who'd caught his imagination and heart.

'Are you all right?' he asked tenderly.

Irene started. 'Pardon?'

'You were miles away. Are you all right?'

She brushed a stray wisp of hair from her forehead. 'Fine. Just thinking.'

'About what?'

'Nothing much. This and that.'

He detected the lie in her voice and frowned. What was she keeping from him? His frown deepened when he wondered if it was to do with Catie. Did she suspect something was going on and that was what she'd been speculating about?

'It's a lovely evening,' Irene commented, gazing out of an adjacent window. It was a Sunday, the one entire day Reith spent around the house.

He also gazed out the window. 'Yes.'

'I adore the gloaming. Don't you?'

He smiled, the gloaming was a traditional time for lovers in Scotland. On many an occasion in the past he and Irene had walked

244

it together, the pair of them hand in hand, surrounded by soft twilight, saying silly and endearing things to one another. 'Yes,' he agreed again. Irene started quietly to sing the old Harry Lauder number about roaming in the gloaming with your lassie by your side.

'I haven't heard you sing for ages,' Reith declared when she'd finished.

She hadn't much to sing about nowadays, she thought bitterly.

'You should do it more often. I like to hear it,' he added.

'Do you?'

'You know I do.'

For a brief moment their eyes locked, then Irene tore her gaze away. 'I simply got out of the habit, I suppose,' she murmured.

He noted how the light was playing in her hair, making it sparkle in places as if tiny fairy lights, flashing on and off, were buried there.

'A penny for them?' she queried.

'Your hair is looking particularly nice right now.'

Irene blushed at the compliment. Reith settled back in his chair, surprised to find himself for once, while at home, strangely content.

'I give up,' Jameson declared to Reith. 'We've been everywhere, spoken to everyone. Nothing. If whoever did those two jobs was local then they're keeping their mouths well and truly shut.' He paused. 'How about you?'

Reith shook his head. 'The same.'

'So what do we do now?'

Reith considered that. 'I honestly don't know. Continue to keep our eyes and ears open, I suppose.'

Jameson sat on the edge of Reith's desk. 'What about Scotland Yard?'

'Same there. Zero.'

'They're still working on it though?'

'According to Dodd they are.'

'It *could* be a London team,' Jameson mused.

'Fanny's perhaps, but not Finlay. And a coshing connects both jobs. It has to be local. I just know it.'

Reith drummed the fingers of one hand lightly on his blotter. 'And I still think they had inside information. But who? That's the question. Who?'

'Who?' Jameson echoed with a smile.

★   ★   ★

'I can't come, I'm laid up with the flu,' Irene said into the telephone.

There was a pause. 'You wouldn't lie to me, sweetheart, would you?' Billy queried suspiciously.

'I've got the flu, I assure you. I'm in a dreadful state.'

'Hmmh,' Billy murmured, still not convinced she was telling the truth. She sounded all right.

'You wouldn't want to catch it, would you?'

He certainly wouldn't, he thought. The last time he'd had flu, while banged up in the Bar-L, he'd suffered for almost three weeks. He didn't wish to repeat the experience. 'I'll ring you at the end of the week, see how you are,' he declared. And hung up.

Irene cradled the phone and leant on it. She'd decided to tell him it was flu rather than merely a germ as she'd thought that sounded more convincing. Also, according to Mrs Murphy, there was quite a bit of flu going around, which would help corroborate her story. She returned to her chair and the latest edition of the *People's Friend* she was reading.

Billy cruised slowly past the Douglases' house, peering up the driveway and noting that a single light was on, then went further down the street and turned round again. He parked the car, got out and walked towards the driveway. It was a quiet street, particularly at that time of night, with no-one else about.

Irene's Jag wasn't in the driveway so he padded quietly over to the garage, going straight to the window inset in one wall. From his pocket he produced a torch and shone it through the window. The Jag was there, which meant what? Only that she hadn't gone out in it. She could be with Douglas himself, or could have taken a taxi. He decided to give her the benefit of the doubt and believe she was laid up.

Before leaving the driveway he stopped and stared at the house silhouetted in the moonlight. Someday he'd have a house like that, he promised himself. A big house, Rolls Royce, servants, the lot. He wanted it so much he could almost taste it. Then he began to wonder what was in the house. There must be oodles worth nicking.

Somewhere nearby a dog barked, making him tense. Guard dog? If it was roaming the Douglases' property and came at him he'd brain the bastard. Dogs didn't frighten him.

He kept hold of his torch as a potential weapon as he silently retraced his steps to the street. Seconds later he was sliding into his car and closing the door. The dog barked again and he realized it was coming from an adjacent property. There hadn't been any danger after all.

He shone his torch on his wrist-watch. He was meeting Cliff Kelman later, as the pair of them had to do a burglary together. Or so Cliff believed. Billy smiled crookedly in the darkness.

'Have you heard the news?' Desperate Dan Henderson queried as Billy joined him and others in the Caley Snooker Hall.

'What news?'

'Cliff Kelman was murdered last night. Knifed to death.'

Billy pretended to be shocked. 'You're joking!'

'It's true,' Mo Drysdale nodded.

Billy leant back in his seat and reached for his cigarettes. 'Cliff dead,' he murmured, lighting up.

'They found him in an alleyway,' Mo added.

'Have the polis any idea who did it?'

'Not that we know,' Mikey Sullivan replied.

'Makes you think, doesn't it?' Mo said. 'You never know the moment till the moment after.'

'I still can't believe it,' Billy sighed. 'Cliff was one of the best, a real pal. Who would want to kill him?'

'He might have been up to something, double crossed someone,' Desperate Dan reflected. 'There again, this is Glasgow, after all. He might simply have been in the wrong place at the wrong time.'

'Aye,' Billy agreed. 'Who found him?'

'A couple of beat polis. He'd been stabbed, then had his throat cut.'

Billy screwed up his face. 'Nasty.'

'You and he were doing quite well recently, too, weren't you?' Mikey said.

Billy shot Mikey a hard look. 'We were. Pulled off a few nice ones. Nothing spectacular mind, but nice.' He paused, then asked, 'Why?'

'Just stating facts that's all Billy. Just stating facts.'

'I'll miss the sod,' Billy declared softly, almost tenderly. 'He and I went back a long way.'

Billy stood up. 'This has upset me, I'm going for a drink. I take it you'll all be at the funeral, whenever that is?'

'Oh aye,' the others chorused. 'We'll be there.'

Billy nodded his approval before striding away.

247

Chapter Twenty-one

Catie's latest pride and joy was the new washing machine she'd bought, a real luxury if ever there was one. She hummed happily to herself as she began loading it, thinking she'd dash out and do a spot of shopping while it was on the go. She planned to buy several other luxury items shortly, a refrigerator and a television set. My, how they were coming on in the world! She reflected they were a far cry from the poverty and grind of Bridgeton. Those days seemed a lifetime away.

'Now,' she muttered, sorting out the mound of dirty clothes piled at her feet.

Article followed article into the machine. Then she picked up one of Roger's work shirts.

'Damn!' she exclaimed, noticing one had lost a front button. She held the shirt up to check there weren't any more missing. If she hadn't singled out that shirt she might never have caught the faint whiff of perfume lingering on it. But, thanks to the missing button, it *was* singled out, and she did.

Catie frowned and brought the shirt to her nose. It was unmistakably perfume, and not hers. It was a brand she'd never worn. Now why would Roger have perfume on his shirt? And a work shirt at that. There weren't any females in the Midnight Rooms when he was on duty, he worked alone.

'Oh dear,' she exhaled. Surely not! He couldn't be . . . Her arms dropped to her sides and her shoulders slumped. She suddenly felt completely empty inside. No, she thought. There had to be an explanation. Someone he'd bumped into in the pub perhaps? That couldn't be it. The sort of pubs Roger patronized in his work clothes didn't have females in them. They were all male boozers where a woman wearing reasonably expensive perfume wouldn't have been seen dead. A barmaid? That was out as well. Such pubs only employed male staff.

So where had the perfume come from? A hated name she hadn't thought of in a long time popped into her mind. Linda Brasil. It couldn't be her, that had been years ago. But . . . if not Linda Brasil, someone else, someone new who he was . . .

'Careful Catie,' she cautioned herself. 'Mustn't jump to conclusions, girl. Mustn't let your imagination run riot.'

She'd speak to Roger, ask him how his shirt had come to be this way. Nor would she accuse him of anything, she mustn't play the jealous wife. Roger was bound to have a satisfactory and acceptable explanation.

Roger cursed inwardly. Bloody hell! How could he have been so remiss? It was stupid of him. Stupid, stupid, stupid!

He smiled. 'Perfume on my shirt?'

'Here, smell for yourself.'

'You're right. It is perfume. Not yours?'

Catie shook her head.

His thoughts were racing. 'Are you sure?'

'It's not mine, Roger. That's a brand I've never used.'

'Hmmh!' he exclaimed innocently. 'Damned if I can think how it got there.'

Roger furrowed his brow in apparent puzzlement, and slowly shook his head. 'Astrid was here earlier in the week. Perhaps . . .'

'I've already thought of that. It isn't hers either,' Catie informed him.

'Well, all I can imagine is that I picked it up at the club. That it somehow got rubbed onto me there.' He brightened, regarding her hopefully. 'You know what those clubs are like, you work in one yourself. They reek at times.'

That didn't satisfy Catie. 'But how would you have got it on your shirt? That doesn't make sense.'

'Search me,' he murmured.

Catie didn't believe that was the explanation, it simply didn't ring true. 'You haven't been kissing anyone behind my back, have you Roger?' she teased lightly.

'Not me, darling. I swear.'

He wished he could think of something more plausible, but couldn't. 'Anyway, it's hardly important,' he said, dismissing the matter. 'Now what's to eat? I'm starving.'

Catie tossed the shirt aside. He might have dismissed the matter as irrelevant, but she hadn't, not by a long chalk.

Roger found himself sweating as he launched into some idle chit-chat in an attempt to keep Catie's mind off the subject of the shirt and perfume. He didn't succeed, albeit neither shirt nor perfume was mentioned again.

'But I wasn't wearing perfume!' Moira McDonald protested. 'I never do when I know you're coming. That was our agreement.'

'But you must have been for some to get on my shirt.'

Roger was frightening Moira, she'd never seen him enraged before. Up until then their relationship had always been sweetness and light, with never a cross word between them. She didn't like this side of him at all.

'I wasn't,' she persisted.

'It was your perfume all right, no-one else's. I recognized it.'

She backed off in alarm when he stalked towards her. 'You must have been careless, put some on without realizing.'

Was he going to hit her? Please God, no. He was a powerful man, capable of doing who knew what damage to her. And how would she explain any facial marks to Ronnie, her husband?

'Don't touch me!' she exclaimed.

He stopped and glared at her. 'You must have,' he repeated through gritted teeth.

She shook her head. 'I didn't, Roger. I wouldn't make that sort of mistake. I'm far too careful.'

'Then explain the fucking perfume!'

She was at a loss as to how she could do that, convinced she hadn't been wearing any. 'I can't.'

'You can't,' he sneered, twisting his face grotesquely.

'Maybe . . .' She trailed off.

'Maybe what?'

She was watching his bunched hands, praying he wasn't going to lash out. 'Maybe there was perfume already on my clothes. That could be it.'

Roger considered that argument. It was possible. 'Have you got a drink in the house?'

She nodded, and scuttled past him, keeping an eye on his fists.

One thing was certain, she and Roger were finished. She didn't want anything further to do with a man who was capable of hitting her. And Roger, in his present mood, was certainly that.

'Already on your clothes,' he repeated thoughtfully. That could be the answer.

'I really am sorry for any trouble it might have caused,' she said, pouring him a hefty whisky.

Roger let out a long exhalation of breath, and as he did so, he relaxed, his fists unfurling. 'What annoys me most is that I should have picked up the perfume on my shirt. If I had I would have done something about it.'

She handed him the whisky. 'What did your wife say?'

'Asked how it got there of course, for which I had no plausible answer.'

He gulped down some of the contents of his glass. 'It quite threw me, I can tell you. At least she was reasonable about it and hasn't mentioned it since.'

Roger shook his head. 'My mind just went blank, which isn't like me at all. I'm usually fairly quick witted. But not on that occasion, worst luck.'

Still scared, Moira kept her distance from Roger. It would be a pity to lose him, she thought, he was such a wonderful lover. He was far better than Ronnie who was extremely mundane in that department, boring to be exact. Roger could make her feel things Ronnie never had, or would.

'Fucking perfume,' Roger swore vehemently.

'As I said, I'm always so careful when I'm seeing you, Roger. I never wear a drop, just as we agreed early on.' She paused, then added, 'The last thing I wanted was to get you into trouble with your wife, or me with Ronnie come to that. As I've told you before, I'm very fond of Ronnie. He's a damned good provider.'

Roger finished his whisky.

'Would you like another?'

He thought about that. 'No,' he replied. 'That was enough.'

'I think in the circumstances we shouldn't meet for a while,' she suggested hesitantly. 'We don't want any more accidents.'

He nodded his agreement. 'You're right. Just to be on the safe side.'

She took the empty glass from him. 'I'm not in the mood now for lovemaking, Roger. You gave me quite a turn there.'

He wasn't in the mood either, so that suited him. 'All right.'

'I'll see you out.'

When they reached the front door he pecked her on the cheek. 'I'll be in touch.'

She forced a smile onto her face. 'Right.'

He knew he wouldn't be, and so did she.

Moira was highly relieved when he was gone. A sad ending to a fulfilling sexual relationship. But it was over. She shuddered, recalling the look on his face when she'd thought he was about to hit her. She hated violence, especially when it might be directed towards her.

Catie came to the end of her weekly report which always took place with Reith in his office. It was part of her job to recount precisely what had been going on at the tables and how the various dealers and croupiers had done. She was also expected to discuss any problems, professional and domestic, that might be bothering any of the staff.

'Succinct as usual, Catie, very good,' Reith nodded.

He leant back in his chair and regarded her across the desk separating them. 'And how's Roger?'

There it was again, she thought. That knowing look in his eye as if he knew something she didn't. It was so exasperating!

Then she thought again of the perfume on Roger's shirt, and wondered. *Did* he know something?

'Reith . . .'

'Catie?' he smiled.

'Can I ask you a question?'

'Certainly.'

'When you ask about Roger it often seems to me more than merely a casual enquiry.'

He raised an eyebrow. So, it had come out at last. 'Really?'

'Yes,' she stated emphatically.

He didn't reply, preferring her to continue.

'Is there?'

He rose and went to the small bar. 'Drink?'

'This isn't a special occasion and I'm still on duty.'

'I said to you once before, they're my rules to bend whenever I choose. Drink?'

'A small sherry then, please.'

He placed the glass in front of her, then sat down again. 'Is there a particular reason for your asking or is it just idle curiosity?'

She would have to confide in Reith, she realized, not entirely sure, because of their history, that she wanted to. But, in the circumstances, she didn't really have a choice.

'You and I are good friends,' she said.

'Uh-huh.'

'And once upon a time, more than that.'

'Lovers,' he articulated.

'Yes.' She had a sip of sherry. 'This isn't easy for me, Reith. In fact it's damned difficult.'

He thought then with satisfaction that he knew what was coming. She suspected Roger.

'Because of our past?'

'Yes,' she whispered.

'It's Roger, isn't it?'

She stared at him.

'You'll have to say, Catie,' he prompted. 'I won't.'

'So you *do* know something?'

He kept his face impassive, and didn't reply.

She drank more sherry to give herself courage. Then she told him about the perfume.

'That the only time?' he queried.

She nodded. 'I've been examining his clothes ever since and looking out for any other signs that he might be . . .' She swallowed hard. 'Involved with someone else.'

'It isn't much to go on, Catie. It could be entirely innocent.'

'It could be,' she agreed. 'But having caught him out before I'm naturally highly suspicious.'

'Quite. And rightly so.' He hesitated before adding, 'Leopards and spots and all that.'

Her eyes narrowed. 'You do know something, but how?'

'Do you still love Roger?' he prevaricated.

'Yes.'

Reith's heart sank. 'And does he still love you?'

'I thought so.'

'But maybe he doesn't if he's having an affair?'

Catie knocked back the rest of her sherry. 'If he is I honestly don't understand why. I rarely . . .' She glanced away, embarrassed. 'Refuse him. Rather I accommodate him, if you understand me.'

Reith did, only too well. If Roger had been present he could cheerfully have killed him from a combination of jealousy and of retaliation for what he was doing to Catie. He nodded instead.

'And I'm still not bad looking—'

'You're beautiful, Catie,' he interrupted softly, 'absolutely beautiful.'

She blinked. 'Do you really mean that?'

He ached to take her into his arms, stroke her hair, kiss her eyes, nose, lips. For her to be his. Now, to the grave, and beyond should there be such a thing.

'Yes Catie, I do.'

A strange expression crept over her face which made her glance away again. 'Thank you,' she husked.

Reith felt they were closer at that moment than since the time of their affair. No, he corrected himself, she was closer to him.

'I've got something to show you,' he declared, opening a drawer in his desk.

He rummaged through some papers and other items till he found what he was after.

'Read this,' he said, handing her Cairns's report.

While she was doing that he poured them both another drink, watching her face as she read. She'd gone quite pale.

'As you can see from the headed paper, Cairns is a private investigator,' he said when she'd finished.

'You had Roger followed?'

'Yes.'

'But why?'

'Because I wanted to know what was what. It was of interest to me.'

She glanced again at the report, then back at Reith. 'When did this happen? The report isn't dated.'

'Shortly after I bumped into you at Daly's that day.'

She swallowed hard. 'I see,' she murmured.

'I take it this Mrs McDonald isn't a family friend?'

Catie shook her head.

'Ever heard of her?'

'Not before now.'

Reith asked, 'Could there be an explanation other than the obvious one?'

'Not that I'm aware of.'

'And Roger has never mentioned her to you?'

'No,' Catie whispered in reply.

'There might be nothing in it of course. It's only circumstantial evidence.'

254

'But you don't believe that, do you?'

'You'd suspected him on a number of occasions before the Brasil woman, isn't that right?'

'Yes.'

'So, perhaps he's just been a bit more careful since then. Determined not to get caught out again.'

'The bastard,' Catie whispered.

'To be fair to Roger, the report doesn't say he's sleeping with this Mrs McDonald. Only that he regularly visits her. We could be misjudging the man.'

Catie thought bitterly how unlikely that was.

'What are you going to do, confront him?' Reith queried.

'I'm not sure yet. I have to think this through. The last thing I want to do is make a false accusation.'

'He could hardly blame you with his track record,' Reith pointed out. 'I would say a full explanation is in order.'

'In my place would you confront him?'

Reith nodded. 'Without a doubt. But that's your decision, not mine.'

Catie took a deep breath. 'He'll go berserk if he finds out you've had him spied on.'

'Then don't tell him.'

'How else could I explain knowing about this Mrs McDonald?'

'We'll think of something.'

God, she thought, hurt, angry and humiliated at the same time. If he was sleeping with this Mrs McDonald female then . . . She felt sick, just as she'd done all those years ago when Linda Brasil had come to her door. But he could be innocent, she reminded herself. There was certainly cause for doubt. There was no actual proof of infidelity.

She looked at Reith. 'Why didn't you show me this report before now?'

He took his time in replying. 'Put it this way, I had my reasons.'

'You didn't want to hurt me, is that it?'

'Partly.'

'What else, Reith?' She was aware even as she asked the question that it was a loaded one.

Reith rose, picked up his glass and went over to the window where he stood with his back to her. He slowly sipped his drink before answering. 'I still love you Catie and always will. It's all as simple as that.' There, he thought, it was out at last.

She'd guessed of course. There had been so many giveaways, the beaver-lamb coat was a prime example. But it had been more than that, a feeling, the way he brightened whenever she came into his presence, the look in his eyes which he sometimes hadn't been able to mask.

'What about Irene?'

'I told you before, we muddle along.'

'Only you don't love her?'

'It's always been you ever since that night in the fog, Catie. There will never be anyone else.'

That last remark touched her deeply. 'Oh Reith!' she breathed.

He turned to face her, smiling crookedly. 'It's a funny old world, isn't it? I'm successful to the point where I can have virtually anything I want, except what I want most. You.'

'My job, Roger's . . .'

'My reasons there weren't entirely altruistic,' he confessed. 'Having you at Fanny's meant I got to see you every working day.' He paused, then said, 'Do you find that pathetic?'

'Not in the least, Reith.'

'Take it as a compliment then.'

'I do. An immense one.'

'And you are beautiful, Catie.' Then, teasing, he mischievously added, 'Slightly crooked nose, big bum and all!'

'Reith!'

'Your words, not mine. To me both are perfect.'

'Which doesn't alter the fact they're still crooked and big.'

He laughed. 'Vain cow. You really are.'

'Am not!'

He wagged a finger at her. 'But vanity born out of what I ask myself? Could it be insecurity?'

'Possibly,' she admitted quietly.

He studied her thoughtfully. 'You and I are so alike, Catie, and at the same time so different. I find it fascinating.'

She dropped her gaze. 'Do you regret our affair, Reith?'

'No, never. You hurt me more than you'll ever realize. But I don't regret it. And you?'

'Me neither,' she whispered.

'I'm pleased about that. We're both being positive about it, to have felt anything else would have taken away from what we had, which would have been a terrible shame.'

'I thought you might have come to hate me.'

'I'm not like that Catie. I accepted your decision, difficult though it was. But love turning into hate never entered into it. Not for one moment.'

She felt enormous warmth for him then. He was a far better man than Roger, she thought. In his position Roger would have loathed and detested her, gone out of his way to harm her if he could. Reith's reaction had been quite the opposite.

'I think you'd better get back to work,' Reith declared.

She immediately stood up. 'Certainly.'

'Do you want to take that report with you?'

She gazed at the report which she'd placed on top of his desk. 'Do you mind?'

'Not in the least.'

She picked it up. 'Thank you.'

'I'm not certain that thanks are in order, considering what it contains.'

'Circumstantial evidence you said. It could still be that.'

He didn't reply.

Confront Roger or what? she wondered as she returned downstairs. She didn't know yet.

He was going to marry Irene, Billy decided. Why? Well, he didn't love her, but then he'd never loved anyone, not even his parents. He did find her exceptionally attractive though, had done for years. And she was Reith Douglas's wife, the big man himself. A title he wanted, lusted after, just as he lusted after Irene. He wanted what Douglas had, *all* that he had: wife, money, clubs, businesses, everything. And he'd get them or his name wasn't Billy Boyne. It would take time of course, and a great deal of careful, not to mention devious and crafty, planning. But some day he'd supplant Douglas, take his place.

Billy stopped ruminating to gaze round the empty premises which were up for sale. They were perfect for what he had in mind. This was where he'd really start, where *his* empire would begin. It was a pity about Cliff's money, he reflected. If only he could have laid his hands on that. But he knew, from conversations in the past with Cliff, that it was in a dozen different bank accounts all over Glasgow which is where it would stay now, as Cliff had no next of kin. Oh well! he mentally sighed. No use worrying about it. It was beyond his reach and that was that.

First the premises, then the various licences that had to be

257

procured. There wouldn't be any trouble with the latter, thanks to Irene. He knew exactly who to approach, and the amount of 'bung' required.

In the meantime, he focused on another job. A third strike against Douglas. Billy laughed. Douglas was going to be hopping.

She loved Roger, but what did she see in him? Catie wondered, watching him eat. She noted with surprise that he'd put on weight recently, he was showing the definite beginnings of a paunch. Mind you, it was hardly surprising the way he ate nowadays. Without money restrictions to hold it in check, his appetite had increased considerably; it was nothing for him to ask for second helpings, thirds occasionally, despite the fact his plate was always piled high to begin with.

She studied his face, wondering if it was the face of an adulterer? Oh, it had been once, but was it again? How almost angelic he seemed, as though butter wouldn't melt in his mouth. Except she now knew better. Was Reith right? Was he simply being more careful since the Linda Brasil episode? Was Mrs McDonald only the latest in a long line stretching back God knows how long?

'How's the tea?' she asked.

'Fine,' he mumbled in reply through a mouthful of food.

She thought of Reith and his table manners. Although the two men came from Bridgeton there was a vast difference between them at table. Reith held his knife and fork properly, as did she, but Roger . . . Well, being charitable, all she could say was there was great room for improvement.

Was she becoming a snob? Was working at Fanny's and mixing with the people there giving her ideas above her station? She didn't believe so. She'd always been more refined than Roger who had a certain baseness about him that would never change. She winced when he burped.

'Sorry,' he apologized before shovelling more food into his mouth.

What if she did confront him with the report? Would he confess? Hardly likely, that wasn't his style. He'd think of something to explain away those visits, just as he'd done in the past with Linda Brasil and the others. So how did she go about tackling the problem, exacting the truth? She was damned if she knew. She could do a Linda Brasil in reverse, she mused. Knock at Mrs McDonald's door and accuse her face to face. The only trouble with that was, what if the accusation wasn't true? She'd have stirred up a right old hornets' nest then. Roger would be furious with her. So accusing Mrs McDonald face to face was out. Perhaps her best bet was to play the waiting game. See if she could come up with any further tell-tale signs (how that brought back memories!). Yes, she decided. That's exactly what she'd do. Play the waiting game. She always had the report to fall back on should she decide otherwise.

'Anymore?' Roger enquired eagerly.

Smiling, she got up to reheap his plate.

Chapter Twenty-two

'What!' Reith exploded into the telephone. It was early one Sunday evening and he was relaxing over a drink with Irene. He had just arrived in from work a short while ago.

'I see,' he muttered, anger darkening his face.

He uttered a few more terse words, then cradled the receiver. Picking it up again he dialled a number.

Irene watched him in consternation, certain she knew what this was all about. She hastily gulped down the remains of her whisky and soda and crossed to the decanter from which she poured herself another.

She glanced at Reith, watched him wait for his call to be answered. Was there no end to this nightmare? If only Billy Boyne would get run over by a bus, or have a heart attack, anything that would remove him from her life, and poor Reith's.

'Jameson, Reith. Tony Noble was coshed as he was about to put the takings for Fanny's into the night safe . . . No, no, he's OK apparently.'

Reith listened for a few seconds, then said, 'If there was any doubt left this knocks it out the window. They're local and have inside information. How else could they possibly know that the Saturday night takings aren't kept in the safe till Monday any more?' He listened intently. 'That's agreed then. First thing tomorrow I want you out on the streets offering a thousand quid to whoever will turn him or them in. Meanwhile, I'm going back to square one at my end. There's a leak and I'll damned well find it . . . Right, good night. Love to Ena and Ian.'

Reith hung up and stood staring at the telephone, visibly fuming. 'This has gone beyond a joke,' he said, suddenly rounding on Irene. 'The entire Saturday night's takings from Fanny's lifted for the second time.'

He took a deep breath. 'There *has* to be someone in the organization supplying them with information. Nothing else makes sense. Well, God help whoever it is when I get hold of them. And get hold of them I will. You can count on that. As for whoever's doing the coshing, they've got Finlay to pay for apart from anything else.'

'Jesus!' he swore, and smacked a fist into the opposite palm. 'These guys are playing me for a total mug, which they'll regret. Oh yes, they'll regret it all right, I swear.'

'Shall I top you up?' she asked, indicating his glass.

He replied with an affirmative grunt.

Reith began to pace up and down. 'It's partly my own fault, mind, I've relied on my reputation for protection too much. Been too lax, thinking no-one would be stupid enough to pull such a stunt, far less three. Do you know how much money they've now got away with?'

Irene shook her head.

'I don't know the exact figure offhand but a small bloody fortune. A small bloody fortune!'

Irene winced, her hands shaking again as she gave him his topped-up drink. If Reith noticed he probably put it down to the dreadful situation.

'Beyond a joke,' he repeated. 'Beyond a bloody joke.'

A little later he told her to go off to bed, as he intended to stay up and think. She could still vaguely hear him pacing below, before, at last, she sank into a troubled sleep.

'Have you heard the news?' Desperate Dan Henderson asked Billy as he joined them at the Caley Snooker Hall.

'Don't tell me someone else has been murdered?'

'No, nothing like that. We had a chap called Heraghty in here, Douglas has been robbed again and is now offering a grand to anyone who'll finger the guilty party or parties. How about that, eh? A thousand smackers!'

Billy whistled. 'A lot of mazoolah.'

'You can say that again,' declared Mikey Sullivan.

'Anyone any ideas?' Billy queried.

Desperate Dan shook his head. 'None. Not that we know of anyway.'

Billy's face was impassive, but inside he was laughing. Of course no-one knew because the only person who shared his secret – excluding Irene, of course, but she didn't count as the last thing she would do was talk – was dead and buried. He was as safe as houses.

'Well well,' Billy murmured.

Desperate Dan winked at Billy. 'Pulled off a nice little tickle last night. Sweet as a nut.'

'Good for you,' Billy congratulated him.

'How about yourself, how are you doing?'

'I'm going away for a while.'

'Oh aye?'

'Down south. But keep that to yourself.'

'Of course, of course, Billy.' Desperate Dan and Mikey waited for him to elaborate which Billy wouldn't normally have done, but did so now. He wanted to give some explanation as to how he was going to afford to buy and set up a club.

'I've had wind of something really big down there. And I mean, really big.'

Desperate Dan's eyes widened.

'A chance in a lifetime which I'm going to grab with both mitts. If it comes off I'll be sitting pretty when I get back. So wish me luck.'

'All the luck in the world old china,' Desperate Dan enthused, while Mikey nodded his agreement.

Billy leant conspiratorially towards them. 'And not a word. Keep this between yourselves.'

'You bet Billy. You can trust us,' Mikey assured him.

He could trust them all right, Billy thought. Neither would be able to keep his mouth shut. Which was precisely what he wanted.

Jack McCall crouched and signalled Reith to remain where he was. He then gestured he was going forward.

This was proving bloody, Reith thought. Every bit as difficult, not to mention costly, as they'd been led to expect. The Krauts were putting up fierce resistance. He gazed up at a wave of Dakotas flying overhead, similar to the ones which had dropped them only hours before. Hours? It felt like days.

Reith shrank into the wall he was leaning against as a German bullet whined past. There was the unmistakable thunk of it hitting flesh, followed by a deep groan. Who was that? Reith wondered, glancing round. But he couldn't spot the victim.

And then the machine-gun opened up, spraying bullets in a deadly, chattering hail. But it didn't last for long, because a grenade exploded and the machine-gun fell silent.

Grinning, Jack, face dirt streaked like his own, rejoined him. 'Got the bastard,' he declared. 'Now let's . . .' Jack never finished what he'd been about to say. He suddenly jerked and went spinning away to fall, crashing to the ground, his front stained bright red.

Instantly Reith was at his side. Grabbing Jack he swiftly hauled him behind the wall he'd been leaning against. A swift look confirmed the worst.

'Shite!' Reith swore.

Jack opened his mouth to speak and a trickle of blood ran from one corner down his chin. 'I . . . I . . .' The voice was a laboured whisper. Reith bent his head to hear, but Jack uttered no further words. When he looked again at Jack's face he saw that his friend was dead.

Reith exhaled slowly. Somewhere ahead there was another grenade explosion followed by a rapid exchange of fire. Reith was kneeling, rooted to the spot, staring at Jack. He'd never had such a good pal as Jack McCall.

He was still kneeling when there was a momentary pain in his head, as though he'd been swatted. Then nothing.

Reith stood by Charlie's grave, shoulders hunched, hands deep in the pockets of his crombie, tears in his eyes.

'I finally remembered, Charlie, how Jack died. It came back at long last.'

He paused, then went on, 'He died a hero, Charlie, you would have been proud of him. I only wish . . . I could have told you that while you were alive. We were together at the time, he and I. He'd just taken out a machine-gun when he got shot in the back. It was quick, Charlie, he didn't linger. A few seconds at most. I was still by the body when they got me. Only I was lucky, I survived.'

He smiled at the grave, remembering Charlie, remembering Jack. 'You once said I'd become like an adopted son to you, Charlie, Jack would have appreciated that. For we were like brothers.'

'Brothers,' he repeated, emotion choking his voice. Reith waited till the tears had dried, then he wiped his face with a hanky before returning to Jameson and the Daimler.

Catie waited till Roger had fallen asleep before getting out of bed and putting on her dressing gown. Frowning, she stared down at him. Now where had he learned that little trick? She'd thought she'd known his entire sexual repertoire, they'd been married long enough for goodness sake! So where had *that* come from? Mrs McDonald? She considered the matter further. Was it something spontaneous that had simply happened? Possibly. She couldn't entirely rule that out. Such things did happen during lovemaking.

But it was the *way* he'd done it, as though it was part of an established routine and not something new at all. She'd been looking for another sign, another giveaway, and now it seemed to her she'd found it.

'You left word you wanted to see me?' Reith smiled at Catie. It was a quiet night at Fanny's, but then it was still early, so there was plenty of time for things to change.

'Can you spare me a few minutes?'

'Of course. Shall we have coffee in the bar?'

'Now what's this all about?' he queried when they were seated and Charlotte had taken their order.

'I have a favour to ask you.'

'Fire away.'

She glanced around, making sure they weren't being overheard. 'It's about that private detective you hired. Do you think you could do so again?'

When he didn't reply she hastily added, 'Roger and I have a joint account now you see and if I took out the amount of money it's certain to cost in one go Roger would be bound to—'

Reith held up a hand, silencing her. 'The money isn't a problem, Catie, I'll gladly pay for Cairns myself.'

'No, no, I'll pay you back on a weekly basis—'

'I said it isn't a problem, Catie. Now explain yourself.'

She dropped her gaze. 'It's embarrassing, Reith. And, eh . . . could be hurtful to you.'

Again he didn't reply.

'It's something that happened this morning when Roger and I were in bed together. He, eh . . .' Her face coloured. 'Did something different that he's never ever done before.'

'I see,' Reith murmured.

'Don't ask me what, I've no intention of going into detail. But it's more or less convinced me he has been sleeping with someone else.'

She paused, then said, 'You know what it's like being married, you get to know your partner's ways.'

'No need to elaborate, Catie. I fully understand what you're getting at.'

They were interrupted then by Charlotte with their coffee, which Reith thanked her for. Then the pair of them watched her walk away.

'So when do you want the new surveillance to begin?' Reith asked when Charlotte was out of earshot.

'As soon as possible.'

'Mrs McDonald?'

Catie shrugged. 'That's who was named in the report last time.'

Images of Catie and Roger in bed were flashing through Reith's mind. What had Roger done to arouse Catie's suspicions? It was agony to think about.

'I'll speak to Cairns tomorrow morning and set the ball rolling,' he stated.

When she reached across and touched his hand, it was like an electric shock jolting through him. 'Thank you, Reith.'

'Anything for you, Catie, you know that.'

She decided to change the subject. 'How are you getting on with the latest robbery?'

His face immediately darkened. 'Like the others, we're getting nowhere. Even a grand for a name isn't getting any result.'

'What do the police say?'

'That they're doing everything they can. The trouble is there's absolutely nothing to go on. But we'll find whoever's responsible, I swear it.'

The steeliness in his voice, the absolute determination, brought goosebumps out on her arms. 'I'm sure you will.'

He hesitated, then said softly, 'Always remember what I told you in my office.'

'That you still love me?'

'Yes.'

'I'll always remember, Reith. I'll never forget. How could I?'

'That's fine then.'

He took her hand in his and gently squeezed it, wishing they could remain there together for the rest of the evening. 'How about a drive in the country sometime, just you and I?' he suggested.

'Is that a good idea?'

'You tell me.'

She thought about it. 'I don't know, Reith. I honestly don't. To be truthful I'm very confused.'

'About Roger?'

'It's been so wonderful between us since the Linda Brasil business, now this. I really did believe he'd given up his old ways to stay on the straight and narrow.'

Poor Catie, he thought. She deserved so much better than Roger Smith. He smiled, himself to be precise.

'What are you smiling at?'

'Secret thoughts.'

'Concerning me?'

He nodded.

'Do tell.'

'If I did they wouldn't be secret anymore.'

'Nice thoughts?'

'Naturally. I never have nasty ones about you.'

'And Roger?'

'All the time.'

She laughed.

'Do you blame me?'

'No.'

'I'm glad about that.'

'One thing more,' she said. 'Do you think Cairns could get a photograph of this Mrs McDonald?'

Reith smiled again. 'You want to view the opposition. See what you're up against?'

'Something like that.'

'And what if she's an absolute stunner? A complete and utter knockout?'

'I'll be sick. Then I'll rush round and scratch the bitch's face to shreds.'

He regarded her thoughtfully. 'I believe you might just do that, Catie. I think it's in you.'

'Well, you know what they say about a woman scorned.'

'If I was this Mrs McDonald I'd run for the hills,' he said, half joking, half in earnest.

Catie nodded, her expression sober. 'Advice the woman, I won't call her lady, might be wise to heed.'

'I don't care how good-looking she is, she'll never be as beautiful as you, Catie. Not in a thousand years,' he declared.

Her face softened. How sweet he was, she thought, and how good to know someone felt that way about you, saw you in a glowing light. 'Now I'd better get back to work before my boss accuses me of skiving. He's a holy terror you know, a real slave driver.'

Reith grinned. 'Sounds dreadful.'

'Except he does have his moments. Very decidedly so.'

She began to rise and he followed suit.

'Thank you Reith, for everything.'

'My pleasure.' He took her by the arm, savouring the contact, as they left the bar.

For the umpteenth time Reith studied the list he'd drawn up of all those who'd known about Tony Noble and when he'd be using that particular night safe. Himself, Jameson, Milla, several people in the general office. Well it certainly wasn't him, and he'd have trusted Jameson with his life. Milla? She'd denied imparting or mentioning such information to anyone vigorously, as had those in the general office. He certainly couldn't believe she'd leaked facts for personal gain. If she had, he was an appalling judge of character. As for the others . . . And then he was struck by a new thought. What if it was Noble himself who'd carelessly mentioned his whereabouts? Could that be it?

He pressed the intercom. 'Milla, contact Tony Noble and get him on the line.'

'Yes, Mr Douglas.'

He then sat back in his chair and wondered how Cairns was getting on. He couldn't wait for the second report to be delivered.

'Not a word to a soul, Mr Douglas, I swear on all that's holy,' Tony Noble assured Reith, utterly appalled.

'Are you absolutely certain? Perhaps it just slipped out without you realizing?'

'No, Mr Douglas,' Noble replied, shaking his head. 'I've never breathed a single syllable about it to a living soul.'

'Not even the wife?'

'Not even the wife. Everything about your business is kept strictly confidential.'

Reith stared hard into Noble's face, and believed that the man was telling the truth. Damn! he swore to himself. Well, it had been worth a try.

'Besides,' Noble went on, 'I have myself to think about.'

Reith frowned. 'How so?'

'We both know what happened to Finlay. I have no intention of ending up in the morgue like him. I was in the war, too, you know. Remember "Careless Talk Costs Lives"?'

'OK Tony,' Reith sighed. 'You can go.'

'Another bloody dead end,' Reith mused aloud as the door snicked shut.

'No more robberies, you mustn't. They'll have you next time,' Irene said to Billy Boyne, almost hysterical.

'And why's that?'

'He's hired a security firm to take the money from the clubs to the various night safes he now uses. And the chap who's replaced Finlay has four blokes with him at all times, very hard men indeed I can assure you.'

Billy digested this latest development.

'He blames himself for being too lax before. But no more. There's been a complete shake-up.'

So, that side of things was finished, Billy reflected. No matter, he had enough of Douglas's money to do what he wanted.

Irene went over to Billy and grasped his arm. 'Say you won't do anything else. Please?'

'I don't know,' Billy replied slowly, enjoying her anxiety. 'I think I need more persuading.'

'Are you mad?'

His mood changed in an instant. His free hand flashed to crack across her cheek. She cried out in pain and alarm. His dark, glittering eyes were frightening as they bored into hers. 'Don't call me that ever again. Understand, sweetheart?'

She nodded.

'Not . . . *that*,' he hissed.

'All right Billy, I won't. Honest.'

'For . . .' His lips twisted into an evil grin, 'I might just make that call on Agnes after all if you do.'

Irene sobbed, now utterly terrified, not for herself but for her daughter.

★   ★   ★

'Hello Joe,' Reith said coolly as Joe Biles and Jameson entered his office. Biles was one of his runners whom he'd inherited from Charlie.

'Hello Mr Douglas,' Joe smiled, wondering what this was all about.

'Have a seat.' Reith gestured to the chair in front of his desk, waiting till Biles had sat down before doing so himself. Jameson took up a position directly behind Biles.

'So what can I do for you Mr Douglas?' Biles asked.

Reith made a pyramid with his hands and stared at Biles over the apex of his fingers. 'Life's been good to you recently I hear.'

Biles frowned. 'That's right.'

'Been spending quite a bit of money.'

Biles's frown deepened, and suddenly he was uneasy. He became horribly aware of Jameson at his back. 'Some.'

Reith raised an eyebrow. 'More than some I'd say. A fair amount.'

'Isn't a crime, is it?'

That caused Reith to smile. 'Not in itself it isn't, Joe. Though other things are.'

Biles started to sweat. He didn't like this at all. 'What things, Mr Douglas?'

'Robbery.'

'Robbery!' Biles started to rise but was restrained by Jameson who forced him back into the chair.

'What are you getting at, Mr Douglas?'

'This money you've been spending so lavishly. How did you come by it?'

'That's easily explained.'

'Oh?'

'It's my wife's. She came into a wee inheritance, see.'

'An inheritance? Since when did people like you and your wife come into inheritances, Joe?'

And then it clicked with Biles, who wasn't unintelligent, what this was all about. 'You don't think I had anything to do with the robberies you've had recently, Mr Douglas?' he queried, aghast.

'Have you?'

'Absolutely not. I know nothing about them. On my life.'

Reith leant back and studied Biles now shifting uncomfortably in his chair. 'Tell me about this inheritance Joe.'

'From my wife's uncle who did well for himself. Not a great deal mind, though a lot to us. A few hundred nicker. It's all legal and above board, Mr Douglas. We've got a letter at home from the lawyer if that would help convince you.'

'A letter?'

'On headed paper and everything. Addressed to the wife.'

Reith bit back his disappointment, though pleased for Joe's sake. Joe was an old and valued employee which was why he'd had Jameson bring him in so Reith could question him personally rather than leave it up to Jameson. He'd felt he owed that to Joe.

'It would seem you're in the clear then,' Reith stated.

Joe sagged. 'I wouldn't cross you, Mr Douglas, you've always been fair and square to me, so you have. Besides, only a headcase would do that.'

Jameson, still standing behind Biles, smiled thinly.

'I'll tell you what Joe. Why doesn't Jameson run you home and you can show him this letter? That all right?'

'Certainly, Mr Douglas. Fine by me.'

Reith felt sorry for the man who, for a few moments there, must have had a terrible fright. 'Would you care for a dram before leaving, Joe?'

'Oh yes, please.'

Reith signalled Jameson to pour one out, at the same time indicating he wouldn't have any.

Biles drank his dram in one large swallow.

'Reith?'

'What Irene?' He'd just got into bed and had presumed she was asleep.

'Cuddle me.'

He gathered her into his arms. 'What's wrong?'

'Nothing, I just want cuddling.'

Her thin body trembled in his arms. 'I think you should go and see the doctor again. You're still not well.' When she didn't reply he said, 'Is there anything I can do?'

She only wished there was. 'I love you, Reith,' she whispered.

'And I love you,' he lied.

Chapter Twenty-three

Once out of Dumbarton and heading towards Renton and Alexandria, Reith let the Riley Roadster off the leash, the powerful two and a half litre engine growling under the bonnet as the car flew along the road.

Catie laughed with pleasure. 'You're a demon driver, Reith. Who do you think you are, Stirling Moss?'

'Scared?'

'Not in the least. I'm enjoying myself.'

He glanced sideways at her, thinking how adorable she looked. He'd been delighted when, mentioning the subject of a drive in the country again, she'd accepted.

'That's a pretty coat,' he commented. It was a new one she'd bought herself, grey wool cut in the raglan fashion.

'Thank you.'

He changed down through the gears as they approached a sharp bend, then quickly up again when they were round it. 'You should learn to drive,' he said.

'I've thought about it.'

'So what's stopping you?'

'Nothing really.'

'It would make life an awful lot easier for you if you had a car. Shall I buy you one?'

'You can't do that!' she exclaimed.

'Why not?'

'What would Roger say?'

'He wouldn't have to know. Tell him you bought it yourself.'

'He'd know from our joint bank account that I hadn't.'

'There are always ways and means,' Reith murmured, pressing down further on the pedal as they overtook another vehicle.

Now it was Catie's turn to glance sideways at him, her feelings a combination of admiration and tenderness. 'Would you ever cheat on me?' she suddenly asked.

That startled him. 'Never.'

'You cheated with me on Irene.'

'That's different, and you know it. If I had you, Catie, it would never cross my mind to look at another woman.' Then he added, jokingly, 'Well . . . look maybe, but that's as far as it would ever go.'

'Any news of that report yet?'

'Soon,' he replied. 'I instructed Cairns to take his time, make it thorough.'

'Right.'

'Are you hungry?'

'Starving. I could eat a scabby-heided wean.' Reith laughed. That was an old Glasgow expression, meaning scabby-headed child, an expression he hadn't heard in a long time.

'I'll try to do better than that for you,' he declared.

'And you?'

'Hungry all right, and not just for food. I could eat you from top to toe.'

A little shiver ran through her. She always enjoyed the way Reith spoke to her.

Once through Alexandria Reith drove on towards Balloch, their destination, which was on the banks of Loch Lomond. He knew from past experience that the hotel there served excellent food. On reaching Balloch he parked the Riley in the car park and they both got out.

'Shall we have a look at the loch before we go inside?' he suggested.

'If you like.'

'It's what you like, Catie. That's what's important to me.'

'You can be a real smoothie at times,' she teased.

'Not really, and certainly not where you're concerned. I mean what I say.'

For a moment their eyes locked, then Catie glanced away. She found her heart was pounding as they moved towards the lochside where they halted on a bank sloping down to the water.

Catie started when his hand slid into hers. 'Reith!'

'What?'

'I'm not sure—'

'Does it offend you?' he interjected.

'No.'

'Well then.' His grip tightened. 'What excuse did you make to Roger about today?'

'I said I was instructing at the club. I knew he wouldn't question that.'

They stood for a few moments in silence, savouring the tranquil beauty of their surroundings. 'I wouldn't mind living out here one day,' Reith murmured. 'It's one of my favourite places.'

'You'd give up that beautiful house of yours?' she queried in surprise.

He shrugged. 'To come and live here, yes.'

'Irene might not appreciate that idea.'

'Who mentioned Irene?' he smiled.

'I see.'

'Do you?'

She wasn't sure she did. 'What are you getting at?'

'How would you feel about living here? Would it appeal?'

She glanced around. 'Very much.'

'With me?'

She stared at him, hard. 'I don't quite understand?'

'If you left Roger and came to me we could live here together.'

'Oh Reith!' she whispered.

'I'd divorce Irene and you Roger. Then we could get married, be man and wife.'

She didn't know what to say. The thought of living here in a big house was certainly tempting. But there was Roger . . . And what if he wasn't having an affair with this Mrs McDonald? What if he hadn't betrayed her?

'Well?' Reith asked softly.

'I'm still starving. Can't we go in and eat?'

'Of course.'

He never mentioned the subject again that day, nor did she. But as they were driving away he saw a thoughtful, contemplative look in her eyes as she gazed out of the car windscreen and he knew she was considering his proposal, which was enough for now.

Everything was coming along dandy, Billy thought, strolling through the premises he'd acquired. Painters and decorators were everywhere, a veritable swarm of them, and the air was filled with the combined sounds of sawing, hammering and drilling.

Obtaining the various licences he'd needed to open had been a doddle, knowing, thanks to Irene, whose were the right palms to grease. His plan was to open the following month, providing the club was ready, of course, which it would be, or there would be hell to pay.

As for staff, he'd interviewed a number of people and had quite a few more to see. That side of things was also moving along satisfactorily.

Naturally, with the resources available to him, it would be a small club, tiny compared to Fanny's. But The Cat Club was just the beginning.

'The Cat Club,' Reith mused.

'That's right,' Jameson nodded. 'Due to open in a couple of weeks, I believe.'

'Gambling?'

Jameson nodded again.

Reith considered that. 'Who's the owner?'

'A chap called Boyne.'

Reith went very still, and felt the blood drain from his body. 'Christian name?'

'William.'

So, it was him. Irene's old paramour. He hadn't even been aware that Boyne was out of prison.

'I know something about Boyne,' Reith stated casually. 'Opening a club is a departure for him. Any idea where he got the money for it?'

'I thought you might ask that so I made some discreet enquiries. Word is he pulled off a big job down in England somewhere, but I haven't any details.'

'Hmm-hmm,' Reith murmured.

'So, what do you want to do?'

'Nothing for the moment. Let it go ahead, but keep an eye on the place. I want to know what's what.'

'Understood.'

Reith sat back in his chair when Jameson was gone. Boyne, the man Irene had been in love with. *Been?* Perhaps she was still. And now he was out, on the loose again. Did Irene know that? Had he been in contact? And . . . were they seeing each other again?

Reith sighed. A new club and one owned by Boyne needed a great deal of thinking about. Boyne of all bloody people! He remembered his reaction to finding out about Irene and Boyne, the confrontation between himself and Irene, her confession that she loved Boyne and the effect that had had on him.

'Boyne!' he said aloud, loathing the name.

Reith stood staring out of his office window waiting for Catie whom he'd sent for. Cairns's report was on his desk. It had made enormously disappointing reading.

He'd briefly toyed with the idea of scrapping the report altogether, and having similar headed paper run off and falsifying a new report. But he'd come to the conclusion that would be stupid. Accusing Roger of something he wasn't doing simply wasn't on. If Roger was to be hoisted it had to be with a genuine petard.

'Come in,' he called out when there was a knock on the door. It was Catie, as he'd expected. 'Hi,' he smiled.

She stared at him expectantly.

He pointed. 'Cairns's report is there. You'd better read it.'

He went back to staring out the window while she read, and managed to turn round again just as she finished it.

'There's no mention of the McDonald woman,' she stated.

'No.'

'He didn't visit her once while Cairns was following him.'

'So it seems.'

Reith cursed inwardly as relief crept over her face. Damn and blast Roger for being in the clear.

'His visiting her in the first place might have been completely innocent, after all, then?'

'Or they may have ended the affair.'

That was true, she thought. Well, if he'd been involved with Mrs McDonald, and there was no real proof that he had, he wasn't any more. Nor, apparently, was he involved with anyone else.

'What do you think?' Reith asked.

'That I'm back to square one not knowing either way.'

'Are you going to give him the benefit of the doubt?'

'What else can I do? I'm certainly not going to accuse him in any way. That's right out of the question.'

Reith gave her a wry, crooked smile. 'So you'll let things go on as they are?'

275

Catie nodded. 'A whiff of perfume and a sexual variation are hardly hard evidence.'

And us? Reith wanted to ask, but didn't. Anyway, being realistic he told himself, there was very little *us* to talk of. A declaration of love, a drive in the country, speculation about a house, a proposal . . .

'You'd better get back to work,' he declared harshly, and turned his back on her once more.

'Reith?'

'What?'

'I, eh . . . I'm sorry.'

'He's fucking around, Catie, I'd bet on it. And that's not wishful thinking either. Like I've said before, leopards and spots.'

'It might well be wishful thinking, Reith. You want him to be doing what you just said, and because you want it so much you've come to believe it.'

'I don't think so, Catie.'

She went over to him and touched him lightly on the shoulder. 'I won't jeopardize our marriage, Reith, not without proof.'

Proof he'd get, Reith swore to himself, somehow, someway, he'd find proof.

'I take it there isn't a photograph of the McDonald female?' Catie queried, still profoundly curious about her.

'Cairns didn't bother as Roger never went to see her. Why, do you still want one?'

'If it's possible.'

'I'll arrange it then.'

'Thanks, Reith, for everything. Now I'll get back to work like you said.'

She kissed him on the cheek before she left the office.

Roger had been told to expect a new workmate who turned out to be a chap called Alastair White. The two of them shook hands after they'd introduced themselves.

'I can't tell you how delighted I am to have company,' Roger declared. 'It's lonely in here all by yourself.'

'I can imagine.'

A personable bloke, Roger thought. He and Alastair should get on well.

'As no doubt you've had explained, I'm here because of the security shake-up. Two night-watchmen are seen to be better and safer than one.'

276

'It's a good idea,' Roger agreed.

'Did you know this McKendrick who got coshed at Fanny's?'

Roger shook his head.

'Terrible business, eh? And they've never caught the bastards either.'

'I'll show you round. It's a sizeable place,' Roger said.

It was great having someone to chat to, Roger reflected later. The long lonely nights would be a thing of the past. He couldn't have been more pleased.

Reith studied the gilt-edged card that had arrived in that morning's post. Imagine Boyne having the effrontery to invite him to the opening of The Cat Club. Talk about impertinence!

There again, Boyne wasn't aware he knew about him and Irene all those years ago. And it would be interesting to meet the man. Should he go? He'd think about it.

Boyne eased his way out of the company surrounding him and approached Reith, beaming a winning smile. He was wearing a flashy suit Reith wouldn't have been seen dead in.

'Mr Douglas I understand. How good of you to come.'

Reith stared into those dark eyes and knew instinctively he was dealing with a thoroughly bad man. Reptilian, he thought, that's what Boyne was, reptilian.

Billy offered his hand which Reith shook. 'It's kind of you to ask me,' he replied.

'Not at all. It's you who's being kind in coming. You're the big man in Glasgow when it comes to clubs, after all.'

'This is my associate Jameson,' Reith said.

Jameson and Billy shook hands, Jameson's face impassive. 'We met before,' Jameson declared.

'That's right, at the Caley Snooker Hall. You were looking for someone.'

Jameson didn't reply.

'Tell me, did you ever find him?'

Jameson slowly shook his head.

'Sorry to hear it.'

Billy crooked a finger and a scantily dressed waitress carrying a tray of champagne came hurrying over.

'You will join me in a drink?' Billy said, taking two glasses which he handed to Reith and Jameson. He then picked up one for himself.

277

Reith knew it was up to him to make a toast. 'To The Cat Club. I hope it's successful.'

'I'll certainly drink to that,' Billy responded.

Cheap champagne, Reith thought, having taken a sip from his glass. Nasty stuff.

'I didn't know you were a man of means when we met in the Caley,' Jameson commented casually.

'Looks can be deceptive,' Billy replied with a smile.

Not in your case, Reith mused. There was nothing deceptive about Boyne's looks whatsoever. He was an evil villain through and through. What in God's name had Irene seen in him? That was a mystery.

'Will you play?' Billy asked, indicating the gaming tables.

'I'm afraid we can't stop. We only called in for a minute,' Reith informed him.

'Oh, that's a pity.'

Reith gave Jameson his glass to dispose of. 'Anyway, we'll be on our way. Interesting to meet you.'

'And to meet you, Mr Douglas. You're quite a hero of mine.'

'Is that so?'

'Oh yes. I admire what you've done tremendously. You're a real success story.'

'I'm glad you think so.'

Jameson returned without the glasses. 'All the best then,' Reith said, and moved towards the door with Jameson at his side. Billy watched them go, beaming from ear to ear.

'What do you think?' Reith asked when he and Jameson were outside on the pavement.

'Him or the club?'

'Both.'

'He's dangerous, with a vicious streak. Not a man to be trusted under any circumstances. The club . . . well, let's just say it'll appeal to a certain element.'

Reith knew exactly what Jameson meant, and he thoroughly agreed with him.

'What did you make of him, Reith?'

'Reptilian was the word that sprang to mind. He reminded me of a snake, the poisonous variety.'

They climbed into the Daimler. 'Have you found out anything further about that job he pulled in England?' Reith queried as he settled back.

'Not really. Plenty of speculation but nothing concrete. One thing I have been able to establish and that is he did leave Glasgow for a while, and did go south on the London train.'

'Hmm-hmm,' Reith murmured.

'Want me to keep digging?'

'Yes. And another thing, that thousand quid we have on offer for a name, up it to two.'

'Shall do.'

Reith dismissed Boyne and The Cat Club from his mind. He had other, more important, matters to think about.

'How was your smoky?' Irene asked the following morning at breakfast.

'Lovely.'

'There's nothing like a nice Arbroath smoky.'

'No,' he agreed.

'More coffee?'

'Please.'

He watched her pour. 'I went to the opening of a new club last night.'

Irene hesitated for a fraction of a second before replacing the coffee pot on its stand. 'Oh?'

'Called The Cat Club.'

'Any good?'

'Not really. But it'll do business. Owned by a chap called Boyne. Billy Boyne.'

Irene paled. 'Who?'

'Billy Boyne.'

She dropped her gaze and attacked what remained of the fish before her. 'These really are delicious,' she muttered.

Reith lifted his cup and studied her over the rim, noting that her hands were trembling ever so slightly.

She suddenly pushed her plate away and rose. 'Must get on. I'll see you when you get home.' She came to his side and pecked him on the cheek. 'Bye darling.'

'Bye.'

He felt immeasurably sad when Irene was gone. There had been a time when he'd enjoyed taunting her, but not any more. With a sigh he picked up the post and began flicking through it, stopping once he recognized a letter from Cairns.

As he was slitting the envelope it struck him that it might be a

279

good idea to have Cairns, or the man's associates, keep a watchful eye on the house. Burglary was a speciality of Boyne's, after all.

Reith glanced through the list of serious crimes that had been committed in England during the dates that Boyne had been absent from the city, a list supplied by Dodd. There was no clue whatever as to which one Boyne had been involved in. Nothing in Boyne's police record, a copy of which he also had to hand, shed any light on the matter. A huge consignment of furs taken in Birmingham was a possibility, or even a bank robbery in Newcastle. Reith sighed with exasperation, sat back in his chair and gazed up at the ceiling in contemplation.

Catie made sure Roger was fast asleep before taking the photograph she'd been given the night before from her handbag and studying it. Mrs McDonald was a smartly dressed woman about her own age. She wasn't exactly pretty, though she wasn't plain either. She was the sort of woman you would pass in the street and never give a second glance.

Had Roger been sleeping with her? And if so, why? What would attract him to someone like that? One thing was certain, Catie thought with satisfaction. She was far better looking, there could be no doubt about that. Mrs McDonald couldn't hold a candle to her.

Catie couldn't make out what Mrs McDonald's figure was like; her coat obscured it. But it appeared ordinary enough. Her legs weren't bad mind, quite shapely really. Maybe she had large breasts, Roger would have been drawn to those. It wouldn't be the first time he'd remarked on a woman's breasts, saying something like, 'you'd get a right handful with those'. Her own were fairly modest in size, neither large nor small, just perfect she'd always thought.

She sighed. All this was speculation. There was no proof, none at all, that Roger had been to bed with the woman. All she knew for certain was that he had visited her a number of times which could easily be connected with Masonic business or with something else.

The trouble with Roger was he could be such a secretive bugger, that was second nature to him. He was secretive and, dare she say it, slightly sly. Yes, sly as a fox, she thought grimly. That was Roger to a T. There was no slightly about it. Perhaps this Mrs McDonald . . .

'No!' Catie exclaimed softly. This was daft. She'd wanted to see what the woman looked like and now she had. Her curiosity had been satisfied. Mrs McDonald was no bombshell or *femme fatale* but an ordinary housewife who'd probably never been unfaithful to her husband in her life and would have been scandalized at the very idea, not only of being unfaithful but of anyone thinking she might have been.

Catie returned the photograph to her handbag and put on the kettle to make some tea. She'd destroy the picture later she decided. There was no place to keep it at the club and she wasn't going to run the risk of hiding it in the house in case Roger accidentally found it. If only she'd been able to smell Mrs McDonald to find out what perfume the damn woman wore!

'I never knew there were brothels in Glasgow!' Roger exclaimed to Alastair White. Now that he came to think about it he supposed there must be, he'd just never heard of any, that's all.

'Oh aye. I've been using one since the wife ran off and left me, the bitch. And with an Aberdonian at that! I've never yet met an Aberdonian I can honestly say I've liked. They're a miserable lot up there.'

Roger didn't agree about Aberdonians, but that was beside the point. 'Tell me about this brothel, is it expensive?'

'Well, it isn't cheap. But the girls are class, nothing like the tarts you'd pick up on the street.'

Alastair offered Roger his packet of cigarettes and they both lit up. Roger by this time was intrigued.

'I had a real cracker last time I was there,' Alastair went on, Roger hanging on his every word. 'A young Jamaican girl called Candy.'

'Jamaican? I've only ever had white women.' Roger sounded intrigued.

'Well let me tell you, these Jamaican birds, if Candy's anything to go by, are really something. She's wild in bed.'

Roger swallowed hard.

'Best tits I've ever seen.'

'What about her bum?'

'You wouldn't believe that, Roger. A work of art.' He paused in recollection, a smile lighting up his face. 'As for her skin, I think she must oil it because it glistens.'

'Glistens?' Roger breathed.

'Glistens,' Alastair repeated. 'You just don't get skin like that on a white woman.'

'How old is she?'

Alastair shrugged. 'I don't know. Seventeen, eighteen maybe.'

'Seventeen!' Roger choked.

'Round about that. Possibly even younger.'

Roger found that mind boggling. Imagine a seventeen-year-old, especially one as beautiful as Alastair had described. For the rest of the shift he kept returning to the subject of the brothel, pressing Alastair for more and more details.

Chapter Twenty-four

Irene's eyes widened in surprise and alarm as her bedroom door slowly opened to reveal Billy, smiling broadly.

'Hello sweetheart,' he said, coming into the room and glancing around. He flicked off the torch he was carrying and slid it into a jacket pocket.

'What . . . are you doing here?' Irene demanded, appalled.

'I haven't seen you for weeks I've been so damned busy, so when tonight I got the chance of a few hours off I thought, what the hell! I've always wanted to have a dekko round this place anyway.'

She was about to say he was mad, then abruptly changed her mind remembering the threat he'd made the last time she'd called him that.

'How did you get in?' she queried.

'No trouble there for someone with my talents. Easy as pie.'

'You're taking an awful risk coming here.'

'That's what makes it exciting, eh?'

He crossed to her dressing table where he picked up a silver Georgian jewellery box. 'Nice. Worth a few bob,' he commented.

'It was a birthday present.'

'Douglas?'

She nodded.

He replaced the box. 'I invited him to the opening of the club and he came. Did he tell you that?'

'He mentioned it. Wasn't that another terrible risk?'

'Why? According to what you told me he doesn't know about us, now or before. And he certainly hasn't connected me with the recent robberies that have cost him so dear. So where was the harm? He's an extremely powerful figure don't forget, and I want him as a friend, not an enemy. It was a good move inviting him.'

'Please go, Billy,' Irene pleaded, wishing this was a dream from which she'd awake. But it was no dream. It was horrible reality. Billy in her bedroom! She couldn't believe it.

'I had a fair old look downstairs before coming on up. I was impressed sweetheart, very much so. The stuff down there alone must be worth a fortune.'

He took off his jacket and tossed it aside, the jacket landing with a clunk thanks to the torch.

'What are you doing?' Irene queried.

'Making myself at home. That's OK, isn't it?'

'No, it's not, Billy. I'm frightened half to death at your being here.'

He started to undo his tie. 'Know what would amuse me, sweetheart?'

She could guess only too well what was in his mind. 'You can't Billy. Not here.'

'But "here" is precisely what would amuse me. In the great man's bedroom, in the great man's bed, with the great man's wife.'

She closed her eyes. This wasn't happening. Please God make it a dream after all. But of course it wasn't. When she opened her eyes again she saw that Billy had continued to strip.

'I beg you Billy, please leave,' she pleaded a second time.

'Not on your life Irene.' Naked now he began to advance on her.

Oh Reith! She wailed inside herself. What she'd done with Billy previously had been bad enough, obscene in the extreme. But this!

Billy yanked the clothes back and grinned down at her. 'Pretty nightie. Another present from him?'

'No. I bought it myself.'

'Pity. Now take it off.'

'You will be quick, please?'

'We'll see about that.'

She dropped the nightie by the side of the bed, thinking that she'd never wear it again because of the association.

'I like to see a woman shake,' he commented, eyeing her.

'Do you?'

'Oh yes sweetheart.'

'Does that also amuse you?'

'You bet it does. You'd better believe it.'

There were no preliminaries, as already excited he went straight into her, his lips slashing wolfishly upwards when she gasped in pain.

When Reith eventually returned home he found Irene sitting alone in the dark. She blinked when he switched on the light.

Drunk? He didn't think so. There was no smell of alcohol and she didn't look it. 'What's wrong?' he demanded.

She didn't reply, merely shook her head.

He shrugged. He couldn't help her if she wouldn't tell him what the problem was.

'Reith?'

He gazed at her expectantly. She opened her mouth to speak, then changed her mind and shut it again. 'Nothing,' she mumbled.

'Are you sure?'

'Yes.'

Now he shook his head in puzzlement and despair. There were times when she really worried him with her behaviour, and this was one of them.

'I'm going upstairs to bed,' Reith declared, wondering if it was his imagination or had Irene shuddered when he'd said that?

'OK.' Another mumble.

'You coming up?'

'In a while.'

'Suit yourself.'

For a moment he hesitated, tempted to take her into his arms and try to comfort her, for it was clear she was bothered or worried about something. He decided against it and left her to it.

'So, where are we going?' Catie demanded. 'What's the big secret?' She'd met Reith at his insistence. He'd informed her mysteriously the night before that it was important she did so. He'd refused to elaborate on it.

Driving himself, Reith eased the Daimler through the traffic.

'Well?' she demanded.

He turned the car into Garnethill Street. 'We're going to visit an establishment I own. I want you to witness something.'

'Witness what?'

'Wait till we're there and I'm sure of matters and then I'll tell you.'

She glanced at him, slightly irritated. She didn't like being kept in the dark.

'Is it something nice?' she asked.

Hardly that he thought.

'A surprise?' she further probed.

'In a way.'

'What does that mean?'

He laughed softly. 'Patience Catie. It's a great virtue. I learned that in the Army.'

She snorted. She wanted answers, not a lecture. 'Be like that then,' she retorted.

A few moments later he pulled into a side street where he parked. 'We have a short walk from here as I don't want the car to be spotted by the party in question,' he explained.

'What party?'

He ignored her question, but took her arm as they re-entered Garnethill Street, the tall buildings on either side towering above them. Eventually they climbed up some grey stone steps and Reith rang the bell beside a black painted door. It was opened by a well-dressed woman whom Catie judged to be in her fifties wearing lots of make-up and dripping costume jewellery.

'Come in, Mr Douglas,' the woman said, stepping aside.

'I presume he isn't here yet?'

'No.'

'Fine. I was worried he might be early.'

Who might be early? Catie wondered. What *was* this all about?

The inside of the house was gaudily decorated with heavy red embossed wallpaper and an Irish green carpet. The fixtures and fittings were gilt and glass.

'Follow me,' the woman said, and proceeded down a long hallway, with Reith and Catie following behind.

Catie's eyes came out on stalks when a heavily made-up young female wearing a flimsy wrap over nothing at all sauntered out of a doorway to flash Reith a broad smile. Reith ignored her. They passed a large room in which Catie glimpsed other young females all similarly clad with the exception of a blonde who was sporting a black basque highlighted in pink.

'What is this place?' Catie asked Reith in a whisper.

'A brothel,' he whispered back.

'A brothel!' She was shocked to the core.

'As I said, I own it,' Reith went on in his normal voice. 'This and several others.'

Stunned, Catie, very uneasy to be in these surroundings,

continued to follow Reith and the woman up a stairway and into a small sitting room.

'Would you care for a drink while you wait, Mr Douglas?' the woman queried.

'Catie?'

'Is a cup of tea possible?' she answered weakly.

'Certainly,' the woman said. 'And you, Mr Douglas?'

'The same, thank you.'

The woman left them, quietly closing the door behind her.

'I didn't know you owned brothels,' Catie declared to Reith.

'I'm not exactly proud of them, but they are good business and I do ensure the girls are well looked after.'

'Was that woman the . . . madam, I believe the word is?'

Reith nodded. 'Janine. She does an excellent job.'

Catie slumped into an overstuffed club chair. 'I can't for the world imagine why you've brought me here, Reith. A brothel of all places!'

'Perhaps I intend selling you to white slavers,' he teased.

For a moment she was alarmed. 'You wouldn't!'

'No, of course not, silly. I was only joking.'

She exhaled a sigh of relief. 'I could never . . . ever . . .' She broke off and shuddered.

'A fate worse than death, eh?'

'Very much so.'

'Well, there's no need to worry, Catie. What we're here for is to observe.'

'Observe?'

'Before I explain I want to know the party in question has arrived and is doing what I expect him to.'

She was still baffled.

Reith glanced at his watch. 'We shouldn't have to wait too long. In the meantime we can make ourselves comfortable.' And having said that he too sat down in an overstuffed chair that was adjacent to hers.

'How did you come to own brothels?' she enquired, intrigued.

They were still talking about that when Janine arrived back carrying a tray of tea things. 'He's here,' she informed Reith as she set it down.

'Ah!'

'I'll let you know when it's time.'

'We'll be waiting.'

Janine gave Catie a sideways glance, her expression one that Catie couldn't decipher.

'Will you pour?' Reith asked Catie.

He made a pyramid of his fingers and studied her as she busied herself, accepting the cup and saucer which she handed him.

'I've found the perfect little car for you,' he suddenly announced.

She stared at him in amazement. 'Pardon?'

'A little car. I've also arranged some driving lessons.'

'Reith, you can't do that!' she protested. 'For the reasons we've already discussed.'

'I can and I will, Catie.'

'And what if I refuse to accept it?'

'That's your choice. I won't force anything on you. I'd never do that.'

A car of her own! She was thrilled at the prospect. What a difference it was going to make. The freedom it would give her. 'But what about . . .'

He held up a hand, silencing her. 'That's taken care of. You're buying it through a finance company. Everything above board and in your name. Only I'll be giving you a cash sum every month to counterbalance the payments.'

She had to laugh. 'You really are too much, Reith.'

'I'll take that as a compliment,' he replied drily, thinking if things turned out as he hoped that arrangement would be superfluous.

'You spoil me, you know.'

'Not half as much as I'd like to. Or intend to.' He laid his cup and saucer on the floor, the tea untasted. 'There's something else.'

'Oh?'

'Do you remember our conversation that day at Balloch? When we were standing on the lochside?'

She frowned. 'Concerning what?'

'I said it was one of my favourite places and wouldn't mind living there.'

She nodded.

'I made enquiries and as it happens there's a castle nearby for sale.'

'A castle!' she exclaimed.

'Only a small one, nothing too grand or pretentious. And it does need a great deal doing to it. But it's perfectly situated with a stunning view out over the loch.'

She felt the beginnings of panic recalling the rest of that

conversation. He'd suggested he divorce Irene, she Roger, and they live there together.

'Rossdhu Castle has a ring about it, don't you think?' he said.

'Are you serious?'

'Never more so,' he assured her.

They were interrupted at that point by the return of Janine. 'He brought Candy upstairs some minutes ago,' she stated to Reith.

'So it's time we had a peek.'

'I'd say so. Candy doesn't muck about.'

Reith glanced at Catie who'd temporarily forgotten they'd come there for a reason. 'Shall we?'

They both stood up.

'Will you tell me now who I've come to see?' she asked.

'Roger.'

Janine dropped her gaze to stare at the floor.

'Roger?' Catie repeated hoarsely.

'That's right.'

'But he wouldn't . . . no . . .' She shook her head.

'I want you to see for yourself, Catie, so there can be no doubt in your mind. You wanted proof, well I've got it for you, thanks to our old friend Cairns the private eye whom I recently put back on the job. Roger, it transpired, has been coming here on a regular basis, same time every week.'

Turning to Janine he said, 'Take us to the room.'

'I don't want to . . . not walk in on him. Not like that!' Catie protested.

'That's not my intention,' Reith replied. 'Now come along.'

If she'd been stunned when she'd been told she was in a brothel, she was a lot more so now. She followed unprotestingly when Reith took her by the hand and led her through the doorway.

They went along a corridor, made a turning, and entered a bedroom. Or at least a room containing a bed, washbasin and solitary wooden chair. There were a number of risqué prints and framed French Can-Can posters on the walls. Janine removed one of the prints.

'There's a similar device in all these rooms,' Reith explained to Catie. 'It's a safety measure enabling Janine to keep a watch on customers she isn't sure about. If any start to cut up rough she blows the whistle on them.'

Janine peered through the small glass spyhole that had been revealed, then nodded to Reith.

'Your proof, Catie,' he stated quietly.

The last thing she wanted to do was to look through the spyhole, and yet she found herself inexorably drawn towards it, like an iron filing to a magnet. Her heart was thundering, her mouth dry as dust, her feet seeming to have a life of their own. She sucked in a deep breath before applying her eye to the hole.

Reith had given Catie the night off, so she was sitting, staring into the fire. Andrew had already gone to bed which was a profound relief as she'd found it difficult keeping up appearances in his company.

Well, she thought, she'd wanted proof and now she had it. Irrefutable proof at that. Nothing second hand on a piece of paper, but Roger, witnessed by herself, actually in the act.

How could he? she asked herself yet again. How could he? Having an affair was bad enough, but to go to a brothel where goodness knows what he might pick up. Not only pick up but pass on to her. Her skin crawled at the thought of his using such a place. And why? It was the same question she'd asked herself about Linda Brasil. Why? What did a whore have that she hadn't? What could a whore do that she couldn't?

A whore! The very word made her cringe and want to vomit. A piece of flesh used by all and sundry. And now her Roger, the man she loved. Or thought she loved anyway, for how could she love a man who went out and did that, who betrayed her with a common prostitute. How could she?

Catie's expression was stony as she watched Roger finish his mountain of a breakfast. 'Tip top,' he smiled at her.

'Glad you liked it.'

She gathered up his plate and cutlery, took them over to the sink and began washing up. She hadn't slept a wink the previous night, every time she'd closed her eyes she'd seen Roger and the dark-skinned woman again.

'What did you do yesterday afternoon?' she enquired casually.

'Nothing much.'

'Did you go out?'

'I went into town for a while. Just mooched around.'

That was a new word for shagging, she thought bitterly. Mooching around indeed!

'Anyway it's me who should be asking where you were. You

weren't here for tea, Andrew and I had to make it ourselves,' he complained.

'You're quite capable, aren't you?'

He blinked at her. 'We're capable all right, but that's hardly the point.'

'Doesn't do either you or Andrew any harm to fend for yourselves once in a while.'

'What's got into you this morning?' he queried.

'Nothing,' she snapped back.

'Well, you're hardly all sweetness and light.'

'Really?' she replied sarcastically, clattering a plate onto the draining board. She hadn't been able to eat any breakfast herself. A strong cup of tea was all she'd been able to manage.

Roger stretched his arms above his head and yawned. 'I'm beat. It was a long night. Though not so bad now I've got Alastair to keep me company.' He grinned in memory of the previous afternoon, that Candy had really been something! He'd never known a woman like her. Alastair hadn't exaggerated when he'd said she was wild. She'd certainly been worth every penny she'd cost him.

'What are you grinning at? It makes you look half-witted.'

'Was I grinning?' he asked innocently.

She wanted to throw the plate she was holding at him, but restrained herself. 'Yes, you were.'

'Wasn't aware of it, darling.'

Darling! How two-faced could you be? She was no more his darling than he was faithful to her.

'Will you be in tonight to make the tea?' he enquired suddenly.

She regarded him coldly. That was all he ever seemed to think about, his belly and what hung between his legs. God, he was despicable.

'I've no idea,' she replied.

His face fell. 'Well, I hope you are.'

'I'm not your bloody skivvy, you know. I work, and . . .' She said the next bit with relish, well aware of how much it would hurt, 'bring far more into this house than you do.'

He dropped his gaze. 'That's below the belt, Catie. I can't help it if you earn more than me. You earn far more than most men I know. Certainly working-class men.'

'I'm getting a car,' she announced.

'What?'

'A car. C.A.R. One of those things you drive around in and which goes beep beep when you press the horn.'

'But we . . .'

'There's no need to worry. *I'm* paying for it.'

'Even though, the expense.'

'I can afford it. So that's that.'

What had come over her? he wondered. She wasn't usually like this, so aggressive. 'Fine. OK. It's your money, after all.'

'Damn right it is, Roger. And don't you forget it.'

He watched her through partially hooded eyes as she finished the drying-up.

'I'm off out,' she declared, folding the tea towel and draping it over the front of the sink.

'I thought you might go back to bed. Just for a wee while?'

She was still laughing when she slammed out of the house.

Chapter Twenty-five

Reith glanced up when there was a tap on his office door. 'Come in!' he called out. It was Catie as he'd expected. He immediately rose and gestured her to a chair.

'Sit down.'

When she was seated he perched on the edge of his desk. 'So, what did Roger say when you told him?'

'I didn't.'

That surprised Reith. 'Oh?'

'I don't know why, I just didn't.'

'But you're going to?'

She shrugged. 'I'm not certain yet. I'm very confused.'

'Confused! What's there to be that about? The man betrayed you just as he did with Mrs McDonald and the Brasil woman.'

'I can't be certain about Mrs McDonald. That was mere speculation.'

Reith snorted. 'OK, forget her. But you have to accept the fact of the other two.'

She dropped her gaze and began fiddling with her fingers. 'You don't have to sound so bloody pleased about them.'

He couldn't deny that he was pleased at catching Roger out with Candy. He'd been more than that, he'd been delighted, cock-a-hoop. He stared at Catie. There were times when he could read her mind like it was an open book. This wasn't one of them.

'You can't still love him?' he queried slowly.

Catie didn't reply.

'He certainly can't love you.'

She was suddenly angry, and realized it was with Reith. 'I think I'd better go,' she said, starting to rise.

He reached over to place a hand on her shoulder, restraining her. 'Not yet, Catie. We have to talk.'

'About what?'

'Everything. Us.'

Her anger deepened. 'Christ, you can't wait. You're like a vulture attacking a body that isn't dead yet.'

He removed his hand as she sunk back into the chair. 'Sorry.'

'And so you should be. All you're thinking about is yourself. Not me, not how I'm feeling.'

Was that true? He didn't believe it. 'I only want the best for you, Catie, what's right.'

'And you're that, I suppose?' she retorted, glaring at him.

'Wait a minute,' he said, attempting a smile. 'I'm not the one who's done wrong. I didn't go to the brothel and pay money for a leg-over.'

Catie winced when she heard that.

'Did I?'

'No,' she admitted.

'So why attack me?'

'If it hadn't been for you or Cairns I'd never have found out about his visits there. I'd have been blissfully unaware.'

Reith gazed at her in disbelief. 'Is that what you'd have preferred?'

Again she didn't reply.

'Well?'

'No, I suppose not.'

'I was only trying to help, Catie, give you the proof you demanded.'

'While helping yourself at the same time.'

He couldn't deny the truth of that statement. 'You know my feelings towards you, Catie. What I want for us.'

A few seconds ticked by in silence, as she stared into her lap, fiddling with her fingers. When she looked up again there were tears in her eyes.

'Can I get you a drink?'

She shook her head.

'Here.' He pulled a large clean hanky from his breast pocket and handed it to her. She dabbed at her eyes. 'What a mess,' she husked.

294

'Of Roger's doing.'

Her temper suddenly snapped. 'Will you stop going on at him when he isn't here to defend himself!'

Reith was taken aback. 'How could he possibly do that? He's as guilty as hell.'

'You don't know him. Not the real Roger. He has a lot of good qualities. Faults as well of course, but we all have those. You included.'

'I don't . . .' Reith stopped. He was about to say he didn't go around betraying his wife. But he had betrayed Irene once upon a time, with Catie. And how often had he betrayed Irene in his mind, which was just as bad, with the selfsame Catie. If there was a difference between him and Roger, it was that he'd betrayed his wife for love, not lust.

'You can't go on living with him, Catie, not after this.'

'I'll decide what I do, thank you very much.'

'Naturally.'

She had a final dab at her eyes with Reith's hanky, then gave it back to him, which he silently accepted, returning it to the same breast pocket from where it had come.

'It was just so awful, stomach-turning, seeing him doing that to another woman,' Catie said quietly, staring blankly off into space.

Reith could well imagine.

'And a common tart at that.'

Reith's expression became grim. 'Is there anything else I can do?'

'Haven't you done enough already?'

He fought back his own anger. It was clearly a case of retaliating against the messenger, the bringer of bad news. It was something he hadn't foreseen and should have done.

Catie sniffed, and rose to her feet. 'I'd better get downstairs. Unless there's anything else?'

He shook his head.

'See you later, no doubt,' she said, and turned for the door.

Reith swore softly as the door clicked shut.

'Have I offended you in some way?' Roger demanded. 'It's been a week now.'

Catie regarded him with contempt. 'I'm sure lots of couples go a lot longer than that.'

'Well I'm not most men. I need it regularly,' Roger retorted.

295

'Too bad. I don't feel like it.'

'But why?' he demanded. 'This just isn't like you.'

She still hadn't told him that she'd seen him at the brothel, though why she hadn't remained a mystery. One thing she knew was that he wouldn't be allowed in if he went back, she'd spoken to Reith about that and Reith had promised Roger would be turned away from that and the rest of his brothels. Filthy bastard, she thought. Imagine him, her husband, using a whore. And now here he was wanting to use her just as he'd used that tart. Well, he could plead and beg for all he was worth to no avail. She was determined about that.

'Catie—'

'No!' she snapped. 'And that's final.'

'Please?'

'Go to hell.'

He gnawed a thumb in frustration. 'Have I done something?' he asked again.

'Guilty conscience, Roger?'

'About what?'

She treated him to a sweet smile. 'I don't know.'

'No, I haven't.'

Which was undoubtedly true, she reflected. He wouldn't feel guilty at all about what he'd done.

Roger grabbed her, but she immediately struggled to free herself. 'This has gone beyond a joke, Catie. I won't put up with it any longer. You have a duty remember?'

She stopped struggling and laughed. 'Duty! My God.'

'Well, you do.'

'Let me go, Roger. Or so help me—'

'What?'

'I'll knee you right where it hurts.'

He instantly released her and backed off. 'You would, too, wouldn't you. Bitch!'

For a few moments hatred sparked between them, then Roger flung himself into a chair. 'You've changed, Catie,' he declared, a whine in his voice.

'Have I?'

'Out of all recognition. You're nowhere as nice as you used to be.'

Good! she thought.

'You've become hard,' he added.

296

With just cause, she told herself.

'You're not ill, are you?'

'No.'

'Are you sure?'

'I'm not ill, Roger, believe me. Do I have to be ill not to fancy it?'

'It might have explained things,' he muttered, shifting restlessly in the chair.

How weak he was, she reflected. Pitiful, compared to Reith. Now there was a real man, one ruled by his head and heart and not by what was between his legs. But she was still angry with Reith, and he was only too well aware of the fact.

Roger decided on one last appeal. 'Please, Catie?' He winced when she suggested what he should do as an alternative.

Reith leant further back into the plush leather of the Daimler's interior and closed his eyes. So, thanks, yet again, to Cairns he now knew that Boyne had been visiting Irene at their house. Of course that didn't mean they'd restarted their affair, but in his heart of hearts he knew that was probably the case. Which beggared the question, and it made him sick even to consider it, but consider it he must, was she the one giving Boyne inside information? He didn't want to believe that his own wife could betray him, and yet it made sense.

'You all right Reith?' Jameson queried from the driver's seat.

'I'm thinking.'

'Sorry.'

Reith blinked open his eyes and gazed at the back of Jameson's head. 'How's that lad of yours getting on?'

'He's in the pink, Reith. A holy terror.'

Reith smiled.

'Gets up to all sorts.'

'A handful, eh?'

'More than that. Drives Ena ragged at times. But I suppose all boys that age are the same.'

'And Ena. How's she?'

'Says she needs a holiday. I'm thinking of sending her and the lad away for a couple of weeks. Blackpool maybe, or Scarborough. They'd like either.'

Reith thought how lucky Jameson was to be in love with his wife and she with him. The pair of them idolized one another. And despite his handicap, they both idolized their son. They were a truly happy family.

'I'd give you some extra time off to go with them if I could, but I need you for now,' Reith stated.

Jameson's knowledgeable eyes flicked to the rear mirror. 'Trouble?'

'I know who killed Finlay.'

Breath hissed from Jameson's mouth. 'Do you really?'

'Mr William Boyne, owner of The Cat Club.'

'How did you find out?'

'Never mind that for the moment.'

'Is that what you were thinking about?'

'Uh-huh.'

'Want me to take care of him?'

'Not yet. I want to consider the matter further.'

Jameson switched down through the gears. 'Whatever you say, Reith.'

Reith closed his eyes again, ending the conversation.

Reith pointed to the little red car parked at the pavement in front of Fanny's. 'There she is, all yours.'

Catie gazed at it in delight. 'What sort is it?'

'A Mini Minor. They've just come onto the market and from all accounts are going to be a huge success.'

Catie went to the car and tenderly ran a hand over its paintwork. 'It's so different to anything I've ever seen before.'

'That's what I thought. As I said, they've just come onto the market. Designed by a chap called Issigonis whom everyone is hailing as a genius.'

Reith pulled a keyring from his pocket and handed it to Catie. 'Why don't you sit inside and get the feel of her.'

'Can I?'

He laughed. 'Of course, it's yours after all.'

She opened the door and slid onto the driving seat, inhaling that distinct smell of a brand new car straight from the assembly line. A huge, beaming smile lit up her face as she touched, prodded and caressed.

'I wish I could drive it straight away,' she declared.

'I thought you might say that, hence the L plates,' Reith grinned. 'How would you feel about me giving you your first driving lesson?'

'Oh Reith,' she breathed, beside herself with excitement. 'That would be wonderful.'

'Then slip over to the other side and off we'll go.'

Reith drove to a quiet part of the city where there was little traffic. Once he'd parked he instructed Catie to change places.

'Now what do you know about driving a car?' he asked.

'Not a thing.'

'So we'll begin at the beginning and go from there.'

He explained the pedals to her, then the gear box, making her go through it a number of times.

'Now, switch on,' he smiled.

'First gear,' he continued when she'd done that. 'Ease off the handbrake, slowly on the clutch and . . .'

They bumped along the road. He gave her half an hour's tuition, then told her to pull over, believing that was enough for starters.

'Well?' he queried.

'It was fantastic, Reith. You were very patient with me.'

'You're easy to be patient with,' he replied softly, which brought a flush to her cheeks.

'I can't thank you enough for the car.'

'I'm delighted it pleases you.'

She leant across the space between them and pecked him on the cheek.

'Does that mean I'm forgiven?'

'I suppose so.'

'That's a relief. The fact that you were cross with me was starting to get me down.'

He stared at her, drinking her in. How strange life was, he thought. If he'd never gone for that walk in the fog perhaps he'd never have fallen in love with her. It may simply never have happened. Except he didn't really believe that. If it hadn't been the walk in the fog it would have happened another time. He and Catie were destined to be together, he was totally and utterly convinced of that. If only Catie would see it, realize their being together as a couple was inevitable.

'What's the latest on Roger?' he asked.

'I'm making him suffer.'

'How?'

She turned away so he couldn't see her face fully. 'By denying him what he's used to and wants.'

That delighted Reith. 'But you still haven't told him about what you saw?'

She shook her head.

'Are you going to?'

'I'm not sure yet. Probably. When I decide the time is ripe.'

That was beyond Reith who couldn't understand why she should wait. There again, it could be because he didn't want her to wait. When it came to Catie he lost his normal objectivity which served him so well in business and other matters.

'I'm sure you know what's best,' he said, not believing she did at all.

She flashed him a grateful look.

'Now we'd better be getting back.' And with that he got out of the car and went round to the driving side while she again slid across the seats. As they returned into town he said that he'd organized for one of his men to deliver the Mini to Battlefield for her, and that she was to ring the professional instructor he'd engaged and arrange her second lesson.

Reith stared down at Irene, who was asleep. How innocent she looked, angelic almost. And yet this was the woman he was almost certain had divulged details of his business interests to that reptile Boyne, an act that had not only cut him personally to the quick but had resulted in the death of Finlay.

He wanted to condemn her roundly, but couldn't. For hadn't she been driven by love? That same overwhelming and illogical force that had made him betray her with Catie, a betrayal he would gladly and wholeheartedly repeat at any time if Catie were willing. He sighed softly. What a mess. What an unholy, Godawful mess. Or fankle as the Scots would say.

Irene stirred, and smiled in her sleep. Dreaming about Boyne? he wondered, going cold all over. Was she recalling one of the occasions they'd been to bed together?

It was the pot calling the kettle black, he told himself. For how often had he dreamt about Catie, fantasized about her – times without number. There again, he reminded himself, there would probably never have been a Catie if Irene hadn't cuckolded him in the first place. If fault regarding their predicament had to be laid at any door it was surely hers.

And Finlay was dead leaving a widow and three bairns, there was no getting away from that. A death that had to be avenged. If it turned out as he believed, then Irene would have to pay, though nowhere as heavy a price as Boyne. An eye for an eye after all, a death for a death.

'Boyne,' he whispered, hating, loathing, detesting the man.

Leaving Irene asleep, he went into a spare room where he'd been sleeping since he'd first found out about Boyne's visits to the house. His excuse was that his old headaches had returned, bothering him mainly at night, and he didn't want to disturb her rest by continually moving in bed, getting up and switching on the lights.

When Irene woke up the following morning she found, as had so often been the case recently, that Reith had already left home.

'Parks,' Reith said into his telephone. 'This is Reith Douglas.'

'Hello Mr Douglas. What can I do for you?'

'A little while ago you granted a licence to a Mr William Boyne regarding premises called The Cat Club. Is that correct?'

There was a pause, then Parks replied hesitantly, 'That's correct, Mr Douglas.'

'I want it revoked.'

There was an even longer pause during which Reith heard Parks begin to breathe heavily.

'That might be difficult,' Parks said.

'I take it from that that an exchange of cash took place.'

'Yes,' Parks croaked, glancing swiftly round to make sure the conversation wasn't being overheard.

'Return the money and I'll ensure you aren't out of pocket. But I want that licence revoked. OK?'

Parks wiped a faint sheen of sweat from his brow. 'I presume this is necessary, Mr Douglas?'

'Don't presume anything, just do it.' And with that Reith hung up. He smiled grimly to himself. Parks was in no position not to comply with his wishes. It would be the end of the man's job and career if it ever got out he was 'on the take'.

'Please Catie, I can't stand it any more. Please?' he begged the moment the door clicked shut behind Andrew as he left to go to work.

'Forget it,' she replied from the cooker where she was making his breakfast.

'But why? That's what I want to know. Why for God's sake?'

'I've told you before. I don't feel like it.'

'But what about me? I bloody feel like it.'

'Tough.'

He clenched and unclenched his fists. Then stopped still as it suddenly struck him. 'You're not pregnant, are you? Is that what this is all about?'

Catie laughed. 'If I'm pregnant it's news to me.'

'Then what is it?'

'If you're so randy why don't you go and screw another whore?'

It took several moments for that to register. He gawped at her in blank astonishment. 'Eh?'

'I said, if you're so bloody randy, Roger, why don't you go and screw another prostitute?'

Roger swallowed hard as Catie began heaping his plate high with several slices of fried bread, black pudding, white pudding, bacon, mushrooms, sausages, tomatoes all topped with two fried eggs, his usual mountainous breakfast.

'What are you talking about?'

Lifting the plate she turned to smile at him. 'Do you deny it?'

'Deny what?'

'That you shagged a whore.'

'Of course I do!' he protested. 'I've never used a whore in my entire life. The idea's ridiculous.'

She regarded him pityingly. 'You're such a poor liar Roger. You shouldn't even bother trying.'

'I'm not lying.'

'Oh yes you are.'

He thumped the table. 'I'm damn well not!'

She arched an eyebrow. 'Garnethill Street mean anything to you? A certain house there?'

He was shattered. 'Garnethill Street?' he echoed, not believing what he was hearing.

'Right, Roger. Garnethill Street.'

'That's, eh . . . Let me think.'

'Up behind Sauchiehall Street. Charing Cross end. That help?'

'Oh yes. I know it now.'

'You knew it well enough to go there three weeks ago. Or have you conveniently forgotten?'

Jesus! he swore inwardly.

'You were seen, Roger, dear husband.'

'There's some mistake—'

'No mistake. It was you all right.'

'No, no,' he declared, shaking his head. 'A mistake.'

'Your arse in parsley sunshine. You went to a brothel in Garnethill Street, and you weren't merely sightseeing either.'

302

'I deny it. It's a fabrication. Someone's out to get me.'

She crossed over to him and, still smiling, emptied the contents of the plate she was carrying onto his lap, causing him to yelp and jump to his feet, scattering food in every direction.

'I want you out,' she stated.

'Eh?'

'Out. O.U.T. On your bike.'

'Out?' he repeated, dazed.

'Packed and gone when I get back in a few hours' time.'

'But . . . but . . . I've nowhere to go!'

'Try Garnethill Street. Maybe you can stay there on a full-time basis. You'd never be short of nookie then.'

'Be serious,' he retorted, attempting to wipe some of the clinging debris from his trousers.

'But I am, never more so. My mind's made up. It's finished between us. We're through.'

'That's what you think. I'm not leaving.'

'Oh yes you will. For if you don't all I have to do is have a word with Reith and he'll send round a couple of his heavies to persuade you otherwise. Fancy taking them on do you?'

Roger blanched.

Catie laid the plate on the table then went through to the hallway where she shrugged into her coat. Before leaving she rummaged in Roger's jacket pockets, found his house key and pocketed it.

'A couple of hours Roger. Bye!'

Gibbering, Roger felt as though he'd been poleaxed.

Chapter Twenty-six

'What!' Billy exploded.

Nervously Parks, who'd had a couple of stiff whiskies to give him Dutch courage, went on apologetically. 'I really am sorry, Mr Boyne, but there's nothing I can do about it. The whole matter's unfortunately now beyond my control. Your licence has been revoked and that's that.'

'For what reason?'

Parks coughed. 'Your criminal record. I was able to gloss over that when your application went forward. Sadly it's come to light and the decision to revoke has been made by my superiors. There's nothing I can do.'

Billy glared at Parks. The bastard was lying, the fact stood out a mile. 'And what about the bung I gave you?'

Parks hastily produced a wad of notes which he pressed into Billy's hand. 'I'm returning it, of course. No question about that.'

Billy threw the money aside, he didn't care about that. It was the gaming licence which was important. 'Your superiors, eh?'

Parks nodded.

'And who might they be?'

'Surely that's unimportant?'

'Not to me, it isn't.'

'They're beyond reproach, Mr Boyne. There would be no point whatever in contacting them.'

'Why don't you let me be the judge of that?' Billy hissed.

Parks ran a trembling hand over his mouth. He was thoroughly frightened of Billy whose dark glittering eyes bore into his own. He couldn't wait to escape from The Cat Club and promised himself a few more stiffeners before returning to work.

'You mustn't contact them, Mr Boyne. If they thought . . . had an inkling, well, it would be the sack for me.'

'Really?'

Parks nodded again.

Billy reached inside his jacket to produce a cut-throat razor which he lazily flicked open. Parks stared at it in horror. He'd seen what Glasgow's best-loved weapon could do to a man's face, it could turn him into a monster.

'Well?' Billy demanded.

Parks found he was having trouble breathing. He recoiled slightly when Billy turned the razor so that the sharp, cutting edge was pointed directly towards him.

'Please, Mr Boyne, don't get in touch with them. I've a wife and child to support.'

'Have you indeed? Boy or girl?'

'Girl.'

Billy gave a thin, leering smile. 'I wonder what she'd think of a daddy who'd been badly "marked". She'd probably run screaming from the room the first time she saw you.'

Billy suddenly grabbed hold of Parks and pulled him close, waggling the razor under Parks's nose. 'Why do I think you're lying shitebag? Why is it I've got that impression, eh?'

'I don't know,' Parks croaked.

'Now I want the truth, or else . . .' He trailed off, moving the razor closer to Parks's nose.

Parks had no doubt that Billy would use the razor. There was no bluff about this. Billy was the type of Glasgow hard man who didn't make idle threats. He'd have to confess, literally to save his skin. 'I was told to have your licence revoked.'

'That's more like it. By who?'

Parks licked his lips. 'Can this be between you and me?'

'Of course. You have my promise on that. All I want is the truth.'

'Douglas rang instructing me to revoke it. There's no arguing with him, Mr Boyne. At least not if you're me . . .'

'Because he's bunged you often in the past, right?' Billy interjected.

Parks nodded again.

'I take it you're referring to Reith Douglas, owner of Fanny's and other night spots?'

305

'That's right.'

'Just so there's no mistake. I'd hate to hold the wrong Douglas responsible.'

'I had to do it, Mr Boyne, do you understand?'

'Oh, I understand all right. He's a big man round town, when he says jump you jump. Whereas I, well, I'm only small fry.'

Parks didn't make any comment.

Billy considered marking Parks out of spite, but decided against it for a number of reasons, all in his own interest.

He released Parks who staggered back a few steps.

'Get out,' Billy said.

Parks didn't need to be told twice. He fled.

'Douglas,' Billy spat. How typical that the rotten lousy bastard should do this. The reason was clear enough, Douglas didn't want competition. Not even on the scale of The Cat Club.

Well, his gaming licence might be revoked, but he wasn't through yet. Not by a long chalk. The razor flashed and a plastic backed seat was slit neatly open along its entire length. Not by a long chalk.

'Can you imagine it refurbished?' Reith enthused to Catie. The pair of them were standing in a spacious drawing room inside Rossdhu Castle.

She gazed about her, awed at the thought of living in such a place.

'Any ideas?' he queried, watching her in amusement.

'I don't know,' she demurred.

'Oh come on. You must have some!'

'To be honest, Reith, I wouldn't have a clue where to start in a house like this. I couldn't possibly do it justice.'

'We could bring in an interior designer, of course. But the final word would have to be yours.'

She went to the closest window and stared out over the loch. It was a sunny day, light sparkling on the water. Over on her right a small rowing boat was slowly making for the shore.

Reith joined her, laying a hand on her shoulder. 'A penny for them, Catie?'

'I wasn't thinking about anything in particular.'

'No?'

She turned to him, her expression one of concern. 'You mustn't rush me, Reith. I don't want that.'

'Sorry.'

'I may have kicked Roger out but that doesn't mean I'll come and live with you.' She paused, then added, 'At least not yet.'

'So, there's hope for me?' he teased.

'You're a lovely man, Reith. I really do like you.'

'Just *like*?'

She hesitated, then said softly, 'Perhaps more than that. I'm not sure.'

'You love me, Catie. I'm convinced of it.'

It was now her turn to tease. 'Are you?'

'Oh yes. You simply have to admit it to yourself, that's all.'

'A lot of velvet,' she smiled. 'One thing I do see for this house is a great deal of velvet.'

'What colours?'

'Ones that'll brighten up these rooms. Some of them are definitely on the dull side.'

'And how about a four-poster bed? I've always rather fancied one of those.'

'A huge one?'

'Not too huge. I wouldn't want to lose the person I was sharing it with.'

She laughed.

'Well, it makes sense, don't you think?'

'Perfectly.'

He placed a finger on her lips. 'I love you, Catie. With all my heart and soul I love you.'

She kissed the finger.

'Shall I buy Rossdhu Castle then?'

Her brow furrowed. He was pushing her again, trying to make her commit herself. 'That's up to you, Reith.'

'You know what I mean.'

'It's still up to you.'

He brushed his lips lightly over hers. 'Then I will.'

Something lurched inside her. 'I'm not making any promises, Reith. You must understand that.'

'I do.'

'Are you certain?'

He answered that with a question of his own. 'Will you help me choose an interior designer?'

'If you want.'

'And work with him or her?'

'Again, if you want.'

'Good.'

Reaching down he took her hand, then enfolded her in his arms, gazing deeply into her eyes. 'You know there are times when we're not together that I can distinctly smell your perfume.'

That delighted Catie. 'Really?'

'Really. It's as though you were actually there beside me. I'm aware it's only my imagination, but I can still smell you.'

'I've told you before, you're a hopeless old romantic.'

'Hey, less of the old!' he protested.

'Well, we're not exactly spring chickens any more, either of us.'

'We haven't exactly got one foot in the grave either. I'd call it, in our prime.'

'Very tactful.'

'No Catie, true. Neither young nor old, but in our prime. At our best. Mentally and physically.'

'Physically! You must be joking. I've had two children, don't forget. I'm nothing like I was.'

Jealousy stabbed him then, thinking how beautiful she must have been when she married Roger. If only he'd met her first, how different their lives might have turned out. There again, better late than never.

He kissed her and groaned as her breasts squashed deliciously against his chest. He brought a hand round to caress one.

'Enough,' she gasped, breaking away and out of his embrace.

'I'll never get enough of you, Catie. Never.'

She smiled at him, a bright twinkle in her eye.

'Remember that hotel where we had lunch?' he said.

'Of course.'

'We could book in for a couple of hours. What do you say?'

She considered that.

'It's time we became proper lovers again, Catie, don't you think?'

She didn't reply.

'Well?' he queried softly.

'I can't Reith.' She shrugged. 'I'm not ready for that yet.'

He bit back his disappointment. 'Will you let me know when you are?'

Smiling again, she nodded.

'In the meantime . . .' He moved to her. 'How about another kiss? To keep me going.'

'Don't be greedy.'

'There's nothing greedy about it. Merely sheer lust.'

She raised her eyebrows. 'I thought you said it was love?'

'Love first and foremost, but also lust. Roger isn't the only randy man around. But in my case, it's only where you're concerned.' Suddenly, he became very serious. 'You'd never have to worry about me straying, Catie. It just wouldn't happen. You're the only woman I ever want.'

That touched her, for she believed him. He meant what he said. It thrilled her to think of the power she had over Reith. She'd never had anything like the same power over Roger, if anything the boot had been on the other foot. But with Reith, he was hers to command.

'So, can I kiss you again?'

Later on they wandered hand in hand through those parts of the house they hadn't already viewed, and then through the grounds.

'Here,' said Reith when they eventually returned to the Daimler, tossing her the keys. 'You drive.'

'Me!'

'I brought along some L-plates especially.'

'But I can't drive a car that size!' she protested.

He laughed. 'It's not that much different, I promise. And I'll be beside you to keep an eye on things.'

'Even though.'

'You'd better start getting used to it in case you *do* decide to come and live with me,' he stated craftily. 'Being able to use it would be one of the perks. Amongst other things.'

She was intrigued. 'Such as?'

'Your own accounts in whatever shops you fancied. You'd be able to have whatever you wanted, within reason that is.'

Within reason, she repeated to herself, mind whirling.

They retrieved the L-plates from the boot, and then she slid behind the wheel while he attached them.

'I feel like a queen,' she murmured a little later as they headed for Dumbarton. Which made Reith smile.

'Why the fuck didn't you warn me?' Billy demanded.

Irene shrunk away from him. 'I didn't know. Honestly Billy, he never mentioned anything about getting your licence revoked.'

He glared at her, fighting back the temptation to slap her round the room. The only fact that stopped him was that it would have left marks on her which she'd have found difficult to explain to Reith.

Instead, he clenched a fist and smashed it into the wall he was standing beside, causing Irene to shiver, imagining she could easily have been on the receiving end.

'Damn the man. Damn him to hell!' Rubbing his hand, Billy rounded on her, eyes starting from his head. 'Well, he'll pay for this. I don't know how yet, but he'll pay. I swear it on my life.'

Billy began pacing up and down, his anger molten lava running through his mind. Irene remained silent, watching him nervously.

Billy halted to light a cigarette, then crossed to an open bottle of whisky and poured himself a large dram. He didn't offer Irene any. He drank the whisky down in one, shook a little, and poured another. He briefly considered taking Irene to bed, but dismissed the idea knowing in his present state he could easily damage her physically. 'You'd better get out of here. Hoof it!' he snarled.

Thoroughly relieved to be dismissed, Irene promptly left.

'The bitch even took my house key, can you credit that!' Roger moaned to his fat cousin Joan and her husband Sammy who'd agreed to put him up over these difficult times.

'She's a bitch right enough,' Joan agreed, vigorously nodding her head.

'She did have some cause to throw you out,' Sammy murmured. He didn't feel as sympathetic to Roger as Joan.

'She was well overreacting if you ask me,' Joan declared.

'Exactly!' Roger exclaimed. 'I mean, it was only a one-off. A small slip from grace. Hardly enough for her to get her knickers in such a twist.' Joan and Sammy were unaware of Linda Brasil and his other adventures from the marital bed.

'But a prostitute. Women can be funny about such things,' Sammy stated mildly.

'Only the once though. Only the once!' Roger replied vehemently.

'It was certainly bad luck that you were seen,' Joan said.

'Bad luck! It was that all right. More than bad luck, a sodding catastrophe.'

'She'll come round in time. She just needs a cooling-off period,' Joan went on.

'Do you really think so?'

'Her pride's been hurt, after all. She's embarrassed, humiliated, but nothing she won't get over or come to terms with. I take it the marriage was in good shape before this happened?'

'Oh aye. Thick as thieves we were.'

'There you are then.'

Sammy wasn't so sure about that, but decided not to say so. He thought it outrageous that Roger had gone to a prostitute. What on earth had possessed the man when he had someone at home like Catie to sleep with? What Roger had done was beyond him.

'How about a nice cup of tea to cheer you up?' Joan suggested.

'Fine. That would be lovely.'

While Joan was putting on the kettle Roger slumped into a chair and worried a nail. He was missing Catie so much it was an actual physical pain. How he missed her! He would have done anything to have her back, anything. It couldn't be over, he reassured himself, it just couldn't.

Roger came awake as a body slid into bed beside him. It was night, when he would normally have been at work, but he'd arranged a few days off on account of 'a domestic crisis'.

'Are you mad?' he hissed when he realized it was Joan. 'If Sammy . . .'

'Sammy's fast asleep and snoring,' she interjected. 'He won't wake, I promise you. A whole herd of elephants could go trumpeting through that bedroom and they wouldn't rouse him. He's like that.'

She reached out and pulled Roger to her ample bosom. 'I thought you might appreciate a bit of comfort,' she said.

He knew what she meant by that. 'I can't, Joan, I'm sorry. But I just can't.'

That disappointed her. 'It's all right,' she crooned.

'I'm so upset, Joan.'

'I know,' she murmured, stroking his hair. 'That's been obvious ever since you got here.'

'She means so much to me. I suppose I'd forgotten just how much. It was only a little bit of fun, you see, a wee fling. Nothing of any consequence.'

'She'll see that eventually. In the meanwhile she's punishing you, and doing a good job of it, too, I have to say.'

Roger couldn't help himself, the closeness of a female body was too tempting. He fondled one of her breasts, then gently squeezed it.

'Like all men you're just a big baby at heart,' Joan commented as he continued.

Roger wished it was Catie's breast he was holding. He longed to be in bed with his wife. As he remembered her, he began silently to weep.

Joan realized what was happening when tears splashed onto her exposed breast. 'There, there,' she soothed. 'There, there.'

'Oh Joan,' he wept. 'I don't think I can live without her. I would do anything to have her back.'

Catie pulled the beaver-lamb coat Reith had given her more tightly about herself and gazed into the large wall mirror, admiring her reflection. What a lifestyle she would have if she went and lived with Reith, she thought. It was beyond her wildest imaginings. Not just one fur, but several. Jewellery of all descriptions. Diamonds that dazzled, pearls that shone, gold that glittered, silver that gleamed. And clothes, clothes to make other, less fortunate women drool with jealousy. Couture clothes from all the top designers. She giggled to think about it. Talk about Lady Muck! She'd out Muck the best of them.

Reith said wealth within reason, but what did that mean? One thing she knew for certain, she'd be able to wind him round her little finger any time she liked. There was nothing she'd ask for that he wouldn't eventually give her.

Cars were another thing. The Mini Minor was OK, fine in the circumstances, and she was delighted to have it. But it would be superb to have access to the Daimler, not to mention the gorgeous Riley. And why not a Jag for herself same as Irene now had? There were also holidays to consider. Trips abroad, America perhaps. She'd always rather fancied going there. They'd travel first class, of course, that went without saying. Out on the *Queen Mary*, back on the *Elizabeth*, with champagne and caviar all the way. As for Rossdhu Castle, that would be quite spectacular. She laughed aloud. A sumptuous castle after Bridgeton, how ridiculous could you get! A real rags-to-riches story, she Cinderella, Reith the dashing, handsome prince.

And what was stopping her having all this? Roger, that two-timing adulterous bastard! What loyalty did she owe him? None at all. Who would blame her for ditching him and going to Reith? Reith who desperately loved her, who would do anything for her, Reith who worshipped the very ground she walked on. Reith who'd marry her in an instant. She thought of Roger with contempt. The years she'd given him, devoted to him, been at his beck and call. And look how he'd repaid her. How could she possibly matter to a man who cheated on her, God alone knew how many times! A man who lied to her, possibly even laughed at her behind her back. Well, the last laugh would be hers. And what a laugh it would be. All she had to do was say yes, that simple word, to Reith.

'Mum?'

She turned to find Andrew staring at her. 'What is it, son?'

He was regarding her quizzically. 'What are you doing?'

'Day-dreaming, I suppose. Thinking.'

'Are you going to make tea? I'm starving.'

'Of course. I'll be through in a minute.'

He started to go, then stopped. 'Mum,' he went on, now in a quiet voice, 'I bumped into Dad.'

'Oh?'

Andrew shook his head. 'He looked awful, Mum. Quite terrible.'

Catie didn't reply.

'I don't know why you chucked him out, Mum, but I wish you'd have him back. It doesn't seem right with him not around. And I . . . I miss him.'

Catie dropped her gaze to stare at the floor.

'Don't you?'

Catie took off Reith's coat and rehung it in the wardrobe. 'Are you going out later?' she asked.

'I might.'

'How are you getting on with that new girlfriend of yours? What's her name again?'

'Penny.'

'That's right. Pretty girl.'

'About Dad, Mum—'

'It's steak and kidney pie tonight. You like that,' Catie cut in breezily, and swept from the room, leaving Andrew gazing forlornly after her.

Rex Hendry was the senior partner of Hendry, Semple, Ogilvie & Son, and Reith's lawyer. 'Sherry?' he asked, having ushered Reith to an overstuffed leather armchair.

'Please.'

Reith smiled at the nicety. Hendry, Semple, Ogilvie & Son were a very old, reputable firm steeped in tradition.

Rex Hendry handed Reith a well-filled schooner. 'So what can I do for you today, Mr Douglas?'

313

'Premises called The Cat Club have come on the market. I want you to buy them.'

Hendry sat, had a polite sip from his glass, set it aside and pulled a large blank pad towards him. Taking a fountain pen from his waistcoat pocket he slowly uncapped it.

'The Cat Club,' he repeated, writing that down.

'Owned by a person called William Boyne.'

'William Boyne,' Hendry again repeated, concentrating on the exquisite copper plate for which he was renowned. In his sixties he gave the appearance of being a fuddy-duddy, but Reith knew better. Behind the bland, somewhat vague, exterior lay a razor-sharp brain.

'For the asking price?' Hendry inquired.

Reith shook his head. 'Below that, as far below as possible.'

'I see,' Hendry murmured. 'And what if there are other potential purchasers?'

'There won't be.'

Hendry pursed his lips, but didn't comment on that last statement. There were times, particularly when dealing with Reith Douglas, when it was best to remain in the dark.

Reith went on. 'Nor do I want the purchase made in my name. We'll use Bryant Ltd again.' Bryant Ltd was a dummy company set up by Reith some years previously, ostensibly owned by two friends of his. The arrangement was that they were paid an annual sum for their troubles which were minimal, consisting mainly of signing various documents provided by Reith.

'I understand,' Hendry said.

'There's no rush. It may take some while for Boyne to get round to accepting my offer which, hopefully, will be considerably less than he paid for the premises.'

'Right! Now, further details.'

When those had been duly noted and it was established that their present business had been concluded, Hendry screwed the cap back on his pen and returned it to his waistcoat pocket.

'Excellent sherry as usual,' Reith commented.

'Thank you. And how's Mrs Douglas?'

'In the pink. And Mrs Hendry?'

'Likewise.'

When the pleasantries were over, and their glasses empty, Hendry personally escorted Reith to the main door of the building, an honour only accorded to the firm's top clients. There was no question that Reith ranked among them.

Chapter Twenty-seven

'Catie?'

She started at the sound of Roger's voice. How had he got into the house? Surely Andrew hadn't let him in or given him his key. She'd told Andrew not to do either.

'Catie, it's me, Roger.'

She realized his voice was coming from the hallway. 'Go away!' she shouted. 'Clear off, I don't want to see you.'

'Open the door, Catie, please. I must speak to you.'

Open the door? She went tentatively into the hallway where she found the door firmly closed and the letterbox opened inwards. Good grief! she thought. He was speaking through the damn letterbox.

'Catie, pl . . ee . . zz!'

'Sod off! I've nothing to say to you.'

'But I've got things to say to you.'

She caught a glimpse of an eye peering through the aperture.

'Catie, I was in the wrong, I admit it. But you must give me another chance. It's agony living without you.'

'I gave you another chance after that bitch Brasil and look what happened,' she retorted.

'It's you I love, Catie, no-one else. I swear on all that's holy.'

'You should have thought of that before shagging your damned tart.'

'She meant nothing to me, only a bit of fun.'

'Well, that bit of fun has cost you our marriage.'

'Catie!' he wailed.

How pathetic he was, she thought grimly. To think she'd once looked up to him, considered him to be absolutely wonderful. How wrong could a woman be?

'I'll do anything to make amends, Catie. Just name it.'

There was a sudden yelp when he lost his grip on the letterbox and it sprang back trapping a finger. He swore volubly.

Catie grinned, served the bugger right. She hoped it hurt, which judging by his wailing, it obviously had.

The letterbox opened again. 'Catie, let me in. I won't touch you, I promise. I only want to talk.'

'Then talk from where you are.'

'It's uncomfortable. And I feel a fool.'

'You *are* a fool, Roger, crouching in front of our letterbox or not. A bloody fool.'

There was a pause, then he said plaintively, 'Have you got a plaster? I've cut my finger. It's bleeding.'

'You can bleed to death for all I care.'

'You don't mean that!' he further wailed.

'Damned tooting I do. Bleed all you like, just try not to make a mess on the doorstep.'

He got angry then and started banging on the door with his fist. 'I want to see you, Catie. I *have* to see you!'

'Stop that!'

'Then let me in.'

'No. And that's final.'

'I'll stay here till you come out. I won't budge. And you have to come out sometime.'

She had the perfect answer to that. 'If you don't leave right away I'll telephone Reith and tell him you're harassing me. You know what'll happen then. He'll send a couple of his men straight round to deal with you.'

Abruptly, the banging ceased. The last thing Roger wanted was an encounter with Reith's heavies, particularly Jameson. Jameson's reputation terrified him. The letterbox opened inwardly again. 'I'm sorry, Catie. I lost my temper.' Mentally he was cursing the fact they now had a telephone.

'Don't be sorry, just go.'

'Catie, I'm so unhappy. I can't sleep for thinking about you. And it's the same at work, with hardly anything to occupy me you're there in my mind all the time.'

'Well, I haven't thought about you,' she lied. 'Not at all. You're out of my life forever and that's that.'

'I can't be, Catie. I love you.'

'Really?' she mocked sarcastically.

'It's true.'

'So you keep saying. But somebody who loved me wouldn't have gone and shagged a prostitute.'

'That was unforgivable and will never happen again.'

'Words, Roger, that's all those are, words I've heard before. Promises to be broken.'

'I'll be faithful from here on in, Catie. I won't stray an inch. Not a millimetre.'

How plausible he sounded, she thought, plausible as well as pathetic. Well, she was having none of it. He'd burnt his bridges. 'I'm going to the telephone,' she warned.

'Don't do that, Catie!'

'Then go away.'

Roger knew he was beaten, having no doubt that she would ring Reith.

'I love you,' he whispered one last time, then released the letter-box.

Catie listened to his footsteps receding, after which she went to a front window and watched him walk disconsolately down the street, shoulders slumped.

'Good riddance to bad rubbish,' she said, not really meaning it. Surprisingly she felt sorry for him. After all, theirs had been a long marriage, containing many close and tender moments.

Then she was hit by the humour of what had just transpired. Roger must have looked such an idiot, crouching at the letterbox. He seemed so pathetic, trapping his finger, asking for a plaster, desperately pleading his cause, the eye she'd glimpsed peering in. Her smile became a chuckle which in turn became a full blown laugh. Throwing her head back she roared with laughter, clutching a chest of drawers to steady herself. The vision of the once high-and-mighty Roger at the letterbox would be with her till her dying day.

Reith was also laughing, though gently and for quite different reasons. He'd just thought how to twist the knife where Boyne was concerned. What was the expression, between a rock and a hard place? That's exactly where Boyne was shortly going to find himself.

He pressed the intercom. 'Milla?'

'Yes, Mr Douglas.'

'Find Jameson and send him to me.'

'Yes, Mr Douglas.'

Beautiful, he thought, leaning back in his chair. Absolutely beautiful.

'Congratulations!' Reith said to Catie who'd come to his office with a twinkle in her eye, to inform him she'd passed her driving test.

'I was so nervous during it, shaking like a leaf.'

'Nervous or not you passed which is all that matters. Did you drive here by yourself?'

She nodded.

'Good for you.'

Delighted for her he pecked her on the lips. 'Tell you what, this calls for a celebration. How about lunch tomorrow at Rogano's?'

'Done,' she enthused.

'I'll meet you there at one as I presume you'll want to drive?'

'One it is. And yes I will.'

This time it was she who pecked him on the lips before returning to work.

The following morning Catie wasn't long out of bed when there was a knock on the door. Roger again? she wondered, going out into the hallway.

'Who is it?' she queried.

'A delivery for Mrs Smith.'

Well, that certainly wasn't Roger's voice. Nonetheless, she didn't want to take any chances as she knew how devious and sneaky he could be, so she slipped on the chain before she opened the door a few inches and peeped out.

It was a delivery man all right holding a huge bunch of red roses.

'Mrs Smith?' he smiled.

There was a card from Reith with the flowers, congratulating her again on passing her test. He'd sent her four dozen of the most gorgeous blooms. But then that was Reith all over, she reflected happily, he never did things by half.

Billy was stunned as he gazed around the smoking ruins of his club, the interior of which had been completely destroyed.

'Jesus,' he whispered.

A fire officer came up to him, smiling apologetically. 'Sorry we couldn't save anything, the fire was too advanced by the time we arrived. At least the building is intact which is something.'

'How did it start?'

The fire officer shrugged. 'Too early to say. Possibly an electrical fault, or there again a carelessly discarded cigarette . . .'

'It couldn't have been that,' Billy interjected. 'The place has been closed down for weeks.'

'Whatever, we'll discover the cause. Never fear, Mr Boyne.'

At least he was fully insured, Billy thought. Thank God for that.

'And it will be proved that it was arson?'

Jameson nodded to Reith. 'Undoubtedly. All the clues are there waiting to be found, the finger of suspicion will automatically point at Boyne. He won't collect the insurance and should go down.'

'Oh, he will if I have anything to do with it,' Reith declared softly. 'A word in the right ear will ensure that.'

Reith was amused by the idea of Boyne taking a large financial loss and going down for something he didn't do. It would be back to the Bar-L for friend Boyne. Reith suddenly became brisk. 'Now, other business that needs attending to . . .'

'I never see you any more, you're always out of the house,' Irene complained.

She looked pretty ghastly, Reith thought. There were deep lines etched on her face while her facial skin had acquired a greyish tinge. If she were involved with Boyne she was hardly blooming as a result of their relationship.

'I've been busy,' he replied, sounding off hand.

'Not that busy, surely?' She studied him, brow furrowed. 'What's happened to us, Reith?'

He shrugged, and didn't reply. When she laid a hand on his arm he nearly pulled it away. 'Why don't you wake me when you get in tomorrow morning? I'd like that.'

'Wake you. What for?'

'You know,' she said softly.

He knew all right. 'I'll be too tired,' he lied.

Irene's face fell. 'Oh Reith!'

'Age must be catching up with me,' he half joked, which was a complete contrast to the earlier conversation he'd had with Catie.

'A cuddle would be enough. Simply show you cared.'

If she was acting it was a damn convincing performance, he

thought. 'We'll see then,' he said, having no intention whatever of waking her the following morning.

'Now if you'll excuse me,' he went on. 'I've got things to do.' And with that he left the room.

Catie stopped in front of an expensive jeweller's window to gaze at the items on display. A diamond and sapphire brooch caught her eye, then she noticed a gold watch with an intricately wrought band for which she'd have died. It tickled her to think that one day she could actually own such accessories, be the proud possessor of a watch like that.

She smiled to herself. This was a game she'd been playing frequently recently, speculating about life with Reith and what would come her way when they were together. It was a lovely game, one she thoroughly enjoyed and which gave her an enormous amount of pleasure. Reluctantly she moved on only to stop at another jewellery shop further along the street. This time she was enraptured by a pearl choker.

'Arson?' Billy blinked at Detective Inspector Hodge, a middle-aged man with a badly pitted face.

'The findings aren't conclusive yet, but it looks that way,' Hodge said, the scarred face impassive.

'But who would do such a thing?'

'We thought you might have some ideas concerning that, Mr Boyne.'

Douglas! Billy immediately thought. Who bloody else? The only puzzle was, why would Douglas do that when he'd already closed down the club. It seemed senseless.

'Well?' Hodge prompted.

Billy shook his head. 'I can't think of anyone with a grudge against me or the club.'

'Hm-mh,' Hodge mused.

'When will you know for certain whether or not it was arson?'

'Soon, Mr Boyne.'

'I see.'

'And you can't think of anyone?'

'Nope,' Billy replied, lighting up a cigarette.

'Well, get in touch if anyone does spring to mind.'

'I certainly will, Detective Inspector.'

Hodge stood staring pensively at Billy for a few seconds, but if he was hoping to make Billy uneasy he was out of luck. Billy remained totally cool. He had had too many dealings with the police in the past to be discomfited or fazed by a little silence.

'Right, I'll be on my way,' Hodge declared eventually.

Arson? Billy reflected when Hodge had taken his leave. If it was that then surely it had to be Douglas. But why?

Irene stood staring down at the black waters of the Clyde flowing below. She'd been drinking heavily for hours, becoming more and more morose and filled with self-pity. How could she go on? she asked herself. She desperately loved Reith who didn't want to know her, who wouldn't even sleep in the same bed as her any more. She'd have done anything for Reith, and had proved her love when you considered Billy Boyne. Between the two of them life had become intolerable. She lived in constant terror of Reith finding out about Billy and of Billy sending that damned note with which he'd so often threatened her.

Billy had used her in such awful ways, degrading her, humiliating her, often laughing as he did. She constantly prayed that somehow Billy would vanish. She hung her head in shame. What had she done to deserve this? What awful, terrible thing had she done?

All she had to do was climb over the rail she was leaning against, and then . . . A few seconds plunging through the air, into the water and before she knew it would be all over. No more pain, no more agony. Just nothingness.

'Nothingness,' she said the word aloud, and sobbed. Was that what she really wanted, nothingness? Death? Of course not. What she wanted was a return to the good, happy days with Reith, the joy of those times, the days before Billy Boyne had turned up again. Except she knew those days were gone forever, vanished like so much smoke in the wind. So why shouldn't she choose death as an alternative to her present torture?

Would Reith miss her? She doubted it. He'd probably be relieved she'd gone, not around to annoy him any more. Her very presence clearly rankled him, that was obvious. Why else did he stay away from home so much? The explanation was simple, he couldn't bear to be in her company. That water looked so inviting, she thought. It would be cold, but that wouldn't worry her for long. Cold and black, rushing her to eternity.

But what of the children, Mathew and Agnes? What would they

think when they learnt she'd killed herself? Would *they* care? Of course they would. They loved her just as she loved them. They'd care all right.

Irene gulped in a deep breath, and straightened up. What should she do? Kill herself or go on living? Choose nothingness as opposed to pain and agony?

'God!' she choked. 'If you're up there, help me.'

Only there couldn't be a God. She'd stopped believing in Him long ago. Heaven was a myth, as was hell. Maybe hell did exist, because wasn't that where she was living right now? With Billy Boyne her chief tormentor. She sighed, and closed her eyes. Below her the black water flowed steadily onwards towards the sea.

'Yes, Mr Boyne, it was deliberate arson,' Hodge stated.

Three of them were in the police interview room, Billy, Hodge and another detective called McCready.

'Do you mind if I smoke?'

Hodge made a gesture with his hand indicating that Billy could light up.

'What do you say to that, Mr Boyne?' McCready asked as Billy exhaled.

'That I'm surprised, I suppose.'

'Surprised?' Hodge queried. 'Surely not?'

'What does that mean?'

McCready gave Billy a crooked smile. 'You lost your licence recently, I understand?'

'That's right. It's why I had to close down the club.'

'And what was the reason for losing your licence, Mr Boyne? You must have been given one.'

Billy stared from one detective to the other. He hated rozzers, without exception they were all scumbags in his opinion, slime of the earth. 'Because I have a criminal record,' he replied.

'Aah!' Hodge exclaimed softly.

'Which I'm sure you knew about.'

'Interesting,' McCready commented.

'Why? I'm going straight now.'

'Are you indeed, Mr Boyne?'

Suddenly Billy realized what they were inferring. Bloody hell! 'You don't think I set fire to my own club, do you?'

'Did you, Mr Boyne?' McCready queried.

'No, I did not.'

'It does happen, you know,' Hodge said.

'Oh yes,' McCready added.

'More often than you might think,' Hodge went on.

'To claim on the insurance,' McCready explained.

'But I don't need to claim on the insurance,' Billy protested. 'At least I didn't, though I'll have to now. The club premises are up for sale.'

'So they are,' Hodge nodded.

'Having trouble selling perhaps?'

'I've had one offer which I've turned down flat as it was well under my asking price.'

'Only one offer?' McCready queried.

'Others will happen, it's only a matter of time.'

'But in the meantime, you're strapped for cash, is that the case, Mr Boyne?'

'No, it's not.'

'You can prove that, of course?'

Billy found he'd begun to sweat. He didn't like this turn of events at all. 'If I have to, I suppose.'

'Have you already put in a claim, Mr Boyne?' Hodge asked.

'The insurance company has been informed of what happened. I did that straight away.'

'Then no doubt their investigators will back up any police findings.'

Jesus! It was a fit-up! They were somehow going to 'prove' that he himself had set fire to the club. Of course, that's what this was really all about. He was being framed. The sweat was now rolling down his back.

'You're not thinking of leaving town, are you?' Hodge queried mildly.

'That wouldn't be a good idea in the circumstances,' McCready added.

Billy shook his head.

Hodge glanced at his partner. 'Right, I think that's all for the moment.'

'We'll be seeing you,' Hodge said to Billy.

A fit-up! Billy inwardly raged as they walked away. It was now as clear as the nose on his face. But why? Douglas knew nothing about him and Irene, which was the most obvious reason. Irene swore blind that he didn't. So why do this to him? Unless . . . it was to make an example of him to scare off anyone else who might think

323

about setting up in opposition in the future. Yes, that had to be it. He was being made an example of. Framed and sent down as a warning to others.

Well, he wasn't going down, not if he could possibly help it. Another spell in the Bar-L after his last long incarceration was just too awful to contemplate. Particularly for something he hadn't done.

'I'll get you, you bastard,' he swore, clenching his hands into tight fists. 'You'll wish you'd never taken on Billy Boyne.'

'I'm only here because Andrew begged me to meet you,' Catie said to Roger. 'Though I think it was a bit underhand of you getting him to do it.'

'He misses me round the house. He told me that.'

Catie's lips thinned, and she didn't reply.

'You look wonderful!' Roger enthused.

Which was more than he did, she thought. He was a right old bag of nerves, who looked peaky with it. 'How are you getting on?' she asked.

'I can't sleep, Catie. I just lie there, staring at the ceiling, thinking about you and what a fool I've been. I'd do anything to turn the clock back.'

'Would you now?' she taunted.

'I swear it.' And with that he crossed his heart the way children do.

Catie had to laugh. 'Clown!'

'Let me come back Catie, please?'

That sobered her up again. 'No. You made one mistake too many.'

'But never another. On my life.'

She snorted.

'Don't let's throw it all away, Catie. That would be stupid.'

'Us!' she exclaimed. 'You mean *you* threw it away, not me.'

'I know, I know. If only you could find it in your heart to forgive me, I'd never stray again.'

'I've heard all this, Roger.'

Tears welled up in his eyes. 'I love you, Catie. You've heard that before, but it's true. And you love me.'

'Do I indeed?'

'Oh yes,' he breathed. 'I'm certain of it.'

'I did once, but no more, Roger. Love went out the window when I found out about you and that tart.' Suddenly, she lost her temper. 'How could you? That's what I've asked myself a thousand times, how could you? And with a tart!'

His head dropped.

'Wasn't I enough for you?'

'You should have been. It was so good between us.'

'Then why the tart and that Brasil woman?'

'Folly,' he whispered. 'Sheer folly. I must have been out of my tiny mind.'

'Tiny is the word for it,' she retorted scathingly.

He wiped the tears from his eyes, his expression one of total wretchedness. Despite herself Catie found herself softening towards him. She wanted to give him a damned good shake.

'Do you know what I miss most?' he said.

'What?'

'Just being in bed with you. The pair of us snuggled up close. That was better than anything else. Just being with you, the pair of us together, a couple.'

Despite her anger, that declaration touched her deeply for she knew exactly what he meant. 'Are you seeing anyone?' she asked.

He was thoroughly shocked. 'Of course not!'

She believed him.

'And you?'

'What do you think?' she prevaricated.

'I don't know what I'd do if you were. The very thought . . .' He broke off and shuddered.

'Here,' she said, opening her handbag and rummaging inside. 'Take my hanky. You're crying like a big wean.'

'Thank you.' He dabbed his face. 'Ridiculous a grown man, and Glaswegian at that, crying, isn't it?'

She didn't think so at all.

'So, what's the verdict?' he queried. 'Will you change your mind? Let me have one more chance? You wouldn't regret it, Catie, not ever.'

'I have to be getting on,' she declared, glancing at her watch. 'I have an appointment.' She didn't elaborate, for it was a lie.

'Andrew told me you passed your driving test. Congratulations. First time too! But there, I wouldn't have expected anything else from my Catie.'

'Take care of yourself,' she smiled.

He suddenly pulled her into an embrace, wrapping his arms tightly about her, laying a cheek against hers. 'Goodbye my darling,' he croaked. As she was climbing into her car she, too, started to cry.

325

Chapter Twenty-eight

Roger was right, she did still love him. Despite everything, she still loved the sod. It was a revelation. She must be out of her head, Catie reflected. How could she even possibly consider taking him back after what he'd done? But the fact remained, he was her man and always would be.

Catie sighed, and ran a hand over her face. Then she turned to stare at the empty space in their bed where he should have been. Visualizing him there, that knowing look of his as he took her into his arms, recalling, only too vividly, the passion and ecstasy that always followed. How she missed lovemaking. Roger touching her, stroking her, moving inside her. Roger whispering in her ear, his body crushed against her own.

But it went far deeper than lovemaking. There was so much more to their relationship than that. Over the years he'd become part of her just as she'd become part of him. She could no more cut him adrift than she could chop off her own arm or leg. Not that everything had always been hunky-dory between them. They'd had their ups and downs like everyone else, their almighty rows, their simmering resentments and sulking silences. But these had always been followed by the joy of making up. And what makings-up they'd had! She smiled in memory.

OK, Roger had his faults, but who hadn't? She certainly did. No-one was perfect, after all. Not that that excused his infidelities which he now genuinely and wholeheartedly regretted. She was convinced of that. Throwing him out had given him the shock of his life. 'Roger,' she whispered, and shivered. She could almost imagine him there beside her.

Then she thought of what she'd be giving up by taking him back. The lifestyle Reith offered, Rossdhu Castle, the Daimler, the expense accounts that would have been hers. All so very, very tempting! And there was Reith himself. Lovely Reith who'd been such a wonderful friend to her, so kind and considerate. The trouble was, if she were honest, that's all he was and ever had been, a friend. Admittedly they'd been lovers at one time, but there was a big difference between being someone's lover and being in love with them. He loved her, but she simply didn't love him and never would. Whereas, she did love Roger.

But she wouldn't take Roger back straight away. No, let him suffer a while longer so that the lesson was driven well and truly home. Another month anyway, she decided. Then a return on trial, at least she'd tell him that's what it was. He'd sworn he'd never stray again, and by God she'd make sure he kept to it. He wouldn't even contemplate the idea once she'd finished with him.

But Reith, that was going to be difficult. Mind you, she'd never made any promises, she'd been careful about that, never committing herself. He couldn't accuse her of reneging on anything because that simply wouldn't be true. She didn't want to hurt him, but she knew this would hurt him to the very quick. But what else could she do?

'I'm sorry, but that's how it is.'

Reith stared at Catie in disbelief. 'You haven't thought this through properly . . .'

'I have,' she interjected. 'Believe me, I have.'

'You prefer Roger? After all that he's done, the grief that he's caused you, the heartache, and you still prefer him? It doesn't make sense.'

'When did love ever make sense? You should know that.'

Catie picked up the bottle of whisky she'd deliberately bought in. 'Will you have a dram?'

He nodded. 'A large one.'

He leant against the mantelpiece, watching her as she poured out their drinks. 'When you asked me here today I thought it was because you'd finally made up your mind about us.'

'I had,' she replied. 'Though not the way you'd anticipated.'

'No,' he agreed.

'Water?'

'Straight.'

She gave him his glass before adding water to her own. 'I wish there had been an easier way of telling you, but there wasn't.'

'I love you.'

'I know, Reith. Except I don't love you. And never will.'

'You can't say that!' he exclaimed in desperation.

'But I can,' she replied softly. 'If it had been going to happen it would have done long before now. You're a sweet, sweet man, the best friend I've ever had, or ever will have. And I care for you enormously. But caring isn't loving. It just isn't the same thing at all.'

'He'll cheat on you again, you know. Leopards and spots . . .'

'No, he won't,' she retorted. 'He realizes only too well what he's lost, or thinks he has. Roger will be faithful from here on in.'

'I don't believe that!' Reith exploded.

'You're angry, that's to be expected,' she commented.

'Angry! I'm more than that because I know you're making a terrible mistake. One you'll come to regret bitterly.'

'You're biased, Reith . . .'

'Of course I damn well am!' he cut in quickly.

'But you'll get over me in time.'

He barked out a laugh. 'You're saying that to salve your conscience. I'll never get over you, Catie. Not in a thousand years.'

She glanced away, unable to meet his gaze.

'Catie?' he whispered.

She forced herself to look at him.

'Don't do this to me. Not a second time. The first was bad enough, but this . . .' He trailed off.

'I really am sorry.'

'A terrible mistake,' he repeated.

'Are you going to fire me?'

He blinked. 'I hadn't thought about that.'

'Or Roger?'

Bugger Roger and his piddling job. But Catie, seeing her every working day, wanting her, thinking about how things might have been. That would be sheer torment.

'I'm not a vindictive person, Catie. Roger can stay on at the Midnight Rooms.'

She breathed a sigh of relief. 'And me?'

'I'll have to consider that. Perhaps it would be better if I had you transferred to another club.'

'Perhaps,' she agreed with a smile.

He saw off the remainder of his whisky and laid the glass on the mantelpiece. He was thankful that Jameson was waiting outside for him in the Daimler. He wouldn't have trusted himself behind a wheel in his present state.

He'd been so sure about Catie, so absolutely certain that he'd even begun negotiations to buy Rossdhu Castle. Well blast Rossdhu Castle! He didn't give a fig about it. Or anything else come to that. All that mattered was Catie. Catie who was everything to him, who'd now rejected him and chosen to stay with Roger.

'I hope we'll still be friends,' she said.

He managed a weak smile. 'Of course. We'll always be that. No matter what.'

'Thank you, Reith.'

There was suddenly an awkwardness between them of which they were both aware.

'More whisky?'

He shook his head.

'I'd better go.' He didn't want to leave, it was the last thing he wanted to do. He wanted to stay, be with Catie forever.

'I never intended to hurt you, Reith. You must believe that,' she stated softly.

'No,' he replied, equally softly.

'Is there anything I can do to help?'

'No,' he repeated.

She sighed.

'A last kiss Catie?'

'Don't,' she said, turning away.

He forced himself to say the next word. 'Please?'

How could she refuse? She couldn't. 'If you like.'

He went and stood opposite her, staring into her face, studying her. 'It was good between us. So right.'

'But just wasn't to be.'

'According to you.'

'According to me.'

He wrapped a hand round her neck, and leant towards her. They both closed their eyes as their mouths met. Her lips were cold, her mouth, when he penetrated it with his tongue, unresponsive. He knew she was deliberately withholding herself, which saddened him immensely.

'See you later at work,' he murmured when the kiss was over.

'Yes.'

He hesitated, then said, 'Catie . . . remember . . . always remember. I love you.'

She nodded.

'If you ever change your mind . . .' He trailed off.

'I know.'

'I'll be waiting.'

She didn't deserve Reith, she thought. He was far too good for her. 'But in the meantime you must lead your own life, Reith. I insist on that.'

'Do you now?' he teased.

'You know what I mean.'

'So it wouldn't bother you if I was to find someone else?'

It would, of course it would. Except she wasn't going to admit that. 'I have no claims on you. Certainly not after today.'

He suddenly straightened up. 'Later then.'

'I'll see you to the door.'

'No!' he said sharply. 'I'll let myself out. Better that way.'

'OK.'

He closed his eyes for a moment, breathing in her scent, feeling the warmth emanating from her body. A body he would probably never experience intimately ever again. A body he craved the way an alcoholic does drink.

'Goodbye,' he said, meaning more than farewell.

'Goodbye,' she smiled, knowing that.

He left quickly, striding from the house to where Jameson was waiting with the Daimler.

'Where to Reith?' Jameson enquired.

'Anywhere,' came the strangulated reply.

Billy clattered down the stone steps leading away from court, thankful to have been allowed out on bail. Thank Christ he'd employed such a good advocate, money well spent. Without Symington he was certain bail would have been refused. What a stitch-up, he thought. He might be as innocent of the charges as a newborn babe, but would go down nonetheless. The evidence against him was damning. Well, screw them and their evidence. Screw the poxy court. And, above all, screw Douglas.

He was off, would do a disappearing act, but not right away. He'd have his revenge first.

★   ★   ★

'What's wrong, Jameson?' Reith enquired. 'Something's clearly on your mind.'

Jameson shifted uncomfortably. 'It's not for me to say, Reith. Not my place.'

'Oh come on! We know one another better than that. If something is bothering you then spit it out.'

'It's about Finlay.'

'Aye?'

'I don't understand why you're letting Boyne off with a prison sentence. He killed Finlay after all, Finlay who left a widow and three kids behind. The man should pay with his life.'

Reith smiled thinly. 'And who says he won't?'

Jameson regarded Reith thoughtfully. 'I'm not with you?'

'Boyne's going down, right?'

Jameson nodded.

'He's going down because I want him back inside that hell-hole and all that that entails. I want him to suffer, *first*.'

'First?' Jameson queried with a frown.

'That's right. And then, just before his time is up, days even perhaps, he'll meet with a nasty, and fatal, accident.'

A broad smile broke across Jameson's face, a rare event. 'Oh, that's good. Very good.'

'Why make it swift for him? That's too easy. I want him inside, and then, when he's done his time and thinks he's about to be released, he pays the last instalment of his debt.'

'I should have known,' Jameson declared. 'It's not like you to be soft.'

Not in business anyway, Reith reflected, thinking about Catie. But personal relationships were different. 'So you approve?'

'Very much so.'

'Another twist of the screw is that when he is inside I'll ensure he's given a hard time, an extremely hard time. He'll think his previous spell there was a bed of roses compared to what he's going to experience. I shouldn't be surprised if before long he's begging to be banged up in solitary, a request I assure you that will be denied.'

Jameson nodded. 'I take my hat off to you Reith. I'd simply have killed the swine.'

'As I said, that's too easy.' Reith changed the conversation.

Reith cradled the phone with satisfaction. That had been Rex

Hendry, of Hendry, Semple, Ogilvie & Son, on the line. Boyne had finally accepted his offer for The Cat Club, as he'd been certain Boyne eventually would.

The man needed money to fight his case, having hired a top Scottish brief, which meant he would have to liquidize his assets. He was playing right into Reith's hands. If Boyne hadn't accepted now Reith would have been prepared to sit back and wait till Boyne eventually did sell. Ultimately Reith would have acquired it, or Bryant Ltd to be precise, for no other offers would have come Boyne's way. Jameson would have seen to that.

Reith hummed tunelessly to himself. He'd at least recovered something of the money stolen from him by downgrading the club's real value. When the club opened again, totally refurbished and revamped, it would be the latest acquisition to his string.

But Reith was wrong about Billy's reasons for selling. Billy did want to liquidize his assets, not to meet impending legal fees, but so he could take the cash with him when he jumped bail.

Nor was Billy stupid, he'd worked out that Reith was somehow behind Bryant Ltd. Why else would there be only one offer on the premises? That was the only way it added up. Particularly when you took into consideration that it was Douglas, who was responsible for him being framed. Billy was now completely convinced of that. It was merely adding more fuel to the hatred Billy felt towards Reith, and became another reason for revenge.

Billy, glass of whisky in his hand, sat staring morosely at the wall. He had to hurt Douglas before he left, really hurt him. But how? That was the million-dollar question.

He could torch the house in Newton Mearns, he thought. Repay fire literally with fire. All those fine things, including the Peploe, up in smoke. That was definitely an idea. Only there again, material possessions could always be replaced. What he wanted was something that couldn't.

There were Douglas's children of course. He could in fact razor Agnes's face, as he'd threatened to Irene. Razor her face to shreds. That was another possibility and one that certainly appealed. He could well imagine the anguish that would cause, particularly as Douglas was such a doting father. He smiled grimly, thinking about it, imagining the pleasure it would give him. He visualized the girl pleading for mercy, cornered, trapped, followed by the deed itself. He'd do it slowly, taking his time, revelling in the agonized shrieks every time his blade sank home. He'd turn her into something that would give Douglas nightmares for the rest of his life.

He could find out the girl's whereabouts through Irene . . . Billy sat bolt upright, eyes narrowing. Forget the girl, how about Irene herself? She was more accessible, all he had to do was pick up the phone and she'd come running.

Douglas loved his wife which was the added spice that would make harming her all the more enjoyable. 'Hmmh!' he murmured thoughtfully, and drank from his glass. The fact was, he didn't fancy her any more, not one little bit, so he'd have no qualms about marking her. None whatever, she was no longer useful to him.

But what if she told Douglas it was Boyne who'd done the marking? Despite not wanting Douglas to know about their past, she just conceivably might talk, if not intentionally then by accident. She could become a hysterical woman babbling uncontrollably. Should Douglas discover he was responsible for the marking then Douglas would pull out every stop in the book to find him wherever he was. The police would be called in, of course, when he jumped bail, which would mean he'd have them and Douglas after him. The solution was simple, he decided. He wouldn't mark her. He'd kill her. Corpses didn't tell tales. At least, not if you were careful, that was.

'Oh yes,' he breathed, a tremor of sexual excitement coursing through him. That was it. Sweet revenge. He'd kill Douglas's wife, the woman Douglas loved. It was perfect.

This time there were no tears or hitting the bottle. Reith just wandered through a great black pit of despair, lonely as a ghost. He closed his eyes and pictured Catie, the ache in his guts almost unbearable. She smiled, and waved, Rossdhu Castle in the background, the place that was to have been their home.

Roger appeared, laughing. Roger shouted to Catie who spun round, and ran to him, arms outstretched. Then they were embracing, Roger smirking at Reith over her shoulder. Now they were walking away and he stared after them as they gradually receded into the distance.

'Stop it!' Reith exclaimed, snapping open his eyes. He was being ridiculous, almost childish. Catie had chosen Roger over him, he had to accept that. But it was so hard to do so. If only she loved him instead of bloody Roger. But she didn't, and nothing would change that.

Reith took in a deep breath, and drew himself up. Catie was in the past, she was over and done with. That part of his life was finished. He'd somehow face the bleak loneliness that lay ahead.

He'd have Catie transferred soon, he decided. He knew he should have done before now. Would it be a case of out of sight, out of mind? That was a joke.

Roger was dead beat after a long shift but knew from recent experience that it would make no difference when he got back to Joan's and into bed. He'd lie there, unable to sleep, thinking about Catie. He'd wonder what she was doing, who she was with, and become consumed with jealousy at the thought she might have met someone else and taken a shine to him.

He lit another Senior Service. How many had he smoked that night? Far, far too many as testified by the dark yellow stains on the fingers of his right hand.

'Christ!' he muttered. Who would have imagined a woman could do this to him? But Catie had. Why, oh why, hadn't he appreciated her more when they'd been together! As he'd told her during their last meeting he'd have done anything to turn the clock back. Except that was an impossibility.

He balled his hand into a fist and smacked it against his thigh. Maybe he should go abroad, emigrate. Get away from Glasgow and all the memories it held for him. Make a completely fresh start. He'd heard there was plenty of work in Canada, so why not go there? Or Australia, that was another option. Go out on one of those ten quid assisted passages.

'No,' he murmured, shaking his head. He couldn't leave Glasgow. The bonds holding him to his native city were just too strong. He'd never cut them. He glanced at his watch. Only a few minutes left and then he could be off. He reached for his coat.

'Damn that Alastair White!' he muttered as he shrugged himself into it. If it hadn't been for him all this would never have happened. He'd still be with Catie, still sleeping with her, everything hunky-dory. It had been just his luck to get White as a workmate and for White to be full of lurid tales about that damned brothel.

He wound a scarf round his neck, for it was bound to be cold outside. Joan would have a huge breakfast waiting for him, most of which he'd leave. Ever since he'd split up with Catie he'd lost his appetite, and not only for food. If a good-looking naked woman were to lie down in front of him she wouldn't interest him in the least. It was only Catie he wanted.

As he left the building he discovered it was raining as well. A right miserable day if ever there was. At least it matched his mood. Deep in thought, filled with bitterness and regret, dog tired, head down against the driving rain, his mind on Catie rather than where he was and what he was doing, he stepped off the pavement to cross the road.

Suddenly there was an almighty squealing of brakes and, for one horror-filled instant, he saw a large car bearing directly down on him.

Chapter Twenty-nine

Catie loathed ironing. It was one of those boring, mundane tasks that just had to be done regardless. At least she didn't have Roger's clothes to deal with at the moment which was something. She paused as she thought about Roger. She smiled, another week and then she'd let him off the hook, tell him he could come home again. But even then she'd prolong the agony. Despite her own feelings she'd make him wait a while longer before allowing him to make love to her. No matter how much he pleaded or cajoled he wasn't having any love until such time as she decided to relent. Her smile broadened. He'd suffer all right. Maybe not as much as he was at present, but continue to suffer he would. It served him right, too! The stupid, randy sod.

She was attacking one of Andrew's shirts when there was a knock on the front door. She hoped it wasn't Reith as she went to answer it. But she doubted it would be, as they'd only spoken profession-ally since she'd told him she was taking Roger back.

Nor was it Reith, but a grave-faced policeman. 'Mrs Smith?'

'That's right.'

'I wonder if I could come in. I have some rather bad news for you, I'm afraid.'

White faced, Catie sat gazing at a heavily bandaged Roger who had a drip running into his left arm. It was his internal injuries that were worrying the doctors most, however, and they still weren't quite sure of the full extent of the damage yet. Catie glanced at her watch. She'd been at his bedside three hours now and he still hadn't stirred. Please God, let him come out of this all right, she prayed.

The accident had been entirely his fault, the police had informed her. The driver of the car had been powerless to stop in time.

A young nurse popped her head round the screens. 'Would you like a cup of tea, Mrs Smith?' she gaily asked.

Catie shook her head.

'Better if you did.'

'No thanks, honestly. I couldn't eat or drink a thing.'

'Right-o then!'

The nurse's jocularity angered Catie. Didn't the bitch realize the seriousness of the situation? When she returned her attention to Roger, his eyes were open, staring at her.

He licked his lips, and swallowed. 'Catie,' he croaked.

Relief flooded through her. 'Hello.'

'What . . . happened?'

'You were hit by a car.'

His expression became puzzled as he searched his memory. 'I remember now.'

'Are you in pain?'

He thought about that. 'A little. Mostly I'm numb.'

'I should tell someone you're awake.' And with that she made to rise.

'No, wait!'

She stopped, and sat down again.

'I want you to myself, for a little while first.'

Reaching out, she took his hand in hers. 'Oh Roger, what were you thinking about to make you so careless?'

The flicker of a smile crossed his face. 'You Catie, I was thinking about you. That's all I've been able to do lately, think about you.'

She felt guilty then. If she hadn't made him wait once she'd decided to have him back, this would never have happened. But how could she possibly have foreseen this!

'How bad . . .' He swallowed again. 'Is it?'

'Lots of cuts, grazing and bruising, but amazingly nothing was broken. There is internal damage however.'

He closed his eyes, then opened them again. 'I love you Catie.'

'I know. And I love you.'

'Even after . . .'

'Even after that,' she interjected with a smile.

'Oh my darling,' he breathed.

337

'You're coming home when they let you out of here. Back to the children and me.'

He sighed. 'That's what I've wanted to hear for so long.'

She squeezed his hand. 'I'll nurse you back to health, Roger. I'll look after you till you're fully better.'

'I'll never stray again, Catie. There isn't a female on earth could tempt me after this.'

He suddenly winced.

'What was that?' she asked in concern.

'A sharp . . . stab. It's gone now.'

'I'd better get someone!'

'Catie . . .' He twisted his hand so that he was now holding hers. 'I can't tell you how glad I am that we're together again.'

'Nor me Roger.'

This time she did get up. 'I won't be a mo'.'

He closed his eyes once more, filled with happiness at their reconciliation.

Catie woke up to hear the insistent ringing of the telephone. With a groan she slid from bed, threw on her dressing gown and hurried to the telephone, wondering who could be calling at such an early hour. Her heart leapt into her mouth when she learned it was Night Sister.

'It's me, Reith,' she sobbed into the phone.

'What is it, Catie?'

'I'm sorry to get you up. I'm really sorry . . .' She trailed off to wipe tears from her face. In the space of a few minutes her whole world had disintegrated.

'Catie?'

'It's Roger. He's . . .' She had to force herself to say the word. 'He's dead.'

'What! What happened?'

'He was hit by a car yesterday and . . . died a short time ago from a massive haemorrhage. Oh Reith!'

Jesus, Reith thought. Poor Catie. 'You never mentioned this accident at work last night?'

'I thought he was going to be OK. The doctor was so reassuring.'

'If you'd said I'd have given you time off.' Reith's mind was whirling. 'Are you at home?'

'Yes,' she choked.

338

'I'll be there as soon as I can.'

'No Reith, I want to be alone. Just talk to me.'

He wanted to go to her, be with her, comfort her. 'Is Andrew there?'

'He's still sleeping.'

'Don't you think you should wake him?'

'Not yet.' She paused briefly, then went on, 'Astrid and he are going to be broken-hearted. Utterly devastated.'

Just as you are by the sound of things, Reith thought grimly. 'I still think I should come round.'

'No, please. Just talk to me.'

And so they talked for nearly an hour, Catie sobbing and crying throughout most of it. Early in the conversation Reith told her to take as much time off work as she needed.

When he finally hung up Reith left the bedroom where he now slept alone, went downstairs to the whisky decanter and he poured himself a large dram. It was only normal for Catie to be so distraught, he told himself. Roger had been her husband after all, if a rotten husband at that.

It was madness, Billy thought, sheer bloody madness. And that's why he'd do it. In one fell swoop he'd be set up for life. He'd still kill Irene of course, that went without saying. But Douglas wasn't to know that. Douglas would be hoping he'd keep his side of the bargain. And Douglas would never know who he was dealing with. As far as Douglas was concerned it would be an unknown blackmailer who'd snatched his wife.

How much was Douglas worth? Billy wondered. It must be millions, although a lot of his money was tied up in property. However he was sure that Douglas could easily lay his hands on a sizeable chunk. Two hundred and fifty thousand, he decided, that sounded about right. And all in cash.

Billy threw back his head and laughed. He was a genius, that's what he was. He'd hurt the bastard not only in the heart, where it counted most, but in the pocket as well. It was perfect! Naturally it would all have to be carefully planned, right down to the tiniest detail. But he was quite capable of that. More than capable if he was honest with himself. He laughed again. Honest with himself! When had he ever been honest? It was one of his little jokes that appealed.

He'd go to the 'Smoke' after he'd collected. High tail it down there and disappear among the teeming masses of England's capital. He'd find an out-of-the-way place, somewhere quiet, and lie low until he could arrange a passage overseas. He'd have to disguise himself which shouldn't be too difficult. He'd have a different hairstyle for a start, wear nondescript clothes, and he'd grow a moustache. He could always think about wearing spectacles with plain glass in them instead of lenses, and those he could easily arrange right here in Glasgow.

If he played his cards right, and he'd ensure he did, no-one would ever connect him with the Irene business. It would have been nice, very nice indeed, to have made Douglas aware of the fact that it was him, but that was a luxury he simply couldn't afford. The revenge itself would have to be enough.

As for going overseas, he'd always fancied somewhere exotic, Mexico perhaps, or Brazil. Either would suit him down to the ground.

'A quarter of a million nicker,' he chuckled. 'La de effing da!'

It was a good turn-out, Reith thought, gazing round the gathering that had assembled to bury Roger. He recognized many familiar faces from Bridgeton. He glanced at the minister who was standing at the head of the open grave, speaking about Roger and Roger's life. To one side of him stood Catie, flanked by Andrew and Astrid. She was bowed and stricken with grief. He knew his own reaction to Roger's death was a callous one, he was only too pleased Roger was gone. Well, he may be many things, but he wasn't a hypocrite. Roger may once have been his friend, but he'd come to despise the man as a person, hold him in contempt. He focused on Catie, thinking how frail she looked, his heart going out to her.

'Tragedy . . .' the minister was saying. 'Taken from us before his time . . . leaving behind a loving widow and two children . . .'

Loving widow, those words pierced Reith, reverberating round and round inside his head. Loving widow . . .

Catie started to shake alarmingly, and for a few moments Reith feared she was going to collapse. Andrew, thinking the same, put an arm round his mother's shoulder and whispered something to her. Catie raised her face to stare directly into Reith's eyes. And in that face he saw the terrible pain and anguish she was going through. It struck him then, as if he'd been shot through with electricity, just how much she'd loved Roger. She loved Roger as much as he himself loved her.

And in that instant he knew that even if she did come to him,

340

become his wife, deep down she'd always be Roger's. The thought sickened him.

Reith and Irene had been invited to the buffet meal held in Battlefield after the funeral. Those asked had been limited to relatives and close friends. Reith was in a corner by himself, Irene in another part of the room talking to an old acquaintance from Bridgeton.

He glanced down at the plate of boiled ham and salad which he was holding. He'd dispose of it at the earliest opportunity, not feeling in the least bit hungry. He'd only accepted the plate because it had been pressed on him by a well-meaning Astrid.

Catie detached herself from the person she'd been chatting with and came across to Reith. 'Thanks for coming today,' she said, her voice husky from emotion. He gazed into her face, seeing again the pain and anguish that had been so apparent at the graveside. There was also an emptiness there, as if something had left her. That something, he guessed, was Roger.

'How are you?' he asked, knowing the answer only too well.

'Bearing up. Just.'

'It went well I thought.'

'Yes. The minister did him proud.'

'I thought so too.' They were making polite conversation he realized. The intimacy between them had disappeared.

'It's good of you to give me so much time off, Reith. I won't abuse it, I assure you.'

He managed a weak smile. 'I'm sure you won't. But don't come back before you're ready. We can cope.'

There was a barrier between them, he further realized. Their conversation was not only polite but somehow stilted.

Catie ran her hand over her cheek, and looked away. 'He's still here, you know, in the house. I can feel and see him everywhere.'

Reith didn't pass comment.

'Strange, isn't it?'

Reith shrugged.

'I can even smell him in places.' Her voice became distant. 'Even though he'd been gone all those weeks before the accident I can still smell him.'

Reith felt as if he was holding a handful of sand that was running away between his fingers. 'If you don't mind I think it's time Irene and I made a move,' he said.

Catie made no reply, she was lost in thought.

He laid his plate aside. 'Catie?'

'Uh!' She came back to him. 'Sorry.'

'I understand,' he declared. And he did, only too well. 'I said, excuse us, but it's time Irene and I made a move.'

She grasped him lightly by the arm. 'You're the best friend a person could ever have, Reith. Thank you for everything.'

Friend! Didn't that say it all.

Catie stood by the graveside, staring down at the freshly dug earth and floral tributes. The headstone had been ordered, but wouldn't be in place for several weeks yet. Tears welled up in her eyes. Would she ever stop crying? It seemed to her that they'd been flowing non-stop since that awful telephone call from the Night Sister. She still couldn't fully accept the fact that Roger was dead. It was as if he'd just gone off somewhere and would return at any moment. It wouldn't have surprised her in the least if he'd suddenly popped up out of nowhere to give her a kiss and a cuddle and tell her what he'd been up to.

She remembered him lying in his coffin, skin pale and waxen, hands folded across his chest. Only that hadn't been Roger. Admittedly, it was his body, but it wasn't Roger. Roger had been elsewhere.

How could she ever have seriously contemplated getting rid of him! She'd been angry, that's why. Angry, let down and very, very hurt. But she'd been kidding herself to think she might leave him. She could no more have got rid of Roger than she could have sprouted wings and flown. Over the years she and Roger, despite their difficulties, had become part and parcel of one another, fused into the same person. And now he was dead, and half of her had died, too. From now on, she'd never be the same again. Years might pass, but she'd never regain what she had now lost.

The most hurtful thing was that it was because of her he'd died and she'd never forgive herself for that. He'd been thinking about her when he'd stepped out in front of that car. If only she'd taken him back when she'd decided to do so he'd still be alive today, still laughing, joking . . . warm.

'I'll come again soon, I promise,' she whispered to the grave. She raised a hand in a small salute then, shoulders slumped, slowly walked away, her mind filled with memories of the good times.

*   *   *

'Reith!'

He halted in his tracks and, with a frown, turned to Irene. 'I'm just off to work,' he said.

'I know. I wanted to catch you before you left.'

'I'm in a hurry,' he answered tightly.

'Have you forgotten what day it is?'

His frown deepened. 'Day?'

'It's your birthday, darling.' And with that she kissed him on the cheek.

'So it is. I had forgotten.'

'Well, I hadn't,' she said brightly, producing a small, gift-wrapped, parcel from behind her back. 'Many happy returns.'

Oh Lord! This was embarrassing. 'Thank you,' he replied, accepting the present.

She saw his hesitation. 'Aren't you going to open it?'

What else could he do? He began undoing the parcel while she watched on eagerly. Inside the outer wrapping was another layer of tissue paper. His frown disappeared to be replaced with a smile when he drew out the neatly folded tie.

'The parachute regiment. You don't have one,' she declared.

He fingered the silk tie, a lump rising in his throat. This was something he'd often meant to buy and had just never got round to.

'It's . . . lovely,' he stated levelly.

She beamed at him. 'I knew you'd like it.'

'Like and appreciate,' he qualified.

He gazed at the tie, touched. It was a thoughtful gift, one he'd treasure, not only because it had been given to him by Irene but also because of the associations and memories it held for him.

'Good.'

To Irene's delight he took off the tie he was wearing and replaced it with her own.

'How are you, sweetheart?' Billy asked affably.

'Fine.'

'Come in.'

Irene was passing him when he hit her with the cosh. Unconscious, she dropped to the floor where she lay sprawled in an untidy heap.

Reith was having breakfast when Mrs Murphy appeared. 'Can I have a word, sir?'

He nodded. 'What is it?'

'Has Mrs Douglas gone off somewhere?'

Reith paused, a slice of toast halfway to his mouth. 'Not that I'm aware.'

'It's just that . . . her bed wasn't slept in last night. I often call into her bedroom with a cup of tea at this time and she wasn't there.'

Irene out all night? That was unlike her, he reflected. What on earth was she up to? Boyne? Could well be. 'She hasn't left a note or anything round the house, has she?'

'I haven't seen one.'

'Check, will you?'

'Of course, Mr Douglas.' And with that Mrs Murphy hurried off.

It needn't necessarily be Boyne, Reith thought. She might have stayed overnight with a friend, that was possible, though she'd never done it before. Or . . . his expression became grim. Could she have gone on a bender and ended up in a police cell?

He dismissed that notion out of hand. If she'd been picked up she'd never have seen the inside of a cell, but would have been brought straight home.

When Mrs Murphy returned later she reported that she couldn't find a note anywhere. Then Reith had another thought. Maybe she'd run off with Boyne? Well, if that was the case good luck to her. It simplified matters enormously.

Catie strode out over the Kilpatrick Hills having driven there in her Mini Minor. It was a gorgeous day, the air crisp and clean without even a hint of wind.

She'd move from Battlefield, she decided, though she had no idea where she'd go. Certainly, she grinned to herself, not back to Bridgeton. Those days were long gone. She was gradually coming to terms with Roger's death, the pain easing with every passing day. There was no point in moping, she'd repeatedly told herself. The past was exactly that, now she had to look to the future. She was certain Roger would have approved.

She might be middle-aged, but that didn't mean her life was over, far from it. She had no intention of wearing widow's weeds until her own passing. That would be a waste.

She picked up a stick and idly swished it through the grass, neatly lopping the head off a dandelion which went spinning away.

A picture of Rossdhu Castle flashed into her mind, making her smile. She could just imagine herself living *there*, lady of the manor and all that entailed. It was a far cry from the poverty of Bridgeton right enough! Why not? she thought. Why *bloody* not? Rossdhu Castle, and the lifestyle that went with it, could so easily be hers. Being married to Reith would hardly be a high price to pay for such luxury. He was the loveliest of men, and was besotted by her. Betraying Roger's memory? She didn't believe so. And if Roger had been there he'd have agreed with her. One had to be practical about these things. Continuous weeping and wailing over his grave wouldn't help matters. Life had to go on as surely as day followed night.

Was she being mercenary? Possibly. Especially with the memory of Roger still heavy within her. That damned rogue! She smiled, then shivered remembering how it had been between them in bed. That was something she couldn't, wouldn't, give up. Celibacy was just not for her. The thought of remaining celibate appalled her. She laughed. If anyone would have understood that it was Roger, the randy sod. Had the positions been reversed and she had been hit by that car he'd have grieved just as she was doing, and as deeply, but it would only have been a matter of time before he'd have started casting round for a new partner.

The lovely thing was she didn't have to cast around. Reith was waiting and willing, and rich to boot. He was such a good friend and perhaps, eventually, she'd come to love him. It could never be as she'd loved Roger, but would be in a gentler, different way. She couldn't ask for more. She needed just a while longer, she decided, to finally make up her mind. Then she'd break the good news to Reith.

Chapter Thirty

Reith stared in disbelief at the letter, marked personal and confidential, which had arrived in that morning's post. Part of him was furiously angry, another part wanting to burst out laughing. Two hundred and fifty thousand pounds, otherwise Irene would be killed. Boyne had to be joking! For who else would have sent such a demand but Boyne.

Were they in this together? he wondered. Would his own wife really try to extort him? It was a nagging doubt. He threw the letter down on his desk and sat back. He could just ignore it of course, treat the threat as a bluff. But he knew he wouldn't. The day of reckoning between him and Boyne had finally arrived.

'Right!' he declared, coming to his feet. He pressed the intercom.

'Yes Mr Douglas?'

'Get me Jameson and any other of the lads you can rustle up. Tell them I want them here as soon as possible.'

He crossed to the bar and poured himself a wee dram, his mind whirling. He'd confide the true situation to Jameson, but not the others. There was no need for them to know what was happening. He was only taking them along in case Boyne and Irene weren't alone in this. A few minutes later Jameson arrived.

'Fish and chips again,' Irene sighed. 'Can't you get anything else?' She was chained by the wrist to Boyne's bed, the chain secured by a stout padlock. She was only released to use the toilet and wash.

Boyne glared at her. 'Stop whining! I hate whining women. And count yourself lucky I'm feeding you at all.'

346

Irene retreated into silence, fearing his wrath. She was only too well aware of what Billy was capable of. Would Reith pay the ransom? She wasn't at all certain he would. At least he didn't know the demand had come from Boyne. And if Reith didn't cough up, what then? That was something she daren't think about. The prospect was terrifying.

Billy ripped his cod apart and began to eat noisily. Irene watched him in disgust. The man was an animal, and ate like one.

Billy froze when there was a knock on the front door. No-one ever called on him except Irene for the simple reason no-one apart from her knew where he lived. But he was wrong to believe that. Reith knew.

Out on the steps leading immediately down from the landing Reith glanced at Jameson. Watt and Heraghty were also present, hidden behind the wall masking the flight of steps leading upstairs. Paul Jack, another of Reith's men, dressed as an official from the Gas Board, was standing on the landing itself. It was he who'd knocked.

Reith wasn't at all certain Boyne would be holed up here, he and Irene might well be elsewhere. But it was a start. And wherever they were he'd find them. His big advantage was that Boyne didn't know he was aware Boyne had sent the letter.

'Who is it?' Irene queried quietly in surprise.

'How the fuck should I know!' Billy retorted in a savage whisper.

Irene shut up.

Billy gnawed a nail. Should he answer it or not? At this point he heard a louder, more insistent knock than the previous one.

'Hello, hello? Is anyone in? This is the Gas Board,' Paul Jack declared.

Gas Board! Billy remained undecided.

Irene briefly wondered if she should shout for help, but decided against it for a number of reasons.

'There's a bad leak in the building. Please open up or I'll have to force entry,' Paul Jack went on, urgency in his voice.

Force entry! That settled it. 'Not a peep out of you or you'll regret it,' Billy hissed to Irene who shrank away from him.

Billy closed the bedroom door. 'Coming!' he called out.

Paul Jack gave Reith a thin smile.

'A gas leak?' Billy queried from behind the front door.

'Thank goodness you're in, sir. All appliances have to be turned off.'

'I'll do that myself.'

'And some tests have to be made which I have to do personally. That's my job.'

Billy swore under his breath. Well, what the hell! Where was the harm? It was an inconvenience that was all. 'OK! OK!' he replied, and cautiously opened the door a crack, relaxing slightly when he saw the man was, as he claimed, a gas official.

'Sorry to disturb you sir. But it is of the utmost importance. We don't want the whole kit and caboodle going up, do we?'

'Come in, then,' Billy said, and fully opened the door.

The next instant he knew he'd made a terrible mistake as Jameson, Watt and Heraghty appeared from nowhere to fly at him. Billy reacted with lightning speed, throwing a punch at Jameson who was in the vanguard. However, the punch never connected. Jameson swayed slightly, and it sailed harmlessly past. Jameson's arm twisted, brushing Billy and turning him round. The next moment Billy was in a full nelson.

But Billy wasn't finished yet. He lashed out with a foot which crunched against Watt's kneecap, sending Watt crashing to the floor. That was enough for Jameson, an expert in unarmed combat. His thumb jabbed a pressure point in Billy's neck and rendered Billy unconscious.

Jameson dragged him over to a chair and slung him into it, Jameson's expression one of contempt. These so-called hard men were all the same, easy as pie in the hands of a pro. Jameson told people he'd been a commando during the war, what he never mentioned to anyone, including Reith, was that he'd graduated into Davis Stirling's SAS.

Reith ignored Billy for the moment and knelt beside Watt who was clearly in pain. 'Anything broken?'

Gingerly examining the smacked kneecap, Watt replied, 'Don't think so.'

'Over here!' Heraghty called from the bedroom door which he'd opened. Irene, eyes standing out on stalks, was visible within.

'What do you want done with him, Reith?' Jameson asked, nodding at Billy.

'Keep him there till I decide.'

'Okay dokay.'

Reith gestured Heraghty away from the bedroom and went inside. He was horrified when he realized Irene was chained to the bed.

'Reith,' she exhaled.

'Yes, it's me. As you can see.'

'Help me,' she whispered.

He stared at the chain, then back at her. 'The key on Boyne?'

She nodded.

He shouted out to Jameson who retrieved the key from Billy's jacket pocket. Billy was beginning to stir. Reith caught the key when Jameson tossed it to him and instructed Jameson to shut the bedroom door again.

Reith released Irene, chucking the chain and padlock aside. 'I thought you and Boyne were in this together,' he said.

She gazed at him in puzzlement.

'You and your lover.'

'Lov . . .' She dragged in a deep breath, then slowly exhaled. 'You knew?'

'Oh yes,' he stated quietly.

'But how? I was always so careful.'

He sat on the edge of the bed and regarded her, confused at having found her chained up. 'I've lied to you for years,' he said. 'A lot more of my memory came back to me than I ever let on. Including about you and Boyne before the war. The man you told me you loved.'

'Oh Reith!' she whispered, stunned by this confession.

'I knew when you started seeing him again. Just as I've known it was him who robbed me and killed Finlay.' He paused, then added, 'I had plans for friend Boyne which this little piece of nonsense has completely buggered up.'

'I never loved him, Reith. I swear. On my life. On Agnes's life, on Matt's. I swear by all that's holy.'

'You told me you did which is why I went off and joined the Army.'

She fought back the impulse to laugh hysterically. 'I was protecting you and the children. That's why I lied. I've never loved Boyne, I loathe him. It's you I love. You, Reith. As much now as I've always done.'

Reith was frowning. 'Protecting me and the children? I think you'd better explain that, lady.'

Irene started at the beginning.

Half an hour later Reith emerged from the bedroom with Irene at his side. His face was white, his expression one of ice cold fury.

Billy smiled. 'Well, if it isn't the big man himself. Has she told you how I've screwed the arse off her . . .'

Jameson's hand flashed, landing a fearsome crack that almost knocked Billy right out of the chair.

'Shut up,' Jameson said mildly.

Billy's nose was streaming blood when he looked at Reith again. The smile returned, more insolent than before.

'Kill him,' Reith ordered Jameson.

'Quick or slow?'

Reith stared directly into Billy's face. 'As slowly as you possibly can.'

Billy wouldn't have believed such pain was possible. He'd been shrieking so long the inside of his throat was shredded. And yet the pain continued. It was a long, long time, an eternity, before he eventually gurgled into the all-embracing arms of welcome death.

'Catie, sit down,' Reith said, indicating the chair in front of his desk. He was pleased she'd asked to see him, he had some good news for her.

'I'll stand if you don't mind.'

He looked mildly surprised. 'Care for a drink?'

'I'm on duty.'

'I've told you before, I make the rules and I can break them. Drink?'

'Please.'

'What would you like?'

'A little red wine would be nice.'

'Coming up.' He poured out the same for himself. 'So, how can I help you?' he queried, handing her a glass.

She took her time replying, slowly sipping the wine first. 'I've decided to accept your offer.'

He was momentarily confused. 'What offer?'

'To be your wife, of course.'

Her words hit him with the force of a sledgehammer. 'I see,' he murmured.

'I couldn't accept while Roger was alive, but things are different now he's dead.'

'Quite.'

She stared expectantly at him, slightly puzzled by the coolness of his reaction. This wasn't at all what she'd expected.

350

He turned away from her and walked to the window where he stood staring out. All he could think about was Irene and what she'd suffered for all those years. The dreadful mental anguish she'd gone through, the physical degradation at the hands of that reptile Boyne, simply because she loved him, and their children.

'Reith?'

'I've a new job for you,' he declared without turning round. 'I can't remember if I mentioned it, but I bought The Cat Club which I'm having totally refurbished. It's opening in a couple of months under the new name of La Ronde. I want you to be the manageress in overall charge, which naturally means a sizeable hike in your wages. It's quite an opportunity.'

'Manageress?'

'That's right.'

'But . . .' She swallowed. 'What about us? Surely what I've just said changes your plans?'

How could he walk away from Irene now? He couldn't. The debt he owed her could never be repaid. And yet, he now recognized what he thought had been love was an obsession. Nothing more. Irene had shown him, these last few days, the meaning of true love.

'Reith?'

He forced himself to turn and face her. 'You loved Roger, Catie. Not me. You told me that.'

'Roger's dead,' she repeated, a little harshly.

'Does that mean you've stopped loving him?'

She couldn't reply to that.

'Of course not,' he said, smiling thinly.

Catie laid her glass aside. The fact that he might refuse her had never entered her mind. Reith was hers for the taking, had been for years. Since that night in the fog. Now this!

'What are you saying?' she queried.

He placed his glass on the desk and crossed over to the bar where he poured himself a large whisky. This situation needed something stronger than wine. He turned to face her again.

'It was a lovely dream, Catie. But a dream that just wasn't to be.'

'You're turning me down?'

'It wouldn't work between us, Catie. Not now.'

Thoroughly shaken, she stared into his eyes, incapable of saying anything.

'Don't worry,' he said. 'I'll always ensure you're OK financially. You'll never want.'

She dropped her gaze to stare at the floor, her face colouring with embarrassment.

Reith returned to the window. 'I don't regret anything,' he stated. 'Do you?'

She thought for a moment. 'No.'

'That's good. Makes it easier for both of us, don't you think?'

Several seconds ticked by during which neither spoke, then Catie turned to leave. 'I never deserved you, Reith. And that's the truth.'

Then the office door clicked shut, and he was alone again.

'Catie,' he whispered. 'Catie.'

Irene glanced up as Reith strode into the room. 'What are you doing home at this time of day?' she queried in surprise. He stopped and regarded her thoughtfully. Although it was only a short while since Boyne's death she'd come a long way to becoming her old self again. She'd gained some weight and was once more taking pride in her appearance. He thought she looked enchanting in the buttercup-coloured dress she was wearing.

'We're going on holiday,' he announced.

'I beg your pardon?'

'Holiday. Or a sea cruise to be more precise. What do you think about that?'

She leapt to her feet, a broad smile lighting up her face. 'It's wonderful!'

'We leave on Monday so you'd better start packing.'

'Monday!' she laughed.

'From Southampton. We're staying overnight in London and then leaving the following morning. We're going to the West Indies.'

She shook her head. 'I don't know what to say.'

He went over to her and curled an arm round her waist. 'We've a lot of wasted time to make up, Irene. This is only the beginning.'

A tear crept into her eye. 'I'm so happy, Reith. Thank you.'

'No, my darling, thank you.'

She closed her eyes in anticipation as his lips came down to meet hers.